ON THE RUN

On the Run

LEFT BEHIND™

>THE KIDS<

Jerry B. Jenkins

Tim LaHaye

WITH CHRIS FABRY

TYNDALE
KIDS

TYNDALE HOUSE PUBLISHERS, INC.
WHEATON, ILLINOIS

Visit Tyndale's exciting Web site at www.tyndale.com

Discover the latest Left Behind news at www.leftbehind.com

Left Behind is a trademark of Tyndale House Publishers, Inc.

Published in association with the literary agency of Alive Communications, Inc., 7680 Goddard Street., Suite 200, Colorado Springs, CO 80920.

Edited by Curtis H. C. Lundgren

ISBN 0-8423-4330-X

Printed in the United States of America

08 07 06 05 04 03 02 01 00
9   8   7   6   5   4   3   2   1

To Kirsten

TABLE OF CONTENTS

What's Gone On Before

JUDD Thompson Jr. and his friends are involved in a dangerous adventure. The global vanishings of millions of people have left them without family. They decide to spread the truth—that Jesus Christ has returned for his true followers.

When the Global Community begins World War III, beloved Pastor Bruce Barnes is killed. The kids realize Ryan Daley is missing.

They discover that Ryan is being held hostage along with Darrion Stahley, the daughter of a high-level Global Community officer. Judd and his friend Vicki find Darrion's father and rush toward Chicago to rescue their friend.

As the bombing of Chicago begins, Ryan and Darrion escape their captors and try to get away. At a Global Community outpost,

Mr. Stahley is mortally wounded, but before he dies he and his daughter express a belief in Jesus Christ.

After finding Darrion's mother, Judd and the others pull together as the world continues to spin out of control.

ONE

Tragic News

"JUDD, *help!*"

The girl sounded desperate. He tried to place her voice, but he couldn't. Judd called back, but she didn't seem to hear.

"Judd, we need you! Hurry!"

"Nina!" Judd said as he awoke. He tried to shake the dream but couldn't. Judd had met Nina in Israel while traveling with Bruce. Because her father was such an outspoken Jewish believer, Nina, her brother, Dan, and Mrs. Ben-Judah were in constant danger.

Nina's helpless cry haunted Judd as he collected himself. There was a pain deep in his chest. Could the previous day have been a dream? Could Bruce really be dead? Judd sat up and listened to voices in the other room. Judd had come to Loretta's—Bruce's secretary at New Hope Village Church—house when he heard Chloe Williams was in trouble. The search for Ryan had been exhausting. Judd had fallen asleep before he found out what happened to Chloe, and now he listened as Loretta and Buck Williams talked in hushed tones in the kitchen.

Loretta wept about Bruce. Buck assured her she wouldn't have to handle the arrangements for Bruce's body.

"But I don't think I can handle the memorial service either," Loretta said. "There's so much to prepare."

Buck said he would take care of both.

"It feels so good to have people in this place again," Loretta said. "Y'all stay as long as you need to or want to."

"We're grateful," Buck said. "Amanda may sleep till noon, but then she'll get right on those arrangements with the coroner's office. Chloe didn't sleep much with the ankle cast, but she's sleeping hard now."

When Loretta left for the church, Judd went to the kitchen to talk with Buck.

"I heard you had quite an experience with Ryan," Buck said. "How is he?"

Judd told him. He asked Buck's advice about Mrs. Stahley and Darrion.

"That's a tough one," Buck said. "You want to get them into hiding as fast as you can," Buck said. "If the Global Community wanted

Mr. Stahley that bad, they'll come looking for the rest of his family. Sounds like they know too much."

"What happened with Chloe?" Judd said.

Buck quickly explained that Chloe had received a message from her father to get out of downtown Chicago. She was talking with Buck on a cell phone with a cop right behind her. Chloe didn't want to stop. Then the bombing began. Chloe's Range Rover was thrown off Lake Shore Drive and landed in a tree. That's where she stayed until Buck found her.

Buck was interested in Ryan's story. Judd explained how they found him and how Ryan helped save their lives. "Mr. Stahley gave his life for his daughter," Judd said.

"We may all be asked to do that," Buck said. "I'm not sure how much Nicolae Carpathia knows about my faith, but he's sure to find out at some point. We have to be ready for whatever comes."

"Is Verna Zee a Christian too?" Judd said, referring to Buck's coworker, also staying at Loretta's house.

"No," Buck said. "I may have put myself in real danger when I brought her here. My hope is that she'll hear the message and respond. If not, I'm in trouble. Carpathia hasn't given any indication he suspects anything, but if Verna tells my superiors, it's only a matter of time."

"Do you talk with Carpathia?" Judd said.

"Last night in fact," Buck said. "He wanted to know about the coverage of the war here. His voice got real emotional when I told him. He said it was a tragedy."

"Makes me sick," Judd said. "Is that all he said?"

"No, he wanted me to come over there and cover meetings in Baghdad and New Babylon."

"You're not going?" Judd said.

"I told him I was working another story," Buck said. "He's getting another guy."

As they talked, Buck turned his attention to the papers scattered across the dining-room table. "Bruce's notes," he said. "Chloe had them with her in the Rover. I have to put them back together."

Judd helped get the transcripts in order. Buck had a huge job ahead of him. He not only had to read the massive pile of pages but also edit it for the church.

"Can I ask about the other story you're working on?" Judd said.

Buck reached for the phone. "Hang on," he said.

Buck called Ken Ritz, a pilot who had flown him to New York just after the disappearances. "I know you're busy and probably don't need my business," Buck said, "but you also know I'm on a big, fat expense account and can pay more than anyone else."

Judd wondered where Buck needed to go so soon after his wife's accident.

"Israel," Buck said to Ken Ritz. "And I have to be back here by Saturday night at the latest."

***

Vicki awoke and heard someone crying. For a moment she couldn't figure out where she was. *Judd's house,* she thought. He had asked them to stay at his house while he went to Loretta's. Vicki had crashed in Judd's parents' room. Chaya sat on the edge of the bed, her shoulders shaking.

"Are you OK?" Vicki said.

Chaya shook her head. "I couldn't sleep," she said. "I called my father about my mother's funeral. He said I shouldn't bother. He doesn't want me there."

"That's all he said?" Vicki said.

"He asked about Bruce; then he told me this would be our last conversation."

"He can't keep you away from your own mother's funeral," Vicki said.

"He said he would turn his back if I came. I have betrayed the Jewish faith by becoming a Christian. I have betrayed him and the memory of my mother."

Vicki put an arm around Chaya as the older girl sobbed. "I prayed that her death would soften him," Chaya said. She was clutching the note she had found in her mother's hand.

"At least you know where your mom is now," Vicki said.

"I know she's in a better place," Chaya said, "but my father . . ."

Lionel and Ryan were in the kitchen fixing breakfast. Ryan held out a plate to Vicki when she sat down.

"You're our guests so we're pulling out all the special food," Ryan said.

"If I can keep him from eating it all," Lionel said.

Ryan and Lionel seemed to be working together. Their rivalry the past year had been fierce at times, bickering and fighting almost daily. Vicki wondered how long the truce would last.

As they ate, although they were sad, they kept remembering funny stories.

"When I moved into Bruce's house, I forgot my toothbrush," Vicki said. "I asked Bruce if he'd take me to buy some toiletries, and he got all serious. He told me he'd never had a teenager in his house and knew there were things I'd need. He was about to launch into this big speech about growing into womanhood when I stopped him and said, 'Bruce, I just need a toothbrush.'"

Everyone laughed.

"What do you think Bruce would say about Darrion and Mrs. Stahley?" Ryan said.

"He'd be proud of what you did," Lionel said. "If you hadn't been there, they might not have made it. They sure wouldn't have heard about God the way you told them."

"None of it would have happened if I hadn't gone to see Bruce," Ryan said. "He started the whole thing."

Chaya had talked with Loretta late the previous night and brought everyone up to date on Chloe and Buck. Though Amanda was safe, Rayford Steele remained with Nicolae Carpathia. Amanda said Rayford was flying to New Babylon.

"Carpathia gives me the creeps big time," Ryan said. "I think he's Satan himself."

"That's not what Bruce told us," Lionel said.

Chaya nodded. "Bruce taught that the Antichrist would not be indwelt by Satan himself until halfway into the Tribulation. The guy's evil, no doubt. But even with the war and all the death, things will get worse."

Darrion rushed up the stairs. "Turn on the television!" she said.

※

"Why Israel?" Judd asked Buck. "I've heard that's the one place the war hasn't touched."

"I'm not covering the war," Buck said.

"Then why go?" Judd said.

"I'm not sure how much I should tell you," Buck said, "for your own safety."

"With what we've been through," Judd said, "I don't think you could tell me anything that would endanger my life more than us hiding family members of a Global Community traitor."

"In the middle of trying to find Chloe yesterday, I got a call from Dr. Chaim Rosenzweig," Buck said. "He's friends with Rabbi Tsion Ben-Judah."

Judd reminded Buck he had met the rabbi's wife and two adopted children on his trips to Israel. Buck looked away.

"We watched the rabbi's televised speech too," Judd said. "And Bruce kept us up to date. It was exciting to watch the rabbi speak to all the new believers in Teddy Kollek Stadium. What's happened?"

"They can't find him," Buck said. "Dr. Rosenzweig said he was going to Nicolae for help and I begged him to leave Carpathia out of it. I haven't heard anything more, but I assume the prophecy from the two witnesses at the Wailing Wall is correct. Dr. Ben-Judah will be protected in spite of the murders. So I feel I have to—"

"Wait," Judd said. "What murders?"

Buck stared at him. "You'd better sit down."

※

Lionel flicked on the television in the kitchen. The Stahley girl looked upset. Mrs. Stahley was there a moment later and watched with her arms folded.

The news anchorwoman was nicely dressed, but the worry showed on her face.

"This report out of Chicago has pushed aside war news," she said. "An international business leader and a high-level member of the Global Community is dead this morning. Maxwell Stahley, who made his fortune in international security, was found dead of a gunshot wound in an office building in a suburb of Chicago."

Video footage showed men carrying Mr. Stahley's body from the Global Community building.

"Mr. Stahley was found alone in a pool of

blood in a first-floor entryway," the woman said.

Mrs. Stahley covered her mouth and turned her head.

"He wasn't on the first floor," Ryan said. "He was on the fourth floor with the other guy."

"Also missing are Stahley's wife and daughter," the anchor said. A picture of the Stahley family flashed on the screen.

"I hate that picture," Darrion said.

"The motive is not clear," the woman continued, "but a source close to the Global Community confirmed that a large amount of money had been taken from one of Stahley's bank accounts in the U.S."

"They found it already," Mrs. Stahley said. "I transferred the funds last night."

"Will they be able to trace it to Judd?" Vicki said.

"I put the money into several different accounts to be safe," Mrs. Stahley said. She looked at Vicki. "One of them was Judd's."

A spokesman for the Global Community appeared on a satellite hookup. He vaguely answered questions about the war, then turned to the Stahley report.

"We must let the investigation run its course," the man said. "This is a great personal loss of a devoted colleague. I do believe it will be important to focus on the mother and daughter at this point. They may be in danger, or perhaps they know something about the murder."

"You wanna find them because they know what's really going on," Ryan said to the TV.

"Are you suggesting his wife and daughter might be responsible for the murder?" the woman said.

"We're not ruling anything out at this point," the spokesman said, "but we would like anyone who has any information on the whereabouts of these two to get in touch with the Global Community immediately."

A phone number flashed on the screen.

"That guy looks nervous," Vicki said.

"My husband left important documents behind," Mrs. Stahley said. "Documents that might save our lives."

"Where are they?" Vicki said.

"That's the problem. They're at our house in a secret place."

The phone rang. Chaya answered. She looked startled, then covered the receiver with her hand.

"It's Loretta," Chaya said. "The police just called the church."

※

"Who was murdered?" Judd said, sitting warily.

"I found this out from Dr. Rosenzweig," Buck said. "He respects Dr. Ben-Judah but couldn't understand why such an educated man would throw away his reputation by proclaiming Jesus as the Messiah. He was afraid religious zealots would kill Ben-Judah."

"And they did?" Judd said, holding his breath.

Buck shook his head. "Chaim called to tell me about the rabbi's wife and children."

"No!" Judd gasped.

Buck's voice grew tense. "All killed," he said. "I'm very sorry."

The words felt like a sledgehammer. The air went out of the room and Judd couldn't speak. Couldn't think. Buck kept talking, but Judd couldn't concentrate.

"Chaim said Ben-Judah's house was burned to the ground," Buck was saying.

"You sure it was them?" Judd managed.

"Chaim says it was a public spectacle. I assume the rabbi is in hiding. At least I hope so."

"That's why you're going to Israel?" Judd said.

"It's not what Carpathia thinks, but yes. I need to find the rabbi."

Judd put his face in his hands. "The dream," he said. "I had a dream about Nina last night." Judd explained his relationship with Nina, Dan, and their mother. They had taken Judd in. They had driven him to historic sights in Israel and explained their social customs. They had eaten together and talked about their faith. Judd had invited them to America. Now they were dead.

Or were they? He could hope. Judd thought a moment. "Maybe they're just trying to lure the rabbi out of hiding. If he thought his family had been killed, he'd come out for sure."

"What could he do if they're dead?"

Judd slammed his fist onto the table. "I don't get it," he said. "The two witnesses promised protection, right?"

"Moishe said anyone who threatened the rabbi would answer to him," Buck said. "I thought the rabbi's family would be protected, too."

"I don't think they're dead," Judd said.

"Dr. Rosenzweig wouldn't have told me that unless it was true," Buck said.

"You said yourself Carpathia has the power to make people believe a lie," Judd said.

"But there's no reason," Buck said. "You've just gone through a gut-wrenching experience with Ryan. You've lost Bruce. Now this.

I don't blame you for being upset. But you have to face the facts."

Judd wanted to keep arguing, but he knew he shouldn't. "I need a favor," he said.

TWO

Suspects

"DON'T panic," Lionel said, though mention of the police startled him. "We don't know what they want."

Chaya looked upset. "The officer told Loretta someone used the church phone to call Mr. Stahley's office yesterday," she said. "Loretta told them it might have been Judd. She hung up and realized he might be in danger."

"Great," Lionel said. "The church was our best hiding place for the Stahleys. Now that's out."

"I was the one who made the call," Chaya said. "They're looking for me, not Judd."

"Doesn't matter," Lionel said. "We're in this together."

The phone rang again. Lionel waved the rest off and looked at the caller ID. It was blank. "Yeah, he's not here right now. Can I take a message?" Lionel said.

"This is the police," the man said. "We're investigating a murder. Do you know where Judd Thompson is right now?"

"I'm not sure," Lionel said. "He was gone all night. What precinct are you with? I'll have him call when he gets back."

The phone line clicked.

"Funny," Lionel said. "Since when do the police not want anyone to know who they are?" He looked at Mrs. Stahley and Darrion. "We need to get you out of here fast."

Before anyone could move there was a knock at the door.

***

"I don't like it," Buck said.

"Don't treat me like a kid," Judd said. "I've been to Israel before."

Buck folded his arms. "That's not the point."

"It can't cost much more to let me fly with you," Judd said. "As soon as we touch down, I'll be gone."

"I'm not against you going to Israel," Buck said. "I'm just not in a position to let you go with me."

"Where else am I going to find a way over there when there's a war on?" Judd said.

Buck sighed. "I don't know. I just can't handle the responsibility of—"

"You don't have any responsibility," Judd said. "All I need is a way to get over there so I can check on Nina and Dan. That's all I'm asking."

"I know this news hurts," Buck said, "but I'm doing something that could get me killed. I just can't take you. I'm sorry."

"If you don't help me out, I'll find my own way," Judd said.

Judd dropped the subject. If God really wanted him to go to Israel, God could work it out without Buck's help.

Judd helped Buck finish organizing Bruce's transcripts. Buck said he was going to pack and then try to reach Dr. Rosenzweig. "The old man knows he's being watched," Buck said. "But I think he's trying to tell me, in a cryptic way, that Dr. Ben-Judah is alive and safe somewhere."

Chaya slipped to the garage with Darrion and Mrs. Stahley. The girl and her mother climbed into the trunk. Chaya waited for Lionel's signal and opened the garage door.

"I hope this works," Chaya said to herself.

Vicki opened the door. A tall, thin woman with glasses greeted her. Vicki remembered the woman from the hearing she had been given at Nicolae Carpathia High School.

"Candace Goodwin," the woman said. Vicki showed her into the living room. As she did, a huge crash of pots and pans clattered behind Vicki. Lionel stood in the kitchen in the midst of the furor. The noise lasted a good twenty seconds as the boy clumsily picked up, dropped, and kicked several pans. Vicki introduced Lionel. Vicki could tell that the social worker was ready to get down to business. Her face was tight, and she looked like she had aged since the last time Vicki had seen her.

"If you recall," Mrs. Goodwin said, "I'm with Global Community Social Services." She pulled out a yellow legal pad and scribbled some notes.

"I remember," Vicki said. "I told my story to you and got sent to the Northside Detention Center."

Mrs. Goodwin grimaced. "I didn't want to do that, but you wouldn't cooperate."

"What are you doing here?" Vicki said.

"It's my job to know these types of things," Mrs. Goodwin said grimly. "The real concern before us is what you're going to do now."

"What do you mean?" Vicki said.

"We received a report about your guardian's death," Mrs. Goodwin said.

"How could you possibly—"

"Do you deny it?" Mrs. Goodwin said.

Vicki bit her lip. "No," she said. "But he wasn't my guardian. He was my adoptive father."

"We have some important matters to discuss," Mrs. Goodwin said. "You're a ward of the state now."

"Does that mean what I think it means?" Vicki said.

"Unless we find a suitable alternative," Mrs. Goodwin said, "you could return to NDC."

Vicki gasped. With the war and mayhem around the world, she had thought she might be able to slide through the cracks in the system. *How could they have discovered Bruce's death so fast?* she thought.

"I have a place to stay and friends—"

Mrs. Goodwin's beeper sounded. She handed Vicki her card. "I need to talk with you about something later," she said. "I'll be in touch."

Judd came through the door as Mrs. Goodwin was leaving. Vicki explained the situation and told Judd about the police call.

"Chaya drove the Stahleys somewhere,"

Vicki said. "I don't know where. We just wanted to get them out of here."

"If it was the Global Community on the phone rather than the police," Lionel said, "we might have company soon."

"Better they find us than Chaya," Judd said.

"I'd rather they didn't find any of us," Vicki said.

Judd called Ryan into the meeting and told them about the Ben-Judah family. The kids were crushed. Ryan said he had been looking forward to meeting Nina and Ben and helping them adjust to American society. Vicki stared off into space.

"I wonder if that's what we'll have to go through," Lionel said. "The persecution of people who believe in Jesus is increasing."

"This is going to hit Chaya hard," Vicki said. "She thought the Ben-Judahs might talk to her father."

Judd told them of his desire to go to Israel. "I want to make sure," he said. "I think God is drawing me back there, and it may be because the family isn't really dead."

"You don't trust Dr. Rosenzweig?" Vicki said.

"I don't trust anyone who says Nicolae Carpathia is a good man," Judd said.

"It's not fair," Ryan said. "You've been to Israel twice, and Bruce promised. You ought to take me."

"Hang on," Lionel said. "You're going to Israel because you have some kind of feeling?"

"I can't explain it," Judd said.

"What if it's a bad piece of pizza?" Lionel said. "Come on, Judd, we can't just go running off whenever we feel like it."

The phone rang. Lionel looked at the caller ID. "No number," he said.

"Let's get out of here," Judd said.

※

Chaya drove Mrs. Stahley and Darrion to Bruce's house and put them in a secluded room downstairs. When they were settled, Mrs. Stahley became emotional. "What will they do with my husband's body?" she said.

"I assume they'll keep it until the investigation is complete," Chaya said.

"I want to see him," Mrs. Stahley said. "It doesn't seem real to me."

"Mother—," Darrion said.

"It's not that I don't believe your report," Mrs. Stahley said. "I need to see my husband's face."

"You have to resist that," Chaya said. "The

Global Community wants you to come forward. If they find you, they'll twist things and make you look like the murderer."

"She's right, Mother," Darrion said. "We must hide."

Judd and the others joined Chaya at Bruce's house. Mrs. Stahley and Darrion excused themselves while the group met. When Judd told them the news about the Ben-Judah family, Chaya shook her head. "When will the insanity end?" she said.

Judd asked Chaya's advice on the trip to Israel.

"Travel anywhere is risky right now," Chaya said.

"I still don't get it," Lionel said. "Why does God want you in Israel?"

"I woke up thinking about the Ben-Judah family this morning," Judd said. "Maybe they're still alive. And who knows, if Buck can't find Dr. Ben-Judah, maybe God will let me help."

"I don't see how it's possible," Vicki said. "Mr. Williams won't take you, and you sure can't get a flight anywhere with the war going on."

"Maybe you're right," Judd said. "Maybe this was all in my head."

"I'm sorry for interrupting," Mrs. Stahley

said, slipping in the room. "I know how you can get there."

"You do?" Judd said.

"The only person who worked with my husband that I trust is Taylor Graham," Mrs. Stahley said. "I wanted to call him when Darrion was taken, but Maxwell wouldn't allow it. He knew Taylor can be pretty high-strung."

"Sounds like my kind of guy," Ryan said. "How can he help us?"

Judd glanced warily at Ryan. "Us?" he said.

"He's been our family pilot for years," Mrs. Stahley said. "He's flown us around the world several times."

"Cool guy," Darrion said. "He's let me fly before."

"Right," Ryan said.

"No, really." Darrion rolled her eyes and smiled. "Okay, it was on autopilot, but it still felt like I was flying."

"Wouldn't they have taken possession of your plane by now?" Judd said.

"We keep it in an underground hangar near the house," Mrs. Stahley said. "Maxwell used the Global Community–supplied aircraft for business, but no one knows where our private jet is. The trick will be getting onto the property. I'm sure the Global Community is watching it."

"Can you get in touch with this guy?" Judd said.

"I can try."

Mrs. Stahley reached the pilot's answering machine, then dialed his pager.

"What do you hope to accomplish with the trip?" Mrs. Stahley said.

"To find out about the Ben-Judah family," Judd said.

"Which brings us back to me," Ryan said. "What happens if you're over there and you get into some real trouble?" Ryan flexed his muscles and Darrion smiled. Judd explained Ryan's wish.

"Judd won't admit I can take care of myself," Ryan said.

"After what you accomplished yesterday," Vicki said, "I would think Judd would jump at the chance."

"I agree Ryan proved himself," Judd said. He held up his passport. "But it's not practical. He doesn't even have one of these."

Chaya's eyes widened. "I'll be right back," she said, running from the room. Soon she returned, holding a white envelope.

"What you said about Ryan going with you?" Chaya said. "It *is* practical."

She handed Judd the envelope. Judd opened it slowly, then let out a low whistle.

"What?" Ryan said, grabbing the envelope.

"It was going to be a surprise," Chaya said. "Bruce told me that on his next trip to the Holy Land he was taking Ryan with him. He filled out the paperwork and sent in Ryan's—"

"That little picture!" Ryan said, his mouth open wide. "Bruce wouldn't tell me what he was going to do with it."

Ryan pulled out the crisp, blue passport and opened the cover to see his picture inside. He touched it gingerly, as if it were a treasure. A yellow Post-it note was stuck to the back. In Bruce's familiar handwriting Ryan read out loud, "For Ryan. It's your turn finally."

Vicki gave Judd a look.

"Don't take sides on this," Judd said. "You know it's too dangerous—"

"Judd," Vicki said, "we watched Ryan dodge bombs and bullets yesterday and save Darrion's life. I'd say he's earned a chance, don't you think?"

"If God wants you to go," Lionel said, "it looks like he wants you to have some company."

Chaya handed Ryan a page from Bruce's manuscript. "I copied this for you," she said.

Over Ryan's shoulder, Judd read the page.

Bruce wrote, *I'm so excited the process is complete. The next time I set foot on Israeli soil, I'll get to take Ryan. He talks constantly about going. I've had to say no twice. This is going to be such a surprise. I can't wait to see his face when I show him the passport and tell him he's going with me.*

Ryan looked at Judd with tears in his eyes.

Judd shook his head. "We don't even know if this Graham guy will fly us," Judd said.

"Us?" Ryan said.

"Yeah." Judd smiled. "Us."

***

Judd and Ryan arranged a meeting with Taylor Graham at a donut shop in Prospect Heights. "I don't want to tell him everything," Judd said. "I know Mrs. Stahley trusts him with her life, but we have to be careful."

Graham looked like a swimmer—tall, tanned, and muscular. They bought coffee and donuts and sat in Judd's car.

"I have to tell you," Graham said, "I didn't know I'd be dealing with a couple of kids."

Judd glanced at Ryan, who rolled his eyes.

"I wouldn't even be talking to you unless the Mrs. had asked."

"I understand your concern," Judd said. "You're safe with us. I assume the Global Community is looking for you, too."

"They found me already," Graham said. "Since my boss was grounded for a few days, which I still don't understand, the GC had me do a VIP run to Dallas yesterday. Didn't get in until early this morning."

"The GC told you Mr. Stahley was going to be grounded?" Judd said.

"Said he was out for at least a few days and might not be back," Graham said. "I do what I'm told, but first thing on the list when I got back was to check with him and find out what's going on."

"So you don't know anything about why Mr. Stahley was out?" Judd said.

"If you know something, tell me," Graham said.

"You sure you can trust us little kids?" Ryan said.

Graham ignored him and listened intently as Judd explained the events of the previous day. Ryan told the pilot how he had gotten entangled in the kidnapping and about some of the kidnappers' conversations on the phone.

"What did the guy in the trench coat look like?" Graham asked.

Judd told him. Graham shook his head. "Corny bit it, huh?"

"What?" Ryan said.

"Cornelius Van Waylin," Graham said. "Supposed to be Max's friend. They were together a few years ago before this whole Global Community deal. Had a falling out. Corny had it in for Max from the get-go."

Ryan described the other man who had gotten away. "Doesn't ring a bell," Graham said, "but Corny had lots of people working for him, inside and outside the GC."

"So will you take us?" Ryan said.

"It's probably about the safest airspace in the world right now," Graham said, "but you have to pass through some hot spots. Why Israel?"

"It's a personal trip," Judd said. "I promised Ryan we'd—"

"OK, you can cut that stuff," Graham said. "I'm not gonna risk my neck on a joyride to Jerusalem because somebody has an itch. I'll ask you one more time. Why are you going?"

Judd was in a corner. If Graham was working with the GC, he and Mrs. Stahley were in trouble. But if he offended Graham, he might lose his best chance for a trip to Israel. Before he could answer, Graham turned to Ryan. "What's your name again?" he said.

Ryan told him.

"I want you to buckle your strap tight around you," Graham said. "Now." He turned to Judd. "As fast as you can, flip the front seat back and climb next to your friend."

"What's going on?" Judd said.

"Two GC guys walked into the donut place after we ordered," Graham said. "I didn't think much of it. When the second car pulled up I got a little antsy. Then I saw someone who looks a lot like the guy you said ran away from sector four last night. I figure we ought to do something."

Judd was in the backseat and barely buckled in when Taylor Graham pulled away from the curb. Judd had no idea his car could move that quickly or that it could look so easy.

"Yeeehigh!" Ryan said.

"While we're in the process here," Graham said, "tell my why you need to go."

"Some friends of ours were killed," Judd said. "I don't believe it. We want to find out what happened."

"You think they're still alive?" Graham said, taking a curve hard.

"Maybe it's blind hope," Judd said, "but I have to know. They'd do the same for me."

Judd couldn't see either of the other cars

now. Graham turned onto a frontage road that paralleled an expressway and sped toward an intersection.

"I'll take you on one condition," Graham said.

"We're not telling where Mrs. Stahley is," Ryan said.

"I don't want you to," Graham said.

"Then what's the condition?" Judd said.

THREE

Taking Flight

VICKI met with Chloe later in the day. Chloe hobbled around on a cane, needing crutches but unable to manage them with her sprained wrist. Chloe brought Vicki up to date on the adult Tribulation Force. Buck's coworker, Verna Zee, was back at the Global Community office and would return later that night.

"We need your advice about Darrion and Mrs. Stahley," Vicki said. "Where do you think they should stay?"

"Here," Chloe said. She told Vicki where to find a key in the kitchen. "Bring them over while we take Buck to Palwaukee Airport. Verna's staying downstairs. You can put Mrs. Stahley and Darrion in the garage apartment. It's not fancy, but no one will find them."

"What about Loretta?" Vicki said. "She'll need to know."

"I'll tell Loretta," Chloe said. "You stay with them and bring whatever they need. I'll have Loretta say you're trying to get over Bruce's death and you need a little privacy."

"That wouldn't be far from the truth," Vicki said.

Chloe put a hand on her shoulder. "Hang in there until the memorial service," she said. "I'm sure that will bring healing to us all."

The phone rang and Chloe handed it to Vicki.

"You'll never believe it," Judd said. The car phone was noisy, and Judd sounded out of breath. "We're on our way to Israel!"

"Great," Vicki said. "When do you leave?"

"The pilot will take us on one condition," Judd said. "He wants to go right now—no packing, no good-byes. Ryan hasn't let go of his passport, and I have mine."

"Why does it have to be all of a sudden?" Vicki said.

"Can't explain," Judd said. "Just be careful. And make sure you get Mrs. Stahley and Darrion to a safe place."

"It's already taken care of," Vicki said.

Vicki told Judd the group would pray for him and Ryan, even though she didn't know exactly what to pray. When she hung up, Buck came in with his luggage. Rayford Steele's wife, Amanda, was there to drive him to the airport.

"I want to ride along," Chloe said.

"Are you sure you're up to it, hon?" Buck said.

Chloe's voice was quavery. "Buck, I hate to say it, but in this day and age we never know when we might or might not ever see each other again."

"You're being a little dramatic, aren't you?" he said.

"Buck!" Amanda said in a scolding tone. "You cater to her feelings now. I had to kiss my husband good-bye in front of the Antichrist. You think that gives me confidence about whether I'll ever see him again?"

Vicki smiled. Buck had been properly chastised. Vicki got in touch with Chaya. "We have a couple people to move," Vicki said.

Judd was impressed with Taylor Graham's abilities behind the wheel. He also had keen insight. Graham whipped the car into a drive-through canopy and let the car idle.

"What's wrong?" Judd said.

"Helicopter," Graham said. When the pilot was sure they weren't being followed, he headed for the Stahley mansion. "The place'll be watched closely, so we'll have to go the long way around," he said. "I hope you guys are in good shape."

On their way, Nicolae Carpathia's voice

interrupted the news reports on the radio. He talked in his usual overly humble manner.

"Make no mistake, my brothers and sisters," Carpathia said, "there will be many dark days ahead. It will take a huge supply of resources to begin the rebuilding process, but because of the generosity of the seven loyal global regions, the world will see the largest relief fund in the history of mankind. This will be given to needy nations directly from New Babylon. The relief effort, under my direct orders, will be handled in a swift and generous way.

"Continue to resist those who speak out against us. Continue to support the Global Community. And remember that though I did not seek this position, I accept it with resolve to pour out my life in service to the brotherhood and sisterhood of mankind. I appreciate your support as we set about to stand by each other and pull ourselves out of these troubled days to a higher plane."

Ryan shook his head. "He's saying that because people want to hear it."

Judd waited to see any reaction from Taylor Graham. The pilot concentrated on the road ahead. Judd explained how he and Vicki had gotten onto the Stahley property.

"You're lucky the dogs didn't tear you apart," Graham said.

Graham drove into a different entrance to the forest preserve, farther from the Stahley estate. Instead of staying in the parking lot, he stopped at a hidden gate in a wooded area. Graham unlocked the gate and drove deeper into the woods. A few hundred yards farther they found a gravel path with warning signs posted every few yards.

"I didn't know this was here," Judd said.

"No one's supposed to," Graham said. "I usually have my four-wheel drive. It can get nasty out here when it's wet."

The car snaked through the underbrush, and the terrain gradually inclined. Finally they went straight uphill until the ground leveled and they came to a clearing. Graham parked the car under a huge willow tree, and the three hiked along the edge of the woods.

"See anything out there?" Graham said.

Judd saw the edge of the Stahley estate in the distance and the iron fence he and Vicki had climbed. Between them and the fence were acres of rolling, green land.

"I see some pine trees and a lot of grass," Judd said, "but nothing that looks like a plane or a landing strip."

"Good," the pilot said.

Graham showed them to a small grove of trees and knelt in front of a brick-sized stone.

Underneath, Judd saw what looked like a fishing-tackle box. Graham opened the lid. Inside was an airtight instrument panel covered with buttons and knobs.

"I'll need you to stay here and work the runway," Graham said to Judd. "Ryan, you come with me, but you have to stay low. When we're in the clearing, we'll be easy to spot."

Ryan smiled at Judd and raised his eyebrows.

"We have an underground tunnel that connects the mansion with the plane hangar," Graham said. "It's hard to find, so I'm assuming the Global Community people haven't located it yet."

Graham pointed to the panel. "This is our backup entrance," he said. "When Ryan and I make it to the entrance, I'll give you a thumbs-up. You press the black button and hold it until we get inside."

"How long will you be in there?" Judd said.

"It'll take a few minutes' prep, maybe fifteen or so," the pilot said. "When you hear the plane start, flip the green switch to the "on" position. Pull the top down and replace the stone, then run like mad straight toward that tree."

Graham caught Judd's eye. "This is important," Graham said. "If something goes wrong, you'll need to find the road and get back to Mrs. Stahley. If we're clear in there, the sound of the plane is bound to alert them. If you're slow and don't make it, I'll leave you in a New York minute."

"I'm not slow," Judd said. "I'll make it."

"Good," Graham said. "There's an old stump about ten yards in front of the tree. The door to the plane will be open. Got it?"

Judd nodded. Ryan held up both thumbs and the two took off, running close to the ground.

Vicki and Chaya helped Darrion and Mrs. Stahley get settled in the garage apartment. Mrs. Stahley had found some clothes in Bruce's wife's closet that fit, but the two had little else.

"The apartment doesn't have a phone," Vicki said, "so we'll get you a cell phone to use in case of an emergency. It does have a complete kitchen, so you won't need to go out."

"This is very kind of you," Mrs. Stahley said, "but where will the hiding end? At some point they'll track us down. And when they do, you'll be caught in the middle."

"God put us together for a reason," Vicki

said. "He wants us to help. We'll take this a day at a time and pray God leads us."

Darrion flipped on the television. The reporter stated that Nicolae Carpathia would speak from New Babylon within the hour. "I can't wait," she said sarcastically.

Ryan watched Taylor Graham give Judd the signal. Before them, a grassy door in the side of the mountain opened. Ryan and the pilot scurried in. Graham hit a button that closed the door.

While the pilot readied the Learjet, Ryan walked around the hangar. The place was massive. Tools hung from one wall. In another area Ryan found fuel pumps. Ryan couldn't believe the interior of the plane. Leather seats complete with video monitors were neatly positioned about the cabin. In the rear of the plane Ryan found electronic equipment.

"We can hook up with satellites," Graham said. "We can hear and see just about anything we want up here."

"Cool," Ryan said.

Graham showed Ryan how to close the rear door once Judd was aboard. "You do what I say," Graham said, "whether your friend makes it or not. Understood?"

Ryan nodded, but he knew he wasn't going anywhere without Judd.

Judd waited for any sign of the plane. He had seen the hill open, but now, as he looked closely, he couldn't tell where the door had been. If Graham hadn't given him the tree as a reference, he would never have found the correct spot. He still couldn't see the landing strip.

A line of geese flew overhead in a perfect V. A squirrel skittered about searching for nuts in the dry leaves. Winter was coming. Instinct told the animals to prepare. Judd felt the same way about his life. He had survived nearly two years of the Tribulation. What lay ahead was more frightening than anything they had been through.

Judd heard an engine and at first thought it was the plane. To his left he saw a four-wheel drive vehicle bounce up the hill and around the tree line. A man with binoculars surveyed the landscape. Judd hit the ground and stayed there. Moments later he heard the engine rev. He lifted his head and saw the car near the willow tree. Two men disappeared beneath its branches.

Come on, Graham. Hurry! Judd said under his breath.

Ryan watched the pilot leave the plane and grab a nozzle outside. "If we didn't have this," Graham yelled, "we'd have to refuel somewhere along the East Coast. Once we're airborne, I'm not stopping until we hit the Holy Land."

Ryan heard something beep behind him.

"Hey, Mr. Taylor, sir," Ryan said, "there's something going on with your computer back here. The one with all the lines on the screen."

The pilot shut off the fuel and replaced the nozzle. He jumped into the cabin and quickly closed the door. He had a worried look on his face as he ran to the cockpit.

"What's wrong?" Ryan said.

"We've got company," Graham said. "Better get strapped into your seat."

"But I thought you wanted me to close the door once Judd—"

"There's no time to pick him up," Graham said. "I just hope Judd has the sense to throw the switch and stay where he is."

"But you can't leave him!" Ryan said.

Ryan's words were drowned by the roar of the jet engine as it came to life.

Loretta was glad to see Vicki. "You can use that apartment as long as you need it," she said.

"I don't want to impose," Vicki said.

"That's the last time I want to hear a thing about it," Loretta said. Vicki smiled, and the two hugged.

Verna Zee joined them at the kitchen table. Vicki could tell by the way Loretta served food and coffee that hospitality came naturally to her. She could also tell that Verna wasn't a people person. When Loretta talked, Verna fidgeted with her napkin. Verna was probably perfect at barking orders in the newsroom, but she was out of her element here over coffee and cookies.

The conversation turned to Bruce. Loretta politely asked if Verna had ever been involved in a church.

"That's a laugh," Verna said. "I've probably been to church about a dozen times my whole life. And that includes weddings and funerals.

"My dad was an atheist," Verna continued. "My mom grew up in a strict home. Her parents said it was evil to watch TV. Couldn't go to dances or drink anything stronger than Kool-Aid, and that may have been too strong, I don't know. When she got old enough, she turned her back on religion and said yes to my father. Then I came along."

"So you never went to church as a child or as an adult?" Loretta said.

"The idea of attending church was never discussed," Verna said. "Wasn't an option."

"And what do you think about God now?" Loretta said.

"I don't think about it," Verna said. "I figure if there is a God out there, a force or a being of some sort, he'll weigh my good and bad points."

"But haven't you ever been curious?" Loretta said. "Most people look for some kind of deeper meaning in life than what they see from day to day."

"I don't have time for deeper meaning," Verna said. "I do what I do and leave it at that."

"That seems kind of sad to me," Vicki said. "Mr. Williams talks about journalism as a noble profession. Seeking truth and all that. But you're saying—"

"Buck Williams and I are different people," Verna said. "If he wants to be motivated by the truth, fine. But I don't do it because a God is standing over me wagging his finger."

Vicki backed off and let Loretta take over.

"I think what Vicki is saying is that without some kind of deeper purpose, life is empty. To do what you do, you have to be motivated by more than your paycheck, right?"

"Look, I'll admit I don't live the happiest life on the planet," Verna said. "I'm skeptical. I see the glass as half empty. But I like being this way."

"What did you make of the disappearances last year?" Loretta said.

Verna shook her head.

Loretta took a long sip of tea and leaned back in her chair. "Verna," she said, "I'd like to tell a skeptical journalist the true story of what happened to me. That is, if you want to hear it."

Verna looked about nervously and sighed. "I guess I don't have anything better to do," she said. "I'm listening."

Judd heard the plane engine come to life. He flipped the green switch to the "on" position as Graham had said. He shut the box, replaced the stone, and kept his head down. The door in the side of the hill opened, and Judd spotted the plane. Then his jaw dropped. The grass in the middle of the clearing moved. As it did, a black line of asphalt appeared as far as he could see.

Judd looked left and saw the two men hop in their vehicle and speed toward the clearing. *Should I run or stay?* Judd thought. *If I hunker down here, they won't find me. But what about Ryan? I can't leave him alone.*

Judd waited until the men were a safe distance past him; then he stood and ran.

"How'd you get the runway to do that?" Ryan said.

"If you look closely at the field," Graham said, "you'll notice that part of the grass is greener than the rest. We put in artificial turf and motorized the strip so it would stay hidden. When I trip the wire at the end of the runway, it triggers the turf to return."

Ryan saw something move in the distance and let out a whoop. Judd was running like the wind.

The pilot cursed. "He should have stayed put," he said.

"He's going to make it," Ryan said.

"Not if those guys see him," Graham said, pointing to a car in the middle of the runway.

Judd ran as fast as he could up the hill, then picked up speed as he reached the clearing. He could see the stump of the tree. To his right, Mr. Stahley's Learjet whistled and picked up speed. To his left were the men in the car. He heard them honking their horn and yelling, but he focused on the tree stump.

He crossed the runway and jumped onto the stump as the jet roared toward him.

"Slow down!" Ryan yelled.

"There isn't time," the pilot screamed.

"He's right where you told him to be!" Ryan said. "It's not fair. Those other guys will get him for sure if we don't pick him up."

"Those guys will get all of us if we don't get out of here right now," Graham said.

The car sped toward Judd. He saw one man pull a gun and hold it out the window. The plane was going too fast. Suddenly it slowed and nearly came to a stop as he timed his jump and fell perfectly onto the cabin floor at Ryan's feet.

"The pilot was going to leave you," Ryan said. "I convinced him to stop."

"Stay low," Graham said from the cockpit. "These guys are armed to the teeth."

"I've never seen you run that fast before," Ryan said, as he buckled his seatbelt and leaned toward the floor.

"I've never had to run that fast before," Judd said.

"Hang on," Graham said from the cockpit. He swerved off the runway and barely missed the four-wheel drive. Judd heard a bullet ping off the glass in the cockpit, and Graham smiled.

"Bulletproof," Graham said. "But I hope he doesn't try for the fuel tank."

The car turned around and followed them. Graham had trouble getting back on the runway, but when he did, the plane shot forward.

"They're gaining on us!" Ryan shouted.

"I'm not worried about them," Graham

said. "I'm worried about those guys up there."

Through the front of the plane Judd could see another car parked across the runway near the end.

"How are you gonna get around that?" Judd said.

"Hang on," Graham said. "We either get this rig in the air now or we're finished."

The plane accelerated and lifted its nose. Judd heard a thud beneath them, and then they were airborne.

"Yahoo!" Ryan shouted. "We're on our way to Israel."

"What was that noise?" Judd said.

"Landing gear," Graham said. "One of the tires clipped the car. We're on our way, but we might have trouble landing."

FOUR

Loretta's Story

LORETTA began with her childhood. She had been raised in the South, where church was part of her routine.

"It was our meeting place," Loretta said. "Social and spiritual at the same time. My father taught Sunday school. My mother led Bible studies in our home. But something was missing, and I didn't realize what it was until the disappearances."

Verna rolled her eyes. "You mean that it was God," she said.

"You said a little bit ago that if there were a God, he could weigh your good and your bad," Loretta said. "I've been a member of this church for more years than I care to admit. I've served on just about every committee and group they have. If some-body had made a list of people most likely to

go to heaven, I'd have been at the top, right
up there with the pastor."

"And you don't think you measured up?"
Verna said.

"I know I didn't measure up," Loretta
said.

Verna shifted in her seat and put her hand
on her chin.

"The night people vanished, I went to the
church and found Bruce Barnes, one of our
pastors. We knew what had happened. We
watched a video the senior pastor made.
That's when I understood my life was a fake.
I wasn't a true Christian."

"This is all fascinating," Verna said, "but—"

"Bruce Barnes taught me everything,"
Loretta continued. "I learned more from him
in the last two years than in the sixty before it
combined. I'm not blamin' anybody but
myself. My daddy had gone on before, but I
lost Mama, all six of my brothers and sisters,
all of their kids, their kids' husbands and
wives. I lost my own children and grandchil-
dren. Everybody.

"A couple of weeks before it happened,
one of my daughters was over here with her
children. I was reading one of those picture
Bibles for little kids to my grandbaby. The
child was no more than three years old, and
she looked up at me with these huge, brown

eyes and said, 'Grandma, do you have Jesus living in your heart?' I was so pleased. I was glad my grandkids were growing up in a good home. And if I'd have listened closer to what that little child was saying, I wouldn't be here today."

"If that were true, then I wouldn't have a place to stay and you wouldn't have a new sermon," Verna said.

Loretta leaned closer. "I had the sermons memorized," she said. "I didn't have a relationship with God."

※

When the plane made it past the East Coast, Judd and Ryan relaxed a little. Judd told Ryan he was lucky he didn't have to endure the scrunched legroom of a commercial flight. In the Stahley jet, they could both get up and walk around.

"There are soft drinks and snacks in the kitchen area," Graham said. Judd made the pilot some coffee and sat near the cockpit.

"I knew the Global Community boys underestimated how tight Max and I were when they asked me to run the Dallas flight for them," the pilot said. "I didn't know what was up, but it was clear they trusted me and not him."

"Did you find out stuff about Carpathia?" Judd said.

"Enough to make me think there was something wrong with the guy," Graham said. "Max felt that way when he was checking out his brother's death."

Ryan looked at Judd. Judd knew what he was thinking. Maxwell Stahley's brother and his wife hadn't died. They had been raptured. Judd nodded at Ryan. "What else do you know about Carpathia?" he said.

"From Max and some of the security taps we had, I know he's not too happy with that rabbi."

"What do you think Carpathia's next move will be?" Ryan said.

"The war has put him in a perfect position," Graham said. "This is what he wanted. With people vulnerable, they'll look for help. The Global Community will give it. With the one-world currency almost in place, he's moving toward a cashless society."

"Everything will be electronic?" Ryan said.

"Exactly," Graham said. "And if he taxes every transaction, you can imagine the billions he'll rake in for his New Babylon then."

"How can people let him get away with all that?" Judd said. "You know he's a fake, right?"

"I know Max had strong suspicions,"

Graham said. "Carpathia wants to own the major media so he can control the press. He'll replace the three ambassadors who revolted with leaders who agree with him. That'll bring the Global Community back to ten regions."

"Ten leaders!" Ryan said. "Can you believe it?"

"What?" Graham said. "Did I miss something?"

Judd wondered again if Graham could be trusted fully. A man who would risk his life for them surely needed to know *why* Nicolae Carpathia was doing these things. *But should he hear it from me?* Judd thought. *Could giving him that information prove costly in the future?*

⁂

Vicki was content to listen to Loretta's story. Chloe and Amanda arrived and joined the others at the table. When Loretta was finished, Chloe told Verna how she and Buck had met because of the Rapture, and how she, Buck, and her father had become believers in Jesus Christ.

Loretta refilled Verna's cup with coffee. Verna warmed her hands over the steam and sighed. "You guys like to gang up on people, don't you?"

Everyone laughed. Verna shook her head.

"Those are interesting stories, but it seems a little wacky."

"What's so strange?" Loretta said.

"The whole thing," Verna said. "My dad warned me there'd be people like you. And not only you, but Buck is mixed up in it too. Nicolae Carpathia trusts him!"

"Verna," Chloe said, "Loretta didn't have to welcome you in here. We didn't have to offer this information. We're telling you this because we care."

Amanda defended Buck. "If there's one person on the planet you should trust, it's Buck Williams," she said.

"You and Buck have been at each other's throats for a long time," Chloe said. "He's told me about your fights."

"I think the war made our skirmishes look petty," Verna said.

"Your skirmishes were petty," Chloe said.

Verna stood and leaned against the wall. "I'll tell you the truth," she said. "I've been a little bit jealous of Buck's assignments. Buck is everything I wanted to be, and the more I look at his copy, the more it steams me. Compared to him, I feel like a college kid trying to put sentences together."

Amanda wandered out of the kitchen, then called for Chloe to come into the living room. Vicki followed and saw a news bulletin on television. People were crowding around an airplane tarmac.

"There comes Rayford," Amanda said. "Thank God he's OK."

The flight crew, followed by seven ambassadors, gathered around the microphone. Finally the camera pulled back to show Nicolae Carpathia descending the steps. Vicki was amazed at the man's ability to strike just the right pose and expression. He appeared concerned, grave, and yet somehow purposeful and confident.

As lights flashed and cameras whirred, Carpathia resolutely descended the steps and approached a bank of microphones. Every network insignia on each microphone had been redesigned to include the letters "GCN," the Global Community Network.

A woman broke from the crowd and ran directly for him. Security guards who stepped in her way quickly realized who she was and let her through.

"Is that Hattie?" Chloe said suddenly.

"Who's Hattie?" Verna said.

"Carpathia's fiancée," Chloe said. "It *is* her."

Vicki thought Carpathia looked embarrassed and awkward for once. He welcomed the woman to his side, but it was clear he was upset. Hattie leaned in to kiss him, and

Carpathia pulled her ear to his mouth and whispered something. Hattie looked stricken.

"Poor girl," Chloe said. Hattie tried to pull away from Carpathia, but he grabbed her wrist and kept her standing next to him at the microphone.

"It is so good to be back where I belong," Carpathia said. "It is wonderful to reunite with loved ones. My fiancée is overcome with grief, as I am, at the horrible events that began a few hours ago. This is a difficult time in which we live, and yet our horizons have never been wider, our challenges so great, our future so bright.

"Even though we have all suffered a great tragedy, I believe we are destined for prosperity if we commit to standing together. We will stand against any enemy of peace and embrace any friend of the Global Community."

The crowd, including the press, applauded with just the right solemnity. It made Vicki sick. Besides, she was eager to see how Darrion and Mrs. Stahley were.

Ryan sensed Judd's uneasiness. The pilot needed to hear the truth, and Ryan wanted to give it. If Graham was interested, Judd could join in. If not, Ryan could play the mouthy kid. Judd flinched when Ryan first began;

then he saw where Ryan was going and backed off.

Ryan told his whole story. When he got to the end and described his last meeting with Bruce, Graham was quiet.

"Must have hurt a lot to lose a friend like that," Graham said.

"More than you can know," Ryan said. "Bruce taught us a lot about the Bible and about what's going to happen in the future."

"OK, I'll bite," the pilot said. "What *is* going to happen in the future?"

"If I'm right," Ryan said, "everyone's going to go through some scary stuff. But people who don't believe are going to be in worse trouble than they could ever imagine."

"Max's brother talked to me once about this stuff," Graham said. "I didn't listen all that closely because I thought he was a kook. But if what you say is right, the end isn't that far off."

"Exactly," Ryan said.

Judd took over. Graham spent the hours throwing questions to both boys. Ryan was amazed at how much they both remembered from Bruce's teaching.

After the press conference, Vicki listened as Chloe pulled Verna aside.

"Verna, the information you know about Buck could ruin his career."

"It could ruin a lot more than that," Verna said.

"Will you keep quiet about what you know?" Chloe said.

"It depends. What do you think Buck would be willing to offer in exchange?"

"You know as well as I do Buck would never work that way," Chloe said.

"I figured that."

"As far as we're concerned, the most important thing is what you decide to do about Christ," Chloe said. "But you know our very lives depend on you protecting Buck from your bosses."

"Cameron's only boss is Carpathia," Verna said. She shook her head. "As much as I admire the man and what he's been able to do for America and the world, I hate the way he controls the news. We journalists are supposed to be fair. Unbiased."

"So you'll help us then?" Chloe said.

"When will Cameron be back?" Verna said.

"Sometime over the weekend," Chloe said. "And one more thing. Promise me you'll come to the memorial service for our pastor."

Verna bit her lip. "I don't know why I'm saying this, but OK. I'll wait till I talk with Buck, and I'll be at that meeting Sunday."

Chloe smiled, then laughed when Verna said, "I just hope the floor doesn't fall through when I walk in."

※

Taylor Graham landed the Learjet on a private airstrip near Tel Aviv. Judd and Ryan prepared for a rough landing. Graham masterfully landed the plane, then got out to inspect the damage.

"Doesn't look too bad," Graham said. "I know a guy who can fix it and keep quiet. We won't have to go through customs, but we'll probably run into some Global Community checkpoints on the way."

"We?" Judd said.

"If you don't mind the company," Graham said, "I'd like to go along. I might be able to help you find the people you're looking for."

Judd stammered. "We . . . wanted to do this on our own."

"Hey, I'll back off," Graham said, putting up both hands. "A little rest by the seashore sounds good to me. I'll wait to hear from you."

Judd conferred with Ryan.

"What about the checkpoints?" Judd said to Graham. "Won't the GC be looking for you?"

"I have a fake ID," Graham said. "My GC connections could come in handy, but—"

"If you're willing to follow our lead," Judd said, "we want you to come with us."

"Hey, I've followed so far," Graham said. "I'll give my mechanic a call and get a car."

Vicki checked on Darrion and Mrs. Stahley. Chaya was with them. She had brought dinner and the cell phone.

"We saw Carpathia," Mrs. Stahley said.

"Made me sick," Darrion said. "That man is the reason my father is dead."

Chaya motioned for Vicki to step outside. "I didn't want them to know this, but there's been a strange car across the street all afternoon."

"You think it's GC?" Vicki said.

"I'm not sure," Chaya said. "I had Lionel create a diversion so I could come over here. The social worker, Mrs. Goodwin, called. She wants to meet with you."

"At the house?"

"I told her you were out and she seemed nervous," Chaya said. "She said she'd meet you at nine o'clock at that coffee place on Rand Road."

"I don't like leaving Mrs. Stahley and Darrion," Vicki said. "Did she say what she wants?"

"She wouldn't tell me," Chaya said. "Just to meet her there tonight."

Vicki told the Stahleys she had to go out and that they should not answer the door if anyone came. Chaya drove Vicki to the coffee shop, and they looked for Mrs. Goodwin. They parked across the street and waited until they saw the woman walk in.

Chaya stayed in the car while Vicki went inside.

"I'm glad you're here," Mrs. Goodwin said when she saw Vicki. "Let's go to my car." The woman looked upset.

Vicki didn't know if she should get in. It could be a trap. Vicki looked inside. The car was empty.

"Is there a problem?" Mrs. Goodwin said.

Vicki shook her head and climbed in.

"What did you want to talk about?" Vicki said.

The woman shook her head. "I know I shouldn't be here," she said. "Your house is being watched by the Global Community. They say you may be hiding a murder suspect."

Judd and Ryan located the garage near the hangar and found three vehicles stashed by Mr. Stahley.

"He was prepared for everything," Ryan said.

Judd chose a late-model sedan that looked like it could move fast. Graham got behind the wheel, and Judd did a double take. The man had sunglasses, a mustache, and a goatee.

"You grow hair that fast?" Ryan said.

"Another precaution," Graham said, with a hint of British accent. "From here on out, I'm Geoffrey Croton. Jolly old chap from just outside London, you know."

"I always wanted to meet somebody who talked like that," Ryan said.

"Sit back and relax," the pilot said, as he revved the engine. "We've got a long drive ahead and who knows what in between."

"Murder suspect?" Vicki said, stunned. Was this woman giving information for Vicki's own good, or was she a pawn in the hands of the Global Community? "Who am I supposed to be hiding?" Vicki said.

"I don't know exactly," Mrs. Goodwin said, "but it must be someone pretty important. I got wind of it earlier this afternoon."

"Why are you telling me this?" Vicki said.

Mrs. Goodwin looked about nervously. "Ever since that day at the school, I've thought of you. The way you handled yourself under the pressure of our questions and the way you talked about what you believe."

"That's why you're here?" Vicki said.

"Partly," Mrs. Goodwin said. "You deserve every chance I can give. First, you need to know about the call that came in about you. All calls are monitored. It was from Barrington, from a Mr. Stein."

"Chaya's dad!" Vicki gasped.

"He told us about your father's death and gave us information about your religious views, things I already knew from your answers at the hearing."

"Did he say anything about me hiding someone?" Vicki said.

"No, that was another source," Mrs. Goodwin said. "All I know is that you're in great danger." Mrs. Goodwin started the car. "I can't stay here. We need to keep moving."

Vicki looked behind her to see if Chaya was following them. She thought she saw her once, but lost sight of the car in traffic.

FIVE

Video Truth

Mrs. Goodwin drove through town and parked on a residential street. "This should be OK," the woman said.

"What are you afraid of?" Vicki said.

"The Global Community," Mrs. Goodwin said. "You have to find another place to stay tonight."

"I have one," Vicki said, "but I still don't know why you're helping me."

Mrs. Goodwin had avoided eye contact with Vicki. Now she turned in her seat and pursed her lips.

"I work with troubled kids everyday," Mrs. Goodwin said. "There are thousands who have been left homeless because of the disappearances. I'm sure a lot of them have fallen through the cracks."

"I wish I had," Vicki said.

"I'm glad you didn't," Mrs. Goodwin said. "I talk with some pretty tough kids. You're the first one who seemed to have more direction than the people trying to help her."

"Ma'am?" Vicki said.

"Your principal, Mrs. Jenness, and the other teacher, Mrs. Waltonen," Mrs. Goodwin said. "They put up a front that they had it together. I could tell they were scared."

"Do you know anything about Mrs. Waltonen?" Vicki said. "I saw her at Judd's graduation, but I haven't heard anything more."

Mrs. Goodwin said that Mrs. Waltonen and Coach Handlesman were both at a re-education facility. Mrs. Goodwin said, "From the moment I heard you, I knew at some point I needed to talk with you."

Vicki held her hands open as if to say, "I'm all ears."

"I've tried to be a good person all my life," Mrs. Goodwin said. "When I was a kid, they called me Goody Two-Shoes. I was at the top of my class academically. I volunteered for social organizations. I was popular."

"You look like you could have been a cheerleader," Vicki said.

Mrs. Goodwin smiled. "Varsity squad. When I went to college, I studied to teach disabled children. I worked with Social

Services and saw how much help they needed, so I took this position."

"How does that fit with me?" Vicki said.

"When you spoke of your faith," Mrs. Goodwin said, "you didn't talk about living up to rules and regulations. That's what I've always thought about religion. You do your best and hope."

"That's what most people think," Vicki said.

"I've cornered the market on helping people," Mrs. Goodwin said. "I've gone overseas to feed the starving; I've worked at soup kitchens in the city. I've even taken people into my home to give them a place to stay. But I've never felt accepted by God. I've never really been sure like you. Over the last few months, I couldn't get what you said out of my mind. I knew I had to talk with you. When the call came about your father, and I got wind of what the Global Community was saying, I had to come."

"I'm glad you did," Vicki said.

"So tell me," Mrs. Goodwin said, "how can you be sure God accepts you?"

✳

The sun was coming up when Ryan, Judd, and Taylor Graham neared Jerusalem. Ryan pointed each time he saw a familiar biblical landmark. He couldn't believe they were so close to the Sea of Galilee. Then came Nazareth.

Judd pointed out other spots he and Bruce had seen from their earlier trips. Ryan asked questions as they passed roads leading to Jericho, the Dead Sea, and the Jordan River. A few miles from Jerusalem, Ryan spotted a sign for Bethlehem.

"Don't get too excited," Graham said. "Look up ahead."

Ryan saw a line of cars and what looked like tollbooths.

"It's a GC checkpoint," Graham said. "Let me do the talking."

They waited in line a few minutes, then pulled forward to a uniformed Global Community officer, who asked the nature of their visit.

"My good man," Graham said in his cockney accent, "we're on holiday. Seeing the sights. Enjoying the safety, if you know what I mean."

Graham laughed and handed the man the passports. "Don't suppose you'd know how we could get in to see those shouting chaps down at the Wailing Wall, would you?" he continued. "We've seen them on—"

"This is not a tourist center," the guard said, looking closely at the passports. "Why do you have the two Americans with you?"

"They're in my charge for a few days," Graham said innocently. "As I said, we're on holiday."

The guard bent down to look at Ryan and Judd. He handed the passports back. "You may go," he said.

"We passed our first test," Graham said. "Now where?"

Judd handed him an address. "We're going to the Ben-Judah house," he said. "I want to see it myself."

Vicki remembered praying that God would use what she had said in the meeting at the school. She hadn't planned on it affecting Mrs. Goodwin.

"You know about my parents and how the rest of my family disappeared," Vicki said.

"And I know about Pastor Barnes and how he helped you," Mrs. Goodwin said. "I want to *know* that God accepts my efforts. And I want to be sure about what's to come."

"God always keeps his word," Vicki said. "The prophecies in the Bible are coming true all around us. So you can be sure that what God says will happen."

"I believe that," Mrs. Goodwin said.

"The Bible says that if you confess with your mouth Jesus is Lord and believe in your heart that God raised him from the dead, you will be saved."

"That's it?" Mrs. Goodwin said.

"That's the beginning," Vicki said.

"So all the good I've done is worthless?" Mrs. Goodwin said. "All I needed to do was believe something?"

"Somebody explained it this way," Vicki said. "Suppose everybody in the world is required to jump to the moon. That's the goal. Some people jump really high. Some people can't jump at all. Some don't even try. But no matter who they are, no one can jump to the moon."

"What's the point?"

"God is holy. He's perfect in every way. So those who want to follow him have to be perfect. But we're not. We sin. And sin separates us from God. The good things you've done are like those jumps. They were a good try, but you're never going to make it unless someone takes you there."

"And that's where Jesus comes in. . . ."

"Exactly," Vicki said. "Jesus was God in the flesh. He lived a perfect life and paid the penalty so you could be accepted by God. That's why I know you can be sure about heaven. Jesus said whoever believes in him will not die but will have eternal life."

Mrs. Goodwin looked toward the street,

deep in thought. "So if you don't do good things to get to God," she said, "why do them at all?"

"When somebody has given his life for you," Vicki said, "you want to love and serve him with everything you have."

Judd gasped when he saw the Ben-Judahs' house. It was nothing but a charred pile. Smoke still filled the air. The area was cordoned off by police tape.

"The reports about the fire were right," Ryan said.

Judd asked Graham and Ryan to stay put while he looked around.

"Be careful what you say," Graham said.

Judd walked the street, asking for anyone who spoke English. He came to the house next door where he, Nina, and Dan had slipped through a secret passage. A boy who looked about fifteen sat in a small garden with a water fountain.

"I speak English, yes," the boy said.

Judd let himself inside the gate and sat down. The boy was average in size, but a little heavy.

"You have seen the news," the boy said. "My house is famous because it's the one next to that mess."

"I'm Judd Thompson," Judd said, as he stretched out his hand.

"My name is Samuel," the boy said.

"Nina and Dan were friends of mine," Judd said.

Immediately, Samuel closed his eyes and let his head fall to his chest. "You could get in trouble mentioning their names in this neighborhood," he said. "I can't talk about them. My father does not permit it."

"I remember your house," Judd said. "Nina, Dan, and I went through the tunnel—"

Samuel put up his hand. "I must go," he said.

"Please," Judd said. "I don't believe they're dead."

Samuel shook his head. "You are wrong," he said softly.

"I've come a long way," Judd said. "Tell me what you know."

Samuel raised his voice. "I am glad they are dead! We are better off without those who would blaspheme the name of God."

Judd saw two men pass near the garden and walk on. Samuel lowered his voice. "Why should I believe you?" he said. "You could be working with the attackers. You could be one of them."

Judd knew he had to be careful, but he felt he should trust this boy.

"I am a believer in Christ, as were Nina and Dan," Judd said. "For some reason, God sent me here. If you know anything that would help, I want to hear it."

Samuel looked toward the street again and leaned close, barely moving his lips. "I will do better than that," he said. "I will say good-bye to you and go inside the house. Wait a few moments, then go to the side entrance. The door will be unlocked."

Samuel stood, shook hands with Judd, and left. A few moments later Judd went inside. Judd heard a noise and found a stairwell leading to a basement.

"Welcome to my hideaway," Samuel said. "My mother no longer lives with us, and my father has left for work. He let me stay home today."

"I'm glad," Judd said. "Now maybe I can get to the bottom of this."

Samuel led Judd to a small room with a computer and some electronic gear. Judd waited while the boy retrieved a video camera.

"You must understand that what I am about to show you must not be revealed to anyone," Samuel said.

"I understand," Judd said.

Samuel hooked up the connections. "You were right about the passageway," he said.

"We allowed Nina and Dan to go through our home. But my father said the risk was getting too great. When the rabbi went on television and proclaimed Jesus as the Messiah, our whole community was under suspicion.

"I have known Nina and Dan for years," Samuel said. "I knew them before their father died and Mrs. Ben-Judah married the rabbi. It was a shock that their stepfather had betrayed the faith, but I never held them personally responsible."

"Do you know anything about what they believed?" Judd said.

"We had many talks in this very room," Samuel said. "After my father sealed up the entrance, I still met with them. They were very frightened."

"And for good reason, it sounds like," Judd said.

"I will tell you about the day it happened," Samuel said. "But I must warn you. You may not wish to hear or see what is on this video-tape."

Judd nodded. "I want to see all of it," he said.

※

Vicki led Mrs. Goodwin in a simple prayer. "God, I know I'm a sinner and I need your forgiveness. I believe Jesus died for me, and I ask you to come into my life now. Forgive me of my sins. I don't trust in myself or my own goodness anymore but in your Son, Jesus. Amen."

Mrs. Goodwin said, "Amen."

Samuel prepared the equipment and sat in front of the video monitor. "Before I show you this, I will tell you about that day," he said.

"I'm ready," Judd said, taking a deep breath.

"I was sick that day. My father let me stay home but told me not to go outside. I couldn't sit in the garden or go onto the patio. I had nothing to do but watch television and read. In the afternoon, I sat near the window and watched traffic, waiting for my father.

"That's when I saw the van. It pulled into a parking space down the street. No one got out. The glass was tinted, so I couldn't see who it was. It just sat there. Mrs. Ben-Judah came outside for something, and I saw movement inside the van, just shadows.

"I had no idea how it would turn out," Samuel continued, "and you should not think I am able to tell the future, but I pulled out my video camera and used the zoom lens to get a better look. As I turned it on, Dr. Ben-Judah's driver pulled up. Nina and Dan got out."

Samuel paused. Judd nodded, and the boy pushed the Play button on the camera.

Mrs. Goodwin drove Vicki back to the coffee shop. Headlights flashed brightly in the rearview mirror.

"Someone's getting out of that car," Mrs. Goodwin said. "Do you want me to keep going?"

"No!" Vicki said, recognizing Chaya. Chaya tapped on the driver's window. She looked angrily at Mrs. Goodwin, then at Vicki.

"Are you all right?" Chaya said.

"It's OK," Vicki said. "Mrs. Goodwin and I were just talking about some really important stuff."

Chaya looked relieved. "Good," she said, "but I need you to come with me, if you're through."

"We're finished." Mrs. Goodwin smiled. She took Vicki's hand and squeezed it. "Find a safe place and stay there." She handed her card to Vicki. "Call me at this number when you get settled. I'm sure I'll have more questions."

"How did you find us?" Vicki said when she was in the car with Chaya.

"I lost you when you turned off the main

road," Chaya said. "I thought she might take you to the detention center, so I went there. I waited a while and then went to Loretta's to see if you were there. That's when I found this."

Chaya handed Vicki a piece of paper. Vicki unfolded it and saw Mrs. Stahley's elegant handwriting.

"They're gone, Vick," Chaya said. "Darrion and Mrs. Stahley are gone."

Samuel's camera work was shaky. Judd could see the unmarked van in the background. Nina and Dan got out of the car and went into their house. They passed the two guards at the front door, posted by Dr. Ben-Judah for his family's safety.

Judd felt queasy watching the video, like there should be an eerie soundtrack to go along with the pictures.

"I turned off the camera, and then it started," Samuel said. "I turned the camera back on as quickly as I could."

The tape jumped to a horrifying scene. Several hooded thugs shot automatic weapons at the house. Judd couldn't see the guards of Dr. Ben-Judah, but there was little return fire.

The camera pulled away from the window, and Judd heard the heavy breathing of

Samuel saying something in Hebrew. There were shouts on the street and confusion.

"I did not know what to do," Samuel said, as Judd watched. "I froze. Then I placed the camera on the windowsill and went into the other room."

With the camera's zoom pulled back, Judd could see the entire scene. One thug stood by the van and waited. Shots rang out inside the house. More shouting. Then Mrs. Ben-Judah was dragged outside. Judd heard Nina cry out. He couldn't watch.

"What did Nina say?"

"She cried for her mother," Samuel said. "I will translate for you."

Next, Nina was brought into the street. *They're making an example of them,* Judd thought.

"Where is he?" the thug said. "Where is the rabbi?"

"I will not betray my father!" Nina screamed.

"Tell us now!" the man screamed back.

Such courage, Judd thought. In the face of death, Nina would not give them any information. Dan was dragged out last. A man ran to the van and brought a container inside the house.

"Spare your life," the thug sneered at Dan. "Tell us where your father is."

Dan stammered and looked into the face of his hooded captor.

"Now! Before it is too late!" the man screamed.

"Let me see your face," Dan finally said.

The man was standing over Dan and facing the camera. He lifted his mask and bent low. Judd could see the man had a heavy, black beard and a mustache. "Now, tell me! Where is Tsion Ben-Judah?"

Dan spat in the man's face.

"You insolent—"

"I would rather die than betray my father!" Dan said.

Those were Dan's last words.

A crackling sound grew in the background. One of the thugs yelled, "The rabbi is not inside. What now?"

"To the university," another said.

As the van pulled away, Judd heard a siren in the distance. Neighbors waited a few moments, then rushed to look at the three lifeless bodies. Then the screen went blank.

Judd could not speak. The horror of what he had seen was too much.

"No matter what one thinks of their beliefs," Samuel finally said, "they died honorably."

"They were treated like animals," Judd choked.

"I do not know where the rabbi is,"

Samuel said. "Maybe his driver saw what happened and found him before the others. No one knows where he took him. On the news, the driver claims he knows nothing."

"The report I heard was true," Judd said. "My friends are dead. We came here for nothing."

"I have not been able to show this to anyone," Samuel said. "Not even my own father. I do not know what to do with it."

Judd heard the front door open, and a man called for Samuel.

"Here he is now," the boy said.

Judd went to the side door. Samuel ran after him. "Take this with you," Samuel whispered, shoving the small videotape into Judd's jacket pocket.

SIX

To the Wall

WHAT'S taking Judd so long? Ryan thought, as Taylor Graham snored. When Judd finally returned to the car he looked worried. Ryan woke the pilot, who suggested they find a hotel. They checked into the King David and found their room.

"I'm gonna crash for a couple hours," Graham said. "Wake me when you need me."

Ryan sat with Judd. He had never seen his friend so depressed. Judd flicked on CNN, but Ryan turned it off with the remote.

"Talk to me," Ryan said.

"Why did we come here?" Judd said flatly. "And with a guy we've just met. It was crazy."

"You know we had to check on the Ben-Judahs," Ryan said. "God wanted us here."

"Maybe he did, maybe he didn't," Judd said. "Looks like a wasted trip to me."

"What did you see in that house?" Ryan said.

Judd told him about the video. Ryan cringed when he heard the details. Judd pulled out the cassette.

"No one sees this, and no one gets access to it," Judd said. "I'm putting it in the safe downstairs."

"Then what?" Ryan said.

Judd shrugged. "As long as we're here, you might as well see the sights," he said. "And the most impressive are at the Wailing Wall."

※

"What do you mean they're gone?" Vicki shouted. "I told them to stay put."

"Read the note," Chaya said.

Vicki couldn't believe what she saw. Mrs. Stahley's beautiful handwriting cut Vicki to the heart.

Dear Friends, the note read, *Darrion and I have appreciated your concern and sacrifice. You have risked your lives for our safety and we thank you. However, our very presence puts you in danger. We cannot do that any longer. We believe God will protect us and you. Thank you for your kindness. Sincerely, Louise Stahley.*

"They must have overheard me when I told you the house was being watched," Chaya said.

Vicki shook her head. "I hope she knows what she's doing," she said.

"Where do you think they went?" Chaya said.

"I don't know," Vicki said. "I just hope we can find them before the Global Community does."

Judd secured the videotape at the front desk. He placed the key in his wallet. Near the elevator Ryan tapped Judd on the shoulder and nodded toward the front of the hotel. Judd saw Buck Williams.

"He's traveling as light as we are," Ryan said.

Buck was shocked to see Judd and Ryan. "You're taking a big chance," Buck said.

Judd explained what they had learned about the Ben-Judah family. "Have you heard anything from Dr. Ben-Judah?" Judd said.

"Nothing firsthand," Buck said. "I just came from the airport and met one of the rabbi's friends. He said Rabbi Ben-Judah called him once and said that I would know where to start looking."

"Where's that?" Ryan said.

"No way," Buck said, shaking his head. "You two are out of this. The authorities are even trying to pin the murders of his family on the rabbi."

"That's loony!" Ryan said.

"I agree," Buck said, "but the people out to get Tsion will stop at nothing. His driver was killed in a car bombing. That's why I'm saying you two should get back to the States."

"If that's so," Judd said, "they're following you right now."

"I've taken precautions," Buck said. "I'm registered here under the name of Herb Katz. I'm going to my room to make a few calls and get some sleep. I'll see you when I get back home."

Vicki and Chaya went back to Bruce's house. Lionel was still there, and the two brought him up to speed.

"If Mr. Stahley had a secret hangar for his plane," Lionel said, "you can bet he had another secret house or cabin somewhere."

"Still," Vicki said, "you have to believe Mrs. Stahley will try to get back to her place for the documents she talked about."

"There's no chance," Lionel said. "The Global Community goons will be crawling all over the place. Plus, we've got problems of our own."

"What?"

"School is back in session starting tomorrow," Lionel said.

Vicki thought a minute. "That might not be a problem," she said.

Judd and Ryan took turns napping in the lobby of the hotel so they wouldn't miss Buck. Near sundown, Buck briskly walked to a cabstand. Judd and Ryan followed.

Judd paid the cabbie when they reached the Wailing Wall. They saw Buck walk toward a wrought-iron fence, where the two witnesses prophesied.

The two men called themselves Moishe and Eli, and truly they seemed to have come from another time and another place. They wore ragged, burlap-like robes. They were barefoot with leathery, dark skin. Both had long, dark gray hair and unkempt beards. They looked strong and had bony joints and long muscled arms and legs. Anyone who dared get close to them smelled smoke. Those who dared attack them had been killed. Several had rushed them with automatic weapons, only to seem to hit an invisible wall and drop dead on the spot. Others had been overcome by fire that had come from the witnesses' mouths.

They preached almost constantly in the language of the Bible, and what they said angered the devout Jews. They preached about Jesus Christ, proclaiming him the Messiah, the Son of God.

Judd had seen the witnesses with Bruce. Hearing their voices again made a chill go down his spine. Ryan was excited at the sight and drank it in. As usual, a huge crowd had gathered, though people kept their distance.

This evening the witnesses were doing as they had done every day since the signing of the treaty between Israel and Nicolae Carpathia. They were proclaiming the terrible Day of the Lord. They acknowledged Jesus Christ as "the Mighty God, the Everlasting Father, and the Prince of Peace. Let no other man anywhere call himself the ruler of this world! Any man who makes such a claim is not the Christ but the Antichrist, and he shall surely die! Woe unto anyone who preaches another gospel! Jesus is the only true God, maker of heaven and earth!"

Judd pointed out all the different people of various races and cultures in the crowd. "They're understanding the message in their own language," he said.

"Unbelievable," Ryan said.

Judd saw Buck edge farther into the crowd of about three hundred. Suddenly, both preachers stopped and moved forward toward the fence. The crowd seemed to step back in fear.

"I think they see him," Ryan said. "They're both staring straight at Buck."

Without gesturing or moving, Eli began to preach. "He who has ears to hear, let him hear! Do not be afraid, for I know that you seek Jesus, who was crucified. He is not here, for He is risen, as He said."

Judd was riveted. Moishe stepped forward and looked directly toward Buck. "Do not be afraid, for I know whom you seek. He is not here."

Eli again: "Go quickly and tell His disciples that Christ is risen from the dead!"

Moishe, still staring at Buck: "Indeed, He is going before you into Galilee. There you will see Him. Behold, I have told you."

The witnesses stood and stared silently for so long, unmoving, it was as if they had turned to stone. The crowd grew nervous, and some left. Some waited to hear the witnesses speak again, but they remained still. Judd and Ryan moved farther to the back so Buck wouldn't see them. Soon, Buck was left standing alone, with the two witnesses still staring at him. The witnesses seemed not even to breathe. No blink, no twitch. Their faces almost glowed with the final rays of sunlight. Neither opened his mouth, and yet Judd heard, plain as day in English, "He who has ears to hear, let him hear."

"What's Buck saying to them?" Ryan said.

"I can't hear," Judd said. "Let's move closer."

Buck asked the witnesses, "If I came back here later tonight, might I learn more?"

Moishe backed away from the fence and sat on the pavement, leaning against a wall. Eli gestured and spoke aloud, "Birds of the air have nests," he said, "but the Son of Man has nowhere to lay his head."

"I don't understand," Buck said. "Tell me more."

"He who has ears to hear—"

Judd thought Buck looked frustrated. "I'll come back at midnight," Buck said, interrupting Eli. "I'm pleading for your help."

Eli backed away. "Lo, I am with you always, even to the end of the age."

Judd and Ryan hid as Buck left.

"Was that something, or what?" Ryan said. "Those were the words Jesus spoke to his followers. You think they'll actually help him find Rabbi Ben-Judah?"

"If anyone can help him," Judd said, "those two can."

※

"You're not thinking about reviving the *Underground,* are you?" Lionel said.

Vicki smiled. "It's a perfect chance to invite those who haven't heard the message yet."

"Wait," Chaya said, "I'm not following either of you."

Vicki told Chaya about the *Underground* and what they had been through with the secret newspaper. Vicki and Judd had paid a great price for their involvement. Since the graduation ceremony in the spring, the *Underground* hadn't made an appearance.

"And you want to invite people to do what?" Chaya said.

"Come to Bruce's funeral," Vicki said. "If we get started on the copy now, we can get it into their hands by Friday. The service is on Sunday, and you know it's going to be evangelistic."

"But if they catch you—" Lionel said.

"I'm past worrying about that," Vicki said. "We're in a war for people's souls now. We can't afford to be careful."

Judd and Ryan didn't want to go back to the hotel. They would let Graham sleep and wait until Buck returned. They wandered the old city, visiting the sights of the ancient world. The newly rebuilt temple was lit up to look like something in a three-dimensional picture show. It seemed to hover on the horizon.

"You know what Bruce said about that place," Ryan said. "One day Nicolae Carpathia will sit in that new temple and proclaim himself God."

Judd shivered. "I wouldn't want to be near that guy for a million bucks," he said.

Judd showed Ryan the Garden of Gethsemane, the Garden Tomb, and the Mount of Olives, where Jesus would return in triumph.

"It won't be too long," Ryan said. "One day we're going to be able to sit down with Bruce and get answers to all the questions we've ever had."

Judd and Ryan ate dinner, then returned to the Wailing Wall before midnight. They came upon a small group of sailors strolling past the fence.

"Where are the two weirdos?" one sailor said.

"Over that way," another said.

Buck drove up in a cab and hurried toward them. Ryan and Judd stepped out of sight. Buck was carrying his overnight bag.

"Looks like he's on the move," Ryan said.

Buck hung back and waited for the sailors to leave. When he moved forward, Eli and Moishe raised their heads and looked directly at him. Buck walked to the fence. He whispered something to the witnesses, and Eli said, "He who has ears to hear—"

Judd inched closer and listened as Buck said, "I know that, but I—"

"You would dare interrupt the servants of the Most High God?" Eli said.

"Forgive me," Buck said.

Moishe spoke. "You must first communicate with the one who loves you."

Judd gave Ryan a puzzled look.

"What does he mean?" Ryan said.

Before Judd could answer, Buck's cell phone rang. Judd heard Buck say "Chloe," and understood. These witnesses knew so much.

Buck got off the phone. Moishe and Eli huddled and seemed to be whispering. They approached the fence.

Suddenly the two began shouting at the top of their lungs. Judd and Ryan stepped back, startled, then listened as Eli and Moishe traded off quoting verses.

"And it shall come to pass in the last days, says God," they shouted, "that I will pour out My Spirit on all flesh; your sons and your daughters shall prophesy, your young men shall see visions, your old men shall dream dreams."

The men looked at Buck.

"What's that all about?" Ryan whispered.

"Shh, listen," Judd said.

The witnesses continued: "And on My menservants and on My maidservants I will pour out My Spirit in those days; and they shall prophesy. I will show wonders in heaven above and signs in the earth beneath: blood and fire and vapor of smoke. The sun shall be turned into darkness, and the moon into blood, before the coming of the great and awesome day of the Lord. And it shall come to pass that whoever calls on the name of the Lord shall be saved."

Buck picked up his bag and moved closer. Judd heard others in the crowd warn him. "Better not do that, you'll regret it!" someone said.

Buck whispered something, and Eli spoke softly. Buck retreated to the crowd. "Did they hurt you, son?" a man said. Buck shook his head.

Moishe began to preach in a loud voice: "Now after John was put in prison, Jesus came to Galilee, preaching the gospel of the kingdom of God, and saying 'The time is fulfilled, and the kingdom of God is at hand. Repent, and believe in the gospel.'

"And as He walked by the Sea of Galilee, He saw Simon and Andrew his brother casting a net into the sea; for they were fishermen. Then Jesus said to them, 'Follow Me, and I will make you become fishers of men.'

"They immediately left their nets and followed Him."

Ryan tugged on Judd's arm. "It's like they're speaking in a biblical code," he said. "They're telling Buck where to look for the rabbi, but nobody knows it but Buck."

Buck drifted from the crowd, lugged his bag to a short taxi line, and climbed into the back of a small cab. "Can a fella get a boat ride up the Jordan River into Lake Tiberius at this time of night?" Judd heard Buck ask the driver.

"Well, sir, to tell you the truth," the cabbie said, "it's a lot easier coming the other way. But, yes, there are motorized boats heading north. And some do run in the night."

Judd and Ryan watched as the driver sped off. "Looks like we're not gonna follow this time," Judd said.

"Why not?"

"I'm almost out of cash," Judd said. "Besides, I think Buck's right. We need to get back home."

Judd headed for a cab and noticed Ryan wasn't budging. "It'd be different if Bruce were here," Ryan said.

"How?" Judd said.

"He wouldn't give up this easy," Ryan said. "God brought us here for a reason. I don't know what it is, but if those two guys can help Buck find somebody, they might be able to help us figure it out."

Judd looked at the witnesses. His first reaction was to tell Ryan to cut the guilt trip. But he knew being in Israel was a dream come true for Ryan.

"All right," Judd said. "Let's see what they say."

Ryan was glad Judd had changed his mind. The crowd was much smaller as they approached. The witnesses were silent. Ryan boldly made his way to the front, and Judd followed.

"This is the chance of a lifetime," Ryan whispered. "I never thought I'd see them this close."

"Be careful, boys," an older man said. "They can breathe fire."

Ryan turned and looked at the man. He had graying hair and wore the clothing of a religious man. "Thank you, sir," Ryan said, "but we don't have anything to fear from these men. They're preaching the truth about Jesus. I believe what they say. He died, was buried, and rose again on the third day. He's alive right now. Those who believe in him don't have to worry about these witnesses. . . ."

A murmur went up in the crowd. People around Ryan stepped back as if they had seen a ghost. When Ryan turned, he saw both witnesses at the fence, looking straight at him.

SEVEN

Arrested

RYAN didn't know what to say. The two witnesses stared at him. Judd stood at Ryan's side.

Eli was the first to speak. "Blessed are those who mourn," he said.

Ryan's eyes widened. "You're talking about my friend, Bruce, right?" he said.

A single tear fell onto the leathery face of the man at the fence. "Blessed are those who mourn," he said again, "for they shall be comforted."

Moishe spoke. "The kingdom of heaven is like a mustard seed, which a man took and sowed in his field, which indeed is the least of all the seeds. . . ." When Moishe said the word *least*, he paused, looked at Ryan, then continued. "But when it is grown it is greater than the herbs and becomes a tree, so that the birds of the air come and nest in its branches."

Eli again: "Assuredly, I say to you, unless you are converted and become as little children, you will by no means enter the kingdom of heaven."

Ryan was awestruck. Judd stood with his mouth open. The crowd had retreated, and the boys were alone with the witnesses.

Eli and Moishe looked at Judd with their piercing eyes. Their lips did not move, but Judd heard them distinctly.

"The Lord is slow to anger and great in power, and will not at all acquit the wicked."

Will not acquit the wicked, Judd thought. God was telling them that he would never let guilty people go unpunished.

Judd and Ryan were quiet on the trip back to the hotel. Their experience had left them speechless. A note from Taylor Graham lay on Judd's pillow.

"You two obviously don't need me hanging around. I found an air strip close to Jerusalem. Call me on my cell phone when you're ready to leave."

"Should we have told him where we went?" Ryan said.

"I'd rather have it this way," Judd said. "I just hope he doesn't take off and leave us."

Judd and Ryan both slept hard through the morning and into the afternoon. When Judd awoke, he found Ryan watching the news. Ryan turned it off and asked to talk.

"The first thing the witnesses said to me was clear," Ryan said. "They knew I was mourning Bruce. It's the part about the mustard seed I don't understand."

"I don't think they were trying to tell you something as much as report it," Judd said. "You've got a lot of faith for a young person. God can use you or anybody who puts their trust in him."

"That makes sense," Ryan said. "What about that stuff about God being slow to get angry?"

"At first I was scared that I'd done something bad," Judd said. "But I can't help but think it has something to do with the tape."

"I don't get it."

"Maybe God is going to judge the people who killed the rabbi's family."

"And he's going to use us to help do it?" Ryan said.

"Exactly," Judd said.

"You're not thinking of going to the authorities with the tape?" Ryan said.

"I know it sounds dumb, but—"

"It's worse than dumb," Ryan said. "It's

suicide. If the murderers are just religious zealots, you're fine. But if they're connected with the Global Community, they'll want that tape. And then they'll want to do away with anyone who's seen it."

"The Ben-Judahs were my friends," Judd said. "They didn't deserve to be killed."

"You want revenge," Ryan said.

"I don't!" Judd said. "I want to do what God wants me to."

Judd called Vicki to check in. He was aghast that Mrs. Stahley and Darrion were gone. He promised to get in touch with Taylor Graham to see if he had any ideas where they might have gone.

"I wanted to call you earlier," Vicki said. "Something really strange happened to Loretta."

"Fill me in," Judd said.

"I was at Loretta's house with Chloe and Amanda. Loretta called and said she was working alone at the church, and she had an urge to pray for Buck. She said she was so overcome with emotion that she stood up, then got dizzy and fell to her knees. Once she was kneeling, she realized she wasn't dizzy but was just praying for Buck."

"Weird," Judd said. "Have you heard anything from him?"

"Just that he's still looking for the rabbi," Vicki said.

Judd told Vicki about seeing Buck the previous night. "Some strange things are happening over here," he said. "It might just be me, but God seems to be working in more direct and dramatic ways all the time."

"He's about to work in more dramatic ways here," Vicki said. She explained their plan with the *Underground*.

"Don't take any unnecessary risks," Judd said.

Vicki laughed. "I could say the same to you."

🌟

Ryan fought with Judd about the tape, while Judd tried to call Taylor Graham.

"I don't see how God could be saying two totally different things to two people," Ryan said. "I've got a feeling that we should head over to the rabbi's office and have a look around. Maybe Buck hasn't found him yet and we can help."

"This is what I've decided," Judd said. "If you don't want to help, you don't have to."

Ryan rolled his eyes. "Pulling seniority again," he said.

"It's late," Judd said. "First thing in the morning we'll head to the police station."

Vicki looked over the *Underground* and smiled. It had been a long time since she had been involved in writing and producing the paper.

The front page dealt with the bombings and what was predicted in the Bible. The story continued inside with specific prophesies that had already been fulfilled. On the back was an invitation to Bruce's funeral Sunday morning. The kids scanned in a picture of Bruce.

Vicki wrote, *He was the only pastor on the church staff to be left behind. But the disappearances of most of his congregation changed his life. The prophesies that appear in this edition were taught by Bruce Barnes, but he left many more. Hear his story and what he believes is coming after World War III Sunday morning at New Hope Village Church.*

"You think they'll come?" Lionel said.

"Wouldn't you want to know what's coming next from somebody who had nailed the future so accurately?" Vicki said.

Lionel nodded. "How are we going to get the paper inside the school? You know how tight security is."

"We have one day to figure it out," Vicki said.

※

Ryan didn't want to hold Judd's passport or wait outside the police station, but Judd was set on the idea. Ryan was glad Judd had compromised with him and left the tape in the vault at the hotel.

"You wait here and if anything happens, call Taylor Graham right away," Judd said.

"As if that's going to help," Ryan said.

"He was probably out of range when I called," Judd said.

"On a satellite phone?" Ryan scoffed. "He didn't answer last night or this morning. He's probably on his way back home without us."

Ryan stood by the door and watched as Judd strode through the door to the police headquarters.

Judd got nowhere being polite. He was an American in a foreign country. He stood in one line, then was told to wait in another. Finally he grabbed the arm of an officer going by. The man looked at him sternly.

"I have information about the murders of the rabbi's family," Judd said.

The man immediately took Judd into a corner office. Judd waited until a police captain arrived.

"Why did you come to our country?" the man said.

"Friends," Judd said. "The Ben-Judah family. I wanted to be sure the reports were right."

"Their bodies are in the morgue now," the man said. "Would you like to see them?"

"No," Judd said. "I know they're dead. But I saw something. The face of one of the murderers."

"And how could you have seen that?"

"First, I need to know that you're serious about finding the murderers," Judd said.

The man stood and picked up a phone. "We are serious," he said. He spoke softly into the phone, then put it down. "I am so serious about this matter that I want you to talk to the people heading up the investigation."

"Who's that?" Judd said.

"The Global Community," the man said. "They have asked us to give them any leads we might find."

Ryan saw a Global Community van pull up to the police station. *If I don't try now, I might never see Judd again,* Ryan thought. He walked confidently into the station and spotted Judd sitting in a holding area. Ryan finally got Judd's attention but didn't dare go close to him.

Judd's eyes darted to the GC officials, then back to Ryan. Judd pointed to his chair.

"What?" Ryan said.

Judd didn't have time to explain. Two men led him outside. He was careful not to look at Ryan.

Ryan waited a moment, then rushed to the chair. It was empty. He moved the cushion. Underneath was the key to the lockbox at the hotel. He grabbed it and ran outside. The van had already pulled away and was lost in traffic.

Please, God, Ryan prayed, *show me what to do.*

※

Vicki and Lionel packed the *Underground* the night before and were ready the next morning. Vicki called her friend Shelly, and the two stayed up late sewing a special pouch into the lining of Lionel's and Vicki's jackets. They hoped that the GC monitors who checked every backpack and duffel bag wouldn't notice.

At school, Vicki and Lionel walked through different entrances. When she reached her locker, Vicki took off her jacket and unzipped the pouch. She took the stack of pages and quickly placed it in the bin where school newspapers were distributed.

At lunch she met with Lionel. "I had a close call at the door," Lionel said. "The metal detector went off when I went through, and they made me take off my backpack and jacket and walk through again."

"They didn't find anything?" Vicki said.

"I thought for sure they'd feel how heavy the jacket was, but they gave it back and didn't say a thing. A bunch of kids in my third-period class had copies."

"Same here," Vicki said. "I wonder what the principal will do this time?"

In Vicki's next class, Mrs. Jenness, the principal, made an announcement condemning the illegal paper. The school secretary then interrupted Vicki's class.

"Would you please send Vicki Byrne to Mrs. Jenness's office?" the secretary said.

Ryan made his way back to the King David Hotel and gave the key to the man at the front desk.

"One moment," the man said.

He returned with the tape. As Ryan walked out, another man called after him. The man had a phone to his ear. "Yes, we just gave him something," the man said into a phone.

Ryan briskly walked toward the revolving door.

"All right, we'll keep him here until you arrive," the man said.

Ryan ran.

"Stop him!" the man yelled. Then Ryan heard on the loudspeaker, "Security to the front lobby!"

A doorman stepped in front of him. Ryan faked left, then ran through the automatic handicapped exit. The doorman gave chase, but Ryan was too fast.

He kept running, not knowing where he was or where he was going. He knew Judd's life was at stake if the tape wound up in the hands of the Global Community.

Ryan ran through crowded streets. Once he thought he saw a security patrol nearby, but he ducked inside a building and hid in the bathroom. When he came out he realized he was in the university where Tsion Ben-Judah taught.

He looked in the directory and found the rabbi's office number. He ran to the third floor and saw the door covered with police investigation tape. A guard sat in an adjacent office.

"May I help you?" the guard said.

"Just looking around," Ryan said. "Whoever had this office must have done something really bad."

"He murdered his family," the guard said. "We're keeping watch in case he tries to come back."

Ryan wandered down the hall, feeling

something strange. Maybe it wasn't an accident that he had stumbled into the university. Maybe there was something in here he needed. He found an empty classroom and camped in the corner. He would wait until nightfall. He had to get inside the rabbi's office.

※

Judd was placed in a holding cell. He knew the Global Community officials wanted to scare him. When they finally brought Judd upstairs he gave them his name and where he was from.

"Where is your passport?" the GC officer said.

"It's probably back at the hotel," Judd said.

"And where is the item you had locked in the hotel safe?"

"What item?" Judd said.

The man tilted his head and looked over his glasses. "Mr. Thompson, we can make this as easy or as difficult as you wish."

"I don't know where it is," Judd said. "That's the truth."

"Who is in possession of it?"

"A friend."

"Would this be your young friend?" The man described Ryan.

"I don't understand," Judd said. "I come here to tell you about a murder you're investigating, and now I'm the bad guy. What's up with that?"

The man nodded to the guard, and Judd was taken back to his cell. Another guard came with some dinner a few hours later. Judd wondered about Ryan. Maybe Buck had been right. Maybe he had endangered both of them needlessly.

After midnight the guards brought a bearded man into the next cell and threw him on the cot. The man was bleeding and had dark bruises on his face.

Ryan waited until it was dark, then slipped into the wing where the rabbi's office was located. He heard the guard snoring at the end of the hall. He placed a stack of books on the railing of the stairwell and attached a spool of thread he had found in a utility closet. He backed into the bathroom and pulled hard on the thread. The books clattered down the stairs, echoing through the massive building. A moment later he heard the guard's keys jangling.

"Who's there?" the guard shouted.

Ryan slipped past the secretary's desk and into the rabbi's office. Ryan gasped. Books lay on the floor. Maps and artifacts had been shredded. Old parchment with funny writing had been stomped on.

The drawers of the rabbi's desk had been ripped out, the contents strewn on the floor. The lock on the middle drawer had been shot through. Framed awards and citations lay broken on top of the desk.

"It would kill Dr. Ben-Judah to see this," Ryan muttered.

He spotted something in the rubble. A small, round picture frame had escaped the thugs. In the picture was the rabbi's wife and their two children. Ryan smiled and put the picture in his pocket.

Ryan heard the jangling of keys outside. He hid under what was left of the rabbi's desk.

*

Mrs. Jenness looked sternly at Vicki. "I had hoped this foolishness would stop with what happened to your friend last year."

"I saw the newspaper in the bin," Vicki said. "Why do you think I had anything to do with it?"

Mrs. Jenness shook her head. "Don't play innocent this time," she said. "We know about your father, or at least your adoptive father."

Vicki fumed.

"We received a call from an anonymous parent who told us about his death," Mrs. Jenness continued. "I'm sorry for your loss. But no matter what emotions you're going through, you must abide by the rules."

Vicki remained silent.

"I don't think you want us to go further up the ladder with this," Mrs. Jenness said. "You know what happened last year. If you'll confess, we'll figure out something, taking into account your . . . state of mind."

Vicki knew if she confessed, Mrs. Jenness would have grounds to send her back to Northside Detention Center.

"I won't confess," Vicki said. "You'll have to call whoever you need to call."

The next morning Judd was again interrogated.

"I suppose you've had time to think about your situation," the man said.

"I'm an American citizen," Judd said. "I came here to find out about my friends.

I wanted to give information to the authorities, but I don't think I can trust you."

"You are a citizen of the Global Community," the man corrected. "You only have the rights granted by such. We know who killed the woman and the children. We do not need your help to solve this crime. As a matter of fact, there is the man now."

The officer pointed a remote-control device to a television in the corner. A picture of Rabbi Tsion Ben-Judah flashed on the screen. The Global Community Network News reported that a Michael Shorosh had been arrested in connection with the harboring of a fugitive from justice. "Global Community spokesmen say that Ben-Judah, formerly a respected scholar and clergyman, apparently became a radical fundamentalist. They point to this sermon he delivered just a week ago as evidence that he overreacted to a New Testament passage and was later seen by several neighbors slaughtering his own family."

Judd watched in horror as the news ran a tape of Tsion speaking at a huge rally in a filled stadium in Larnaca, on the island of Cyprus. "You'll note," the newsman said, as the tape was stopped, "the man on the platform behind Dr. Ben-Judah has been identified as Michael Shorosh. In a raid on his Jericho home shortly after midnight, peace-keeping forces found personal photos of Ben-Judah's family and identification papers from both Ben-Judah and an American journalist, Cameron Williams. Williams's connection to the case has not been determined."

Judd recognized the man named Michael as

the person in the cell next to him. In the photo on television he had no cuts or bruises.

The tape showed Dr. Ben-Judah reading from Matthew. The verses, of course, had been taken out of context. "Whoever denies Me before men, him I will also deny before My Father who is in heaven.

"Do not think that I came to bring peace on earth. I did not come to bring peace but a sword. For I have come to 'set a man against his father, a daughter against her mother, and a daughter-in-law against her mother-in-law'; and 'a man's enemies will be those of his own household.' He who loves father or mother more than Me is not worthy of Me. And he who loves son or daughter more than Me is not worthy of Me."

The news reporter said solemnly, "This was recorded just a few days before the rabbi murdered his own wife and children in broad daylight."

EIGHT

Michael's Story

MRS. Jenness set up an appointment to meet with Vicki and a social worker that evening. "I may need to have someone from the Global Community present as well," Mrs. Jenness said.

"I'll be there," Vicki said.

Vicki was unable to reach Mrs. Goodwin before the meeting. She wasn't surprised to see her walk in with a representative of Global Community Social Services later that evening.

"Mrs. Jenness," Mrs. Goodwin said, "as I told you on the phone, we've been working on Vicki's case for a few days. The evidence you've submitted doesn't implicate her, except that Bruce Barnes was her adoptive father."

"Well, I—"

The social worker spoke up. "Have you made a list of students who attend that particular church?" the man said.

"Well, no, but—"

"I don't mean to tell you how to do your job," the man continued, "but I think I speak for the office on this. We can't waste our time on frivolous accusations such as this."

Mrs. Jenness looked stunned. Vicki thought Mrs. Goodwin would stick up for her, but she didn't count on this much support.

Mrs. Goodwin and the man stood to leave. Mrs. Jenness apologized, then glared at Vicki. "This is the last time you'll embarrass me like that," she seethed.

🌵

When Judd wouldn't talk, he was taken to his cell. The man named Michael was gone, but was roughly returned a few minutes later. Judd pulled close to the bars and whispered. The man looked at Judd, then lay back again.

Michael looked awful. One eye was swollen shut. "I'm a friend of Buck Williams," Judd said.

Michael's voice was low and gravelly. "The Global Community can do better than this. I told you already, I do not know where the rabbi is."

"I'm not one of them," Judd said. He tried to explain who he was and why he was in Israel, but Michael wouldn't listen. "I was there when the witnesses talked with Buck," Judd said in desperation.

Michael sat up. "What did the witnesses say?"

"They quoted verses about going into Egypt," Judd said. "Buck got in a cab and was looking for someone who had a boat who could take him up the Jordan River."

Michael slid close to the bars and looked at Judd with his good eye. "You are not a plant by the Global Community?" he said.

"I'm a friend of Buck's from America," Judd said.

"And you are looking for the rabbi as well?" Michael said.

"I came here to find out about his family," Judd said. Judd briefly told Michael about his trip and discovering the truth about the Ben-Judah family.

"You must be very careful what you say," Michael said. "You are a believer?"

"I am," Judd said.

Michael sat back against the bars. Judd saw a trace of a smile. "We are like Paul and Silas now, except I do not sing very well," Michael said. "Moishe and Eli are my mentors.

I became a believer under their preaching and that of Tsion."

"Are you an evangelist?" Judd said.

"In the manner of Paul the apostle, according to Dr. Ben-Judah. He says there are 144,000 of us around the world, all with the same assignment that Moishe and Eli have: to preach Christ as the only everlasting Son of the Father."

"Tell me about Dr. Ben-Judah," Judd said.

"An escape plan has been in place for some time. For months we thought the guarding of his family was unnecessary. The zealots wanted him. At the first sign of a threat or an attack, we sent to Tsion's office a car so small it appeared only the driver could fit in it. Tsion lay on the floor of the backseat, curled into a ball, and covered himself with a blanket. He was raced to my boat, and I took him upriver."

"He knows about his family, right?"

"Yes, and you can imagine how awful that is for him. When we loaded him into the boat I could hear his loud sobbing over the sound of the engine throughout the entire voyage. I can still hear it in this prison cell."

"What about Buck?" Judd said. "Are they together?"

"They are," Michael said. Michael described his meeting with Buck. "I had killed two enemies of God who were searching for the rabbi. I was prepared to kill your friend. He was more than a little surprised when I pointed a high-powered weapon at his head. He answered my questions, and I showed him where we had hidden Tsion."

"How did you know he was for real and not just a journalist looking for a great story?" Judd said.

"I had my doubts," Michael said, "but when I asked him to describe the fulfilled prophecies of the Messiah, I knew it was more than just a story for him. He was the deliverer."

"Buck?" Judd said.

"God spoke through the two witnesses and assured us a deliverer would come. He would know the rabbi. He would know the witnesses. He would know the messianic prophecies. And most of all, he would know the Lord's Christ. Buck fit the description perfectly."

"What's Buck gonna do with the rabbi?" Judd said.

"He has to get him out of the country," Michael said.

"But the rabbi has to be one of the most recognizable people in Israel," Judd said. "How in the world will Buck get him through customs?"

Michael smiled. "How else? Supernaturally."

Ryan picked up the phone that was still on the floor and dialed the secretary's desk. He heard the guard jump when it rang, then the deep, "Hello?"

Ryan spoke in a whisper. "There's somebody in the stairwell," he said. "A guy with a gun!"

"Who is this?" the guard said.

Ryan hung up. The guard's chair scraped the floor. The man unsnapped his holster. Ryan crept to the hall and saw the guard peeking over the railing. Ryan went down the other stairwell.

"Stop!" the guard called after him, but Ryan was already into the street.

Judd and Michael talked like old friends. They were fellow prisoners, united in their belief in Christ.

"I do not want to tell you too much," Michael said. "If the Global Community thinks you know something about Tsion, they will get you to talk."

"Are Buck and Tsion safe?"

"When you are in the will of God, there is

no weapon formed against you that can pros-
per," Michael said. "God rides with Tsion
and Buck. I believe they will be saved."

Judd sat back against the cell bars. Just
talking with Michael was worth the trip. But
how did God want to use him? Why did he
have him here?

"I have been thinking about the verses
Tsion said were comforting to him," Michael
said. "The joy of the Lord is my strength."

Michael repeated the phrase again and
again. Judd thought about joy. Behind bars it
took on a different meaning. It wasn't just
being happy and smiling all the time. It was
deeper. Joy came from believing God is in
control and knows what he is doing.

"Our God is working his will through
Tsion and Buck," Michael said. "Buck told
me of a dream. That he would leave through
Egypt rather than through Israel. And as we
were praying together, God made his will
clear to us."

Michael bent forward, inches from Judd's
face, and said, "I believe my life is destined
to be short. My assignment is to preach in
Israel, where the real Messiah is hated. But if
God is for us, who can be against us?"

Judd shivered. He was face-to-face with
one of the most courageous Christians on

the planet. It made him want to exhibit courage as well.

"My only concern now is for my loved ones," Michael said. "I have a wife and family. A small child. I pray they do not suffer the same fate as Dr. Ben-Judah's family."

Ryan found a pay phone and called Taylor Graham. This time the pilot answered.

"They probably took Judd to the main headquarters in Jerusalem," Graham said. "Where are you?"

Ryan told him, and the pilot gave him directions. "You'll go past the Wailing Wall on the way," Graham said. "Stay as far away from there as you can. I'll meet you in a half hour right across the street from GC headquarters."

Ryan walked briskly through the moonlit streets. He heard dogs barking. He stayed as close to the buildings as he could, clutching the picture and the tape in his pocket.

When he passed the Wailing Wall he saw a small crowd gathered near the fence where the preachers sat. He wanted to go closer but knew he should get to Judd as quickly as possible.

Then he heard it. Was it inside his head? A whisper? A voice? A thought? Whatever it was, it stopped Ryan in his tracks. He turned and faced the witnesses.

The tape, Ryan thought. *They'll be after the tape. Where can I keep it safe?*

Then the plan was clear to him. He could see it. God's justice. The purpose of their trip. He took the tape from his pocket and ran toward the crowd.

※

Vicki, Chaya, and Lionel met at Bruce's house late that evening. Vicki described her ordeal with Mrs. Jenness.

"Mrs. Goodwin called before you got home and suggested you stay with an adult in the area," Chaya said. "I told her about Loretta's house, and she said that would be fine."

"I was thinking of going over there anyway," Vicki said, "in case Mrs. Stahley and Darrion show up again."

The phone rang. Lionel answered and put Ryan on the speaker.

"What's happening?" Lionel said.

"I need you guys to pray, and pray hard," Ryan said. "I can't go into it all, but Judd's in big trouble. I have to go into the Global Community headquarters and see if I can—"

"Global Community?!" Lionel shouted.

"He was arrested," Ryan said. "Look, just

pray that I'll be able to get him out of there and back to the plane. If I can do that, we'll be back for the memorial service."

"And if you don't get him out?" Vicki said.

"We may have a memorial service of our own over here," Ryan said.

The guard came for Judd, led him upstairs to another office, and told Judd to wait. The same interrogator stepped in the room and left the door ajar. He told Judd to go through his story again and Judd reluctantly did. Another man stepped inside and closed the door. He looked familiar, but Judd couldn't place him.

"We understand you paid a visit to a neighbor of the Ben-Judah family," the officer said.

Judd studied the face of the other man.

"A concerned father called and said his son had talked with an American who knew the rabbi's children," the officer continued. "Would that have been you?"

"I went to the Ben-Judah house to see for myself," Judd said. "There was a kid next door in a garden."

"You took something with you when you left," the officer said. "What was it?"

The video! Judd thought. *That's the man in the mask!*

"What did you take with you?" the officer said sternly.

The man by the door was looking directly at Judd now. His eyes were dark and piercing.

There was a knock at the door. An officer handed the interrogator a note. The man held it out to read it, then glanced at Judd.

"You were expecting a visitor?" he said.

"No, I don't think so," Judd said.

"Stay where you are," the man said.

He left and to Judd's surprise came back with Ryan. Ryan smiled as he sat. The other men left the room. Judd held his finger to his lips.

"You know they can hear us," Judd whispered.

"It's OK," Ryan said. "I had to see you about the tape."

Judd's eyes widened. "Don't do this!"

"I went exactly where you told me to go, but the tape wasn't there," Ryan said. "You have to get out and help me find it."

"I told you it was—"

"I won't listen," Ryan said, sticking his fingers in his ears. "You said the tape would be where we were the other night. With our two friends. Remember?"

Judd stared at Ryan. Finally he understood. "Where should I meet you if I can get out of here?" he said.

Ryan smiled. "I'll be waiting where we last saw the journalist," Ryan whispered. "Meet me there."

"They'll follow you when you leave," Judd whispered.

"I have that figured out, too," Ryan said. He leaned closer. "Vicki, Chaya, and Lionel are praying up a storm. I'll see you outside."

Ryan left and Judd was returned to his cell. Judd told Michael the news.

"I am praying for you," Michael said. "I believe you will see Tsion. I may not see him until we are in heaven together. Tell him I am praying for him. I have told him I would risk everything to protect him. He is my spiritual father. Now may God give you the same. Do not lean on your own strength. Go with God."

Ryan walked out of the Global Community building and hopped straight into a cab parked outside.

"Hit it," Ryan said.

"Yes sir," Taylor Graham said.

Ryan glanced back to see two Global Community guards rush outside. The cab was around the first corner by the time the men made it to their vehicle.

"Where'd you get it?" Ryan said.

"Friend of mine owns a cab company," Graham said. "This is the fastest one they have."

Ryan slid from one side of the backseat to the other as the pilot drove the car through the narrow streets of Jerusalem. With the speed of the cab and the ability of the driver, Ryan knew those following them didn't stand a chance. Now if Judd could convince them to let him go, his plan could work.

"I want to speak with the other man alone," Judd said when the officer came into the interrogation room. The officer looked startled, turned, and said something in another language to the man with the beard.

"It's out of the question," the officer said.

"I have some information I only want to give to *him*," Judd said. "I believe it will clear up the questions you have."

The other man nodded, and the officer reluctantly left the room. The man who had taken the life of Judd's friends now sat before Judd. Judd's palms were sweaty.

"What do you have to tell me?" the man said with a thick accent.

"How does it feel to know you've killed innocent people?" Judd said.

"I do not know what you're talking about," the man said.

"I know it was you," Judd said.

"We are trying to apprehend the real murderer right now—"

Judd interrupted. "I saw you take off your mask before you killed Dan, Dr. Ben-Judah's son."

The man kept his steely gaze on Judd. "Then you are a liar," he said. "You told the officer you arrived from America after the killings."

"I saw a videotape," Judd said.

The man was silent. He scratched his chin. Finally he spoke.

"Where would you come upon such a tape?" the man said.

"Where I found it isn't the point," Judd said. "It proves the rabbi is innocent. And if the media gets it, you're in big trouble."

"There are channels the media must go through—"

"And you know it would embarrass you and your superiors," Judd said. He couldn't believe how he was standing up to this cold-blooded killer, but he was.

"What do you want?" the man said. "I am not admitting anything, you understand. But you must want something."

"I want you to let me out of here with the

promise that I'll have safe passage back to the U.S."

The man scoffed. "If I am the man you say I am, why wouldn't I kill you right now?" he said. "What would prevent that?"

"Because you don't have the tape," Judd said. "And that little kid who just walked out of here knows exactly where it is. And if I don't show up within a half hour, he'll hand it to those headline-hungry journalists."

"We are following the young man as we speak." The man smiled.

"And I'd be willing to bet a few minutes of video that your guys have lost him," Judd said. "Go ahead and check. I'll wait."

The man picked up a phone and dialed a number. He spoke softly, then raised his voice. He finally put the phone down gently and turned to Judd.

"Was I right?" Judd said.

"We have failed to locate him for the moment," the man said. "It is only a matter of time."

"Yes, it is, isn't it," Judd said knowingly.

The man leaned forward. "You will take us to the tape," he said. "You will hand it over and be safely on your way."

NINE

Justice and the Witnesses

JUDD waited nervously while the men finished the paperwork for his release. As far as Judd could tell, the man who had killed the Ben-Judah family wasn't an official Global Community officer, but he was working closely with them.

Judd questioned the man again before they led him to the car. "When this is over I'm free, right?" he said.

"You have my word," the man said.

Judd sat alone in the backseat of the car. Judd glanced behind them as they pulled out. A van followed that looked like the same one used in the Ben-Judah murders.

So the whole crew is here, Judd thought.

🌾

Taylor Graham drove Ryan through the exact streets he and Judd would need to take to get to the airstrip. "It's pretty secluded outside of town," Graham said. "I'll have the plane running and ready to go. You just keep the directions straight."

They drove back to town and parked in a line of cabs near the Wailing Wall. It was the wee hours of the morning and there were only a handful of people looking at the witnesses.

"Are you sure Judd'll be here?" Taylor Graham said.

"As sure as I can be of anything right now," Ryan said.

"For what it's worth," the pilot said as he got out of the car, "you two don't act like any kids I've ever known. See you at the plane."

Judd didn't tell them they were going to the Wailing Wall. Instead, he gave them directions as they came to each intersection. Finally, Judd told them to stop.

"What is this?" the man said.

"You wanted the tape, right?" Judd said. "This is where it is."

The driver pulled his gun. "This is a trick," he said. "He has no tape."

Judd tried to remain calm. He didn't know exactly where Ryan had put the tape, but he had an idea. He opened the door and slowly got out. The driver jumped out and held his gun on Judd.

"Put that away," the other man said.

"I've kept my end of the bargain," Judd said.

"You haven't given us anything," the man said.

Judd pointed toward the witnesses. "The tape's over there. I told you it was in a safe place."

The van pulled up, and several men exited. They didn't have black hoods, but Judd placed each of them as the masked gunmen.

The driver started forward, but the leader stopped him. "If he wants to be released," the man said, "he'll have to bring the tape to us himself. Everyone wait here."

Judd scanned the cabs and noticed one at the end with no driver. Then Ryan popped his head up and winked.

Judd made his way to the front of the small crowd, then inched further. "Don't let their stillness fool you," someone said. "They'll kill you if you get too close."

Judd spied the tape lying near the fence. Moishe and Eli appeared to be sleeping, their leathery skin rising and falling with each breath. Judd got close enough to bend down and grab the tape when he heard a voice.

"God shows his anger from heaven against all sinful, wicked people who push the truth away from themselves," Eli said. "Stand back."

Judd stood and left the tape. The small crowd had retreated when they heard Eli's voice.

"What are you doing?" the leader called behind Judd. "Bring it here."

"I can't," Judd said, moving away from the fence. "If you want it, you'll have to get it yourself."

The driver reached for his weapon and the other man held his arm. He stepped forward and slowly pushed his way through the crowd.

Ryan started the car when he saw Judd move away from the fence. "Just like I thought it would be," Ryan said to himself.

※

Vicki joined a nervous Chloe and Amanda at Loretta's house. She asked that they pray for Judd and Ryan. Then Chloe filled them in on Buck's situation.

"I talked with him briefly, but I have no idea where or how he is," Chloe said. "My dad said I shouldn't worry, but I think something's wrong."

Chloe punched the number of Buck's cell phone.

"Do you know if he found the rabbi?" Vicki said.

Amanda shook her head.

"Buck! It's Chloe!"

Chloe listened, frowned, then tried to talk. "But Buck—," she sighed. "You call me when you're safe," she said.

"What did he say?" Vicki said.

Chloe was busy dialing more numbers. "He said to not ask questions. He's safe for now, but everybody needs to pray. And he wanted me to get on the Internet and find the phone number for an airport in the Sinai desert. There's a pilot there—"

Amanda grabbed Chloe's hand and squeezed hard. Chloe's father, Rayford, answered, and Chloe told him the story. Chloe asked Rayford to get the phone number and call the pilot. Rayford agreed.

"Hurry, Dad," Chloe said.

Judd stepped a safe distance from the fence. The leader of the group was seething. "You will regret this," the man said.

"What do you mean?" Judd said. "You told me—"

"You didn't actually think I would let you out of the country, did you?" the man said.

"You and your little friend in the cab will be dealt with most severely."

The man strode toward the fence and picked up the videotape. He turned to leave but stopped when Moishe's voice thundered behind him.

"We proclaim the power of God Almighty," Moishe said, "whose majesty is over Israel, whose power is in the skies."

"Woe to you, evildoers," Eli said. "Woe to those who shed the blood of the innocent."

Judd watched the man's face turn white with terror. He clutched the tape to his chest and turned. People behind Judd fell to the ground.

"The blood of the righteous cries out," Moishe thundered.

The man stiffened. "What do you want with me?" he cried. "I have done nothing to you!"

Eli and Moishe looked with piercing eyes at the man. The man gasped at their faces and turned to run.

"Behold, the Lord says vengeance is mine," Eli and Moishe said in one, loud voice. "I will repay, says the Lord."

With that, the two witnesses opened their mouths, and fire gushed forth, engulfing the man. Judd was so close, his clothes were singed. The tape in the man's hands melted instantly. Judd stumbled backward. People behind him fled.

Judd heard a gun blast. A bullet whizzed past him. Eli and Moishe turned their gaze on the men at the van. With lightning accuracy the two opened their mouths and consumed the entire company of murderers. One man fled to the van, only to have it catch fire and explode. The driver of the car had barely pulled his handgun from its holster when the fire fell. The gun melted in the man's hand.

Judd ran toward the last cab. He dodged several burning figures. As he got in, he looked toward the witnesses. Eli and Moishe looked straight at Judd and nodded. Without moving their lips Judd heard them say, "May the glory of the Lord be your rearguard."

Ryan's hands were shaking when Judd got in. Nothing could have prepared him for that horrifying scene. Judd got behind the wheel and Ryan pointed the way. He heard sirens behind them.

Judd tried to drive like Taylor Graham, but the streets were unfamiliar and the car felt stiff. As they rounded a corner, Ryan yelled. A Global Community patrol car careened out of an alley and pulled behind Judd.

"We can't stop now," Ryan said. "We're almost at the airport."

"But we can't lead them to the plane," Judd said. "We'll have to lose them."

"How?" Ryan said.

Judd saw a man with a gun leaning out the window. Just as he fired, Judd swerved. The patrol car followed, nearly sending the man out the window.

"They're shooting at our tires," Judd said.

"Can't you go any faster?" Ryan said.

Judd took an alley, then another, but the patrol car stayed right behind them.

"Don't take too many of those or I won't be able to remember the way to the airport," Ryan said.

"Call Taylor and tell him we've got company," Judd said.

Ryan dialed the number. "He says there's an access road around the back that might help," Ryan said. "We can drive right onto the runway from there."

Judd floored it and pulled slightly away from the car. When they neared the airport, another GC vehicle with its lights flashing joined the chase. Judd saw the plane taxiing to the end of the runway.

"When I get close," Judd said, "we're both making a run for it."

Judd barrelled through a sandy area and onto the runway. He screeched to a halt beside the plane. Ryan jumped out and ran up the stairs. Judd put the car in reverse and jumped out. The plane was moving as he entered the cabin. While he and Ryan pulled the stairs up, Judd saw the two GC cars swerve and narrowly miss the taxi.

"Take a seat fast," Taylor Graham shouted as the plane picked up speed. The cars pulled to within fifty yards of them, then faded in the distance as the plane took off.

Judd and Ryan explained what happened at the Wailing Wall. The pilot seemed impressed.

"How did you know to take the tape there?" Graham asked Ryan.

"I can't explain it," Ryan said. "I knew God would take care of us."

When they reached cruising altitude, the pilot suggested Judd and Ryan check the GC frequencies in the rear of the plane. They played with the knob, hearing static and foreign languages. Finally, Judd found a transmission from an Egyptian border guard.

"He just slammed on his brakes and sent me off the side of the road," an officer said.

"We have backup coming, as you requested," another man said. "The road-block is in place at the airport. How many are on the bus?"

"Did he say bus?" Judd said. "Michael said Buck and Tsion are on a bus."

The radio squawked. "I'm not sure," the first man said. "I am now in front of him and—" There was a crash, and the transmission ended.

"What happened?" the other man on the radio said.

"He rammed me! I have lost my hood, but I'm giving chase."

"You should be able to see your backup soon," the other man said.

"What's going on?" Taylor Graham said from the cockpit.

"The Global Community guards are chasing Buck," Judd said. "I'm assuming he has Tsion Ben-Judah with him. They're headed for an airport in Egypt."

"Probably Al Arish," Graham said. "It's south of the Gaza Strip on the Mediterranean."

"Unable to stop him, sir," a different voice said on the radio. "We'll turn around and give chase."

"How far to the airport?" a man said.

"We can see it now," a guard said. "Less than a kilometer."

Judd and Ryan held their breath.

"The blockade is in place, sir," another man said. "There is no way he can get into the airport from here. We can see him now."

The radio went silent. Ryan looked at Judd. "They're caught," he said.

"Unit one, report," a man said.

There was static on the man's transmission. Judd could make out the words *bus* and *fire*, but little else. The leader was frantic, calling for information. Finally a man in a squad car broke through.

"The bus ran into the roadblock and scattered the officers," the man said. "It nearly tipped over, then burst into flames. Several officers are down."

"What about the occupants?" the first man said.

"We opened fire into the bus immediately," the second man said.

"Have you found their bodies?"

Silence. Then, "I'm sorry, sir, officers are firing again!"

"Go to a secure frequency," the base said.

Judd and Ryan scanned the frequencies but couldn't find more information.

"I hope they made it," Ryan said. "I can't imagine losing Bruce *and* Buck in one week."

Vicki answered the phone when the pilot of Buck's plane, Ken Ritz, called a short while later. She handed the phone to Chloe, who was relieved to hear that Buck and Tsion were on their way home.

Later, Buck called Chloe and assured her that when she heard the whole story she would understand. Chloe told Vicki and Amanda that no one outside the Tribulation Force but Loretta could know about Tsion.

"Buck didn't know Verna had moved out," Chloe said. "He's really uptight about her knowing about his faith."

"He'll be even more surprised if he sees Verna at Bruce's memorial service," Amanda said.

Ryan heard Taylor Graham's satellite phone ring. "I'm so glad to hear from you, Mrs. Stahley," he said. "We heard you moved."

The pilot listened intently and briefly told the story of their trip to Israel. Finally, he handed the phone to Ryan.

"Ryan it's me, Darrion!"

"Are you guys OK?" Ryan said.

"We are for now," Darrion said. "We've had some pretty close calls."

"Where are you?" Ryan said.

"I can't say," Darrion said. "My mom told Taylor we were in Wisconsin, but that's not true. Don't tell him, though."

"Why not?" Ryan said.

"My mom was worried about you guys," Darrion said. "She thinks she might have set you up."

"How?" Ryan said.

"It's a long story," Darrion said. "Just make sure he doesn't land at the strip near our home. If my mom is right, Taylor is working with the Global Community."

"But that's not possible," Ryan said.

"I can't tell you any more," Darrion said. "But when you land, we think Taylor will suggest he be taken into custody, then he'll try to help you two escape somehow. If that's what he does, it's a trap. They'll follow you to try and find us. Be very careful, OK?"

"We will," Ryan said. "Thanks."

Ryan hung up. "What was that all about?" Taylor Graham said.

"She said she was sorry she left our friends," Ryan said. "She wanted to thank me for what I did when she was kidnapped."

"Is that all?" the pilot said.

"Yeah, that and something about a reunion she wants to have in Wisconsin or someplace," Ryan said. "I don't know how we're gonna pull that one off."

Ryan jotted a note to Judd. *Darrion says the*

pilot is dirty. He placed it on a tray and handed it to Judd.

"Care for a cookie?" Ryan said.

❋

It was as if Tsion Ben-Judah was in some international witness protection program. Vicki was at Loretta's home when he was smuggled in under the cover of night. Amanda and Chloe greeted him warmly and compassionately. Vicki had talked with Judd briefly from their plane and knew the truth about his family. She stayed in the background and watched.

Loretta had a light snack waiting for all of them. "I'm old and not too up on things," she said, "but I'm quickly getting the picture here. The less I know about your friend, the better, am I right?"

Before anyone could answer, Tsion said, "I am deeply grateful for your hospitality."

Loretta soon trundled off to bed, expressing her delight in offering her home in service to the Lord.

Buck and Tsion had been injured. Chloe hobbled with them into the living room, followed by a chuckling Amanda. "I wish Rayford were here," she said. "I feel like the only one who can walk without a limp. I'm going to have to do every chore that requires two good legs around here."

Chloe leaned forward and reached for Tsion's hand with both of hers. "Dr. Ben-Judah, we have heard so much about you. We feel blessed of God to have you with us. We can't imagine your pain."

The rabbi took a deep breath and exhaled slowly, his lips quivering. "I cannot tell you how deeply grateful I am that God has brought me here. I confess my heart is broken. I cannot deny God's presence, yet there are times I wonder how I will go on. I must pray for relief from bitterness and hatred. Most of all, I feel terrible guilt that I brought this upon my wife and children. I don't know what else I could have done, short of trying to make them more secure. I could not have avoided serving God in the way he has called me."

Amanda and Buck each put a hand on Tsion's shoulders. They all wept and prayed. They talked well into the night, Buck explaining that Tsion would be the object of an international manhunt, which would no doubt be approved by Nicolae Carpathia himself.

TEN

Race for Home

RYAN was dying to tell Judd more of what Darrion said, but he couldn't risk it. If Taylor Graham saw them whispering or passing notes, he'd know something was up. Ryan went to the front and asked if he could watch. "I just put it on auto," Graham said. "The thing will fly itself."

Ryan climbed into the tiny cockpit and put on the headset. The pilot showed him what not to touch. The sun was sneaking up behind them, and it put a purplish glow on the horizon ahead. *I have to tell Judd*, Ryan thought. *But how?*

※

Vicki went back to Loretta's apartment to get some sleep. She couldn't believe she had just met the rabbi. She had trouble sleeping and turned on the television. The reports of the war around the world continued. Already, Nicolae Carpathia was putting his spin on it.

"World health care experts predict the death toll will rise to more than 20 percent internationally," the reporter said. "Global Community Potentate Nicolae Carpathia has announced a new health care plan. He and his ten global ambassadors have outlined the new regulations. Here is renowned heart surgeon Samuel Kline of Norway."

"The current agencies cannot handle disease and death on this scale," Dr. Kline said. "Potentate Carpathia's plan is not only our only hope for survival, but also a blueprint for the best health care agenda ever."

Vicki was distressed over the reports of the war, but for some reason, this doctor scared her.

"Should the death toll reach as high as 25 percent," the doctor continued, "we will need these new directives to govern life from the womb to the tomb. Our planet can be brought from the brink of death to a shining new state never before imagined."

Right, Vicki thought. *Carpathia kills 25 percent of the world's population and we're all healthier for it.*

Ryan stayed at the controls, loving the feeling. The pilot tapped him on the shoulder. "I'm gonna catch a little nap," Graham said. "Wake me in twenty minutes, OK?"

Ryan said he would. When he could hear the pilot snoring he motioned for Judd to join him. Ryan whispered what Darrion had told him, making sure the pilot was really asleep.

"Why would he rescue us in Israel if he's with the GC?" Judd said.

"They must think we know where the Stahleys are," Ryan said. "Darrion and her mom are priority one."

"If Graham is working with the GC," Judd said, "he knows almost everything about us."

"And he also knows about Buck getting Dr. Ben-Judah."

"It just doesn't seem right," Judd said. "He seemed genuine, like he was really trying to help."

"How about when he took off from the hotel?" Ryan said. "You think he was really mad at us, or was he using that chance to communicate with the Global Community?"

Judd grimaced. "How did you know where to find me after the GC took me from the police station?"

"I tried to follow you, but they went too fast," Ryan said. "I called Graham and he told me."

"That's what I thought," Judd said. "We could use a couple parachutes right now."

"What can they do to us when we get back?" Ryan whispered.

"I can cover for you," Judd said, "but they're gonna have my record on file. They could slap me on the wrist and say I can never go outside the country again. . . ."

"Or what else?"

"Remember what happened to Coach Handlesman?" Judd said. "They could send me to one of their reeducation camps. And I'd probably be there a long time."

"So what are we gonna do if he wants to land at the Stahley place?" Ryan said.

"How good are you at acting?" Judd said.

Judd woke Taylor Graham. "It hasn't been twenty minutes, but I need your help," Judd said frantically. "Something's wrong with Ryan."

Graham shook himself awake and followed Judd to the bathroom. Ryan was leaning against the sink, beads of sweat on his forehead.

"I didn't feel well when I got on," Ryan said, "but I thought it was just all the excitement."

Graham felt his head. "You're burning up," he said. Graham retrieved a first-aid kit with a thermometer. Ryan passed out on the floor.

Judd and the pilot moved Ryan to a seat

and made it recline. Judd asked what Graham thought it could be.

"It might be food poisoning," the pilot said. "I've also seen guys with a bad appendix act this way. Could be a hundred things."

"We'd better get him to a hospital right away, don't you think?" Judd said.

"I wanted to make it back to Chicago so we'd be safe," Graham said. "I'd like to touch down at the Stahleys' landing strip."

Ryan writhed in pain and moaned loudly.

"Let me check where we are," Graham said.

※

Vicki saw Buck embrace Rayford Steele at the house later that day. Amanda had picked Rayford up in Milwaukee after his exhausting flight from New Babylon. "I'm really fighting the jet lag," Rayford said. "I'm going to try and stay up until tonight so I can go over what you've put together for Bruce's funeral."

Rayford looked awestruck when Buck took him to Tsion Ben-Judah.

"It's truly an honor to meet you," Rayford said.

"I have heard much about you as well," the rabbi said.

Rayford, Buck, and Tsion moved downstairs while Vicki talked with Amanda.

"We might need to use the apartment for another visitor," Amanda said. "I don't want to kick you out or anything—"

"That's fine," Vicki said. "Who's coming?"

"We hope a woman named Hattie Durham will be here in a few days," Amanda said. Amanda explained that Hattie had been Rayford's senior flight attendant on the night of the Rapture. Since then she had taken a job with the Global Community.

"She's romantically involved with Carpathia," Amanda said gravely. "And from what Rayford tells me about their talks on the plane coming over here, she's struggling with a lot of decisions she has to make."

Judd was relieved to see Ryan's pains pick up as they entered North American airspace. They seemed to become unbearable the closer they got to Chicago.

"I'll divert to Indianapolis," the pilot said. "I thought we might make it to Chicago, but he's in too much pain. Did you get a read on his temperature?"

"It's really high," Judd said.

Graham declared an emergency, and an ambulance met them at the gate of the airport. "They'll take you straight to the hospital," the pilot said. "I'll need to stay with the plane."

"You've been a lot of help," Judd said. "We'll call you when we get back."

"No, I feel I should stay until I make sure he's OK," the pilot said. "Mrs. Stahley would want it that way."

"OK," Judd said. "We'll meet you over at the hospital."

"I'll be there as fast as I can," Graham said.

The paramedics put an oxygen mask on Ryan and checked his vital signs as they sped to the hospital. Judd stayed in the back with Ryan.

"Your heart rate and blood pressure look normal," the man said. "Are you feeling better?"

"A little," Ryan managed to say.

"I'm going to start an IV," the man said.

"No, don't," Ryan said. "I'm feeling a lot better."

"It'll help—"

"No, I don't want you to stick me if you don't have to," Ryan said.

Judd was watching the roadway for car rental dealerships. "Stop!" Judd shouted to the driver. "You have to stop!"

The startled driver pulled over, his lights still going, and Judd quickly had Ryan off the gurney and out of the ambulance.

"We're really sorry about this," Judd said as he shut the door. Judd glanced back as they ran through the parking lot and saw the paramedics watching them with opened mouths. One was talking on the radio.

Judd and Ryan darted into the car rental office. "We're in a really big hurry," Judd said. He quickly filled out the forms, paid for the car, and left.

Three hours later they were nearing Chicago and trying to make sense of their trip. "That was a pretty convincing job of acting," Judd said.

"I always wanted to be a movie star," Ryan said.

"I noticed your acting ability ended when that paramedic was going to stick a needle in your arm."

"What are we gonna do?" Ryan said.

Judd shook his head. "We have to take it a step at a time," he said. "We'll check in at Loretta's house first. I have to know about Buck."

"The memorial service is tomorrow," Ryan said. "Will it be too risky, since Graham heard us talking about it?"

"I don't know," Judd said. "We'll have to get everybody together and go over our options."

Back home, Judd went to Loretta's house and found Vicki and Amanda in the front living room. Judd and Ryan were relieved to know Buck was alive and were thrilled to hear that he, Rayford, and Tsion Ben-Judah were downstairs preparing for Bruce's memorial service.

"Let me take you to return the car," Amanda said. "You can meet him a little later."

After returning the car, Amanda dropped the three kids off at Bruce's house. Lionel and Chaya were overjoyed to see Judd and Ryan and listened to their story.

"I hope Buck has time to tell us what happened to him," Ryan said. "We heard about his chase from the border guards."

Judd and Ryan listened as Vicki explained what had happened to them while the two were gone. Judd paced as she talked.

"We're under suspicion of hiding Mrs. Stahley and Darrion," he said, "which is true."

"But they didn't do anything," Vicki said.

"Which is also true," Judd said, "but the truth doesn't make any difference to the Global Community. Also, the pilot who took us to Israel knows a lot more than we want him to. It's pretty clear he's mixed up with the GC, and he might have had something to do with Darrion's kidnapping and Mr. Stahley's death."

"Which makes Mrs. Stahley look pretty smart for getting away from us," Vicki said. "After she made those calls to her pilot, somebody started following us."

Judd sighed. "We might have to do something drastic," he said. "Relocate. Maybe all of us move back together."

"I don't care how much trouble we're in," Lionel said, "I'm not missing the service tomorrow for Bruce."

Judd agreed. "We need to be there," he said. "But now I want to hear Buck's story and meet Dr. Ben-Judah."

Ryan wanted to hear Buck's story too, but he was more excited about meeting the rabbi.

When they arrived at Loretta's house, Rayford Steele met them. "We need to go over a few things," he said. "Tsion is an international fugitive. I can't tell you everything I know, or how I know it, but the Global Community wants Tsion dead. One slip could cost him his life."

The kids said they understood.

"Buck can't speak in public," Rayford continued. "And with all the suspicion surrounding you kids with the Stahley situation, I'm wondering if it would be smart to have you guys go underground."

"You mean like, disappear?" Lionel said.

"Not forever," Rayford said, "but until things cool down, it's best to be safe."

Judd glanced around the room. "I don't mean to be disrespectful," he said, "but are you going underground?"

"I know what you're thinking," Rayford said, "but the fact is—"

"We had this same conversation with Bruce," Judd said. "He finally understood that God can use us just like he can use grownups."

"I'm not saying God can't use you," Rayford said.

"We want to live for Christ," Judd said. "We don't want to be foolish or careless, but we want to be bold and believe in God with all our hearts."

Rayford nodded. "I know you do. But you have to be careful not to think everything you feel is straight from God. The trip to Israel turned out OK for the moment, but the final results aren't in."

"I understand," Judd said. "Knowing God is more than a feeling."

Rayford nodded. "I believe in you guys. God will show you what's best. I've heard you all know something about the shelter Bruce built."

The kids nodded. "We understand we won't be able to go there or know how to get in," Judd said. "We'll never tell anyone about it."

"Good," Rayford said. "I'm tired and need to prepare for tomorrow. I know you want to see Tsion, but he's very emotional right now."

"We won't stay long," Ryan said.

Rayford led the kids downstairs, where Buck and Tsion sat at a table. Buck greeted the kids warmly and smiled at Judd and Ryan.

"Good to see you two," Buck said. "We'll trade stories later."

"It's a deal," Judd said.

Buck introduced Tsion to Lionel and Chaya. Chaya said something in Hebrew, and Tsion embraced her. He spoke with a thick Israeli accent.

"Praise God!" Tsion said. "I am so happy to know God is calling the Jewish people all over the world to himself through Jesus."

Vicki shook the rabbi's hand, then Judd's.

"You knew my daughter," Tsion said.

"I did," Judd said. "I'm very sorry for your loss."

Tsion wept. "Forgive me," he said. "Looking at you reminds me of what I have lost. But I know that today my wife and children see God. Part of me very much wants to die so I can be with them. Only God's grace keeps me going. Only God can take away my thoughts of revenge."

Judd looked at Ryan.

"I feel called to serve God, even in my grief," Tsion continued. "I do not know why he has allowed this. God must have something new for me to do with the time I have left. I am grateful for your friendship and for your prayers."

"What will you do now, sir?" Vicki said.

"I know my life is worthless in Israel. My message has angered all those except the believers, and with the silly murder charges against me, I had to leave. If Nicolae Carpathia wants me dead, I will be a fugitive everywhere. But if God wants to use me to help others know him better, I will go anywhere and do whatever he calls me to do."

Tsion craned his neck. Ryan had been standing slightly behind Judd as he listened.

"And who is this young man?" Tsion said.

"My name is Ryan, sir." Ryan put out his hand, and the rabbi clasped it in his own.

"I have something for you," Ryan said. He pulled out a crudely wrapped package and handed it to the man.

"A gift for me?" Tsion said.

"I didn't do a very good job with the paper," Ryan said, "but I think you'll like it."

Ryan hadn't told Judd about the picture. Judd frowned and elbowed him.

"I think we need to get back to our meeting," Rayford said.

"No, let me open the gift," the rabbi said,

as he gingerly tore at the package. When he
could see its contents, he gasped and reached
for a chair. The rabbi put his face in his
hands and wept.

"What did you do now?" Judd said.

"I think that's enough," Rayford said.

The rabbi put up his hand. "Please," he
said after a few moments. "What he has
given me is priceless."

Tsion held up the picture frame and
showed the others his wife and children.
"I kept this on my desk in my office at the
university," Tsion said. "I do not know how
you were able to find it, or who you bought it
from, and I will not ask you. But I thank you."

Tsion hugged Ryan hard. Then he turned
the picture over and opened the back of the
frame.

"I was overcome because I remembered
the occasion my wife used to give me this
picture," he said. "I was well into my research
about the Messiah. The disappearances had
taken place. I knew I had been left behind.
And I knew my decision to follow Jesus
would cost me greatly.

"My wife also knew the reality of such a
decision. I explained my studies to her and
the children. I also explained the dangers. If
they followed me in faith, they could
become outcasts.

"One by one, I prayed with them. My wife, then my son, and then Nina placed her trust in Jesus."

Tsion stopped and bowed his head, his whole body shaking with emotion. Ryan looked at Vicki. Her eyes filled with tears. Finally, the rabbi continued.

"The next day, my wife went to the photographer's studio and had this portrait taken of the three of them. And on the back," Tsion choked, "she wrote a note to me. I had thought it was lost forever."

Ryan and the others listened as Tsion read the note in Hebrew, then translated.

To my beloved Tsion, the rabbi read, *you have shown us the way of life, the path of peace. May God grant you wisdom and courage in the days ahead. May he be, to you, Jehovah Jireh.*

"What does that mean?" Ryan said.

With tears in his eyes Tsion said, "*Jehovah Jireh* is a name that means 'the God who provides.' In the Old Testament God provided for his people again and again. And God will provide the strength I need at this time of despair." Tsion looked at Ryan. "This means so much to me. I have artifacts in my office, texts of ancient manuscripts that are priceless. But you have given me back what is most valuable."

Tsion hugged Ryan so hard he picked him up off the floor.

Judd led the others to Loretta's living room. He knew trouble might be ahead. How long would it take Taylor Graham to find them? And after him, the Global Community? Would the people from Nicolae High show up at the service tomorrow? Would Buck's coworker, Verna Zee, be there? And what had happened to Darrion and Mrs. Stahley?

Tomorrow, Judd thought. *We have to make it through tomorrow.*

ABOUT THE AUTHORS

Jerry B. Jenkins (www.jerryjenkins.com) is the writer of the Left Behind series. He is author of more than one hundred books, of which six have reached the *New York Times* best-seller list. Former vice president for publishing for the Moody Bible Institute of Chicago, he also served many years as editor of *Moody* magazine and is now Moody's writer-at-large.

His writing has appeared in publications as varied as *Reader's Digest, Parade,* in-flight magazines, and many Christian periodicals. He has written books in four genres: biography, marriage and family, fiction for children, and fiction for adults.

Jenkins's biographies include books with Hank Aaron, Bill Gaither, Luis Palau, Walter Payton, Orel Hershiser, Nolan Ryan, Brett Butler, and Billy Graham, among many others.

Six of his apocalyptic novels—*Left Behind, Tribulation Force, Nicolae, Soul Harvest, Apollyon,* and *Assassins*—have appeared on the Christian Booksellers Association's best-selling fiction list and the *Publishers Weekly* religion best-seller list. *Left Behind* was nominated for Book of the Year by the Evangelical Christian Publishers Association in 1997, 1998, and 1999.

As a marriage and family author and speaker, Jenkins has been a frequent guest on Dr. James Dobson's *Focus on the Family* radio program.

Jerry is also the writer of the nationally syndicated sports story comic strip *Gil Thorp,* distributed to newspapers across the United States by Tribune Media Services.

Jerry and his wife, Dianna, live in Colorado.

Limited speaking engagement information available through speaking@jerryjenkins.com.

Dr. Tim LaHaye (www.timlahaye.com), who conceived the idea of fictionalizing an account of the Rapture and the Tribulation, is a noted author, minister, and nationally recognized speaker on Bible prophecy. He is the founder of both Tim LaHaye Ministries and The Pre-Trib Research Center. Presently Dr. LaHaye speaks at many of the major Bible prophecy conferences in the U.S. and Canada, where his nine current prophecy books are very popular.

Dr. LaHaye holds a doctor of ministry degree from Western Theological Seminary and the doctor of literature degree from Liberty University. For twenty-five years he pastored one of the nation's outstanding churches in San Diego, which grew to three locations. It was during that time that he founded two accredited Christian high schools, a Christian school system of ten schools, and Christian Heritage College.

Dr. LaHaye has written over forty books, with over 22 million copies in print in thirty-three languages. He has written books on a wide variety of subjects, such as family life, temperaments, and Bible prophecy. His current fiction works, written with Jerry Jenkins—*Left Behind, Tribulation Force, Nicolae, Soul Harvest, Apollyon,* and *Assassins*—have all reached number one on the Christian best-seller charts. Other works by Dr. LaHaye are *Spirit-Controlled Temperament; How to Be Happy Though Married; Revelation Unveiled; Understanding the Last Days; Rapture under Attack; Are We Living in the End Times?;* and the youth fiction series Left Behind: The Kids.

He is the father of four grown children and grandfather of nine. Snow skiing, waterskiing, motorcycling, golfing, vacationing with family, and jogging are among his leisure activities.

The Future Is Clear

In one shocking moment, millions around the globe disappear. Those left behind face an uncertain future—especially the four kids who now find themselves alone.

Best-selling authors Jerry B. Jenkins and Tim LaHaye present the Rapture and Tribulation through the eyes of four friends—Judd, Vicki, Lionel, and Ryan. As the world falls in around them, they band together to find faith and fight the evil forces that threaten their lives.

#1: The Vanishings Four friends face Earth's last days together.

#2: Second Chance The kids search for the truth.

#3: Through the Flames The kids risk their lives.

#4: Facing the Future The kids prepare for battle.

#5: Nicolae High The Young Trib Force goes back to school.

#6: The Underground The Young Trib Force fights back.

#7: Busted! The Young Trib Force faces pressure.

#8: Death Strike The Young Trib Force faces war.

#9: The Search The struggle to survive.

#10: On the Run The Young Trib Force faces danger.

BOOKS #11 AND #12 COMING SOON!

Discover the latest about the Left Behind series and complete line of products at

www.leftbehind.com

A hand touched her shoulder.

Laura couldn't turn to look at the person behind her. She knew it was Jesse Cooper. She knew that hand, the touch. Firm but comforting, in a detached way.

"You okay?" he asked.

She nodded and swallowed the pain, the truth. "I'm good."

"I think you probably aren't."

He wouldn't ask who she'd been on the phone with. She turned, swiping at her eyes and managing a wavering smile to prove it didn't hurt.

"I was talking to my little girl."

"You have a child?" His eyes narrowed but continued to focus on her face, continued to be kind.

"Yes, I have a daughter. They put her in foster care. I can have her back once I have a job, a place to live and once I prove that I'm clean. Which is rather ironic, since I've never done drugs."

It registered, the truth. She saw it in his eyes and then he nodded.

And for some crazy reason, she felt relief flood her because he believed her.

Books by Brenda Minton

Love Inspired

Trusting Him
His Little Cowgirl
A Cowboy's Heart
The Cowboy Next Door
Rekindled Hearts
Blessings of the Season
  "The Christmas Letter"
Jenna's Cowboy Hero
The Cowboy's Courtship
The Cowboy's Sweetheart
Thanksgiving Groom
The Cowboy's Family

The Cowboy's Homecoming
Christmas Gifts
  *"Her Christmas Cowboy"
**The Cowboy's Holiday
  Blessing*
*The Bull Rider's Baby
*The Rancher's Secret Wife
*The Cowboy's Healing Ways

*Cooper Creek

BRENDA MINTON

started creating stories to entertain herself during hour-long rides on the school bus. In high school, she wrote romance novels to entertain her friends. The dream grew and so did her aspirations to become an author. She started with notebooks, handwritten manuscripts and characters that refused to go away until their stories were told. Eventually she put away the pen and paper and got down to business with the computer. The journey took a few years, with some encouragement and rejection along the way—as well as a lot of stubbornness on her part. In 2006, her dream to write for Love Inspired Books came true. Brenda lives in the rural Ozarks with her husband, three kids and an abundance of cats and dogs. She enjoys a chaotic life that she wouldn't trade for anything—except, on occasion, a beach house in Texas. You can stop by and visit at her website, www.brendaminton.net.

The Cowboy's Healing Ways

Brenda Minton

Love Inspired

™ LOVE INSPIRED BOOKS

Recycling programs
for this product may
not exist in your area.

ISBN-13: 978-0-373-81673-6

THE COWBOY'S HEALING WAYS

www.LoveInspiredBooks.com

Printed in U.S.A.

Now faith is the substance of things hoped for, the evidence of things not seen.
— *Hebrews* 11:1

This book is dedicated to my kids
because they always make me laugh.

To Janet Benrey. Our last book as agent and author!
Thank you for standing by me
and for giving me a chance.

To Rick (king of the pinewood derby) and Darla.
Thank you for everything,
even for getting me on that plane.

To Stephanie and Shirlee
for keeping me something close to sane.
I love you both.

Chapter One

Rain pelted the windshield of Laura White's car and the wipers worked hard to keep up, making a horrible scraping sound with each swish. Laura leaned in, trying to see the road. This had been going on since shortly after she left Tulsa, and in the past ten minutes it had gotten worse.

She glanced at the clock on the dash. Almost 10:00 p.m. Her head ached from straining to see the dark, rain-soaked highway. Hopefully her aunt Sally wouldn't mind the unannounced visit from a niece she hadn't seen in a dozen years. Laura didn't want to think ahead to what she would do if her aunt turned her away.

Ahead of her, headlights flashed, the beams catching on the sheets of rain. Laura slowed, trying to adjust to the dark, the lack of visibility. She reached to turn the defrost on High and the headlights became a car. The big sedan pulled out of a side road, right in the path of Laura's car. She opened her mouth to scream but the sound choked and wouldn't come out.

The car loomed large in front of her, her own headlights catching the expression on the face of the woman behind the wheel. Laura yanked the steering wheel to the right and sent her car off the side of the road, bouncing as it hit the ditch. Laura hit the brakes and held tight to the wheel as the car tilted. The fence flew at her window, the barbed wire sliding across the glass. Finally she came to a bone-jarring halt, slamming her head against the steering wheel.

Laura groaned and leaned back. Eyes closed, she focused on breathing, on getting her head clear. After a few minutes she unbuckled her seat belt. Nothing seemed to be broken. She reached for the door handle and gave it a good shove. It creaked open and she turned to get out. A woman stood next to her car.

"Oh, honey, I'm so sorry. I didn't see you coming." The woman, older, with gray hair peeking out from under a rain bonnet, reached for Laura's hand. "Maybe you should sit there for a minute."

"No, I'm good. I just wanted to see if my car is tangled on anything or if my tires are flat."

"In this weather? Come on, let's go to my

car and we'll call the police and have them get a wrecker out here."

"No, let me just get my bearings and I'll figure out how to get my car out. I don't have far to go."

"You can't drive that car. Goodness." The woman still held her hand. She gave a pull and helped Laura to her feet. The rain poured down, drenching them in no time flat. "Let me call my grandson. We'll get this car out of here, get the fence repaired and make sure you're okay."

"I'm really fine. I'm going to my aunt's in Dawson. I should be close."

Arm in arm they trudged up the embankment to the car idling on the shoulder of the road. The woman opened the door for Laura and helped her in. A moment later she got in on the driver's side.

Laura leaned back into the soft leather and shivered as the heat from the car hit her. Her head ached. She touched her forehead and her fingers came away with blood.

"Here, let me." The woman handed her a pretty handkerchief.

"I can't use this."

"I have plenty and that's a nasty gash." She tsk'd a few times. "My name is Myrna Cooper and I am just so sorry that I wasn't paying better attention. Did you tell me your name?"

"Laura White. And really, it was just an accident."

Myrna already had her phone to her ear, nodding as she talked. She patted Laura's leg. A moment later she slipped the phone back in her purse. "My grandson is going to tow the car and fix the fence. I'll take you on home with me."

"If you want, you could drop me at my aunt's."

Myrna shifted into gear and pulled onto the road. "Of course, but first I want a doctor to look at that cut on your head."

"I'm really okay." And losing ground fast. Laura leaned back, holding the handkerchief to her head and fighting a wave of nausea that came out of nowhere.

"Now, who is your aunt?"

"Sally White."

"Oh." Myrna Cooper nodded and then repeated, "Oh."

"Is something wrong?"

"Honey, has it been a while since you saw Sally?"

"Yes. After my father passed away, we lost touch."

"Laura, your aunt Sally is in a nursing home. She has Alzheimer's."

Laura closed her eyes. Every bone in her body ached and the nausea rolled through her stomach and up into her throat. She wanted to cry. For the first time in a long time, she wanted to give up. She'd been strong through everything, but this might be the last straw. She'd wondered what a last straw felt like.

It felt like falling.

It felt a lot like never having anyone to lean on. When was the last time someone had been there for her? Who was the last person she'd turned to for help? There hadn't been anyone in years and she had hoped Aunt Sally…

A hand touched her arm. "Now, don't you worry. Sally happens to be a friend of mine and any niece of hers has a place with me. Not only that—I do kind of owe you."

Laura wanted to shake her head, but it hurt to move.

"Laura, honey, hang in there. We're almost to my house."

As they pulled up the drive to a garage, Laura threw her door open and emptied the contents of her stomach, which wasn't all that much since she hadn't eaten dinner. A hand touched her back. Myrna spoke in soft, mothering tones. Laura closed her eyes at the sting of tears. She hadn't been mothered in years. At twenty-eight, she should really be past this.

"Let's see if we can get you inside." Myrna parked the car and a moment later she stood on the passenger side, a hand held out. "Let's go. And I promise, this isn't the end of the world."

"I think it might be." Laura got out of the car.

A truck pulled into the drive as they walked up the sidewalk to the front porch that wrapped around two sides of what would probably be a beautiful home in the daylight. On a dark, stormy night, it loomed large and rambling, a few lights glowing in the many windows.

The truck stopped behind Myrna's car.

"That would be my grandson, Dr. Jesse Cooper. He'll have you fixed up in no time." Myrna unlocked the door and pushed it open. "Go on in."

Laura stepped into the house, her vision blurring with tears and pain. A little bench in the entry was as far as she could make it on legs that shook. Myrna walked around the living room, turning on lights, talking sweetly to a couple of little white and yappy balls of fluff.

The door opened, bringing cool air and a few stray drops of rain. The wind had picked up, blowing the rain at a slanting angle. The man in the doorway slipped off boots and hung a cowboy hat on a hook by the door. She watched as he shrugged out of his jacket and hung it next to his hat.

When he turned she blinked a few times and stared up at a man with lean, handsome features and dark hair that brushed his collar. He looked as comfortable in this big house as he did in his worn jeans and flannel shirt. His dark eyes studied her with curious suspicion. She'd gotten used to that look. She'd gotten used to people staring, wondering, whispering behind their hands as she walked past.

But second chances and starting over meant wanting something new, a new reaction when people met her. She wanted to be the person people welcomed into their lives. She wanted to be the woman a man took a second look at, maybe a third, and not a suspicious look.

Jesse Cooper took a second look, but it was full of suspicion.

"Jesse, I'm so glad you're here." Myrna had returned with a cold washcloth that she placed on Laura's forehead, holding it tight as she talked to her grandson. "It seems I had an accident."

"Really?" Jesse smiled a little, the gesture shifting his features, warming the coolness in dark eyes that focused on Laura.

"I pulled right out in front of her. She drove her car off the side of the road to keep from hitting me."

Laura closed her eyes, leaning her head against

the wall behind her. A cool hand touched hers, moving the washcloth and touching the gash at her hairline.

"Let me see this."

She opened her eyes and he was squatting in front of her, his expression intent as he studied the cut. He looked from the gash to her face. Laura swallowed as he continued to stare, and then he moved and stood back up, unfolding long legs with graceful ease. Laura clasped her hands to keep them from shaking.

A while ago there had been an earthquake in Oklahoma. Laura remembered when it happened and how for a few minutes everyone had wondered if they'd really felt the earth move or if it had been their imaginations. She was pretty sure it had just happened again. The earth had moved, shifting precariously as a hand touched her face and dark eyes studied her intently, with a strange mixture of curiosity, surprise and something else.

"Let's get you in the kitchen where I can get a better look." Jesse held out his hand. "Can you tell me your full name?"

"Laura Alice White." She put her hand in his and he pulled her to her feet.

"What day is it?"

"Friday."

"And where were you heading on a night like tonight?"

She hesitated and didn't look at him. "I was going to rob a bank."

"Too bad. Dawson doesn't have a bank." He smiled a little and steadied her with a hand on her back.

"I was going to visit my aunt." Laura closed her eyes as another wave of nausea hit.

"Are you sick?" He stopped walking. "Dizzy?"

"Everything aches."

"Who is your aunt?"

"Sally White."

"You know she's in the nursing home, right?"

"Your grandmother told me."

"You didn't know?" He glanced down at her, dark hair and tired-looking dark eyes. She looked away because she had blood dripping down her face, smelly breath and a prison record. Sounded like three strikes to her.

They entered a long, narrow kitchen. The cabinets were dark cherry, and the countertops were black granite. It was warm and welcoming. He grabbed a stool shoved into a corner by the fridge and placed it in the center of the room. Myrna flipped on the overhead lights. Laura blinked to clear her vision as she adjusted to the glare.

"Why wouldn't you know that your aunt is in

the nursing home?" he asked as he looked her over, cleaning the cut on her forehead and placing a bandage on it.

Laura started to give a nonanswer but Myrna stepped forward, her lips pursed. "Jesse Alvarez Cooper, watch your manners."

"Sorry, Gran." His long fingers touched Laura's chin and he tilted her face. She tried to turn away but he held her steady with his left hand and with his right he flashed a light at her eyes.

No matter what, she wouldn't let him see her cry.

Jesse finished examining the woman sitting in his grandmother's kitchen and then put his medical bag on the counter. He tried to pretend he hadn't seen the glimmer of tears in her eyes. He'd never been good at ignoring a woman's tears.

He sighed and turned to face the other problem at hand. His grandmother. The fact that she had caused this accident troubled him. There were definitely a few missing pieces to the puzzle.

"Gran, what were you doing out so late on a night that isn't fit for dogs?"

She tossed him a "mind your own business" look. For the first time he noticed that she was wearing a pink skirt and jacket, not her typical jeans and T-shirt.

"You're not here about me. I'm fine. What do you think about Laura? Should she go to the hospital?" She leaned in close to study Laura White, conveniently avoiding his question. "Maybe she needs a CAT scan."

"I don't think so, Gran."

He switched his attention from his grandmother to the woman still sitting on the stool. She trembled and bit down on a quivering bottom lip. He didn't think she had serious injuries; more than likely it was a virus coupled with the shock of the accident and a few bumps and bruises.

Like his grandmother, she'd been out pretty late, driving in a serious storm. He wondered why it had been so important for her to get to her aunt's house, an aunt she obviously hadn't seen in years.

"Should we take her to the hospital, just to make sure nothing is broken?" Granny Myrna wrapped an arm around the woman and held her close, as if she were a long-lost child.

He loved that about his grandmother. The Coopers were the most loving, accepting bunch of people in the state, as far as he was concerned. He'd spent the first years of his life in

South America trying to survive before they'd brought him here to be a part of their family.

"Nothing is broken. I took her temperature and I have a feeling the nausea and body aches have more to do with a virus than the accident."

Laura shivered and he studied her face, pale with big gray eyes. She had long auburn hair that curled down her back. Her clothes were decent but worn, and she was thin, too thin.

"I need to get my car." She shivered again. He looked at his grandmother. She was already scurrying away, probably to get a blanket.

"Even if your car will run, where do you think you'll go?"

"I'm not sure. Back to Tulsa, I guess." Her voice was soft, almost sweet.

"You have a home there?"

She looked at him, gray eyes misty, and she didn't answer.

His grandmother rushed back into the room, an afghan in her hands. She draped it around her guest's shoulders. "She's staying right here."

"Gran."

She shushed him. "Jesse, I'm a big girl and I have a duty to take care of this young woman. I could be in the morgue right now if she hadn't run off the road to keep from hitting me."

She might have a point, but that didn't mean

she should put herself in harm's way, taking in a stranger. "Gran, really."

Laura White touched his grandmother's arm. "What your grandson is trying to say is that taking in a stranger is dangerous. Mrs. Cooper, you shouldn't. You don't know me from anyone."

Jesse's grandmother looked closely at her. "I'm knocking on the door of eighty-five and I know a good girl when I see one. You've had a few setbacks, but I see goodness in your eyes."

"I'm not going to argue because I won't win." Jesse walked over to the sink to wash his hands.

Behind him his grandmother and Laura White were having a discussion about Laura staying. He knew how this would go. He squirted dish soap in his palm, lathered up and rinsed under the hot tap water. The towel hanging over the door of the cabinet was damp. He found a clean one in the drawer.

"Is there a hotel in Dawson?" Laura asked as he turned back around. His grandmother shot him a look.

Jesse shook his head. "Nope."

She started to stand but wobbled, and he caught hold of her arm. He eased her back on the stool and placed his wrist on the back of her neck. Her fever had spiked. He grabbed the thermometer out of his bag and pushed the thick strands of auburn hair behind her ear to slide the thermometer in. She closed her eyes, opening them when he moved his hand and withdrew the thermometer.

He shook his head. "You need to be in bed."

His grandmother smiled big because she knew she'd won the argument. He had to smile, too, because his granny Myrna loved a new project and he could tell she didn't plan on letting this one slip out the door. His grandmother was dead set on fixing the person who had crashed into her life.

"Let me get the spare room ready and then you can help her upstairs."

"Sure thing, Gran." He watched his grandmother, still spry in her eighties, hurry out of the kitchen. He heard her singing as she headed upstairs to ready the guestroom.

"I really can go."

"No, you'll stay. Your car is being towed to the garage. Besides, my grandmother is a determined lady." He helped her up. "But don't hurt her."

"I'm not going to hurt her. I just wanted to get to my aunt's house tonight."

"I take it you're not close to your aunt."

"We lost contact after my father died."

He held her steady and they walked through the living room to the stairs. "And you decided to visit tonight?"

She sighed, stopping at the foot of the stairs.

"There was a rift when my mother remarried. I thought maybe if I came here…" She shrugged. "I need a place to start over. I need a job and a place to live."

"Dawson is a good place to start over, but there aren't too many jobs."

She shivered in his arms and he pulled the afghan closer around her shoulders. Years ago he would have loved having a woman like her in his arms. He had to admit, it still wasn't the worst feeling in the world.

These days he leaned toward caution because he had learned the hard way that people in a relationship weren't always feeling the same thing. Some people fell hard and fast while the other person sometimes didn't fall at all.

They started up the stairs, making it halfway before she paused to rest, a weak kitten, holding the rail.

"Are you going to make it?" He touched her back, holding her steady.

"Of course." She wavered again, turned to look at him and then down she went. Jesse scooped her in his arms, carrying her up the remaining stairs and down the hall to the door where his grandmother waited.

"Is she okay?"

"She will be. I think it would help if we got some food in her." She was light in his arms.

"I'll go heat up a can of soup." His grandmother pulled back the blankets and he placed her guest in the bed, backing away to let his grandmother continue fussing.

"I'll make the soup." He kissed his grandmother's cheek. "You get her settled."

Jesse walked down the stairs and back to the kitchen where he found Laura White's purse still hanging on the stool. He picked up the leather bag with frayed seams and thought about snooping. After a minute he listened to his better self and set the bag down on the counter.

He wouldn't snoop, but he'd stay and make sure his grandmother remained safe. And he'd make sure Laura White recovered.

After that, he'd let his grandmother take over. She was good with projects. His plate, however, was pretty full.

Chapter Two

Morning sun soaked the room in bright light and warmth. The rain had ended. Laura stretched in the softest bed she had ever slept in, but her relief didn't last. Her head ached and she felt as if lead weights had been placed in her arms and legs. She rolled over and squinted to look at the clock.

She was in Myrna Cooper's home. She had made it to Dawson. But now what? She had nowhere to go. She had no money and no real friends.

Dressed in the same clothes she'd worn the day before, she tried to run her fingers through her hair and make herself presentable. Her suitcase was in the trunk of her car, wherever that happened to be. She shivered and reached for the afghan that Myrna had draped over her shoulders the night before. Light-headed and achy, she walked down the hall to the wide stairs.

As she walked through the living room a quilt-covered lump on the couch moved. She paused as he rolled over, flopping an arm over his face. He had stayed. Not because he wanted to make sure she was okay, but because he'd been worried about leaving his grandmother alone with her.

Laura didn't blame him. Instead she liked that he was the kind of person who would stay, spending the night on an old Victorian sofa just to make sure his grandmother was safe.

The aroma from the kitchen pulled her away from the good doctor and back to her goal. Food. She could smell coffee and bacon. As she walked through the door, Myrna turned, smiling. She flipped a pancake and pointed to the coffeepot.

"Help yourself to coffee and the pancakes will be done shortly."

"Thank you." Laura turned and coughed. "Is there anything I can do?"

"I've got it handled. How are you feeling this morning?"

"About the same." Her body still ached, and her throat burned. She was looking forward to the coffee. "I should make arrangements, though. To go somewhere."

She needed a plan and she didn't have one.

This had been it for her. This had been her last resort.

"You'll do no such thing." Myrna handed her a plate of pancakes. "Sit down and eat."

She took the plate, her hands trembling as she moved to the counter. She spread butter and then poured syrup across the golden-brown cakes. Her mouth watered as she thought about the last time she'd had pancakes, good pancakes.

From the living room she heard shuffling, mumbling and then footsteps. Myrna shook her head and then poured more batter on the griddle. A moment later Jesse walked through the door, disapproving but gorgeous with his chocolate-brown eyes still sleepy, and shadowy whiskers covering his lean cheeks. His straight, dark hair went in all directions, and he must have known because he was trying to brush it down with his fingers.

Laura took a bite of pancake and looked away from the barefoot cowboy in his faded jeans and flannel shirt, sleeves rolled up to the elbows. She glanced quickly at her faded jeans and fuzzy sweater, both from a decade or two past, trying hard not to make comparisons.

"How are you this morning?" He walked straight to the coffeepot and grabbed a mug from the cabinet. He looked at her and pulled out another one. "Want coffee?"

"Please." She glanced in Myrna's direction. Myrna flipped another pancake on the platter and then scooped bacon out of a skillet.

Jesse turned from the coffeepot. He set a cup of coffee on the counter next to her. "You can sit in the dining room."

"I'm good."

He shrugged one shoulder and turned away from her. With an ease that she envied he walked up behind his grandmother, gave her a loose hug and pulled a plate from the holder on the counter.

"Do you have anywhere to go?" He leaned against the counter, watching her.

She swallowed a syrupy bite and shook her head. No time like the present to just get it all out there. She wouldn't hide her story or her life from them, not after they'd been so kind. Well, Myrna had been kind. Jesse… She watched as he poured syrup over the stack of pancakes on his plate. He didn't look at her.

Jesse had been kind, too.

"I don't have anywhere to go." She sighed and pushed the plate away, unable to eat the last few bites. A place to go, a job, she needed those things. Had to have them in order to fix her life.

The headache she had thought gone returned with a vengeance, pounding behind her eyes and in the back of her head. She rubbed her forehead.

"I had hoped Aunt Sally would give me a place to stay until I could get back on my feet."

As she'd talked, Jesse opened a cabinet door and pulled out a bottle of pills. He shook a couple into his hand and handed them to her. Laura took them, smiling her gratitude and washing the medicine down with her coffee.

"Well, now, honey, why don't you tell us what knocked you off your feet?" Myrna turned from the stove, wiping her hands on the corner of her apron. "And we'll see if we can't make a plan. Sometimes everything looks dark because we haven't had friends to help us put our situation in a better light."

"I've been living in a halfway house for the past month."

"And before that?" Jesse asked as he leaned against the counter, his plate in his hands.

"Before that I was in jail."

"Jail?" Myrna's eyes understandably widened and she glanced from Laura to Jesse. Of course he had an "I told you so" look on his face. His dark brows arched and he frowned.

Laura scraped her plate in the sink and turned on the water and then the garbage disposal. She gave it a few seconds and flipped the switch off.

That gave her a little time to gather her thoughts and prepare herself.

How much did she tell? Did she tell the truth or the court's version of the truth? A jury hadn't believed her, so why should anyone else? Evidence, beyond a shadow of a doubt, pointed to her guilt.

"I was in jail on a drug-dealing and possession charge." She looked away. She wanted to pretend this wasn't her life and that people didn't look at her with surprise, disgust and every other emotion she'd seen in the past month.

From now on this would be her story.

"You sold drugs?" Myrna scoffed and shook her head. "Now, I might be old, but I'm not naive. I'm having a hard time picturing you selling poison."

Laura raised her chin a notch and blinked back the sting of tears the well-meaning words brought to her eyes. Myrna Cooper clearly wasn't like everyone else. She was a tall woman with every gray hair in place. This morning she'd donned jeans and a sweatshirt, not the pretty pastel suit she'd worn the previous evening.

Laura wanted to think of everything but the three months she'd spent in jail. She could still hear the clank of metal doors. She could still imagine herself surrounded by gray and steel.

Three months of being alone and trying to tell herself she'd survive. And she had. Somehow she'd survived.

"Laura?" Myrna stepped to her side and placed a gentle hand on her shoulder.

A quick glance in Jesse Cooper's direction and Laura knew he had no intention of giving her a pass. His brown eyes were no longer sleepy or soft. She had never wanted this to be her life. He'd obviously grown up here, in a safe and loving family. He had no idea.

The "ifs" would drive her crazy. If her mother hadn't died. If her stepfather hadn't been abusive. If she hadn't let her stepbrother stay in her apartment when he showed up six months ago. That decision had cost her her freedom, her good reputation, her job and her apartment.

Because no one believed her when she said her brother had put the drugs and the money in her purse as she got pulled over that day. He'd bailed on her, running down a side street and disappearing. She'd reached into her purse to grab the bag and the police had caught her as they walked up to her car. More drugs had been found in her apartment.

"I need to go now." She slid past Myrna Cooper.

"Wait a second, young lady." Myrna's voice held a commanding tone that Laura couldn't ignore. She turned, her vision swimming. She leaned against the wall and waited.

"I'm sorry, Mrs. Cooper. You've been very kind to me. Now I need to go."

"Your car is at the local garage, so you really can't go anywhere unless you plan on walking." Myrna sighed. "Tell me what happened."

"I was convicted of felony possession and distribution. There's really nothing more to tell."

"That isn't an answer."

"It's the finding of the court and the ruling stands." Laura stood, holding the back of the stool. "I really need to get my car."

"I think you need to sit back down." Jesse moved away from the counter he'd been leaning on. He moved with power and ease, and she felt very weak and small.

"Laura, sit down."

She nodded and did as he commanded. "I should have called before coming to Dawson."

"Well, I for one am glad God put me in your path last night." Myrna hugged her tightly. "We'll figure this out."

"No, I really should go." Laura glanced at Jesse and then back to Myrna. "I should go because having me here is the last thing you need."

"Jesse, you're the doctor—tell her she can't leave in this condition."

Jesse smiled and shook his head. "I'm not

getting in the middle of this argument. Gran, you're right—she needs to rest. Laura, you have to do what you think is best. My opinion probably won't count for much."

Laura folded the afghan and placed it on the stool. "Myrna, thank you for everything."

"Where do you think you'll go?" Myrna asked.

"I'll find a place." Laura wanted to hug the older woman, but she couldn't. She thought she'd fall apart if Myrna comforted her in any way.

It had been too long since anyone in her life had cared. She picked up her purse and stood for a moment in front of Myrna, wishing she'd had someone like this woman.

"I don't like this, not one bit." Myrna shook her head, looking from Laura to Jesse.

"Thank you for letting me stay the night." Laura turned away and headed for the front door, walking fast and blinking furiously to clear her vision.

As Laura left, Jesse hugged his grandmother, the sweetest woman he knew. She stood stiff in his arms, her mouth in a tight and unhappy line.

"Gran, we don't know her. You don't know the whole story."

"She told us the whole story and I know her

aunt. Jesse, people have stories. That doesn't mean they are stuck in that story. People make mistakes. They do what they have to in the situations they're in. Now, how can we call ourselves Christians if we aren't willing to give someone a second chance? You've had second chances."

"What do you want me to do?"

His grandmother's eyes filled with tears. "She needs help and a place to stay."

"I can get her a room in Grove and then we'll see if we can get her some assistance. You're right—no one knows better than I do about second chances. The other thing I know is how dangerous the drug trade can be. People get angry. They get revenge."

The front door clicked, ending their conversation.

"Go after her, Jesse." His grandmother put a hand on his back, moving him forward.

"I have to get my shoes."

"Well, you'd better hurry. She's sick with nowhere to go. If something happens to her…" His grandmother's face paled and she shook her head a little. "I'm sorry."

"Don't worry about it." He slid his feet into his boots and grabbed his jacket. "I won't let anything happen to her. I'm also not letting anything happen to you."

He hurried out the door, putting his coat on as he went. Laura White stood at the end of the drive, a tall woman with auburn hair blowing in the light breeze. She shivered and hugged herself tightly, turning to look at him with a wan smile on her pale face.

Okay, he wouldn't get the Samaritan of the Year award. But what in the world was he supposed to do with her? He walked to the end of the drive, thinking through options and not coming up with much. He guessed he could take her to his parents.

As he approached, Laura's chin came up a notch, a little pride coming to the surface. He remembered being a kid, digging deep to find that pride to get past his own humiliation. He knew what it took for a person to find that strength.

"I can walk. I'm just not sure where I'm going or how I'll get my car. I can't afford to pay for repairs." She turned, coughing into her shoulder before facing him again. The cold weather made her nose red and her gray eyes sparkle. "I don't have insurance."

"I'm sure Gran is going to pay for the repairs. She did pull out in front of you."

"She didn't see me. The rain was unbelievable."

"She really wants you to stay here."

Laura shook her head. "I can't."

"Then I'll drive you to Grove. We'll get you a hotel room and find some way to help you get back on your feet."

She looked past him, her eyes damp with unshed tears. "You really don't have to do this. I can get a ride."

"No, you're not okay. You're sick. It looks like we're going to get more rain and you have nowhere to go." Jesse adjusted the hat he'd put on before walking outside. "I'm going to be honest. I'm not crazy about my grandmother bringing in strangers. But I'm also not about to let you walk off without help."

She shivered. Jesse shrugged out of his jacket. He draped it across her shoulders and she huddled into it.

"Let's get in my truck before the rain hits." He put a hand on her arm and steered her in the right direction.

When they reached the passenger side of his truck she turned away from him, coughing again. The cough racked her thin body and when the spell ended she leaned against his truck, breathing deeply to catch her breath.

"You okay?"

"I'm good." She turned, smiling, her face pale and her eyes huge but rimmed with dark circles.

"Right." He opened the door and she climbed

in. "When we get to town we'll stop at the store for some cough syrup and maybe herbal tea."

"You don't have to." She clicked the seat belt in place. "Look, you can stop pretending you're my appointed keeper. I don't need one. I'm good on my own. I've been on my own for a long time."

"I'm not pretending anything. I'm just trying to help you." He started the truck and shifted into Reverse, glancing into the rearview mirror as he backed down the driveway. "I'm trying to make sure you're going to be okay."

"I'm trying to let you off the hook." She closed her eyes and his big coat enveloped her. "I'm so tired."

"I know you are. On both counts." He drove through Dawson and headed toward Grove. "You don't have to let me off the hook."

He glanced her way and then turned his attention back to the road. "Do you have job experience?"

"Yes."

"And?" He drove out of Dawson, wondering if she was being purposely vague.

"I worked in an office and then as a manager for a cleaning crew. I was going to school to be a nurse."

"Hmm." He didn't know what else to say. It seemed like a lot to throw away.

"Now I'm a felon and no one will hire me. I can't even rent an apartment."

"There has to be somewhere you can go."

She sighed. "In a perfect world there would be justice and I would get a do-over."

"There are those things—sometimes they're just hard to find."

She nodded but didn't respond. He found himself wanting to know a whole lot more about her than she seemed willing to tell. The curiosity grew when she reached into the side pocket of her purse and pulled out a tiny framed photo. She held it tightly and closed her eyes.

Everyone had a story, his grandmother liked to remind him. They all had things they wished they could do over. He would have been more careful with other people's feelings.

When they reached Grove, he pulled up to the grocery store. "Let's run in here and we'll get what you'll need for a few days."

She didn't answer. He leaned to touch her shoulder. She opened her eyes wide and moved back a little.

"I didn't mean to scare you. I'm going in. You stay here and rest." He reached into the back seat of the truck and grabbed a blanket. "I'll trade. Blanket for the jacket."

She took off his canvas jacket and handed

it to him. He draped the blanket over her. She smiled a weak smile.

"Back in a few."

She nodded and he got out of the truck. As he crossed the parking lot he remembered that he'd left his keys in the ignition. He looked back and saw her in the passenger side, leaning against the door. Sleeping.

His truck would either be there when he came out, or it wouldn't. He sighed and walked through the automatic doors of the store, shooting one last glance in the direction of his truck.

The things he let his grandmother get him into. He'd never learn.

Laura woke up in an empty truck parked in front of a grocery store. She remembered Jesse telling her he would be back soon. She glanced at her watch and pulled the phone out of her pocket.

She dialed the number she had memorized. This phone call was all she could have for the time being. It wasn't enough, but it was better than nothing.

After a few rings a woman answered.

"Mrs. Duncan, this is Laura White." She coughed a little and then cleared her throat. "I'm so sorry."

"Laura, you sound terrible. Are you okay?"

"I think I have the flu, but I'm good. Things are good." She hated the lie, but she couldn't admit that her life was falling apart. She wasn't even close to where she needed to be.

"Did you find a place in Dawson?" Mrs. Duncan hesitated, then cleared her throat. "Do you have a job?"

"Not yet." She glanced out the window at the grocery store. "I'm getting a place to stay, but it isn't permanent."

"Oh, I had hoped this would work out for you."

Laura closed her eyes. "Me, too."

"Okay, let me get Abigail."

And then there were shouts, laughter, her daughter. "Mommy."

"Abigail, I miss you." She swallowed the tight lump in her throat and fought the burning sting of tears.

"I miss you, too."

"What have you been doing?" Laura closed her eyes, remembering her daughter's face, how it felt to hold her. Abigail had dark brown hair and gray eyes. Laura held the memories tightly. "How's school?"

"I made all As and Gina gave me money and we ate pizza. I made cookies last night with the other kids."

Normal moments. A normal life. Her daughter should always have those things. "That sounds like fun. And I'm proud of you."

"I'm proud of you, too, Mommy. Okay, I have to go. When do I get to see you?"

"Soon. Very soon." Promises she hoped she could keep.

"I pray for you, Mommy."

Laura nodded and her throat ached. "I know. Me, too, sugarplum. Bye." She whispered the words as her daughter rushed through another "I love you" and hung up.

She cried. Holding the school picture she kept in her purse, she cried. Abigail prayed for her. She thought back to childhood stories of faith and God. She hadn't thought much about either since her mother died. Her stepfather had been abusive and Laura had left and taken to the streets, believing life on her own had to be better than under his control.

A string of boyfriends, a marriage that hadn't lasted long enough to change anything, a stepbrother who put her in prison and now this. She'd had plans and dreams for her life. She'd wanted more than this, more than barely getting by. She'd wanted more for Abigail. She still wanted more for her daughter.

She shivered in the cool truck and closed her eyes against the bright sky. Nothing was the way she'd planned. She'd really thought her aunt

Sally, a woman she remembered from childhood, would be here to help pick up the pieces of her life, to help her believe again. She'd prayed that she would find something here, a way to get Abigail back.

Instead she had the kindness of a stranger and little more than she'd had the day before. She rested her forehead against the cool glass of the window and thought through the list of things she had lost. She used to believe in people. She used to believe in herself. A long time ago she'd had faith.

She closed her eyes and prayed to get all three back. She had never been a quitter. She wouldn't quit now, not on life or herself. She wouldn't quit because of Abigail.

Chapter Three

Jesse walked across the parking lot and watched as the woman in the passenger seat of his truck wiped at tears streaming down her cheeks. He didn't know how to help her. He shook his head and shifted the paper bag to his other arm. The last thing she needed from him was a promise he couldn't keep. He knew he couldn't fix her life.

He walked up to the passenger side of his truck and peeked in. Laura didn't look up. In her hand she held a school photo of a little girl. He stepped away from the window and walked to the back of the truck to store the groceries in the metal toolbox in the bed of the truck. When he opened the door, Laura wiped the last of her tears. She smiled at him, a watery smile.

"How do you feel?" He shifted into Reverse and then looked her way for a quick moment.

"A little better."

"I bought cold medicine." He didn't know what else to say. "Who's the little girl in the picture?"

She closed her eyes and shrugged. When she looked at him, the pain in her gray eyes was tangible. He drew in a quick breath before he looked away, focusing on the road.

"She's my daughter."

The words hit him hard. He shook his head and kept driving.

"Where is she?" None of his business, but he had to ask.

"They took her. When I was in jail. Of course they took her." She sniffed and when he looked, her face was buried in her hands, auburn hair falling forward. "She's in a foster home."

"You'll get her back?"

She pushed her hair back with pale hands that trembled and nodded as she looked at him.

"Yes. When I get a job and a permanent home. I didn't think it would be this hard. Trying to get her back. Trying to find a normal life again."

"It isn't easy."

"No, it isn't. Someone else is taking her for pizza, praying with her, tucking her in. It should be me. If I hadn't let my stepbrother…" She shook her head. "I have to stop blaming him. I let him move in. I knew it would be a mistake, but I felt sorry for him."

He nodded and kept driving.

Laura continued to talk. "Which is why I don't blame you for not wanting me in your grandmother's house. You don't know me. You don't know what I've done, what is or isn't true. People lie."

"Sometimes we have to trust people." He cleared his throat and looked at her. "Sometimes we have to give them a chance to prove they can be trusted."

He pulled into the parking lot of a motel with a sign that said they rented by the day, week or month.

"Sometimes," she said in a soft voice that told him trust was hard for her.

He parked, sighing because he couldn't leave her here. She had a daughter she didn't want to let go of. She had gray eyes that didn't beg him to give her a chance but begged him to trust her. Believe her.

"I could use someone to help me at my place," he said as he stared at the little motel that had been around longer than either of them had been alive. He switched his attention to look at the woman sitting next to him.

"I'm not looking for a handout. I need a job. I'm willing to work."

"It isn't a handout." He turned in his seat to face her. "I work odd hours and sometimes take shifts at a hospital in Tulsa. I'm also the doctor on call for the local residential care facility. On top of that I might be going out of the country."

"A vacation?"

"No, I'm thinking about going to the mission field, to Honduras."

"For how long?"

"A year."

She nodded. "And so the job would be?"

"I have a small house on my place at the lake. You could have that home and a small salary. In return, I could use a housekeeper and if you aren't afraid of horses, someone to feed my livestock when I'm not there."

"A job and a house." Her voice tightened with emotion. "But do you really want me on your property? I'm a convicted felon."

"Tell me your side of the story and I'll decide."

"I didn't know that my stepbrother was a drug dealer. He used my apartment that last day to make meth while I was gone. The police had been watching him and they thought I was involved. Ryan jumped out of my car and they never caught him. I got busted with meth, some prescription drugs and the money. I was just naive when it came to Ryan. I saw him the way I saw myself—as a victim of our childhood." She shrugged thin shoulders. "I wanted to fix him."

As she finished he nodded. "I believe you."

She nodded and looked away, her hand coming up to swipe at tears. "That's good to know."

"This will be good for both of us. I need a housekeeper and you need a home."

"Why haven't you hired someone? There would have to be any number of people who would want a position like the one you're offering me."

"I interviewed a few people but most of them know my family. The older women feel as if they have to mother me and watch over me." And the younger women wanted a husband.

"I don't know what to say."

"Will you take the job?"

She nodded. "Yes."

The battle with her tears was lost. She swiped at her eyes but tears streamed down her cheeks. Jesse found a napkin in the console between the seats and handed it to her. The most impulsive decision he'd made in years was sitting next to him crying, and he couldn't take back the offer. Not when a child was involved. Because Laura was a mom who wanted to keep her little girl.

Jesse started his truck and pulled out of the parking lot of the motel. He told himself he'd done the right thing. He'd let her clean his house. He'd provide her a home. No strings, no attachments. Easy.

Laura wiped her eyes and tried to think through what had just happened. Too good to be true? In her life strings always seemed to be attached. She couldn't remember the last time anyone had done anything for her that didn't require something back.

She closed her eyes tight and tried to think, which was hard to do in her present condition. First, she had to consider Abigail—not just getting her back, but keeping her safe. She had so much at stake. She couldn't take chances, not with her future or her daughter's.

With a sigh she faced the man who had offered her the opportunity of a lifetime. "Why would you do this for me?"

He shrugged and pulled out on the road. The truck eased through the traffic and he didn't answer for a few minutes.

"Because you deserve a second chance." He paused to make a left-hand turn. "I want to help you out because your little girl deserves to have you."

"How do you know that?"

He looked at her for a brief second, then refocused on the road. "I've seen a lot in my life,

Laura. I've seen the best and worst of humanity. I think I know when someone is decent and really needs a second chance."

She knew there was more to his story. She saw it in the sometimes-lost look in his eyes, as if he might have been a little boy needing a mother. But she had to remind herself that he was a man, not a little boy anymore. And in her experiences with men, limited as they were, there were usually consequences.

"Where are we going?" She touched the phone in her pocket, reassured by its presence.

"If you want the job, I thought I'd take you out to the house." He glanced her way again. "I think we're both going to have to make a stab at trusting."

She nodded, glancing out the window. They were close to Dawson when he turned down a paved road with signs giving directions to different points of interest. A few minutes later he turned into a driveway, hit a remote on the visor of this truck and the gates in front of them opened wide.

Laura shivered in the blanket wrapped around her shoulders and watched out the window. A few deer jumped from the woods and ran across the road in front of them. Her breath caught as she watched the creatures bound out of sight.

A few hundred more feet and the woods gave

way to grass. And then a tiny house surrounded by a picket fence. Ahead she could see a small stable and barely could make out the exterior of a house surrounded by tall trees.

"This is the original house." He pulled in the drive. "It isn't much, but it's in good shape, easy to heat and cool. Two bedrooms and it's furnished."

She swallowed the lump of fear that said this couldn't be real. Things like this didn't happen, not to her, not in this life. She remembered a prayer that God would help her find faith again—that He would provide a way for her to get Abigail back.

"We can go in." Jesse pulled the keys from the ignition and he had his hand on the door.

Laura looked at him, at the house. She could trust him. He was Myrna Cooper's grandson. He was a doctor. And she didn't have a lot of options. She had to take this chance if she meant to get on her feet again.

She reminded herself that decent men existed. Laura barely remembered her real father, but he'd been one. He'd been kind, caring, always worried about his family. After he passed away, her life had been filled by men who were sad replacements. She'd known selfish men, abusive men, users.

"Are you okay?" He had opened his door but

pulled it closed again. "Look, there are other options if you don't think this is what you want."

"I'm fine—just amazed and worried that I could never repay you."

"It isn't charity. You're going to work for this."

"You don't understand. This means everything. I have a daughter who I haven't been able to bring home with me for months."

He smiled, the gesture settling in his chocolate-brown eyes. "Laura, I get it. Let's go in and see if you're going to be okay living here."

Laura got out and met him at the front of the truck. The yard was pretty and neat. The leaves on the trees were budding and still the bright green of early spring. She walked through the gate and up the sidewalk to the front porch of the little white house with the green roof.

Jesse reached into his pocket for the key and after opening the door, he motioned her inside.

Laura stepped into the tiny but bright living room. She walked around the room, touching soft chenille-upholstered furniture and lingering in front of the wide window that overlooked the lawn, the driveway and, across the way, a tiny view of the lake. She drew the blanket around her shoulders a little tighter.

Jesse walked up behind her. He touched her shoulder and she turned a little, smiling at the man who had offered her this place, this chance at a real life and the real opportunity to get Abigail back.

She looked into his deep brown eyes and saw a flicker of something, just before he shook his head and stepped back, his hand dropping from her shoulder.

"Let me show you the rest of the house."

She followed him from the living room to the kitchen, a bright room with white cabinets and ceramic tile floors. Down the hall were two sunny bedrooms. She stood in the center of one of those rooms, hugging herself, thinking she might possibly wake up from a wonderful dream where things went right in her life only to find herself still in the halfway house praying for a way out.

"Are you okay?"

"I'm good." She looked around the room with the quilt-covered bed, windows overlooking green fields and hardwood floors covered with a few deeply colored area rugs. She shook her head. "No, I'm better than good. And I'm waiting for the catch."

"The catch?"

"Things like this don't happen for people like me." She tried to smile but it hurt and her eyes filled with tears that she blinked away before they could fall.

Chapter Four

"Heard you hired a housekeeper."

It had only taken two days for the news to spread. Technically she hadn't really started working until today. The past two days she'd been on the couch of the cottage, sometimes feverish. He'd kept her drinking hot tea and taking cold medicine. This morning she'd stepped out of the house to greet her new life.

Jesse closed the stall door and turned to face the brother who had managed to sneak in on him. Not that Blake typically sneaked. Sneaking would be something Gage would do, or Jackson, maybe Travis. Of all of his brothers, Blake was the one most likely to keep his nose out of everyone else's business. Probably because he didn't want them in his.

Blake stopped at a stall door and ran his

"There's no catch. You need a job and a place to stay. I need help because I can't keep up with housework and laundry."

"No catch?" She walked to the window. In the distance she could see the shimmering waters of Grand Lake.

"None at all." He stepped back into the hall. "You should rest. I need to get some work done around here but I'll stop by later to check on you. Don't forget to put away the milk and other groceries that I left on the counter."

She followed him to the front door. "Jesse, I'll never be able to repay you. Thank you for doing this for me."

"You're welcome." He tipped his hat and walked from the porch to his truck. And she was alone.

But less alone than she'd been in years.

hand down the sleek neck of the mare Jesse had just bought.

"Yeah, I hired a housekeeper." Jesse opened the stall door of the gray, snapped a lead on her and led her out for Blake to look over.

"I still can't believe you're raising Arabians." Blake shook his head. "What were you thinking?"

"They're great animals." Jesse shrugged it off, the way he'd been doing for six months, since he brought home the Arab stallion and mare.

"Right, I'll let you raise your girly horses and I'll stick with a good, strong quarter horse."

"And I'll outride you on an Arab any day of the week."

Blake ran his hand down the mare's back and shook his head. "I think we'll have to put them to the test."

"We can do that. What brings you out here?"

"Thought I'd stop by. It's been a while."

"I'm not buying that. You never stop by because it's been a while."

Blake walked away. He stopped in front of the stallion's stall. The big horse moved restlessly around the stall and settled in the far corner.

"I found my daughter." Blake turned as he made the announcement.

"How?"

"I hired a private investigator. He isn't sure if he found her or if Jana allowed him to find them. He said it was pretty easy once he got on the right track. She's in South Africa."

Jesse whistled and shook his head. Blake's ex-wife had taken off years ago, filed for divorce and then hightailed it out of the country with their little girl. Blake had been chasing leads for ten years, trying to get his daughter back, or at least hoping for a chance to see her.

"How old would Lindsey be now?"

"Twelve."

"Man, Blake, I don't know what to say."

"Yeah, me either."

"Let me know if there's anything I can do."

Blake nodded and walked down the wide aisle between rows of stalls. He stopped at the open double door.

"I'll let you know. And I thought I'd warn you that I stopped to visit our grandmother and she's on her way out here." Blake shot a look toward Jesse's house.

"That's good to know. I'm sure she only has the best of intentions."

Blake actually smiled. Maybe because he enjoyed their grandmother focusing on someone other than himself, or because he felt some amazing relief, knowing where Lindsey was. "See you later, brother."

Jesse waved and went back to work.

When he walked up the steps to the back door of his house, he knew Laura would earn her keep and more. The deck had been swept, the flowers were no longer wilting and the patio table where he liked to drink his morning coffee had been wiped off. He headed for the door but it opened before he could reach for the handle.

Laura jumped back and her hand went to her heart. "I didn't see you."

"Sorry about that." He hung his hat on the hook next to the door and swept his hand through his hair. "I'm going to fix a sandwich. Do you want one?"

"No, I can run up to my place for lunch."

"I'll make us both a sandwich. There's no need for you to walk down there."

She walked out the back door to the edge of the deck and shook a rug out. After several hard shakes, she turned to look back at him. "I really don't need to be taken care of."

"I know you don't. But I really don't want you to work more than a few hours today. You need to get your strength back." He studied the little garden at the side of the house. The garden he'd been meaning to plant something in for as long as he'd had this house. "Did you plant flowers?"

She nodded a little. "I should have asked. It's just that I saw the plants on the table in your utility room and they were starting to look bad. You had tomatoes, too, and a few pepper plants."

He motioned her inside. "I'm glad you planted them. I do this every year. I buy plants, consider planting them, get busy, think about them once or twice and then I forget them until they're brown and long past saving."

"A doctor who can't keep a plant alive." She smiled as she said it. He ignored that smile— with effort.

"Exactly." He touched her back as she moved ahead of him into the kitchen. The house smelled like pine cleaner and fresh air from the open windows. "This is great. I'd forgotten that a house could smell this good."

"It wasn't really messy, just…"

He stopped when he reached the kitchen. "The word you're looking for is *neglected*. And what's in the Crock-Pot?"

She walked past him and lifted the lid. "Roast. I hope you don't mind. I found it in the freezer and thought it would be an easy meal for you. It'll be done by six this evening and if you don't want it tonight, I can put it in a container and you can reheat it tomorrow."

"Amazing." He'd lived the bachelor life since he'd left home for college. He'd forgotten what a woman's touch did for a place.

A car door interrupted his musings. He glanced out the window and saw the corner of a silver car. He pulled ham and cheese out of the fridge. Behind him he heard the water running and Laura washing her hands.

"You have company."

"That would be my grandmother, here to check on you." He put the luncheon meat on the counter and found bread in the cabinet.

Laura turned from the sink, a towel in her hands. "Does she know that I'm working for you?"

"I'm sure everyone in town knows. I bought two meals at Vera's two nights in a row." He handed her a paper plate. "Don't worry about it."

Her eyes widened and pink stained her cheeks. He felt bad about teasing her, but in the past two days he'd learned that she was easy to embarrass, and when that happened, pink crept up her neck to her cheeks.

"Well, I hadn't planned on worrying until you said something. I don't want people to get the wrong idea."

"They won't." He grinned because she was watching the door. "Relax, I'm just teasing."

Before his grandmother could knock, he called out for her to come in. She did. The door banged softly behind her and he heard her mutter something about needing to kick off her shoes before she tracked in mud. The comment reminded him and he looked down at his boots and cringed. Even the hems of his jeans were caked with mud. When he looked up, Laura smiled and shook her head.

"I tracked in on your clean floor." He reached for a roll of paper towels and she stopped him.

"The mop is still damp. I'll clean it up after you're finished with lunch."

Granny Myrna stepped into the kitchen. She eyed the two of them and helped herself to a cup of coffee.

"Now, isn't this cozy?"

"Gran, it isn't what you…"

She raised a bejeweled hand and shook her head. "I know that. It's just…very domestic. I'm glad to see this place clean and smelling of something other than that dog of yours."

"Thanks." He offered her a sandwich and she shook her head.

"I'm not here for lunch. I'm here to see if Laura wants to ride into town with me. I thought we'd check on her car and then we can go by and see her aunt Sally."

Laura had stopped fixing her sandwich. Her hands stilled over the bread and she glanced his way, as if seeking his permission.

"I really need to finish up. I haven't mopped the upstairs bathrooms."

Jesse offered her a bottle of water. "Tomorrow. Eat and go with Gran. I promise she's usually a very safe driver."

Laura smiled up at him, a shy smile. "Thank you. And I trust her."

He grinned at that. "Suit yourself. But trusting her driving, way overrated."

She turned pink again. He looked away but caught his grandmother watching him, an all-too-knowing look in eyes that probably saw too much, even if she did say they weren't as good as they used to be.

Ten minutes and just a few miles later, Laura had lost that trust in Myrna's driving. A ride to town brought new fears and a renewed belief in the power of prayer.

"Relax. And try breathing. By the way, don't wear yourself out cleaning Jesse's house. I don't think you're over that virus." Myrna slowed and pulled into the parking lot of the Lakeside Residential Care Facility. The building was one level, a long, low building with brick siding and multiple windows.

Laura smiled at Myrna.

"It's been a long time since I've seen or talked to Aunt Sally."

"Does that mean my driving has nothing to

do with your pale face or the death grip on the door handle?"

Laura relaxed her grip and smiled. "Maybe a little."

"It's always been a problem for me. I get behind the wheel and something takes over. Mort and I, back in the day when there was a local dirt track, raced. I had a powder-puff car and I could rip up that track."

"You raced?"

"Don't look so shocked. I wasn't always a grandma."

They got out of the car and walked up the sidewalk together. Myrna touched her arm. "Have you talked to your little girl?"

"Abigail." Laura nodded. "I was supposed to see her on Saturday but I'm not sure if I'll be able to."

"Why ever not?"

"It depends on my car." She hated to mention it.

"Well, of course you'll see her. I'll make sure of it—if I have to drive you myself."

Laura choked back a laugh and a sob. "Thank you, Myrna."

"Don't you mention it, sweetie. Now, let's go see how Sally Ann is doing."

Laura followed Myrna down the hall, and Myrna seemed to know right where they would find her aunt. They stopped at a small room with several tables and a few women with jigsaw puzzles in front of them.

Aunt Sally was one of the women. It had been years, but Laura knew her aunt immediately. She wore a pale blue housedress and her dark gray hair was freshly permed. Her wire-framed glasses slid down her nose as she stared at the puzzle pieces in front of her.

"She probably won't remember you." Myrna patted Laura's arm. "I guess you know that."

Laura nodded, tears filling her eyes as she stared at a woman she remembered from childhood, a woman who had been from Dawson but lived in Tulsa at the time. They would visit on weekends and Aunt Sally would make cookies and show Laura how to crochet granny squares out of multicolored yarn.

She approached her aunt, taking the empty seat next to her. Myrna stood behind Sally, a hand on her shoulder. Sally looked up at Myrna smiling and then offered Laura a vacant smile.

"Hi, Aunt Sally. I've come to visit you. I know it's been a long time."

"I can't talk long. I have to go to work." Aunt Sally held a puzzle piece in her hand.

"That piece goes here." Laura showed her the spot.

Aunt Sally shook her head. "I don't see it."

"Here." Laura pointed.

Aunt Sally placed the piece in the spot in the puzzle and looked up at Laura. "Are you taking me home? They have my car and they won't give it to me."

"No, I'm sorry, I can't take you home. I'm your niece, Laura White."

"I thought you were Abby. She married my nephew. You look like her."

"I'm Abby's daughter, Laura."

"I haven't seen her in years." Sally picked up another puzzle piece. "I remember them."

"I'm glad you do, Aunt Sally."

"So when are we leaving? I want to get out of here. They steal my clothes. Sometimes they put me in a dark closet and leave me there for days."

"We can't leave right now." Laura helped her aunt place another piece down. "But I'm going to live close by so I can see you more often."

Aunt Sally looked around. "Live here? Do they have apartments for rent?"

"No, I have a job in town. I'm going to live in a house nearby."

"I'll have to pack my bags."

A nurse walked in, smiling at Laura as she rounded up the women who were still working on the puzzle. "Time for snacks, ladies."

"Will you have a snack with me?" Aunt Sally reached for her hand.

"I would, but I have to go now. But I'll be back soon. I love you, Aunt Sally." She kissed her aunt's cheek. "And I'm sorry it took me so long to get here."

"They do like punctual workers."

"I know. I'll be on time from now on."

Aunt Sally stood, wobbling a little as she reached for a walker. "See that you are. And make sure you feed the cat."

Her aunt left with the other women. After a few minutes Laura got up and left the room. She had no idea where Myrna had gone. Rather than wait in the empty activity room, Laura walked down the hall. She passed a room where someone cried out, the words unintelligible. A familiar voice with a comforting tone and comforting words followed the cry.

Laura turned back to the room and peeked in. Myrna sat on the edge of a bed, holding the hand of the woman in the bed. Laura started to walk away, but Myrna saw her.

"You can come in."

Laura stepped into the dimly lit room, very aware of every scent, the heaviness of the air, the shades pulled over the window. Myrna stood, but she still held the hand of the woman in the bed.

"This is Gayla."

Gayla didn't move but she smiled just a little.

Laura couldn't guess her age. Maybe twenty. Maybe thirty. Her blond hair was pulled back in a ponytail, her body curled in the fetal position.

"Hello, Gayla." Laura touched the hand that curled in. "I'm Laura."

Myrna smiled and leaned to brush back the blond hair of the woman in the bed. "We have to leave, but Jesse will be here tomorrow."

Gayla no longer smiled. Her eyes watered with unshed tears.

Myrna shook her head and reached for Laura's arm. They walked out of the room together. Questions formed but Laura didn't want to ask. Who was Gayla? Family? A friend? Someone special to the Coopers?

Or to Jesse?

"She's a local girl." Myrna led Laura down the hall. "She's been here for years. Her mother had to move to Tulsa and there's no other family. We visit her when we can."

"What happened to her?"

"Car accident." Myrna pushed a code into the front door. It buzzed and she pushed it open. Laura followed her through the door.

"That's terrible."

Myrna stopped on the sidewalk. Her light

hazel eyes caught and held Laura's. "It's a tragedy that has touched several lives."

Laura didn't know what to take from that. Didn't know what Myrna wanted to tell her. Rather than asking the questions, she got in the car and Myrna cranked the engine to life.

Their first stop after the nursing home was the garage where Laura's car had been towed. The mechanic walked over to Myrna's car and leaned in the driver's-side window.

"It doesn't look good, Myrna." He wiped his face with a rag and slipped it back in his pocket.

Myrna shook her head. "Will, I thought you said you could fix anything."

"I usually can, but sometimes fixing is more expensive than the car is worth." He offered Laura an apologetic smile. "Sorry, ma'am."

"Well, then, you see what you can find to replace it."

Laura put a hand on Myrna's arm. "No, Myrna, it's okay. I can save up money and buy something pretty cheap."

"Nonsense. Will, you see what you can find. Something decent and dependable, not a lot of miles."

He saluted and backed away from the car. "You're the boss, Myrna."

"Don't you forget it." Myrna shifted into Reverse and backed out of the parking lot. "How about coffee and pie at the Mad Cow? It's Wednesday. Vera has coconut cream on Wednesday."

"That sounds good, but I should probably get back to work."

"Nonsense. Jesse already said he wants you to take it easy for a few days. You need to listen to him."

A few minutes later they pulled into the black-and-white-painted building with Mad Cow Café painted on the front in red letters. Laura hadn't been in the restaurant but had eaten the meals that Jesse had had delivered.

"Here we are." Myrna parked the car in an empty space at the side of the building. "You coming in?"

Laura nodded and unbuckled her seat belt. "Of course."

Cowbells clanged to announce their arrival as they walked through the door of the restaurant. Although it was well past lunchtime, there were several full tables. A group of ladies took up the long center table. Two tables were taken by older men.

"Men gossip more than women ever thought of," Myrna announced as she walked past the group of men. She touched the shoulder of one man and he smiled up at her. Myrna took off his ball cap and hung it on the back of his chair. "Take your hat off when you're inside."

"It's the Mad Cow, Myrna," he grumbled as he ran a big hand through thinning gray hair. "I tell you, women are a lot of trouble. Who's your friend? Is she as ornery as you?"

"Of course she is. And her name is Laura."

A woman walked out from the back of the restaurant. Her dark hair was shot through with gray and pulled back in a neat bun. Her white blouse and jeans were hidden behind a red apron.

"Well, look who came in for coconut cream pie." The woman hugged Myrna. "Here, sit back here away from these men."

"Thank you, Vera, we will. And I'd like for you to meet Laura." Myrna pulled Laura forward.

Vera nodded and then she smiled. "You're Jesse's housekeeper. How you feeling, honey? Did my chicken soup help?"

"It did."

"Good, well, the coconut cream pie will make you feel even better. You girls have a seat. I'll be right back with pie and coffee."

Laura squeezed into the corner booth, sitting opposite Myrna. Vera returned a few minutes later with three pieces of pie and the coffeepot.

"I brought another piece of pie on out. I saw

Jesse pull in a few minutes ago. I figure he'll want pie."

The bells clanged and the glass door opened. Jesse pulled off his cowboy hat as he walked in and ran a hand through his dark hair. He glanced around the room and when he saw Laura and Myrna, he smiled. Laura choked a little on her coffee and Vera gave her a sympathetic look.

"There's definitely something going around." Vera smiled as she made the comment. "I hope it isn't too contagious."

Chapter Five

Jesse knew he'd start a few new rumors by walking in and sitting next to Laura. He'd considered sitting by his grandmother but she didn't seem to be inclined to move over. Laura looked up, her coffee cup still in her hand. She glanced at his grandmother, then at him. After a long pause Laura scooted and he sat next to her.

"Now, look at that, Laura—my grandson is a gentleman. See how he took his hat off and left it on the hook by the door."

Jesse knew the comment wasn't for him. His grandmother looked at the table of farmers having their afternoon coffee and he wondered which one she meant that comment for.

"Gran, I know you'd still take a switch to my hide if I stepped in here wearing my hat."

She smiled at that. "Vera brought you a piece of coconut pie."

Laura moved the plate and a roll of silverware in a napkin in front of him. "It's really good."

"Best in Oklahoma." Vera returned with the coffeepot.

"Jesse, how are you today?"

"I'm good, Vera." He watched the owner of the Mad Cow, wondering what she was up to. "How are you?"

She smiled and poured his coffee. "I'm just dandy. Are you bringing Laura to church tonight?"

"I have to go in to work this evening."

"That's too bad. The singles group is starting a new Bible study."

Then Jesse got it. He looked from Vera to Laura, and from the shade of pink crawling up Laura's cheeks, he figured she got it, too. Vera was trying to match them up, make more of the situation than there was. From the pleased look on his grandmother's face, she was hoping he'd be the next Cooper she offered an heirloom ring to. He considered putting the rumors to bed right then, but he didn't.

For some crazy reason, he kept his mouth shut. He sat there next to Laura, her shoulder brushing his and her sweet perfume, springtime and fresh, teasing his senses, and he didn't say a word.

"I doubt I'll be able to make it, Vera," he finally managed. "But I can drop Laura off if she wants to attend."

Laura's gray eyes widened as she looked at him. He grinned and lifted his brows. She shook her head.

"I don't think I'm up to it." She turned to smile up at Vera. "But thank you."

"That's a shame." Vera shook her head and looked at his grandmother. "Isn't that a shame, Myrna?"

"It *is* a shame." His grandmother glanced at the table of farmers then at her watch. "Look at the time. I forgot I have an appointment in Grove. Jesse, can you give Laura a ride back to your place?"

"Of course I can. Where are you going in such a hurry?"

His grandmother stood and for a second she seemed a little lost. She touched the back of a chair to steady herself, then smiled big as if nothing had happened. Jesse wanted to believe nothing had happened, but he wasn't wrong.

"I've just got an appointment." She smiled again.

"Gran, are you okay?" Jesse pushed the pie back and Laura was already moving out of her seat. But they were too late. His grandmother walked away.

"I'm fine, Jesse. Make sure Laura gets home."

He watched her walk out the door, head held high. But he wasn't convinced. Later he'd call and have a talk with his dad.

Laura moved to the other side of the table. He watched her settle in the spot his grandmother had vacated.

"Worried what people will say?" he teased.

"People are already saying it, aren't they?" She scooped up another bite of pie.

"Probably, but they'll move on soon enough, once they figure out there isn't a story. How's your car?"

"Dead, apparently."

"What about your appointment Saturday, to see Abigail?" He remembered that she'd gotten a phone call the previous day arranging her supervised visitation.

"I'll reschedule." She looked away as she said it and he knew it wasn't that easy. He could see the heartbreak in her eyes, in her expression.

"I can take you."

"You don't have to do that. You've given me a job and a home, Jesse. You don't have to take on this responsibility."

"I don't mind." He started to tell her how easy it would be but his phone buzzed. "Let me get this and we'll make a plan."

He glanced at the caller ID and hesitated. But then he answered. He had to answer. Gayla's mom seldom called him unless there was a problem. He held up a finger to Laura, hoping she'd understand, and he walked outside the diner to take the call.

"Jesse, I wanted to call and let you know that I'm moving Gayla to Tulsa. I've been looking for a place and I finally found one that's close, so I can see her every day." Jamie's voice sounded apologetic, concerned. He knew the concern was for him.

"I understand. Is there anything I can do?"

A long pause and then she sighed. "No, Jesse, nothing. Just move on with your life. Gayla made a choice that night. You weren't responsible for what she did."

"I know, but if I'd realized…"

"What? If you'd realized that a young woman would build dreams of marrying you after two dates? You've been paying penance for something you didn't do. I'm moving her to Tulsa, Jesse."

Jesse heard the cowbell over the door clang. He turned as Laura walked out of the Mad Cow. She studied his face, offered a sweet smile and walked away. But she waited. She stood at the corner of the building, waiting.

"I'll go over and tell her goodbye." He brushed a hand through his hair, then remembered his hat. He opened the door of the Mad

Cow, pulled out money for the pie and coffee, and handed it to Vera before grabbing his hat.

"Jesse, this is for the best."

"Okay, Jamie. Thanks for letting me know." He hung up. For a minute he stood there in front of the Mad Cow. A truck drove past and honked. He watched as they loaded feed in the back of a truck at the feed store across the street.

Laura walked up behind him. He knew it was her because the smell of springtime reached him first. Jamie had been right. He knew she was right, but that didn't make it easy.

"Are you okay?" She touched his arm and he turned to face her, adjusting his hat and smiling as easy as he could.

"I need to run by the nursing home."

"Okay." And she left it at that.

He led her across the parking lot to his truck. "I dated Gayla."

"I see."

"Twice. We went out twice."

"I'm sorry."

"Yeah, me, too." He'd been sorry for a very long time. Jamie was right; he had to let go of his guilt. He'd thought he had, but every now and then it pulled him back.

A few minutes later they pulled up in front of the nursing home. Laura had remained quiet.

When he pulled the keys from the ignition she smiled at him.

"I can wait out here."

"There's no reason for you to do that." He opened his door. "I could be a while."

They got out of the truck and started toward the building.

"What happened?" Laura walked next to him. "Your grandmother said it was a car accident."

"After two dates I broke it off with her. I had plans for medical school. She wanted someone to marry. I didn't know at the time that her dad was an alcoholic and abusive at times. He passed away a few years ago. That's when her mom moved to Tulsa to find a job."

"And you visit her."

"Yeah, I visit her." He started walking again and Laura remained next to him. They entered the building and walked down the hall together.

At the door to Gayla's room, Laura reached for his hand. He stopped and looked down at her, surprised by the gesture, surprised by her. She squeezed and let go.

"I'm going to check on Sally." She bit down on her bottom lip and looked up. "If you need anything…"

"Thank you." He touched her arm and then he turned and walked into Gayla's room.

* * *

After finding her aunt sleeping, Laura wandered down the hall to the activity room. Several older men were playing checkers. One of them winked at her as she walked through the door. She smiled and winked back.

"You want to play the winner?" He pushed his wheelchair back and pointed at the board.

"No, I'll watch." Laura stood at the end of the table. The two men reset the board and started a new game. They bickered. She pulled up a chair and they gave her a look but kept playing.

"I have a daughter who looks a lot like you." Her new friend sat back in his chair. "She lives in Arizona. She's a teacher."

"You must be proud."

He moved again, blocking his opponent.

Her friend shook his head. "I am proud. I'd be even prouder if I got to see her and the grandkids once in a while. Been a year. Maybe two."

"Do you have other children?"

He shook his head and triple jumped with a big smile. "Nope, just Kelly. My wife passed about five years ago."

Laura looked at her smiling new friend and saw his loneliness. It was etched into his features, caused his shoulders to sag. Life had forgotten him.

"Are you from Dawson?"

"Nope. This is just the closest place they could find for me. I lived about an hour from here. I was a teacher. Forty years in the same school."

She touched his hand. "Is there anything I can get you?"

"New legs? I had a car wreck." He raised his left hand by using his right. "Pretty useless."

"But you still play a mean game of checkers."

"That I do, sunshine, that I do. You know, if you're here visiting someone, just look in on old Charlie from time to time."

"I can do that, Charlie."

Jesse walked past the room. He looked in, saw her and came back. He smiled at her, then at her new friend. Charlie smiled back and raised his right hand.

"Hey, Doc."

"Hi, Charlie." Jesse pulled out a chair and sat down. "How are you?"

"Better since you took me off that sleeping pill."

"I knew you'd feel better with one less med in your system."

"I guess I do. But sometimes I don't think they want me to feel better. They like for me to go to bed early."

"Well, Charlie, I think you're a grown man

and if you want to stay up and watch the late news, you should watch the late news."

"Thanks, Doc." Charlie reached for Laura's hand. "I have a new friend."

"So do I." Jesse smiled at her and winked.

Charlie looked from Laura to Jesse and back to Laura. "Don't tell me she's your girl. Here I was thinking I might ask her to the play this evening."

Jesse laughed and his gaze hooked hers and held it. Then he smiled at Charlie. "She isn't my girl, Charlie—just a friend."

Charlie leaned toward Jesse. "Then I think you're more senile than Bob, and I beat him at checkers every single time we play."

"Hey!" Bob glared at Charlie. "I'm not playing with you anymore."

Charlie pounded the table with his right hand and laughed.

"He says that every day."

Jesse stood. "Charlie, you're one of a kind."

"You'd better believe it. And I'm telling you, don't let this one get away."

"Thanks for the advice." Jesse patted the older man on the back. "See you next week."

Laura joined him to walk out the door. He touched her back to guide her down the hall. Behind them Charlie whistled and laughed again.

"He's quite a character." Jesse walked next to her past the nurses' station to the front door.

"Yes, he is. He doesn't have anyone to visit him?"

"Not to speak of. He has a sister in Tulsa that gets over here every few months."

"It's sad, isn't it?"

"More than most people realize. Some residents never have a visitor. They wait for holidays when the churches and schools show up to sing for them or bring them cards. Other than that, they have the staff and the staff becomes their family."

"Aunt Sally has been here awhile and I had no idea."

"She has friends from the community, people she went to church with." He touched her arm. "Now she has you."

Laura walked to her side of the truck and Jesse got there first to open her door.

"I really can do this myself," she said as she climbed in.

"I've been taught two important rules, Laura. Take my hat off when I'm at church or in a restaurant, and open doors for ladies."

A minute later they pulled out of the nursing home parking lot.

"Does Gayla understand that she's being moved?" Laura asked.

"Yes, she understands."

"I'm sure she's upset."

"She is."

Laura started to ask how he was handling it, but she didn't. She'd known him since Sunday night. That didn't give her the right to push her way into his life.

When they got to her little house, he jumped out of the truck and came around to open her door. She smiled at the unexpected chivalry and how it made her feel. He helped her down, his hand on her arm.

"I'll take you to Tulsa Saturday. I don't want you to miss this visit with your daughter."

"I appreciate that, Jesse. I just don't know how I'll repay you."

"You don't have to repay me. You have a daughter who needs you. I'm glad I can help."

He had a story. She saw it in his eyes. Didn't everyone, though? And she couldn't let herself get tangled in his.

She couldn't. But she stood on tiptoe and kissed his cheek before she turned and hurried up her sidewalk.

Chapter Six

When they set out for Tulsa Saturday morning, rain fell in sheets and the sky was a blanket of gray as far as the eye could see. Laura wore a soft jacket that someone in the Cooper family had donated to her. They'd sent a box of clothes with Jesse after a family dinner. There were things for her and for Abigail. She'd been touched by the generosity, but also humbled, embarrassed.

She'd also been amused because someone in the Cooper family thought she needed a stunning "little black dress" and heels so high she would have towered over most men. Jesse had warned her that Mia had contributed to the box and she should probably discard anything his little sister sent along. But Laura hadn't. Instead she'd hung the black dress and another of pale gray, hoping someday she'd have a reason to wear something so soft and shimmery.

Today it helped to think about the clothes, the dress and Mia, whom she'd never met. Anything to keep her mind off visiting Abigail. It had been two weeks. A lot could change in the life of a child in that amount of time.

"You okay? Want to stop for coffee?" Jesse glanced her way and then nodded in the direction of a fast-food restaurant.

"Coffee would be good. And I'm fine." She shivered and he reached to turn up the heat. "I think I'm fine."

"It can't be easy."

She agreed with a sigh. "It isn't. I'm so worried that I'll never get her back. And then I worry that she won't want to come back. What if she loves this family and wants to stay with them? What if it's easier there, never worrying about having enough, never struggling?"

"Not having her mother to tuck her in at night?" He said it with the slightest accent, his voice husky. She remembered he had a story. He hadn't been born a Cooper.

And she hated that she'd just become an emotional mess in front of him, spilling her deepest, darkest fears. She needed to get out more, to make friends and to remember that Jesse

Cooper had a life and hadn't signed on to be her shoulder to cry on.

"You're right." She offered what she hoped looked like the smile an optimist would wear. "Of course you're right."

"I know I'm right. You're her mom. I love being a Cooper, don't get me wrong, but when my mom first dropped me at the orphanage, and even for the first six months here, I could only think about seeing her again, finding her."

"Did you ever find her?" Laura let go of her story and focused on his, on a little boy who must have been afraid.

"No." He pulled up to the drive-through. "Do you want breakfast?"

"No, I'm good."

He ordered two sausage biscuits. "I'm not pulling rank, but as your doctor, I'm telling you, you need to eat."

"It's hard to eat." She'd lost twenty pounds since her arrest. She didn't tell him that.

And yesterday her stepbrother, Ryan, had called. She'd made the mistake of answering and he'd asked for money. He'd apologized for running and leaving her to take the blame. She thanked him for that and hung up.

"Coffee." Jesse pulled her back to the present by handing her a steaming cup of coffee and a paper-wrapped biscuit.

"Thank you."

He pulled back on the road and a few minutes later they were parking at the office where Laura was scheduled to meet with Abigail and the caseworker.

The sausage biscuit Jesse had insisted she eat now settled in the pit of her stomach. She sipped coffee and told herself that worry was pointless. Whatever happened happened. Right?

"It'll be fine." He glanced in the rearview mirror and smiled. "There they are."

For a second she focused on that smile. His smile made it easier. His smile made her forget, just for a second, that her stomach was tied in knots and her heart had a hole in it the size of Abigail.

"Do you want me to stay for a few minutes?" He hit the button and unlocked the doors that had automatically locked when they took off from Dawson.

"No, I'm good. And she would just wonder who you are." She managed to laugh. "She's a girl. At her age they believe life is a fairy tale and in her eyes you'd be a handsome prince who has come to rescue us."

His smile grew and her heart did a funny thump. "You think I'm a handsome prince?"

"I said *Abigail* would think that. I don't want her to get the wrong idea."

"Gotcha." He handed her the purse she'd thrown in the backseat of the truck. "I'll be back at noon. Right?"

"Right."

Laura smiled a last thank-you and got out of the truck. As she did so, Abigail ran to her, throwing little-girl arms around her waist and holding on tight. Laura looked back at the truck she'd just climbed out of. Jesse tugged the brim of his hat and nodded just slightly.

She mouthed thank you as he backed out of the parking space and then Abigail had all of her attention, pulling her toward the building and the caseworker.

"Can you braid my hair, Mommy?" Abigail led her into the room where they would spend their quality time—a large room with green carpet, chairs meant for children, boxes of toys, a table with crayons and coloring books.

"Of course I will. I even have new hairbands for you."

"Pink ones?"

"Pink ones."

The caseworker took one of the few adult-size chairs. She pulled out a book and a notebook and watched them as they talked, did each other's hair and then sat together and read books. Abigail wanted to do everything. So did Laura.

She wanted to do everything they hadn't been able to do in the months they'd been apart.

After they'd done everything else Abigail climbed up on her lap. "I want to go home with you, Mommy."

"I know, honey. Hopefully soon." She glanced at the caseworker, who had stopped reading and was writing in that ever-present notebook.

The caseworker had a name. Annie. Laura even liked her. She was doing her job. She wasn't the enemy.

"Let's read another book," Laura suggested, hoping to get both of their minds off the reality that they would soon be separated again.

Annie moved to the chair next to them. She sat quietly while Laura read and then she asked Abigail if she wanted a snack. Another woman appeared and Annie smiled and pointed for Abigail to go with her.

"Liz will get you a sandwich." Annie gave Abigail's hand a light squeeze. Before she ran off with the other worker, Abigail hugged Laura tight.

"She's doing really great, Laura. The foster home she is in is one of our best. Though I know that doesn't make it any easier."

"No, it doesn't. I miss her. I need her back."

"I know. We're going to have a caseworker from your new county of residence stop by your home and talk with you. We want to inspect the home, of course. We want to talk to your employer. Of course, we'll do another lovely drug test."

"They'll always be negative."

Annie touched her arm. "I know. Believe me, I'm on your side. If it was up to me, Abigail would be with you, no question."

"Thank you." Laura closed her eyes tight against the sting of tears. Because someone believed her. Someone believed in her.

"We have to do this in the proper way, but I promise, I'm going to move through the steps as quickly as possible."

"Oh, Annie, thank you."

"Laura, thank you for making my job so much easier. I don't always get to reunite children with parents. And I don't always get to feel good about it when it does happen."

Abigail returned, her smile wide as she bit into peanut butter and jelly. She walked to the window and looked out.

"Is that the man who brought you here, Mommy?" Abigail climbed back on her lap.

"It is. That's my new boss. I clean his house. And he has horses, dogs and cats."

Annie smiled "Tell her about the home you live in, Laura."

"It has two bedrooms, Abigail. Your new bedroom has a pretty bed with a quilt and a white dresser. You'll love it. When you look out the window you can see horses. There's even a trail to the lake and we can go fishing together."

"I want to go now, Mommy." Abigail leaned into her, the peanut-butter sandwich forgotten.

"Not today, but soon."

"When is soon?" Abigail sobbed into her shoulder.

Laura looked to Annie for an answer because she wouldn't give her daughter false hope. All too often things didn't work out as she planned.

Annie brushed Abigail's dark hair back from her face. "Soon means as soon as I can make it happen, Abigail. I hope by the end of summer."

Months. Laura closed her eyes at the reality of not weeks but months. She wanted weeks. She needed weeks. Or even days. Abigail moved in her arms. She looked down to see Annie taking her daughter from her lap.

"Time to go, Abigail. Your mommy has a lot to do to get that room ready for you. And I think you're going to eat pizza this evening and play miniature golf. Won't that be fun?"

Abigail didn't nod; instead she shook her head vehemently.

"I want to go with my mommy."

"I know." Laura whispered the words that came out hoarse as her throat tightened.

Annie held Abigail tight. "Let your mommy kiss you goodbye, sweetie."

Laura leaned to kiss her daughter. "Be brave, Abigail. I love you."

She ran from the room, from her daughter's heartache, from her own pain, from the tears falling down her cheeks. She ran out the door and straight into the arms of Jesse Cooper.

Jesse had watched the scene unfold inside the building where Laura said goodbye to her daughter. He'd watched her tears, the heartbreak of her daughter. He had gotten out of the truck to open her door when she ran straight into his arms.

He moved her to the side of the truck away from the window, out of view of those inside, and he held her as she cried. She leaned into his shoulder, sobs shaking her thin body. He brushed his hands down her back and held her close.

"Shh, it's going to work out," he whispered close to her ear.

She shook her head. "No, it won't. How can it work out when it could be months before I get her back? What if she doesn't want to come back with me by then? What if she can't forgive me for doing this to her?"

"You didn't do this to her and she knows that. She loves you."

She continued to cry, wiping at her face with the back of her hand. "I wanted to take her, Jesse. I wanted to grab her up and run from that building with her."

"I don't blame you." He leaned close to her face, brushing a light kiss across her brow. And then he pulled back, before someone saw and got the wrong idea.

Before he got wrong ideas. And that would be too easy with Laura in his arms. That realization took him by surprise.

"We should go before she comes out." Laura put more distance between them. She trembled and hugged herself tight. "I'm so sorry for that."

"Don't be." He opened his door. "Can you climb through to your side?"

"I think so."

He stood back as she climbed in and then slid across to the passenger seat. Inside the building the caseworker had stood but she still held Abigail in her arms.

"Where to now?" Laura's eyes were still on the building they were backing away from.

"I ran errands while you were visiting Abigail. We can go home, unless you have something you need to do in Tulsa."

She looked down at her phone as if she had

something on her mind, and then she shook her head. "No, I'm good."

"You're sure?"

"Yes, I'm sure."

He glanced both ways, waited for a few cars to speed past and then pulled onto the road.

"It won't be long and you'll have her home with you." He offered the assurance that he knew sounded like empty words when her heart had to be breaking."

"I know." She let out a deep sigh. "It's been so long. I know it isn't her entire childhood, but at this point it feels as if it is."

"I'm sure it does."

She let out a shaky breath and smiled at him with tears still hovering in her eyes. "Let's talk about you."

He grinned at that. "Sure, why not?"

Before she could ask questions, her phone rang. She glanced at it and shook her head. Jesse shot her a questioning look that she didn't seem inclined to notice.

And he wasn't inclined to let it go, not when she looked about ready to jump out of her skin.

"Who is it?"

"No one," she whispered and looked away.

He had half a notion to pull the truck over but thought it would push her to the point of jumping and running. Instead he gave it a minute, let her settle down, and then he tried again.

"Laura, if it was no one, you wouldn't have that look on your face. I'm asking because maybe I can help."

She glanced at the phone again and he thought she might be about to toss it out the window. Instead she shoved it in her purse. He kept his eyes on the road but glanced her way from time to time.

"It's my stepbrother."

"Have you talked to him?"

A quick nod. "Yes. He needs money. I told him I don't have money so he's on his own."

"Has he threatened you?"

"Not really. He asked how Abigail is doing in foster care and told me he'd heard that her foster family is real nice."

Jesse gripped the steering wheel a little tighter. "That isn't a threat, but it does sound like he's trying to make you think he knows where she is for some reason."

"I know. So on top of not having her with me, now I'm worried every second of every day that he'll do something to her."

All of his life, Jesse had been pegged as the calm one in the Cooper household. He knew how to let things roll off his back. He could handle pressure in the emergency room of a hospital or in the middle of a Cooper-brother fight. He'd always taken that calm for granted and thought it was as natural as breathing. Until that moment. Looking at Laura, her face awash in fear for her daughter, he lost control.

"We'll take care of this." Now he wanted to pull over and do more than talk. He wanted to pull the woman he'd hired as a housekeeper into his arms and make her feel safe.

Messed up, that's what this situation had become. He'd done a good deed for his grandmother and the ball kept rolling.

"I'm fine, Jesse. I can handle it."

Because that's what she did, he thought. She handled her life, her problems, her fears. Alone.

"Laura, you have people who can help. It's your choice. Hide your fear. Hide what's going on. Or let the Coopers do what they do best."

"What's that?"

"We circle the wagons. And it's a good feeling, to have the family circle the wagons around you." He glanced at the clock on the dash of the truck. "As a matter of fact, Mom called earlier and said we should stop by for supper. We're going to be a little early, but that's okay. We'll get this figured out."

She sniffled and glanced away. He let her have the moment to pull it together because he remembered what this felt like, to suddenly have people he could count on. He'd fought it for a while, thinking he still had to take care of himself. Then he'd given in and let the Coopers be his family.

They'd do the same with Laura because that's who the Coopers were.

Chapter Seven

Somehow Laura fell asleep. When she woke up they were driving up a tree-lined drive. Ahead of them she could see a two-story brick home, Georgian-style with a covered front porch flanked by shrubs. Jesse pulled the truck into a parking space in front of the two-story multi-car garage.

"Here we are." He shot her a cautious look. "Good nap?"

She nodded and continued to stare at the house because it was easier than looking at Jesse. Not that he wasn't easy on the eyes. He was her boss and a decent man who didn't mind helping out a woman in need. Caring came easy for him. She didn't want to confuse caring with any other emotion, even attraction.

"Yes, good nap." She looked at her watch. "We're a few hours early for supper."

"I know. I thought I'd show you around. And I know the best way to get your mind off your troubles."

"What would that be?"

He smiled that megawatt smile that could melt a girl's toes if she wasn't strong. Laura liked to think she was strong.

"Do you know how to ride?"

She shook her head. "Sorry, never been on a horse. I grew up in the city. I can ride a bus but not a horse."

"Then it's time to learn."

"I don't know."

He opened his door to get out. "Trust me."

She wanted to, but her heart ached and she was all out of trust. It had been used up, poured out, stepped on and depleted long ago.

She joined him on the walkway that led to the house. As they drew closer to the huge home, her breath tightened in her chest. Jesse glanced down and smiled.

"Breathe." He reached for her hand.

"I'm breathing." Barely. His hand on hers didn't help. She knew he meant it to comfort her, give her strength. Instead it made her feel weak. Mostly in the knees.

When they walked up the front steps of the house the door opened. A man a little older than Jesse stepped out. He nodded first to her, then

"Mom." Jesse hugged the woman and she stood on tiptoe to kiss his cheek. "This is Laura White."

"Laura, I'm so pleased to finally meet you. And I'm so glad you're feeling better." She patted Jesse's arm. "And since we haven't been officially introduced, I'm Angie Cooper, Jesse's mother and Myrna's daughter-in-law."

Laura held out a hand, which Angie Cooper took in hers and held.

"It's nice to meet you, Mrs. Cooper."

"Call me Angie—everyone does."

"Angie." Laura bit down on her bottom lip and then managed a smile rather than the tears that stung her eyes.

Angie shot Jesse a look. He had moved to the stove and had a dipper in a pan that steamed and smelled wonderful. "Stay out of that soup."

Jesse lowered the dipper and grinned. Laura looked away, choosing to study the details of the large kitchen with its many windows and shelves lined with planters overflowing with herbs of all types. At one end was a large table, and French doors led to a patio where a swimming pool reflected the blue sky on its shimmering surface.

"I hope you like the soup, Laura. It's a new recipe. And I have homemade bread rising."

"I'm sure it will be wonderful."

to Jesse, and he shook his head. "Housekeeper my foot."

Jesse muttered something in Spanish. The other man laughed and kept walking but he glanced back as he headed down the steps. Laura stumbled over the slight step into the house.

"Ignore Blake. He's in a good mood and taking it out on everyone around him." Jesse led her through the living room, barely giving her time to study the family pictures on the walls or the massive fireplace that stretched across the far wall.

"Blake is one of your brothers?"

"Yes." He led her through a dining room with two long tables set end to end. "He recently found his daughter."

"Found her?"

"Her mother took off with her years ago. There have been a few phone calls, some pictures. He hired a P.I. who found her living in Africa."

"Amazing." She could sympathize because she knew how it felt to lose a daughter. She couldn't imagine years without Abigail.

And then they were in the kitchen. A woman turned from the sink, her smile bright and welcoming. She wiped wet hands on a towel and then brushed back her short brown hair.

Jesse leaned against the counter, casual, relaxed. "Dad home?"

"No, he's in Grove picking up another silly llama. I don't know why he has this sudden thing for those animals. They growl."

"He says he's giving one to each of his grandkids for Christmas."

"Craziness." Angie picked a few basil leaves and rinsed them before crumbling them in the soup. "Did you need to talk to him?"

Jesse looked from his mother to Laura, and Laura had to look away. His eyes were kind, considerate. This was how it felt to have wagons circled.

"Laura's stepbrother is making her feel a little threatened." Jesse turned to pour a cup of coffee. He handed it to Laura and she took it, more for the warmth it offered than anything else. "He's making her feel like her daughter might be in danger."

"Where is your daughter, Laura?"

"In a foster home in Tulsa." Laura's voice felt weak, shaky. "I'm sure Ryan won't hurt her."

"Are you?" Angie Cooper stepped close, putting a hand on Laura's back. "Because you look like a mom who's scared to death for her child."

"I'm…"

Angie took the coffee cup from Laura's hands

and set it on the counter before enveloping her in a hug. "Don't you worry—we'll help you."

It was a strange feeling for Laura, being in this house, with these people, a family of strangers. Angie Cooper stood next to her and Jesse leaned his hip against the counter. Laura refocused on Angie.

"I'm not sure what we can do." Laura looked out the window, mesmerized by the glimmering waters of the pool. "The system isn't going to change its policy for one person. And I don't know that she'd be any safer with me. Or even that he'd hurt her."

"I know a thing or two about how this system works." Angie smiled and patted her arm. "I'm very good at pulling strings and moving mountains."

Laura stepped back, wiping her eyes again. She reminded herself that once, a long time ago, her mother had made promises that everything would be better. She wanted to crush the old negativity, the voices telling her not to trust.

Her stepbrother had said he would get a job and help pay the rent on her apartment in Tulsa.

Her stepfather had promised more than once to quit drinking, to quit abusing, to get a job. He'd never done any of those things for more than a week.

As much as she wanted to believe people

were really as good as the Coopers, Laura knew she'd have to fight a lifetime of being let down in order to trust.

She looked up to find Jesse watching her. His expression said he understood. She wondered how he could.

He pushed away from the counter, standing tall again, making her feel small in comparison. It wasn't so much his height as his presence. The doctor she'd met just days ago had morphed into a cowboy, the son of a rancher. His jeans were worn and his boots were scuffed. He had held her and made her feel safer than she'd felt in years.

"I'm going to take Laura out and show her the stable."

His mom shot him a look, her eyes narrowing as she glanced from Jesse to Laura. And Laura felt heat slide up her cheeks. Because that look implied something that Laura wanted to openly deny. But how desperate would it be to open her mouth and tell Angie Cooper that there was nothing between Jesse and herself?

Angie's smile returned, easing the worried lines that had creased her brow. "Don't saddle Willie. He's had a tendon problem that Jackson is doctoring."

"Thanks." He kissed his mom's cheek, then nodded toward the door. "Let's go. And, Mom, when Dad gets back, tell him we need to talk about Gran. I'm worried about her."

"Okay, Jesse."

Laura smiled back at Angie Cooper, hoping it wasn't worry that she saw in that woman's eyes. Because to Laura, worry equaled a woman not wanting her son to get involved with the wrong person.

They walked out a back door into sunshine and the sound of bees buzzing around clover in the grass. Jesse walked with an easy stride, comfortable in his own skin and his place in this world.

"If you stay tense like that, you'll make yourself sick." He smiled as he made the comment and Laura managed a deep breath that she let out slowly, hoping to relax.

"I'm not tense."

"Enough to snap." He touched her back only briefly and then dropped his hands to his sides.

"Your mom is great." Laura let her gaze travel over the ranch, the rolling hills, the white fences, cattle grazing in the distance and horses in a nearby field.

Ahead of them lay the stable, a huge building with several paddocks or corrals attached. A truck and a SUV were parked out front.

"Mom is great. She's the glue that holds this family together."

"I can imagine." Laura slowed her pace as they neared the stable. "I don't have boots. And I'm seriously scared to death."

"There are boots in the tack room, and the fear will be gone as soon as you settle into the saddle."

"You think?"

He grinned at her. "I know."

He opened the stable door and motioned her inside. She walked into a world she'd never experienced but immediately loved. The stable was wide with stalls on either side of the center aisle. There were several doors midway down on the left. She assumed it was the tack room and whatever else could be housed in a building such as this one. To the right was an opening that led to the rest of the building. She slowed to get a look at the arena.

"They're bucking out a few bulls that Jackson recently bought," Jesse explained as he led her past the opening to the arena.

"Bucking out?"

He smiled and turned her down the aisle and to the edge of the arena. On the opposite side were risers for spectators to sit on. To the left were chutes, and behind them were a few pens. Bulls bellowed and loud voices could be heard over the sound of the animals.

"Bucking out." Jesse pointed to the chutes

and she saw a bull being run in. "Basically a practice session. My brother Gage rides, or gets tossed, depending on the week. We have a couple of neighbor kids who are learning. They'll ride the bulls—it gives them and the bulls some training."

"I see." She leaned to watch. The chute opened and a gray bull spun from the opening. The rider on his back moved with the spins and bucks, holding tight with one hand, the other in the air. The men clinging to the gate near the chute yelled at the rider as a man in the arena stayed close to the bull. The arena filled with the sounds of hooves pounding, men shouting and then the buzzer.

"Do you ride bulls?" she asked as she watched the commotion.

"Nope. I guess Blake and I are the only two Coopers who haven't."

The rider jumped and fell and the bull turned on him. The man in the arena threw his hat at the bull, distracting him for a second but not long enough. The bull went back for the rider, gave him a good shove and began to stomp with hooves that looked deadly as far as Laura was concerned. A couple of guys jumped over the gate and into the arena as the bull continued his rampage and the rider crawled fast to get clear of the animal.

Jesse opened the gate and hurried into the arena as the bull ran from the enclosure and back to his pen. Laura followed Jesse to the rider, who had made it to the fence but remained on his hands and knees, head down.

Jesse squatted next to his brother. "Gage, you with us?"

Gage took off his hat and brushed a hand through shaggy blond hair as he turned and sat. "Yeah, I think. Help me up."

Jesse ran a hand down his brother's neck. "Neck and head okay?"

"Yeah, he didn't get my head. He went for my legs." Gage reached for the fence behind him, straightened his left leg and pulled himself to a standing position with Jesse holding his arm. "Why do I keep doing this?"

"That's always been my question." Jesse slipped an arm around Gage, and Gage leaned on him. Laura stood nearby, unsure, eyes watering, mouth opened. He doubted she'd ever be a fan of bull riding after this.

"Who's the woman?" Gage leaned in close and whispered so loud people in the next county heard.

"Laura works for me." He smiled past Gage, connecting his gaze with Laura's and winking in hopes she'd relax and not go all female on him.

"She's a nurse?"

"Housekeeper," Laura answered as she moved in close. "But I'm a good shoulder to lean on if you need more help."

Gage winked and Jesse felt a strange urge to slug his brother.

"I'd love to lean on you but not because of a bum knee." Gage shot Jesse a smirky grin. "But I wouldn't want to make Jesse mad. He acts all cool, but I've seen him knock a guy to the ground before."

"Whatever." Jesse walked a little faster and Gage had to hop to keep up.

"Hey, slow down. I'm serious about the knee."

"The faster we walk, the sooner I can take a look."

"Or kill me." Gage stopped. "Seriously, Jesse, you took some kind of 'do no harm' oath, so give me a break."

Jesse dragged out a sigh for Gage's benefit and eased him to the gate and then out to the nearby bench. "Sit down and let me take a look."

He glanced back at Laura. "There are crutches and elastic bandages in the tack room. Do you think you could find them?"

"Prepared for accidents, are we?" She smiled an easy smile that took him by surprise.

"With this crew, always."

He watched her walk away and then he turned his attention back to Gage, pushing his jeans up to the knee to get a look at the injured leg. Travis and Jackson had taken care of the bulls and sent the neighbor kids home. The brothers were next to him now and both whistled when they saw Gage's knee.

"Gage, this didn't just happen today." Jesse touched his brother's normally knobby knee that was now red and swollen. "Have you had this checked?"

"Yeah, right now, by you." Gage leaned back, his eyes closed and his mouth tight with pain.

"You need to get yourself to the hospital. You know you can't keep riding like this."

"I don't have time for surgery, Jesse."

"Do you have time to blow out your knee?"

Laura reappeared, handing him the elastic bandage that wouldn't do much good. She leaned the crutches against the wall. Jesse smiled his thanks and quickly wrapped his brother's knee.

"Go to the doctor, Gage." Jesse knew the warning would be ignored until it was too late.

Gage reached for the crutches. "I'm outta here."

With an angry glare over his shoulder, Gage left the arena, faster than any of them could have managed. He was an old pro on crutches. Jackson shook his head and went after him, probably to pound some sense into their little brother.

Jesse turned to Travis. "What's up with him?"

"He's been like that for months. No one knows why."

"Someone better find out or he's going to end up in worse shape than this."

Travis swiped an arm across his brow. "We've all tried. Dad had a long talk with him the last time he was in town. The problem is, he takes off when we confront him. He won't even talk to Reese."

Gage and their brother Reese had always been close.

"Have you all noticed that this started about the time Reese got hurt?" Jesse asked.

"Yeah, why?" Travis pushed his hat down on his head and picked up the Kevlar vest Gage had yanked off and left on the ground.

"Just something to think about." Jesse turned, looking for Laura.

Travis nodded in the direction of the door leading out of the arena. "She headed that way when we started talking. She's the housekeeper, huh?"

"I'm not sure what you all are implying with that tone."

Travis laughed, flashing white teeth and dimples. "I'm not implying, and I think you know you're done for."

"I'm not done for anything. I've hired a housekeeper because my place is a mess and I need someone living there if I go to South America."

"Still going through with that?"

"I think so. I have to give Isaac an answer in the next couple of months." Jesse took off his hat and brushed a hand through his hair. "I'm going to teach Laura to ride. What horse should I use?"

"What's wrong with those fancy Arabs of yours?"

"Well, we're here for supper and I didn't want to drive out to the house."

"And you don't have one that's broke well enough for a beginner."

"Nope." He followed Travis back into the main part of the stable. "So, what horse do you recommend?"

He spotted Laura in front of a stall. She reached to pet the buckskin inside, and the horse inched his dusty yellow head close to hers. She rubbed the animal's face and neck.

"Looks like she's picked her own horse." Travis indicated with a nod. "Jackson's old gelding is as gentle as any. I'd let her ride him."

"You're sure?"

"Not a better horse on the place. Jackson would probably let you take Buck on up to your place if she likes him and can ride him okay."

The door at the end of the building opened. Jackson walked back in, looking pretty agitated and talking to himself as he headed their way.

"Any luck?" Travis asked as he opened the stall door and led Buck out, holding tight to the halter he'd slipped over the animal's head. Laura had moved back, close to the wall, as though she thought the horse might run her over or worse.

"None." Jackson eyed his old horse. "What's up?"

"Laura's going to learn to ride." Travis snapped a lead rope on the horse's halter. "I told Jesse that Buck is the best for a beginner."

Jackson ran a hand down the horse's neck. "He's as good as they come. If it works out, take Buck on over to your place. Better for her than an Arab."

Jesse blew out a breath. "I wish you guys would lay off."

Both brothers laughed.

"Not on your life." Jackson headed for the tack room. "Does she need boots?"

"Yeah." Jesse smiled at Laura. "And she can talk. Let's go see what we can find."

Laura gave the horse a last look. "He's bigger out here."

Jesse laughed at that. "Yeah, he's pretty big. You'll be fine, though."

They found boots and she slipped them on, her jeans staying tucked inside. When she stood, he gave her the once-over and nodded.

"Do I pass?" she asked with a soft smile.

Jackson left the room. Jesse pulled a hat off the shelf behind her and settled it on her head. "You pass."

Maybe he really was done for, the way his brothers said. He wished it was that easy. He wished a woman could walk into his life and make him feel settled and ready to stop searching for a past he couldn't grab hold of and a future he couldn't stop second-guessing.

He looked up and Laura was watching him, questions in her gray eyes that looked as if they might match the questions he couldn't find answers for.

Chapter Eight

"Where are we going?" Laura held tightly to the leather reins Jesse had handed her after she first mounted.

The horse walked with a steady, plodding gait. From time to time Buck shook his head, rattling the bit. When he did that, she grabbed the saddle horn and waited for the inevitable, meaning her on the ground, broken and bruised.

Jesse shifted in his saddle to look at her. "You can relax."

"Can I?" She took a deep breath and let it out slowly. She shook her head. "Nope, sorry, I can't."

He laughed, the sound husky, raspy and a whole lot sexy. He looked good on a horse.

"You will relax. Just trust the horse."

He said it so confidently. Of course he was confident—he'd grown up this way. She'd watched him saddle his horse, then swing a leg over to land easily in the saddle as the horse sidestepped and shook his powerful head.

"Okay, I will relax. I will enjoy this." She said it with a conviction she didn't feel.

He moved his horse a little closer to hers. "You will. I promise."

He promised. She swallowed the lump that lodged in her throat and thought about promises so easily spoken, so easily given and, in her life, so easily broken.

They continued to ride along the creek and eventually up a slight rise onto a paved country road. Ahead of them she could see buildings and what looked like a church.

"Is that the community church you attend?"

He shook his head. "No. That's the community center. My brother Jeremy Hightree bought it a couple of years ago. He'd planned on tearing it down, but I guess God and Beth had other plans."

"Beth?"

"His wife. She talked him out of bulldozing it down and instead they turned it into a community center."

They rode a little farther before she asked, "Why is his last name Hightree, not Cooper?"

Jesse glanced her way, smiling a little. "You ask a lot of questions."

"I'm sorry—that's probably personal."

"It is, a little, but everyone knows the story. He's a Cooper, but he isn't Angie's son."

"Oh." Laura didn't have all of the pieces but she got it. All families had stories.

The horses picked up the pace, breaking into a bone-jarring trot. Jesse pulled back on his reins and rode next to her.

"Ease him back a little and try to get in rhythm with the gait. He'll smooth out a little when you get him settled into the right pace."

"Promise?" She managed a smile through clenched teeth and eased back on the reins the way Jesse had taught her when they first took off. And he was right.

"See?" Jesse grinned and pushed back his hat a little. She had pushed hers down tight to keep it on her curls and to keep it from flying off in the breezy weather.

"You love being right, don't you?"

"I do." He eased the horse back to a walk. "But I can admit when I'm wrong."

Her heart tugged her in his direction but she pushed back, unwilling to let herself take a chance on being hurt. She worked for Jesse Alvarez Cooper, she reminded her heart. She couldn't possibly fall in love with him. And she wouldn't let his kindness fool her into thinking she meant more to him than someone he wanted to help.

In a few short months he would leave for South America and she'd be the person taking care of his home while he was away.

End of story.

They rode into the yard of the community center and the door opened. The man standing on the porch of the building smiled big and waved.

"Hey, you're just the person I needed to see." He walked down off the porch, taking the steps two at a time.

Jesse rode a little closer, his black horse pawing at the ground restlessly when he pulled back on the reins. "What's up?"

"We have a few sick kids. Beth noticed it earlier and took the baby home to keep her from catching it." The man she guessed to be Jeremy Hightree tipped his hat in Laura's direction. "You must be Laura."

She wished for a cool breeze to ease the heat from her cheeks, but it didn't happen. "I am."

"Good to meet you. I'm Jeremy Hightree."

"Good to meet you, too." Her horse moved forward, stopping next to Jesse's.

"So what's up with the kids?" Jesse took the conversation back to where it had been left.

"A couple of them have a pretty bad cough. One of them loses his breath every time it hits."

"Where are they now and where are their parents?" Jesse swung his right leg over the back of his horse and landed easily on the ground. He reached for Laura's horse and she attempted to do the same but when she came down, her left foot was still in the stirrup. Jeremy rushed to her rescue and held her shoulders as she pulled her foot free.

"Pull your foot out before you swing your other leg over. You wouldn't want a spooked horse with your foot caught like that or you'll go on a ride you weren't expecting."

"Thank you." She stood next to the horse and waited for her legs to feel like muscles and bone again, not the jelly that they seemed to be made of.

"The parents don't have any money, Jesse." Jeremy had moved back to the front of her horse. "I called and told them the kids need to see a doctor. But they're strapped."

Jesse handed his reins and then the reins of Laura's horse to Jeremy. "If you want to put these horses in stalls, I'll take a look at the kids. But I'll need for you to call their parents and have them come down here."

"Sounds great. There's a room downstairs

that has plenty of light. I'll get on the phone
with the mom."

Jesse led Laura into the church and to a door
that led to the basement. She stayed close to his
side, glancing around the building.

"Nice, isn't it? We went here when I was a kid
and then it closed down because they couldn't
get a pastor. Everyone started going to Dawson
Community Church."

The basement was a buzz of activity. A few
adults and a dozen or more kids were settled
around a long table doing a craft project. The
woman at the head of the table smiled at Jesse.
"Hey, we were just talking about you."

"I heard." His arm brushed Laura's and she
sidestepped the touch and the reaction. "Where
are the kids?"

"Jeremy quarantined them in the other classroom with Peggy. He was going to call you."
She looked over the rim of her wire-framed
glasses. "Did he call you, or did you just show
up?"

"I just showed up. You know how us super-
heroes are."

She laughed and shook her head before returning to the project and showing one of the
children where to apply glue.

Jesse washed his hands in the sink and then
motioned for Laura to follow him.

"This way." Jesse led her to the room where the kids were being kept.

Laura watched as he took over, smiling at the kids and talking to them as they sat, wide-eyed, staring up at him. The worker handed him a bottle of antibacterial gel. He squirted a big glob in his hand and then handed it to Laura.

As she rubbed the gel over her hands Jesse sat down on the table and started talking to the children. She listened as he talked and the children lost their nervousness and began to tell him all about their cough and how they felt.

He did that with people, she realized. They trusted him, depended on him. Because he could be trusted? She watched him and smiled. Yes, he could be trusted.

Jesse didn't have to wait long for one of the children to have a coughing fit. He sat back and listened to the wheezing sound and then rubbed the girl's back as she continued to try to get her breath after the coughing spell. Her lips were slightly blue by the time she gasped that first breath of air back into her oxygen-starved lungs.

The parents walked through the door a few minutes later, followed by Jeremy. Good people—he'd known them for years. The dad, Bob Layton, farmed and did carpentry work when he could. The mom worked at the diner as a cook. They were concerned but didn't quite know what to do.

"What do you think?" Jeremy planted himself next to the dad and looked to Jesse for answers.

"These kids are all about the same age? Maybe a few years difference?" Jesse ruffled the hair of a boy close to him and smiled to ease the panicked look on the mom's face.

She nodded and told him the children's ages.

Jesse wished he had his medical bag with him, but he had a pretty good idea what was wrong with the kids. "We've seen cases of whooping cough at the emergency room."

The mom gasped and drew her daughter close. "But we had immunizations."

"Yes, unfortunately the immunization for whooping cough loses effectiveness when kids are hitting the preteen age."

"What do we do?" The dad mopped at his brow with a worn handkerchief, and Jesse had to agree—the room was warm.

"We'll get them a prescription and take some other precautions. We'll let Mom take the kids home and we'll talk. But these aren't all your kids, are they?"

The farmer nodded, his smile kind of vague. "We adopted my sister's kids about a year ago. They're ours now."

Jesse watched the woman walk out with the

brood of kids, all of them somehow tucked under her thin arms the way a chicken tucks chicks under her wings. He sat the dad down, gave him instructions on how to take care of the children, told him what warning signs to look for and then promised prescriptions for the kids would be waiting for them at a nearby pharmacy.

"What do I owe you?"

Jesse shook his head. "Not a thing, Bob. I'm glad I was here and could help."

The farmer shook his hand for a long moment and then left.

Jeremy sat down on the table next to Jesse. Laura walked out with the dad of the kids, leaving them alone. He watched her go, wondering about her, about her quietness, her steadiness.

"Housekeeper?" Jeremy chuckled and shook his head.

"Don't you start."

"Okay, I won't. Hey, did you ever consider that we need you here, in Dawson, not in South America? I mean, if you're called to go down there, that's great. But maybe you're supposed to be here helping people like the Laytons?"

"I hadn't really thought about it. Those are usually the people we treat at the E.R."

"And that costs them hundreds of dollars they don't have. If they had the money, they would have gone to urgent care or a family clinic."

"I do know that, Jeremy."

"I'm just saying—I would build you a clinic and I think people in town would chip in on supplies. We could have a fundraiser. Maybe people who could afford to pay could drop money in a jar. People who could pay more could give more for those who can't afford anything."

"Sounds amazing. I just don't see how it would work."

"Would you consider staying if I could make it happen?"

Jesse let his gaze head for the door, the door Laura had walked through a few minutes earlier. Open doors. He shook his head because a long time ago he'd thought about a clinic similar to the one Jeremy had proposed. He'd forgotten that idea and moved on to what he thought was a greater need.

"I don't know, Jeremy."

"Think about it." Jeremy pounded him on the back and stood to leave. "And thanks for helping out."

"I'm glad you caught me. Whooping cough can be serious. A couple of those kids are pretty sick. If you see their parents, tell them to give me a call if they have questions."

"Thanks."

Jesse walked out the door and didn't find Laura waiting. He wandered up the stairs to the sanctuary of the church. She was standing in front of the old pulpit reading the inscription. She smiled as she turned.

"It's a lot of history."

"Yes, it is." He glanced at his watch. "And if we don't head home, Mom will have the posse out looking for us."

He touched her back to guide her down the aisle of the church, and the moment took him by surprise. Few things ever surprised him. When she stopped at the entrance to the church and turned back, the late evening sun catching her face and hair, he had to admit to being beyond surprise. She looked up and he knew without a doubt that she'd felt it, too. Whatever "it" was.

They were on the horses and headed back to Cooper Creek when she finally spoke. "Why work at the E.R. and not a family practice?"

He kept his horse next to hers. "I've always liked the freedom the E.R. gives me. I work three twelve-hour shifts. It makes for long days, but then I have time off for horses, a rodeo every now and then and mission work."

"You've done mission work before?"

"A few short medical mission trips. One to Africa and another to a reservation in the Dakotas."

"I thought that when I got my degree, I'd do

something like that." Her tone took on a wist-fulness that etched into his heart.

"Why don't you finish your degree, Laura? Who's to say you couldn't use it?"

"Would you hire me?"

"I don't have that power, but I'd definitely help you finish your schooling."

She smiled at him, another surprise moment. He wanted to ride a little closer, let his leg brush hers, maybe hold a girl's hand the way he had when he was a teenager and he hadn't given consequences or breaking a girl's heart a sec-ond thought.

"Thank you. That means a lot to me."

"You're welcome. And think about getting that degree." He let his horse pick up the speed a little and she kept up. "You're doing a great job for someone who has never been on a horse."

"I always wanted to ride." She still held the reins tight, as if she expected the horse to take off with her. "When I was little I read all of the horse books. I dreamed of having ponies from Chincoteague Island or an Arab straight from the lines of the Godolphin Arabian."

He smiled at the familiar names. He'd had to learn English, but those books had been among his first, too.

They reached the barn with the sun low on

the horizon. Jackson walked out the front door of the stable.

"Mom's been trying to reach you."

Jesse dismounted and then held the head of the buckskin for Laura as she dropped to the ground.

"We were over by Back Street and phones are useless there. What's up?" Jesse handed the reins to Laura and she took them and stepped close to the old gelding.

"Nothing. Supper is ready and she thought you were on your way back. She's been on the phone today. I think she has news for Laura."

"News?" Laura looked up, her eyes searching, instantly troubled.

"Good news." Jackson pulled keys from his pocket. "I have to get home. Jade has a softball game tonight. See you all later."

Jesse slid the double door of the stable and they led the horses inside. "You can go on to the house."

Laura shook her head. "No, I'm good. I'll wait for you."

"You shouldn't be worried. My mom knows how to move mountains. She has some amazing faith."

"I know." She smiled up at him, the gesture not so confident. "I'm trying to have faith of my own."

The stable was shadowy and smelled of cedar, hay and horses. Jesse moved a step closer to the woman who tempted him the way no other woman had and in ways he hadn't imagined. She tempted him to take a chance, to open his heart and to stop holding back.

She tempted him.

He closed the distance between them until she was close enough to tuck beneath his chin. She looked up and he had to think about what he was about to do. But he didn't want to think. Her lips were parted and her gray eyes were luminous in the mixed light of the stable. Dust swirled on a beam of sunlight shining in from an open stall door.

His heart tripped on what he wanted and what he told himself he should back away from. The horse moved behind him and her horse pulled on the reins she held. Jesse touched her cheek and she closed her eyes.

He leaned, still touching her cheek, moving his fingers to her neck where her pulse fluttered.

A kiss could mean anything.

Or it could mean everything.

His lips touched hers. A kiss could make a guy think of forever. He moved his hands to the back of her neck where his fingers tangled in the luxurious softness of her auburn hair, releasing the scent of wildflowers.

She kissed him back and her hand had moved to his arm, her fingers light on his sleeve.

The door to the barn opened. They pulled apart and Jesse could do nothing more than stare at the woman who had just changed everything.

Chapter Nine

"Are the two of you coming in for supper or what?" Blake Cooper stood in the doorway, a massive man in a blazer, dark jeans and a cowboy hat. He grinned widely as he looked from Laura to Jesse.

Laura moved back, still trying to make sense of what had just happened and what it would mean to her future, her job, the security she had been starting to feel here in Dawson. Jesse stared down at her, and the only way to describe that look was shock. He took the reins she held and shot Blake a look.

It was easy to see him withdraw emotionally, as if the moment they had shared and what it could mean had just hit him. They both had too much at stake.

"We'll be in shortly."

Blake shrugged. "Suit yourself."

The door closed. Jesse let out a long sigh and Laura wanted to echo the gesture but her lungs and her heart were frozen. She could barely get oxygen in, let alone sigh and let it all out.

"I'm sorry," Jesse didn't smile as he made the apology. "I shouldn't have done that."

"It never happened." She smiled, as if she could say the words and make it so. She had to keep the tone and the mood light and pretend it hadn't mattered. They could go on as if it hadn't happened.

She couldn't lose her job. Not when everything was hanging in the balance. Her daughter. Their future. Everything depended on this job.

"Didn't it?" Jesse asked as he led the horse away.

Let it go. Move on. Don't make a kiss into something that it isn't. Laura let the thoughts roll through her mind and she considered saying a few of them. Instead she shrugged it off.

"I'm not sure."

Jesse tied his horse to a ring on the wall and moved in her direction. She knew he wouldn't kiss her again. After all, it never happened. It fell under the category of *huge mistake.* He stopped in front of her, tall and relaxed but oozing power and confidence.

"Jesse, we should go inside." Her hands trembled on the reins. The horse had moved close, resting his head close to her arm. She looked at the big golden animal with the sleepy eyes.

"We should." He took the buckskin's reins. "And I want you to know—I don't typically do things like this."

She laughed a little. "I think you should stop talking. I don't know if you're sorry, disgusted or ready to fire me."

"None of the above." He walked away and she leaned against the door of the empty stall, watching him cross-tie the horse he'd been riding and unsaddle it. "But we do need to get inside before the talk in there gets out of control."

"Right."

He glanced back as he removed the saddle. "That didn't come out right. I'm out of practice, Laura. This has blindsided me."

"I know." She still held the reins. "Can I do something to help?"

He had the saddle and bridle off his horse. "Do you want to brush him while I unsaddle your horse?"

"I think I can do that."

"Of course you can." He walked back into the tack room and returned with a brush. He gave her a quick lesson in horse care.

It didn't take long to finish up and turn the horses back into their stalls. Laura had been able to let go of the nerves tangling in her stom-

ach, but as they walked through the door of the
Cooper home, her heart raced ahead of her and
her mind insisted on jumping to horrible con-
clusions.

"There you are." Angie Cooper smiled big as
they walked into the kitchen with its many windows and early evening sun casting everything
in a yellow light. She left the sink of dishwater
and hugged Laura.

"What's up?" Jesse grabbed two bottles of
water out of the fridge and Laura took the one
he handed her.

"I made a few calls." Angie's smile faded. "I
hope you don't mind."

Before Laura could answer, an older man
walked into the kitchen. She knew immediately
that he had to be Tim Cooper, the father of the
brood of Cooper children. His brown hair was
touched with gray and his eyes were kind in
his weathered but still-handsome face. He shot
Laura a smile and shook his head.

"She isn't sorry she meddled." He walked to
the sink and turned on water to wash his hands.

Angie smiled at him but then turned back to
Laura.

"I called a friend and managed to pull a few
strings. Laura, you won't have to make any
more trips to Tulsa to see Abigail. They're going
to move her here."

"Here? To Dawson?" Laura's heart tilted sideways. Her mind had a difficult time wrapping around what Angie Cooper had just told her.

"She's coming to Cooper Creek. We're a licensed foster home and so they'll place Abigail with us while the caseworker does a home study on your new place. I know this isn't the same as having her with you, but you'll be able to see her. You'll have weekend visits with her. I'm hoping that in the next month or two she will be back with you on a permanent basis."

Laura's throat tightened and tears flooded her eyes. She blinked quickly, trying to stop them. From a few feet away, Jesse smiled. Angie moved close to her side.

"Laura, I hope this is okay with you. I know I tend to overstep my bounds, but I wanted to help you."

Laura sobbed into her hands, embarrassed by the flood of emotion. "I'm so sorry. Yes, of course I'm glad you made that call. I'm just…" She shook her head and wiped at her eyes. "Your family has overwhelmed me with support. It's been so long since I've had this."

From across the kitchen Jesse smiled and then he turned to stir the soup. She had to force herself to focus on Angie, but her gaze kept drifting back to Jesse, to the way he distanced himself.

She wondered if he thought she was using his family. He'd given her a job. Now this.

Conversation continued and she got rolled along in it, giving the right answers but worrying the entire time about what Jesse was thinking. She pushed it aside because in the end it didn't matter. He had given her a job and she would do that job.

Most important, she would get Abigail back. Her daughter meant everything to her. If all of this got taken away, it wouldn't matter. She would go on.

If she lost Abigail…

She couldn't think about that. Instead she smiled and said a silent thank-you to God for the doors He had opened and for Angie Cooper.

She even thanked him for Myrna because without Myrna, she might not have stayed in Dawson.

After supper Jesse got a phone call. He excused himself and left the table. Laura watched him walk away, the phone to his ear.

"Laura, is there anything you need for Abigail or to help you get started in your new home?"

Laura glanced up from her plate and smiled at Angie. "No, I think we're good. I'm sure once Abigail gets here we'll find things she needs."

Angie covered Laura's hand with hers. "He's used to emergency calls. It's usually a resident at the nursing home. Sometimes they need him at the E.R. if they get slammed with patients."

Laura realized she had followed Jesse's departure with her eyes. "Oh, of course. I'm sorry, I just got distracted."

"That happens." Angie stood and started clearing dishes. Laura jumped up to help and Angie shook her head. "I can do this."

"I want to help."

Laura was at the sink when Jesse walked back into the kitchen. She glanced at him and then returned to the pan she'd been scrubbing.

"Problem?" Angie loaded the last plate in the dishwasher.

Jesse shrugged one shoulder and reached for his water. "No, not really. Isaac needs me to make a decision a little sooner. He has another doctor that's interested in going to the Honduras. He wants me to go with him to a culture-and-language school in a few weeks."

"Wow, he is moving fast, isn't he?" Angie leaned against the counter, a dish towel in her hands. "Don't let him rush you into this. Sometimes people in their excitement try to push…"

He kissed his mom on the cheek. "I know and thank you. It'll be my decision, not Isaac's."

Angie smiled up at her son. "I just worry."

Laura stepped away. "I'm going to peek at the puppies Mr. Cooper told me about."

Angie reached for her. "Call him Tim, and you don't have to leave. We're not a private family."

Jesse laughed. "Understatement of the year. There is absolutely *no* privacy in this family."

"I'm not sure why that bothers you kids." Angie smiled a sweet smile and Laura remembered her mom, the two of them having conversations that ended with laughter and teasing. There had been few of those moments in the years after Laura's father's death but she cherished the memories.

"I'm not sure why it bothers us." Jesse stepped away from his mother. "I'm going to take Laura back to her place. She looks pretty wiped out."

"Don't use Laura's health as an escape route. But you're right, she does still look pale." Angie leaned toward her son. "But never tell a woman she doesn't look good."

Laura got it now. There was no privacy in the Cooper family. Even for non-Coopers.

On the way home Jesse kept quiet because he knew that anything he said at that moment would come out all wrong. He didn't want to apologize for a kiss he wasn't at all sorry about. He didn't want to think about leaving. But he would leave. That had been his plan for years.

A day that had some pretty decent moments had turned itself inside out on him.

"Your family is in Honduras, aren't they?" Laura asked, breaking the silence.

Jesse glanced her way. In the dark cab of the truck, illuminated only with the dash lights and the occasional security light in a passing yard, he couldn't make out her features.

"As far as I know, my mother and sister are still alive."

"I'm really very sorry. I know that must be difficult."

Difficult. Yeah, that was one word for it. Not knowing, also not easy. Over the years he'd spent a lot of time coming to terms with his life and how he had ended up here, so far from the life he'd been born into. He guessed he was in good company. Moses and Joseph were good examples. God had seen a reason to remove them from their families. He'd had a purpose for Moses in the home of Pharaoh and a purpose for Joseph in Egypt.

They were driving through Dawson. He pulled into the Convenience Counts convenience store and parked.

"I have a family, Laura. The Coopers are in every single way my family. I don't want to find my birth mother because I need a mother. I have one. There are just spaces in my life. I remember my little sister and I wonder what happened to her. I worry about the lives they've lived while I've been here, being a Cooper."

"I'm sorry." She shrugged as she said the words and he knew it was because there wasn't any more she could say. He got that.

"I'm going to run in and get us a couple of colas. Do you want anything else?"

"No, I'm good."

He got out and walked up the sidewalk lit with bright fluorescent lighting. Bugs swarmed. At the edge of the parking lot a few kids had parked their cars and trucks and were sitting on the tailgates of the trucks and talking. Country music played on one of the stereos, a George Strait song.

Jesse didn't need a cola, he needed a minute to get his head on straight. He grabbed the colas and a couple of chocolate bars. Fortunately the girl working the register wasn't talkative. Instead she kept peeking out at her peers who seemed to be having a good time while she worked.

When Jesse walked back to his truck, Laura looked up, her eyes bright and her smile soft. He couldn't not think about that kiss. And that bugged him. He wasn't a teenager with his first crush. He was a grown man who knew a thing or two about women. He got in and handed her a can of soda and a candy bar.

"Here you go—just what the doctor ordered."

"Thank you." She smiled, turning sideways in her seat to face him. "I would ask if this is a first date, but I don't know if you could handle that joke right now."

He laughed. "Well, since you just said it."

"I did, didn't I?" She unwrapped the candy. "I know it isn't a first date. It's a distraction because you don't want to think right now."

"Very astute." He leaned back in the seat and he couldn't help but look in the rearview mirror. The teens were laughing and joking. One of the girls had plopped down next to a boy he knew and they were arm in arm, falling in love. Not that it was really love, he guessed. More like chemistry. Maybe they'd get married and have a few babies. Maybe they'd end up brokenhearted. More likely they'd figure it out in a few years and find the right person.

He'd been waiting for the right person for a long time.

"Let me tell you about being a Cooper."

She crumpled her empty wrapper. "I thought you didn't want to talk."

He grinned and shook his head. "You're not as nice as I thought."

They both laughed and he thought back to

being one of those kids on the tailgate of a truck. Those days had never been easy, not as easy as people pretended.

"I'm nice," she said after a few minutes. "You're just used to me being quiet. But tonight I think I got the best gift ever and I'm in the best mood ever."

"Abigail?"

"Yes." She touched his arm. "Did you think I meant the kiss in the barn?"

"No, of course not. See, that's the trouble growing up Cooper."

"Being the boy, the guy, the man that every girl dreams about?"

"You're not giving me a break, are you?"

"Not at all."

"Okay. Yes, you're right. I'm just trying to tell you this without sounding arrogant."

Her smile faded. "You aren't arrogant."

"The name Cooper means something in Dawson. And as a teenager it meant a lot of things. It meant people expected certain behavior from the Coopers. They expected certain actions. There's some pressure to being a Cooper."

"And?"

"And there is the other side of the coin. My brothers and I learned at an early age that girls like Cooper guys."

"I've met a few now, so I can understand that. You're good-looking men. You're also very kind."

"Among other things." He didn't want to go into it. The money, the ranch, the rodeo and the name.

"I do understand." She smiled again, but this time he noticed a definite sadness in the look and it lingered in her eyes as the smile dissolved. "I lived on the opposite side of the coin. I was never quite good enough. I wasn't a cheerleader or an athlete. I didn't have the right last name. I studied hard, made good grades, had a few close friends and got ignored by the boys in my high school."

"The moral of the story is to give people a chance to be who they are and not who the world says they should be." Jesse started the truck. He glanced back and she followed the look, smiling at what he saw—teenagers in the middle of the courting ritual.

"Dating is a lot of work, isn't it?" Laura sighed. "I remember being in my early teens and what I thought about dating. It was all about finding someone to love me forever. Someone to take me away from my situation. Girls are wired differently."

"I learned that the hard way."

Laura leaned across the truck and kissed his cheek. "I know this is none of my business, but let yourself off the hook. And I promise, one kiss doesn't mean I'm going to start buying wedding magazines. We shared a very sweet moment, that's all. I don't want it to come between us. I don't want it to become awkward."

"Because you need a job and I need a housekeeper?"

"Exactly. It's as simple as that." Her voice grew soft at the end of the sentence and she turned to look out the window.

"Yeah, of course." It was as simple as that.

Chapter Ten

A few days after Angie Cooper moved mountains, Laura was walking down the paved driveway from Jesse's house to hers, dreaming of the day when Abigail would be here with her. Jesse had left early that morning to drive to Tulsa and visit Gayla. Laura had cleaned his house, finished his laundry and now she had her own chores to finish. And she was planting a garden. Her very first.

As she walked up the sidewalk to her front door, the phone beeped, telling her someone was at the gate. She loved gadgets, but it still shocked her each time it buzzed to announce a visitor. She asked who it was and the person responded.

"Jolynn Smith. I'm here to see Laura White."

"I'll let you in. It's the white house on the left."

So when they said they would be around in

a few days for a home visit, these casework-
ers meant it! Laura rushed inside to put away
dirty clothes, wash her face and slip into a clean
shirt. She'd barely finished when the caseworker
knocked on the front door. Breathless, Laura
rushed to the door and swung it open to a fresh-
faced young woman in dress slacks and a pretty
blouse.

"Hello." Laura opened the door and motioned
the caseworker in.

"You didn't have to kill yourself trying to
make it spic and span for me." Jolynn smiled a
"gotcha" smile that was friendly, not accusing.
"Really, get a drink of water. Make that two,
and we'll talk. Laura, this isn't about finding a
speck of dust on your furniture."

"Just a meth lab in my kitchen?"

Jolynn, probably close to Laura's age, blushed
a little. "I'm sorry."

"No, I'm sorry." Laura let out a sigh and led
Jolynn into the kitchen. "I've been a lot of things
in my life, but I've never been a drug addict.
But now, that's what people think I am. Yesterday I got called in by my probation officer for
a random drug test."

"Which came back clean, by the way." Jolynn,
with her cute hairstyle and office attire, took the
glass of water Laura offered her.

"The tests are always clean." Laura closed her

eyes and waited for the wave of anger and desperation to pass. Futile, hopeless, out of control. She wanted a day when she didn't feel as though these were the words that described her life.

A hand touched her arm. "I grew up in foster care. My parents were drug addicts."

Laura didn't know what to say. "I'm sorry."

"Don't be. I got a great deal. I had amazing foster parents. It was the best thing that could have happened to me. Now we're going to do the best thing for your daughter. We're going to do our best to get her here in time to help you harvest those tomatoes growing in your garden."

Laura's eyes overflowed and Jolynn rummaged in her purse and pulled out a tissue that she pushed into Laura's hand.

"Thank you."

"You're welcome. Now, let's take a look around this very pretty and very clean house of yours, and then we'll have a talk about what's going to happen."

Laura led Jolynn through the house. They inspected the bedrooms, the closets, the safety of the bathroom cabinets. Laura then led her out the back door to the beautiful deck with the porch swing.

"How did you find this place?" Jolynn sat on the swing and her feet didn't touch the ground. Laura smiled because she'd never had that trouble. If anything she'd always felt too tall. In high school she had stooped a lot so that she wouldn't tower over boys who hadn't had their growth spurt yet.

"It's an amazing story." Laura watched as a rabbit hopped slowly into the yard to nibble on clover. "I was coming here, to Dawson, to find an aunt. I couldn't stay in the halfway house in Tulsa any longer. I couldn't get a job that paid enough to rent a place. And apartment complexes willing to rent to felons are few and far between. I just didn't see a way to get Abigail back. After a lot of prayer, I headed this way."

She recounted the rest of the story, the crash, the Coopers.

"God does work in mysterious ways. And tomorrow, Abigail is being delivered to the Coopers." Jolynn turned to face Laura, her expression now serious, professional. "You may visit her at any time as long as the Coopers are there and you do not leave with her. This weekend you'll have your first home visit. I'll bring her here on Friday afternoon and she has to go back to the Coopers on Sunday."

"This weekend?"

Jolynn's smile returned. "Yes, this weekend."

"I can't thank you enough. This means everything."

"I know. And I know I don't have to tell you

to make the right choices. You've finished your parenting classes and passed the supervised visitation process. You're doing great." Jolynn looked at her watch. "And now I have another appointment to keep and it won't be as nice as this. Take care of yourself, Laura, and I'll see you Friday."

As Jolynn backed out of the drive, Jesse pulled up and parked. He nodded at the social worker and waved as he got out of his truck. Laura danced a little, excitement bubbling out of her. Jesse headed up the sidewalk. Laura barely held back. She wanted to hug someone, dance them in circles and scream.

Poor Jesse made it to the porch and she couldn't take it any longer. She grabbed him and twirled him in a circle, her arms tight around him. He stared, blinking fast as she laughed and laughed. She hugged him again and his arms loosened and hugged her back.

"I get Abigail this weekend!"

"You should really try and be happy about this."

"I know!" She hugged him again and then re-alized what she'd done. "I'm sorry. I just had to hug someone. You were the person who showed up."

"So I was just the right guy at the right time?"

She wanted to agree. It would have been fine

to hug anyone. A stranger. His mom. Myrna. As much as she would have hugged anyone, it was Jesse she wanted to share this moment with. But Jesse was the last person she should be sharing moments with.

"Yes, anyone, of course." But she couldn't stop smiling.

"I think we should celebrate." He held up an envelope. "I got the information on the training course for the mission trip."

"Wonderful." But the news brought a sudden seriousness to the celebration. If he decided to go to Honduras, he would be gone soon. "What if I fix you dinner?"

"That sounds great. I need to walk up to the stable. Do you want to come with me?"

"I should. I think the more time I spend with the horses, the less I'll be afraid when you leave."

"Probably true. And I arranged for a neighbor kid to come over and exercise the horses a few times a week. The stallion is being sent to Texas. A friend of mine is interested in boarding him for a year."

"Let me get my shoes." She walked back into the house. He followed her. "How was Gayla?"

"Not good. I'm not sure what will happen, but I'm glad she's close to her mom."

"I'm sure that will be good for them both."

"I got a call from Jeremy," Jesse said as they walked out the door.

"And?"

"He's moving ahead with his idea for a clinic."

"He doesn't take no for an answer, does he?"

Jesse walked next to her. "Not at all. That's the Cooper in him."

"Maybe when you get back from South America?"

"Maybe. It's just a matter of blocking all of the voices trying to persuade me to go the way they think I should go."

Laura kept quiet. She didn't want to be one more person with an opinion about what she thought he should do. And she was the last person to really have a say in the choices he made.

Jesse opened the gate to the corral and walked up to the mare he'd been watching the past few days. Heavy with foal she stood in the corner of the white fenced enclosure, her head down, her sides heaving.

"Not much longer, Fancy." He ran his hand down her side. He didn't think she'd foal tonight, but she might. He'd moved her to the barn and this corral weeks ago to get her off the new spring grass.

He turned and walked back to the gate. Laura leaned on the top rail of the white vinyl fencing, her gray eyes settled on the mare, not him. He knew where her mind had gone. From that faraway look, he guessed she was thinking about Abigail's arrival at Cooper Creek and about their first overnight visit this coming weekend.

He stayed inside the enclosure, watching the mare and then turning to look at Laura.

"What?"

He turned back to the mare. "Just thinking that we shouldn't cook or mess up either house. I'll take you to the Mad Cow."

"You don't have to do that." She stepped back, allowing him to push the gate open. "I have chicken thawing. I don't mind cooking."

"You've been cooking for me all week. Let me feed the horses and I'll take you out."

"Jesse, really." She bit down on her bottom lip and then met his gaze. "I don't think we should. I'm not even sure about dinner."

"We have to eat."

"I don't want to mess up. I want to be able to work here, stay here. More than that, I have to protect Abigail. Once I get her back, I want her to feel safe. I want her to know that I'm here for her and she's the most important thing in my life. And—" She smiled weakly. "This is embarrassing..."

"Go ahead."

"I don't want her to think you're more than

my boss. She's a little girl and at this foster home, for the first time really in her life, she's had what she's always wanted. She's had a dad."

He whistled at the revelation that came from left field. He'd expected her to say she wasn't interested or she didn't want to be used. But she had a whole other list of reasons not to get tangled in a "going nowhere" relationship. And for the first time in a long, long time, maybe ever, he thought he'd met the kind of woman he would want to go places with.

That was about the last thing he needed to tell her when her eyes were full of doubt.

"I get that."

He did. He should agree. She was making it easy, the way he'd always liked relationships. Instead he wanted to convince her why dinner together made sense. When he looked at her, he knew that the choices they made now would have a serious impact on both of their lives.

"It's just dinner, Laura. I know you work for me. I know you need this job. I really get that you want to protect Abigail and that you don't want her to think there's something between us." But what if there was?

She followed him into the feed room.

"Jesse, I don't want to let myself believe there's something between us. I've got a record.

I have a child to raise. I've been through a lot and I don't think I can deal with anything else."

"What if we go out as friends, no promises, no expectations?"

"My brain says no."

"What do you say?"

"It's been a long time, maybe forever, since I've had a friend."

It had been a long time since Jesse had wanted to hold on to a woman the way he wanted to hold on to her. And friendship was only the beginning. But he knew her boundaries and the reasons for them.

Her phone rang as they walked back to her place and his truck. She looked at it and didn't answer.

"Problem?"

She shook her head but the tense line of her mouth said otherwise.

"Laura?"

"It's Ryan. He's still trying to get me to give him money. It isn't easy, telling him no. He's my stepbrother, but he was just a little boy when our parents got together and I've always felt responsible for him."

"He's an adult now and his actions put you in jail."

"I know." She stopped at the door of the truck. "I'm afraid of him," she whispered.

"He isn't going to touch you here. I'll make sure of that."

"Thank you." She stood on tiptoe and kissed his cheek.

"No problem." He pulled the keys out of his pocket. "Dinner in town?"

She nodded and he opened the door of his truck for her to climb in. She stopped short of getting in. "Jesse, don't hurt us."

"I won't."

When they got to the Mad Cow, it looked as if half the town had decided to let Vera cook for them. He spotted his brother Reese's truck. He and Cheyenne must have decided to eat out. And Blake was there, too.

No backing out now. He'd deal with his siblings and the town.

"Second thoughts?" Laura paused with her hand on her seat belt.

"We should be prepared for the looks, the speculation and the inevitable gossip."

"You mean it hasn't started yet?"

He pulled the keys from the ignition. "Not even close. At least two of my brothers are here."

"We can handle it."

When they walked through the door all conversation seemed to halt. Jesse knew it had to be his imagination. Laura stepped close, nearly shrinking into his side. Yeah, not his imagination. A few people greeted them, two or three smiled knowing smiles and a few went ahead with the gossip.

In a booth on the back wall, Cheyenne nudged Reese and whispered something. Reese turned, his dark glasses covering his sightless eyes. He smiled and raised a hand in greeting.

"Sit with us?" Cheyenne moved the baby's seat off one of the chairs and put it next to her in the booth.

"Yeah, Jesse, join us. We need to catch up." Reese grinned like a cat with a mouse cornered in the barn. "I haven't talked to you in weeks."

"Last Sunday at church," Jesse corrected. "And you aren't going to talk to me now. We're going to have dinner without a game of twenty questions."

"We?"

Jesse held Laura's hand. "Laura White, my brother Reese and his wife, Cheyenne."

"Laura, good to meet you."

Reese reached for her hand. "Jesse, maybe give me a call soon. We should at least get together before you leave the country."

"I will." Jesse led Laura to a corner booth that had just been vacated by a young couple. He didn't see Blake.

"You should have let me fix the chicken," Laura leaned to whisper after they were seated and the table had been cleared.

"I'm starting to think that might have been smarter. But Dawson gets kind of boring and people need something to keep them entertained. Eventually they'll figure out we're just friends."

"I have a feeling you typically aren't the Cooper they're talking about."

"I do try to fly under the radar."

"Which will make this even more interesting for them."

He started to reach for her hand but knew that would be a mistake in this crowded room. "It will."

They were eating fried chicken when Jeremy walked through the door and straight to their table.

"I've been trying to call you." Jeremy pulled up a seat and sat at the end of the booth. He reached for one of the rolls still in the basket. "Man, I'm starving."

"Help yourself." Jesse handed him a leftover chicken leg. "No, really, I'm done."

Jeremy grinned and took the leg. "Why didn't you answer your phone?"

Jesse felt his pocket and shrugged. "Left it in my truck, I guess. What's up?"

"Two things. I have a building going up and donors for a clinic. I think we could do one day a week and not overwork you. Right?"

"Jeremy, I'm not committing to something I might not be here to do."

"Right, yeah, I know." Jeremy put the chicken leg on a napkin. "Listen, you have to do what you have to do. But I really feel like this is something *I* have to do. If it works out that you can be involved, then that's even better."

"I get that. I can check around and see who might be able to help. You might be able to find more than one doctor, maybe even a physician's assistant, and that would mean being open more than one day a week. Or alternating doctors so one guy isn't pulling the whole load."

"Right, good idea. And while we're on the subject…"

Jesse interrupted his half brother, who had taken a bite of chicken and reached for a napkin. "Were we on the subject? Because the last time I checked, I was having dinner with a beautiful woman and you were interrupting."

Jeremy smiled at Laura and then smirked at

Jesse. "Oh, sorry, I didn't realize this was a date. I thought maybe this was a business meeting."

Behind them a few people chuckled.

Jesse leaned toward Jeremy. "I'm going to take you outside and…"

Jeremy, not at all offended, leaned in and whispered, "And lose your Christian witness?"

"Yeah."

Jeremy wiped his hands on a napkin and stood. "I have a kid at Back Street with some pretty nasty poison ivy."

Jesse glanced from his brother to Laura and she gave a slight nod.

"Let me pay for our dinner and we'll be up in five minutes. Are you happy?"

"Mucho."

"Don't speak Spanish, please. You always end up butchering the language."

"Right, okay." Jeremy grabbed the bill that the waitress had left on their table. "I'm buying. Unless you were going to write it off as a business meeting."

"No, Jeremy, I wasn't. Go!"

Jeremy walked away, still laughing. Jesse leaned back, wishing he had time for a cup of coffee and a slice of Vera's pie. A minute later the waitress was back with two pieces of pie in takeout containers.

"Your brother said to bring you this. You

don't have time to eat it, he said, but you can have it later while you enjoy your view of the lake from your deck." She turned pink as she set the containers on the table. "And he left me a tip. But he said not to tell you that."

She went from pink to red as she relayed the message.

Jesse pulled out his wallet and left the girl a second tip. He stood and waited for Laura to slide out of the booth. "I guess we should go."

That was the way a guy started rumors in Dawson. But right now, Jesse didn't care.

Chapter Eleven

Laura watched Jesse with the little boy Jeremy had asked him to examine. She guessed Teddy to be about eight years old. He wore jeans shorts a few sizes too large and a pajama top for a shirt and his bare feet were cut and blistered.

She found a towel in the kitchen of the Back Street Community Center and while the little guy sat on the table waiting for Jesse to finish the examination, she wiped off his feet and applied salve and bandages to two of the cuts. He smiled at her and didn't look at all upset by his condition, even though his left eye had swollen nearly shut due to poison ivy and he couldn't stop scratching the sores on his arms.

His mom stood behind the table, her smile hovering between gratitude and tearful embarrassment. Laura offered her a smile of encouragement. Moms had to stick together. Laura knew from her own experience that everyone judged, everyone speculated, and people didn't always want the whole truth.

"You're going to have to learn the difference between poison ivy and mint, Teddy." Jesse wrote out a prescription for the mom. "He needs to take this entire prescription. Even if he looks better, he has to take every pill exactly the way the pharmacist tells you."

"I can do that." Her cheeks turned pink and she looked from Laura to Jesse. "How much do I owe you?"

"Nothing." Jesse helped Teddy off the table and ruffled the boy's curly brown hair. "Stay out of the poison ivy, Teddy."

"Okay, Doctor." Teddy saluted and laughed before he turned and ran from the room. His mom apologized and ran after him.

"Cute." Laura watched them run up the stairs together and her heart ached because it had been months since she'd had such normal moments with her own daughter.

But it wouldn't be much longer. Tomorrow she'd be allowed to visit Abigail at the Coopers'.

"Ready to go?" Jesse walked over to the sink and turned on water. Laura joined him because just the thought of poison ivy made her itchy.

"I'm ready." She waited until he reached for the towel to wash her hands.

They flipped off lights and headed up the stairs. Jeremy was waiting for them in what was once the church sanctuary but now served several purposes, Laura had learned. They sometimes had music, sometimes plays or special speakers.

"Looks like Teddy will live." Jeremy walked next to Jesse as they left the building. "You two make a good team."

Jesse shook his head. "Jeremy, stop trying to help God. If this clinic is supposed to happen, it will. And God will supply the medical staff."

"Right, wait on God." Jeremy pulled keys out of his pocket. "I need to head home or I'm going to have a wife praying the wrath of God down on me. But thanks, Jess. All kidding aside, I appreciate you doing this. Even if you're not the guy, at least you helped me to see the need."

"I didn't help you see the need—you latched on and refused to let go."

"Yeah, some people think that's a good quality. You make it sound like an insult."

Jesse shook his head. "Not at all. To show you I'm not upset, I was thinking you could be my partner this Saturday at the arena."

"Team roping?" Jeremy reached for the helmet on his motorcycle.

Laura walked away as the two brothers finished their conversation. She headed for Jesse's truck, eager to get home and work on Abigail's room. Not that she had a lot to do. She'd been working on the room since she moved in. She'd hung posters on the walls, put away the clothes they'd been given and found a few new dolls because most of Abigail's toys had been boxed up and disappeared during the months Laura had spent in jail.

Jesse got in the truck and waved to Jeremy one last time. The Coopers were a close family. She wanted that for Abigail. A real family that held on to each other and helped one another. She'd tried to be that for her brother.

Her phone rang as they were heading for Jesse's place. She glanced at the number and let it go to voice mail.

"Was that Ryan again?"

"Yes. I'm not sure what he wants me to do for him. He's left a few messages saying that he needs my help. I'm the only person he can count on."

"Do you think changing your number would help?"

"I'm not sure. I don't know how he found this number. I've thought about giving him money. Maybe he'd leave me alone if he had the money to go away."

"That isn't the way it works, Laura."

"I know. He'd just be back for more."

"Exactly." He stopped at the gate to his place and punched in the code. "I don't know if I've told you but the gate is monitored by an alarm company. I want you to know that so you won't be worried out here alone. There's an alarm on your place, too. I'll get it activated tomorrow."

"Jesse, you don't have to. I'm not worried about Ryan."

"It's for more than Ryan. I'll feel better about leaving you and Abigail if the alarm is activated. I'm sure you'll sleep better at night."

She smiled at him in the dusky interior of the truck. "I have slept pretty well until now, thanks."

He tipped the brim of his hat a little and smiled. "Glad to oblige. What do you think about coffee to go with our pie? The lake is beautiful this time of night."

Coffee on the deck overlooking the lake. Sitting with Jesse in the stillness of late evening. Dreaming of something she should know better than to dream of.

She shook her head. "I need to get a few things done at my place."

He eased into her driveway. "Is there anything you need for Abigail?"

"No, I'm good."

She had expected to get out and walk up to her front porch. In her mind she would wave goodbye and go inside alone. She'd been alone a long time.

Jesse turned off his truck. "I'll walk you up to the door."

He didn't have to. The words were on the tip of her tongue.

But she let him.

Jesse opened the door to the little cottage. She had turned off all the lights. He flipped on the living room light and walked with her through the house to turn on lights in the kitchen and hall.

It made him feel better, to walk through the house and see for himself that Ryan hadn't managed to get inside.

She set her container of pie on the counter. Her hair hung loose tonight, framing a face that was no longer pale. Her smile radiated, touching her gray eyes with warmth. This place suited her, he thought. The house, the garden, even the horses.

"Thank you for dinner." She met his gaze, her lip between her teeth in that shy way that did more to a man than she realized.

"I think that's my cue to go."

"I'm really okay. I promise."

He knew she was.

"Call if you need anything. I don't go in to work until eight in the morning."

"If there's a problem, which there won't be, I'll call you." She walked with him to the door, even stepped out on the porch with him. Jesse stood on the porch, his keys in his hand, Laura next to him.

They both studied the moon. He told himself to take a step away. He needed to let this go. Over the years he'd gotten good at letting things go. He knew how to keep a relationship easy and uninvolved.

Or he *had* known, until now. Man, he wasn't a kid. He knew all about high school romance and crushes. He knew how to be an adult and just take a woman for dinner. Laura was teaching him a new lesson.

Now he knew for the first time what kind of woman it would take to change his ways. The woman who didn't seem to want to stay in a man's life seemed to be the one. This woman who needed to protect her heart and her child.

He pushed his hat back and turned to face her. Her pale gray eyes were smoky in the dark of the porch with just the glow of a lamp behind her. Her lips parted, as if she meant to say something.

He'd kissed her one other time, on impulse. He could do it again. At that moment he figured he could take one step and she'd take the other. But looking at her standing there, vulnerable in a way he'd never seen before, he knew better.

He knew she needed exactly what she'd said she needed. She needed a friend, not someone complicating things.

"Jesse." His name was soft on her lips and she looked up at him. He took off his hat and backed a step away.

"Laura, I'm going to leave now. It isn't what I want to do." He touched her cheek and she shivered. "I don't know if it's what you want. But I know one thing—it's what I have to do to keep this uncomplicated. I brought you out here to give you a job and make your life easier. I didn't plan on making it harder."

"Thank you." She stepped away from his touch and he let her go.

"Good night." He had a feeling it would be anything but good. He smiled and pretended. "Call me if you need anything."

"Jesse, I'm fine. I've been alone a long time. I'm not afraid of the dark."

"Of course." He walked out to his truck and when he got in to start it, she had stepped back into her house. She stood at the door and watched him go.

He'd been alone a long time, too. It no longer appealed to him.

Chapter Twelve

Laura stepped out of the little blue sedan Myrna had had delivered for her that afternoon. A replacement, Myrna had called to inform her, and would brook no arguments. Laura would argue but not now. Now she had only one thing on her mind—Abigail.

Laura's daughter stood on the front porch of the Cooper home, Angie Cooper holding her hand. As Laura crossed the yard, Abigail rushed to her, throwing her arms around Laura's waist and hanging on tightly. Laura lifted her daughter to hold her close. She inhaled her presence and her softness. They were both crying. Laura wiped at Abigail's tears.

"I love you," she whispered close to the little ear.

"I love you, too, Mommy." Abigail sobbed hard against her, breaking Laura's heart again.

Since all of this had started, Abigail had been strong. They'd probably both worked too hard at not crying, not showing the other they were hurting. Both had tried too hard to be strong.

It came out in that moment, in tears and sobs.

"I think we should go inside." Laura carried Abigail up the steps. "You're getting big. I think you might have to walk."

Abigail shook her head against Laura's shoulder. "Not yet."

"Okay, not yet." Laura kissed Abigail's cheek. "I've missed you so much."

"I missed you, too." Abigail leaned against her. "Can I show you my new room?"

"Of course you can." Laura smiled at Angie Cooper, who waited inside the door for them. She mouthed the words, "Thank you."

Angie nodded and rested a hand on her back. "I think she's excited to show you her room. I told her she's going to have a very nice room at her new house, too."

"I was up all night cleaning it," Laura admitted, avoiding the details of why she'd been up all night. What would she tell Angie Cooper?

She could tell her the obvious—that Jesse was one of the most decent men she'd ever met. She could tell the easy truth—that it felt good to be in his arms and to pretend that she could be the woman he wanted in his life. But the reality was he was considering a year in the mission field and Laura had to protect Abigail.

She needed stability for her daughter, not a relationship that lasted a few months and ended with her losing her job and her heart.

She shifted Abigail to her left side as they walked up the stairs to the room Angie had opened to her daughter. It was the type of room every little girl dreamed of, with white furniture, a lot of pink and a basket of toys and stuffed animals.

"What a great room." Laura hugged her daughter. "I'm going to let you walk now so you can show me everything."

The minute Abigail's feet touched the ground she became animated, leading Laura around the room and showing her every amazing thing. Laura swallowed the lump that slid up her throat, swallowed the jealousy and the regret. So many people were contributing to her daughter's happiness. So many people had helped them.

Focus on the good, Laura told herself. Be thankful for the people God had sent into their lives to help them. She had to remind herself again as Abigail pulled out new dresses for church.

Angie Cooper walked up behind her, resting a hand on her arm. "You're all she needs."

Laura swallowed and blinked away tears that stung her eyes.

"I know. Well, I think I know." She laughed a shaky laugh.

Angie reached for Abigail, and Laura's daughter looked up, her eyes wide. "Abigail, let's go down and we'll show your mom the pizza crust we're making."

Abigail found something new to be excited about. They were going to make pizza. Laura followed her down the stairs and to the kitchen.

"The crust is in the fridge. It's rising," Abigail explained. She opened the refrigerator door and pointed to the bowl with the mound of pizza dough covered with plastic wrap.

"We'll have to get Mrs. Cooper's recipe so we can make this at home." *Soon,* she wanted to promise. *Very soon.* But she couldn't because she didn't want either of them to get their hopes up and then find out that it wouldn't happen for months.

"Mrs. Cooper wrote the recipe on a card." Abigail showed her the card on the counter. "It's for you."

Laura slipped the index card into her pocket.

The front door closed and a few minutes later they were joined by Jackson Cooper. He took off his hat and gave her daughter a big smile.

"Now, there's the girl I was looking for. I have

a brand-new baby calf and I thought you'd like to see him. I also have something else out here, but your mom has to okay it."

"What color is the calf?" Abigail quickly forgot about pizza.

Jackson laughed. "Well, what color do you want him to be?"

"Spotted." She giggled.

Jackson shook his head. "I'm afraid I don't have a spotted calf. This calf is red with a pretty white face."

"Can my mom come with us?"

"Of course she can. Big girls like calves, too."

Abigail let out a whoop and grabbed Laura by the hand. "We're going to see a calf that's red with a white face."

Laura smiled and she wanted to tell Abigail about the new foal at Jesse's and the path that led to the lake. But later—they'd talk about all of that later.

"You're quiet." Jackson spoke as they were walking past the stable and in the direction of the field. "Everything going okay?"

"I'm good." She smiled and watched Abigail run ahead of them, the border collie at her side. "I'm better than I've been in a long time. This is the first time I've spent the day with her in months where we weren't being supervised in an activity room at a state office."

"It had to be rough. But it won't be long and you'll have her home for good."

Laura nodded and managed to not cry. "I know."

Jackson glanced back over his shoulder. Laura turned, hearing the vehicle at the same time. They moved to the side of the driveway and Laura called for Abigail to stay in the grass. Jesse's truck slowed to a stop and he got out.

"I thought he had to work until later." Laura bit down on her bottom lip, surprised she'd said it out loud, surprised she sounded like someone who knew his schedule, his comings and goings.

Jackson gave her a funny look but didn't say anything, not to her. "Hey, brother, what are you doing? Playing hooky from work?"

Jesse shot Jackson a look. "I had a break and I wanted to check on things here."

"We have a new calf." Jackson nodded in the direction of the field and the spot of red in the grass next to a grazing cow.

"Nice calf." Jesse smiled at Abigail, who had returned to Laura's side. "Has Abigail seen the puppies?"

Laura held a hand out to Abigail, who stood close to her side peeking up at Jesse. Her little fingers tightened around Laura's. Laura smiled at the daughter who had suddenly turned shy and gave her hand a comforting squeeze.

"Abigail, this is Jesse."

Abigail freed her hand and held it out to Jesse. He took her hand in his and squatted in front of her, his smile tender and making all the difference in ways Laura hadn't imagined.

"Abigail, I am so glad to finally meet you." He remained at her level. "Are you on your way out to see that new calf?"

She nodded and smiled at him. "My mom said there are horses here, too."

"There are horses, and even a pony or two for big girls like you."

Her eyes widened, and Laura remembered being six and wanting a pony. She wanted to jump in and stop Jesse from making promises. She waited, breathless, hoping that here in Dawson, with the Coopers, Abigail would learn that sometimes promises were kept. Men were strong and could be there for a woman. She wanted Abigail to know those things.

Laura didn't dare include herself in that dream.

Jesse stood and Abigail didn't remove her hand from his. Laura watched, amazed at how her daughter had taken to him. But then, Jesse was easy to like. He was soft-spoken and kind, and his eyes were warm and gentle.

"Will you go with me to see the calf?" Abigail held tightly to his hand, as if she didn't plan on ever letting him go.

"I will, and then I have to get back to work."

"We're making homemade pizza," Abigail told him as they opened the gate. "Do you want some?"

"I'd love homemade pizza, but I won't be here."

"We'll save you some."

"I'm counting on that."

Laura closed her eyes briefly and thanked God for this new chapter in their lives and for people around them who kept promises.

And for Jesse. She smiled when he turned to wink at her. She could add him to the list. She was thankful he'd given her a chance.

Jesse didn't want to go back to work. That didn't happen often. As he walked back to his truck after seeing what Abigail called the most beautiful calf ever, he wanted to stay on the farm. Laura walked a short distance away. Abigail raced ahead, picking daisies, dandelions and anything else that looked like a flower. She handed them all to her mother, and Laura took them with a teary smile.

Jackson had walked next to him but when they got to the stable he stopped. "I've got some work to get done. I'm going to let you walk Laura and Abigail back to the house."

Jesse shook his head but he didn't argue. He almost thanked his older brother for his discretion, his unusual insight. But then, maybe he shouldn't be so thankful. Ahead of him Laura slowed her steps and he caught up with her. She held the little bunch of flowers, sniffing a less than fragrant bouquet of what some would have called weeds. When she looked up at him, he laughed.

"What?"

He pulled her to a stop next to him. "Hold on. I know that years ago it was fun to rub a dandelion under another kid's chin and ask if they liked butter, but I don't think you want to spend all day—" he rubbed her chin and her cheek with his thumb "—with yellow pollen on your face."

He stopped rubbing and his fingers moved from her chin to her neck. She swallowed and shook her head. "Jesse."

"No, you're right." He let his hand drop to his side just as Abigail ran back to join them.

The little girl looked from him to her mother.

"What's wrong?" Abigail gave him a suspicious glare.

Laura reached for her daughter's hand. "I had yellow pollen on my face."

"Pollen?"

"From the flowers," she explained, and Abigail still looked suspicious.

Jesse knew it was time to make his escape. "I'm going to head back to work. Abigail, it was nice to meet you."

"We live at your house." Abigail's smile was big.

"Well, not really at my house. You have your own house, but it's near mine."

"Do you have horses, too?"

Jesse nodded. "I have horses, too. When you come to spend the weekend with your mom, I'll show them to you. I think we can even find one for you to ride."

"I get to spend the weekend and go to church with her."

"I know." Jesse couldn't help but think about the dad who had walked out on the little girl standing in front of him. He was missing out. Jesse's gaze returned to Abigail's mother. Yeah, that guy was missing out.

"Bye, Jesse." Abigail was obviously done with him. She had another fist of flowers and she turned and headed for the house and probably his mom.

"Bye, Abigail," he called out after her. He smiled and turned back to Laura. She held the wilted bouquet in her hand and watched her daughter. When she looked at him, the look didn't connect.

"Jesse, I have to ask you something."

"Shoot."

She bit down on her lip and her gaze drifted away, back to the house, to the door closing behind her daughter and the dog sitting on the front porch waiting for the little girl to return.

"Jesse, don't make her promises. I know that's hard for you to understand. I'm sure you have the best of intentions. People have kept their promises to you. But…"

He shook his head. "Laura, I'm not going to make promises I don't keep."

But what if he couldn't keep promises? What if he let them down?

About the only thing he could promise her was a job and protection from the stepbrother who seemed determined to use her every chance he got.

Laura touched his hand, grazing her fingers against his.

"I know you wouldn't mean to. It's just been a hard few years for us and not a lot of good things have happened."

"Eventually you have to stop living in the disappointments of the past. If you don't, you won't enjoy what you have now. You'll always be waiting for something to go wrong, for someone to hurt you."

She looked away. Jesse stood his ground. She lifted the flowers again, wrinkling her nose at the smell. The breeze picked up, blowing her hair, and she turned to smile at him.

"You're right. But I have to stand my ground on this. It's easy to make promises to a little girl, but she wants so much more. She has dreams about…"

"About?"

She shook her head. "I have to go inside and tell her goodbye."

Dreams about what? Jesse said goodbye and walked back to his truck. As he drove to work, he ran through his mind everything Laura might have been about to say.

Only one thing really made sense. He'd been a kid in an orphanage and he remembered what he'd wanted more than anything. A family. A whole family.

Laura was telling him she didn't want Abigail to think the three of them would be a family.

He got it.

As he pulled in the parking lot of the hospital, his cell phone rang. He answered as he parked and got out of his truck, pocketing his keys and grabbing his jacket.

"Isaac, what's up?" Jesse stepped aside at the door and let a young family walk out.

"Just checking to make sure you're still going to the training school with us."

"I've got that week slotted for vacation time."

Long pause. Jesse stepped through the door and waited.

"So are you still thinking this is what you want to do?"

"Have you been talking to my family?" Jesse smiled as he asked, but he didn't feel it.

"No, I haven't. I just know you. I know that when you see a need, you want to meet the need. If you're called to do this, you know I'm thrilled to have you on board."

Jesse nodded at the receptionist and the couple standing at the desk filling out paperwork. "Isaac, I promise you, I'm not going to take one step if I don't feel like I'm supposed to go."

"I've never doubted that."

Jesse ended the call and pocketed his phone. He stepped into the quiet of his office where he could think and say a quick prayer before he started the next half of his shift. His own words rolled through his mind. He wouldn't take one step if he didn't feel like he was supposed to go. Six months ago this mission trip had felt like the next step in his life.

He'd been planning missions for as long as

he could remember. Since he'd been a kid of about twelve and missionaries had stayed with their family for a week. He'd looked at pictures of kids a lot like himself. Kids who were sick, hungry, alone, the way he'd been before the Coopers adopted him.

He'd made a promise to himself and to God that he would help those children. As he sat there on the edge of his desk thinking back, he remembered just days ago and the family with whooping cough. Kids in need lived everywhere. But where did that leave him—and his plan?

Chapter Thirteen

❧

At three o'clock on Friday afternoon, Jolynn arrived at Laura's house with Abigail. Laura had been sitting on the front porch for an hour waiting impatiently. When the car stopped in her driveway she ran down to open the back door of the sedan.

Abigail took her seat belt off and crawled out fast.

"Mommy, there's a gate that we had to drive through."

"I know." Laura kissed her daughter and hugged her tight. She smiled over Abigail's shoulder at the caseworker. "Thank you, Jolynn."

"No problem. I'm going to leave the two of you alone. Have a good weekend and I'll leave it up to you to deliver her to the Coopers on Sunday afternoon."

"We'll be there." Laura kissed Abigail's cheek again. "Won't we?"

Abigail smiled at the caseworker. "This is my new house. And there are horses and a dog. And kittens."

The caseworker smiled. "I know you'll have a lot of fun. Have a good weekend."

Laura barely heard the goodbye. Her daughter grabbed her hand and pulled her toward the house.

"I want to see my bedroom and the barn and the lake." Abigail tugged on Laura's hand.

"We will see everything, but you have to calm down. We can only do one thing at a time."

Abigail groaned and put a hand to her forehead. "You're killing me."

Laura laughed and laughed. She had her daughter back. She wanted to do a happy dance around the yard. And, like Abigail, she wanted to do everything all at once. She drew in a deep breath and fought for control.

"I have homemade cookies. Does that make you feel better?"

Abigail nodded and the two of them rushed through the house to the kitchen. Laura opened the container of cookies and put it on the counter.

"Do you want milk or water?"

"Water, please. I had milk for breakfast." Abigail shuddered and scrunched her nose.

"Water it is."

As she poured milk she heard a truck pull up out front. She walked to the door and peeked through the living room window. Jesse got out of the truck that happened to be pulling a horse trailer.

"Be right back." She walked to the front door.

Jesse had made it up the sidewalk to the front porch. He had Friday afternoons off and on Fridays he looked like a cowboy in his faded jeans, T-shirt and scuffed leather boots. He pulled off a hat and swiped his hand through his dark hair, brushing it back from his face before replacing the hat.

Laura opened the door.

"Hey, I didn't expect to see you."

"I wanted to make sure she got here okay and let you know about the rodeo tomorrow. You might want to bring Abigail."

She stood in the door. He stood on the porch. She looked back into the house, where there was no sign of Abigail.

"She would like that."

A tiny whinny escaped the horse trailer. Jesse grinned, then he turned that sheepish look on her. Laura melted a little because he looked so much like a little boy with a scraggly bouquet behind his back. But he hadn't brought flowers. She had a feeling he'd brought something far more complicated.

"Is that a new horse?" She stood on tiptoe trying to see inside the trailer. "A tiny horse?"

"I shouldn't have." He cleared his throat.

Laura closed her eyes and shook her head. "No, you shouldn't have."

"I don't want to complicate things. But little girls and ponies, they kind of go hand in hand, and this one needed a home. His owners had to move—their daughter has moved on to bigger and better things, mostly boys. They were getting ready to send him to the auction."

"I see." She saw her heart getting broken. She didn't want her daughter's heart broken.

"I can take him back. Or maybe haul him over to Camp Hope."

She nodded. The camp was owned by former football player Adam McKenzie and his wife, Jenna. He could take the pony there. But what would a pony hurt? Abigail had always wanted a pony. He was right—every little girl wanted one.

"Don't take him back." She smiled and it wasn't the easiest smile. Looking at the man standing in front of her, she had to let her eyes connect with his, even though it hurt deep down inside where little-girl dreams still lived.

Those dreams were about more than ponies. Little girls dreamed of handsome princes, pretty homes, happy-ever-afters. And being loved and protected.

He looked like a man who would make all of those dreams come true for a woman—someday. But not her, the felon who had crashed into his life with a past and a daughter.

"He can be your gift to her, Laura. I'm the person delivering him."

"No, he's from you." She met that dark gaze of his and saw warmth in his brown eyes. "I'm okay with that."

He smiled. "Can we give him to her now?"

Laura nodded and glanced back into the house. "Abigail, are you finished with your cookies?"

"You have cookies?" Jesse leaned in close, and his scent, all country and earthy, wrapped around her. One step closer and her face would be in his neck.

He stepped back, adjusting his collar. He wore a heavy silver chain with a cross around his tanned neck. She focused on the chain, on the cross, and then tore her gaze away. He cleared his throat and her eyes moved up to his teasing smile. She answered the question about cookies.

"I do. Would you like one?"

"I would love a cookie."

Laura led him into the house. Abigail ran down the hall, grinning, her pigtails bouncing.

"I have the prettiest room ever," she announced with six-year-old enthusiasm.

Laura opened the container and held it out to Jesse. He took several chocolate chip cookies and winked at her daughter.

"I have something outside that goes pretty great with a new room and chocolate chip cookies." He winked at Abigail again, and Laura watched as her daughter gave her heart to Jesse Cooper. It was in those big eyes and the smile that spread across her face.

"What's outside? Is it a puppy?"

"A puppy?" Jesse's eyes widened and Laura shook her head. Jesse reached for Abigail's hand and the two of them hurried for the front door, leaving Laura to follow.

"We don't need a puppy," Laura mumbled as she hurried to catch up. Jackson had already promised one, though.

Soon Jesse had the back of the trailer open and Abigail hurried back to Laura's side. The two waited as Jesse stepped inside the trailer and talked in low tones that barely carried. Then the clomping of hooves was followed by Jesse stepping out of the back of the trailer, a pretty dappled gray pony at his side.

Abigail squealed and the pony's ears pricked to attention. The little animal turned to look at Laura's daughter.

"He's a perfect pony." She sounded breathless and her hold on Laura's hand tightened to a grip that went beyond her years and tiny frame.

"He *is* perfect." Laura wiggled her fingers and Abigail loosened her hold.

"Can I ride him?" Abigail looked from Laura to Jesse, her eyes wide.

Jesse grinned. "You certainly can. Let me get his saddle and bridle. Do you want to hold his lead rope for me?"

Laura hurried forward to reach for Abigail as her daughter raced to Jesse's side.

"She can't. She's never held a horse. She doesn't know how."

"Laura, she's fine. He's just going to stand here like the prince he is. He's going to tug on the lead rope and try to grab a big mouthful of that clover and he's going to wait for me to come back."

"But what if something scares him?"

Jesse winked at Abigail. "It'll take her time to get used to the idea of you being a cowgirl."

Laura shot him a look. "I'm her mother and I don't want her hurt."

Jesse's smile faded. "I won't let her get hurt. Prince is fifteen. He's been around a long time and he's taken care of a lot of kids in his life."

"I'm just…"

"A mom." Jesse handed the lead rope to Abigail. "Stand right here by your mom. Don't wrap this rope around your hand and don't let him tug. If he tugs you, pull him right back to your side."

"I can do it." Abigail held the rope the way he showed her, careful not to wrap it around her hand. "Why can't I wrap it around my hand?"

Jesse had made it to the back of his truck. He pulled out a bridle, tiny saddle and saddle pad. "Because if he runs and that rope is around your hand, he could drag you or hurt your hand."

"Oh." Abigail's attention now focused on the saddle and bridle with the silver trim. "It's the prettiest saddle ever."

Jesse set the saddle down and took the rope from Abigail.

"It is a pretty saddle. Now let's tie him right here and I'll show you how to saddle him up."

"And then I can ride him? All by myself?"

"I think I'll help you to begin with." He smiled at Laura and winked. "Because I think your mom and I would both feel more comfortable if you had a little help starting out."

Abigail stood at his side, smiling up at the dark-haired cowboy who towered over her tiny frame. He gently explained the entire process of saddling the horse. Abigail asked a million questions. And Laura was pretty sure she fell in love.

That frightened her more than sounds in the

night, worse than storms, worse than spiders. She swallowed at the thought and watched as Jesse helped her daughter onto the back of the pony named Prince.

Jesse led Abigail on Prince around the yard. The pony minded his manners perfectly. Jesse's friend had assured him that Prince would be the best pony a little girl could start out on. Jesse smiled back at Abigail and he couldn't have been prouder of her.

"You're doing so well, I think you need to learn how to ride him on your own." Jesse stepped next to the pony and showed her how to rest the reins on the pony's neck to get him to turn. He showed her how to gently pull back on the reins to stop Prince.

"But not hard because I don't want to hurt him." Abigail grinned.

"Exactly."

A phone rang. He turned as Laura pulled the phone from her pocket and walked a short distance away. He focused his attention on Abigail, on showing her where and how to ride. But he overheard bits and pieces of a troubling conversation.

"You can ride him around the yard and I'll be right here if you have a problem."

"I won't have a problem because Prince is perfect."

Jesse patted the horse's rump and Prince took off at a sedate, somewhat sleepy walk.

Laura stood at the edge of the yard, the phone back in her pocket, her focus on her daughter. Jesse walked to her side and stood with her, shoulder to shoulder. From time to time Abigail waved and smiled. Laura managed to look excited.

"You okay?" Jesse kept his attention on the pony and child.

Laura shook her head. "That was Ryan again. He says he needs money and he knows I can get it from the Coopers. I don't know how he knows where I am, but I don't have money and I can't associate with him. I won't risk losing Abigail again."

"Let's have his number blocked from your phone."

"I'm not sure how he's avoided the police as long as he has." Laura watched her daughter. "I won't let him hurt her."

How long had she carried everything, all of the worry and the responsibility, on her own? How much did it cost her to trust him and let him help?

"You have people to help you now, Laura. I know it's hard to let go, but we're here."

"You've done so much for me, Jesse." She turned from watching her daughter and smiled up at him. "It isn't your responsibility to take care of us. You gave me a job and a home. That's more than enough. I have to take care of this."

Abigail, obviously thinking she might be on her way to a championship in barrel racing, kicked Prince into a jolting trot that had her grinning from ear to ear. She took the pony around a pole and headed back toward them. Jesse took a few steps in her direction, just in case.

"Abigail, slow him down," Laura warned, stepping past Jesse.

Jesse let her go, but he knew that the pony wouldn't take a wrong step. Prince trotted up to Laura and reached for her to pet his nose. The pony leaned in close, and she did. Jesse kind of envied the animal—Prince obviously had a way of winning females that he didn't.

"What do you think, Abigail? Should we keep him?" Jesse walked up and reattached the lead rope to the halter he'd left under the bridle.

"Forever." Abigail leaned and hugged the pony.

"I agree. Would you like to help me take care of him? After we ride we always brush our horse down, feed him and turn him out to pasture. I have a small field for Prince where he'll get to hang out with other horses."

"Can I help, Mommy?" Abigail reached and Laura set her daughter on the ground.

"I think you should definitely help. If you're going to ride a pony, you should know how to take care of him."

Together the three walked to the barn, leading Prince. Jesse tied the lead to a hook and while Abigail watched, he unsaddled the pony and brushed him down. After a few minutes he handed the brush to Abigail.

"You get to brush his neck." He moved Abigail a little closer to the pony's side. "Just like this, nice and easy but hard enough that he knows what you're doing."

Abigail smiled up at him, changing his world.

"You'd make a good daddy." She dropped the brush and hugged him tight.

Jesse touched the little girl's dark hair and did his best not to say the wrong thing. Which meant keeping his mouth shut.

Laura smiled at her daughter and turned more than three shades of pink. "Someday he will make some little girl a great daddy, Abigail. And he makes a great friend for us."

Abigail released him from the bear hug and reached for the brush she'd dropped at his feet. "I know that, Mom."

Big-girl voice and a roll of the eyes. Jesse could handle that a lot easier than sunshine and pigtails looking for a daddy. He cleared his throat and took a step back.

"I'm going to feed the other horses and make sure Prince has water in his new field. Abigail, wait until you meet Prince's new friends."

"A pony has friends?" She stopped brushing.

"He certainly does. Let me check on the other horses and I'll introduce you to his friends. And while you're waiting, you might check that empty stall right there." Jesse pointed to the middle stall. "I heard what sounded like a bunch of kittens in there."

Abigail ran to the stall and when she couldn't get the door unlatched she looked at him. "I can't get it."

"Crawl under. There's nothing in there but the kittens."

On all fours, Abigail crawled fast under the door. They couldn't see her but she let out a happy shout and informed him that there were four kittens. Jesse smiled at Laura and she met his gaze with those gray eyes of hers. They were more than gray—they were storm clouds, mixed with dark and light blue.

"Walk with me." He held up the lead rope and nodded for her to follow. "Abigail, we're going to turn Prince into the field. You stay with the kittens and we'll be right back."

"Okay." She peeked out from under the stable door. "I'm watching you two."

"Abigail." Laura shook her head. "I'm so sorry. I'll talk to her."

"Don't apologize. If I had kids, I'd want them all to be just like her."

That brought a return of her smile. "Thank you. And you know how she feels about you."

He glanced back and Abigail was still watching, a tiny kitten held up to her cheek. She nodded and he winked and reached for her mother's hand. Abigail smiled and crawled back under the stall door with her kitten.

Chapter Fourteen

Music played on aging speakers and the tempting aroma of hamburgers on the grill greeted Laura and Abigail as they got out of their car at the Dawson arena. Cars were parked in a grassy field. Behind the arena were a couple of rows of trucks pulling horse trailers. The Coopers would be in that crowd.

"I want to see the horses." Abigail pulled on her hand but Laura stood her ground.

"We can't go back there. That's for people who participate—not for people like us."

"What's us?" Abigail looked up, her eyes narrowed.

"City people who watch." Laura winked and led her daughter across the grassy area to the arena. "Do you want a hamburger or a hot dog?"

"Hamburger. And we're not city people. I have a pony and we live on a farm."

Laura smiled down at her daughter. "Yes, you have a pony."

At the concession stand she paid for two burgers and two colas. At the back of the line, she saw a hand wave. Laura peeked around the crowd and smiled at Myrna Cooper and a woman about Laura's age.

"Who is that?" Abigail still held her hand.

"That's Jesse's grandmother. Her name is Myrna. You may call her Miss Cooper or Miss Myrna."

"Oh."

Their order number was called. Laura stepped to the window and picked up the food. When she turned, Abigail was gone. Her heart thudded as she scanned the crowd for Abigail and then for Ryan. What if he'd taken her? What if a caseworker saw it and turned Laura in as unfit?

And then she saw her.

Laura joined Myrna and the young woman, a Cooper who Laura hadn't met. They had Abigail between them.

"Mom, Granny Cooper said I can go back and see Jesse's horse and the bulls that Jackson brought to the rodeo." Abigail smiled. Laura handed her daughter the food and introduced herself to the other woman.

"I'm Laura White."

"Heather Cooper. It's really nice to meet you and Abigail."

Laura smiled down at her daughter. "Yes, and Abigail needs to apologize for running off. I didn't know where you went."

"I'm sorry." And she truly did look sorry. "Can we eat and go say hi to Jesse?"

"I don't know that we should bother him."

Heather shook her head as they stepped forward to order. "I promise, it won't bother them if you go back there. We'll save the two of you a seat."

Laura nodded and turned to say something to Myrna. But Myrna wasn't listening. She didn't seem to be with them. She wobbled a little and Laura caught hold of her arm.

"Myrna, are you okay?"

Myrna blinked and then refocused on Laura. "Of course I am. I just need to eat."

Laura looked from Myrna to Heather, who wore a worried expression that Laura imagined looked a lot like her own. "I should get Jesse."

Myrna grabbed her arm with a hand that felt cool. "No, you will not."

"But, Myrna…"

"I'm very able to make that decision. No." But the words sounded weak.

"Myrna, do you have a headache? Are you dizzy?"

"I'm hungry." Myrna raised her chin and stepped right past Laura.

"Okay then." She motioned Abigail to her side. "Abigail and I are going to go see Jesse and the bulls."

And they would also tell him about his Granny Myrna, but Laura wasn't about to tell her friend that she planned on telling Jesse whether she liked it or not.

They finished their burgers as they walked. Laura slowed her steps as she scanned the area. Men were saddling horses, putting on chaps or standing in groups talking. There were women in jeans, boots and button-up Western shirts. A couple of them smiled, and several gave her curious looks that asked her what she thought she was doing in their world.

She wondered the same thing. But the tiny hand in hers couldn't be denied. Laura thought about all the times she'd rejected an offer to go out because she hadn't wanted to leave Abigail or hadn't wanted her daughter to think there was more to a relationship than just dinner and a movie. She was losing control.

And why? She spotted him standing next to a horse trailer, and his brothers Jackson and Jeremy stood nearby. A woman walked up and she looked as if she belonged in their world. She talked to Jesse for a minute, smiling a carefree smile that said she probably didn't have a child at home.

Laura started to turn around but Jackson waved and called out to her and to Abigail. Laura held tightly because she knew that Abigail would try to make a break for it and run across the open area. With the trucks and livestock, that would have been a mistake.

"Stay with me." Laura glanced down at her daughter and then back at the Cooper men. The woman waved and hurried off, back to a trailer where a beautiful, nearly white horse had been left tied.

"Hey, you made it." Jesse held out a hand and Abigail barreled herself at him. He picked her up and put her on the back of his horse. "Are you going to watch me show these guys what an Arabian can do?"

Abigail smiled at Jeremy and Jackson. "He's going to show you guys."

Jackson laughed and shook his head. "Schooling the kid in your crazy love of Arabians. This is a new low, Jesse."

"I need someone on my side." He leaned to buckle his chaps. "Who better than Abigail?"

"Who better?" Jeremy rested a hand on the horse's rump. "I need to saddle my horse. We're the second-to-last team so we have a while."

"Thanks."

Jackson also made his excuses for leaving. Laura watched the two brothers walk away and then they were alone. She didn't fit into this world.

But it didn't matter. Myrna mattered.

"Jesse, I'm worried about your grandmother."

Her words stopped him. He'd been coiling a rope and he looked up.

"Why?"

"We were in line with Myrna and Heather at the concession stand and I'm not sure what happened. It seemed like she wasn't with us for a second, and she lost her balance. Plus her speech was a little slurred."

"You're sure?"

"Positive. She snapped at me and told me she just needs to eat something."

He ran a hand down the horse's neck. "Abigail, time to get down."

"What are you going to do?"

He lifted her daughter down from the back of the horse and reached for the girth strap. "I'm taking her to the hospital. Could you go tell Jeremy and Jackson? I'll call my parents."

"And when do you tell Myrna?"

"As I'm walking her out to her car."

Laura watched him unsaddle the horse. "I'll go tell your brothers."

"Thanks, Laura. I mean it. I'm glad you were watching. I've been worried for a while."

She nodded and reached for her daughter's hand. "Let's go, kiddo."

Abigail looked up, her eyes narrowed in worry. "What's wrong with Miss Myrna?"

"I'm not sure yet, sweetie, but Jesse will figure it out."

Jesse put his horse back in the trailer and when he stepped out, Jackson was waiting. "Did Laura tell you?"

"She did. Jeremy said he'd take the livestock home. Unhook your trailer and he'll put your horse in with his and mine. Bart is going to drive the bulls back to my place."

Jesse nodded and went to unhitch the trailer. "She's going to be mad."

Jackson laughed at that revelation. "You think?"

A few minutes later they walked up the steps to sit on the wooden seat next to their grandmother. She gave them both a look and then her wrath turned on Laura, who had taken a seat next to her.

"Tattletale," Myrna whispered.

"I'm sorry, Myrna, but I want you safe and healthy." Laura rested a hand on her arm.

"Gran, we're going to the hospital to have you checked out." Jesse reached for her hand to help her to her feet. She pushed herself up without his assistance.

"I can walk my own self down these bleachers. I've been doing it longer than you've been alive, Jesse Alvarez Cooper."

"And that's my name when I'm in big trouble."

Her eyes misted and she sniffled. "I don't want to be sick."

"I want you to be healthy and that's why we're going to the emergency room."

His grandmother glanced back at Laura. "Well, are you coming with us?"

Laura shook her head. "Myrna, you have family. They'll all be there with you. We would just get in the way."

Jesse started to tell her to come with them, but he couldn't. He knew why she was trying to keep her distance. Their gazes connected and she smiled and nodded once.

Myrna reached back for her hand. "I want you there with me. I might not have much longer…"

"Of course you do, Myrna." Laura hugged his grandmother. "You're stronger than anyone I know."

Jesse saw it coming and he couldn't stop it. His grandmother smiled and patted Laura's cheek and then she turned to pat his with a bejeweled hand.

"Jesse, tomorrow I need for you to go to my house and get the sapphire ring out of the safe."

"Gran, you're going to be fine."

"In case I'm not, that's your ring." She looked from Jesse to Laura. "You'll take good care of her."

Jesse saw the light dawn and spread across Laura's face. Her mouth dropped and her eyes widened. "Oh, Myrna, no."

He didn't have time to worry about it. His grandmother wobbled a little as she started down the steps, he and Jackson on either side of her. People in the stands cleared the way and whispered about what was happening to Myrna Cooper.

He didn't have time to look back and see if Laura would follow. Heather was with her. They would make a plan. As he helped his grandmother out of the bleachers and down to his truck, which they'd pulled close, he could tell that her left leg dragged a little and her hand on his felt weak.

"Gran, you okay?"

She turned to look at him. Her left eye drooped, as did her mouth. "We're just going to put you in the ambulance and get you there a little quicker."

He waved at the paramedics and they jumped in the ambulance and pulled the door closed.

Jesse spoke quietly to his grandmother, assuring her that he'd be right behind them in his truck. She whispered about Laura. He told her Laura would be with him.

As they loaded her into the ambulance, she reached for his hand.

"What is it, Gran?"

"I want…Tim." Her slurred speech gave him greater cause for concern. He gave the paramedics directions on what he wanted her to receive and then closed the door and headed for his truck. Jackson stayed with him.

As they backed out of their parking space he saw Laura get in her car with Abigail. He thought she'd be heading home. And he understood.

He never expected her to walk through the doors of the emergency room a short time later. She searched the room and Abigail let go of her hand and headed for Jackson's daughter, Jade.

When she saw him she smiled, and it floored him. Every tense muscle and nerve in his body relaxed. For the first time in an hour he took a deep breath. He stepped away from the rest of the family that had gathered. Before he could think it through he walked her outside and off to the side of the building.

No words. He didn't need words. She wrapped

her arms around him and held him tight. He didn't want to think. He just wanted this moment with her when everything felt right.

They stood that way for a long time and finally he exhaled and kissed the top of her head, then her cheek and then a soft kiss that sealed the moment.

"Thank you," he whispered close to her ear. She nodded.

"She's going to be okay."

"Of course she is." He held her hand and they walked back to the doors of the E.R. She slipped her hand from his before they walked back inside. "Of course."

Abigail. He got it.

"Was it a stroke?" Laura asked as they stood outside the doors that had opened at their nearness.

"She's having TIAs." Precursors for a larger stroke. "We'll get her on the right meds and then Mom and Dad will take her to Tulsa for more testing."

"I'm so glad she's okay. She means a lot to me."

He brushed her hair back, letting the strands of auburn silk curl around his finger. "Yeah, you obviously mean a lot to her."

At that Laura smiled. "I'm really sorry she's

doing this to you. Maybe we should be more careful around Abigail and around your grandmother."

"I think that might be a good idea."

Laura leaned to peek inside. Abigail was sitting on Jackson's wife's lap. Madeline said something and Abigail laughed.

"I should go." Laura rested a hand on his arm. "But I'll be here if you need me. And if your mom needs to make other arrangements for Abigail, tell her to let me know."

Jesse let her go. He had to. She moved her hand from his arm and walked back inside. He watched her talk to Madeline, to Heather and his newly married sister Sophie. His older brother Lucky was with their grandmother, and their parents would be there soon.

Abigail hugged Madeline and Jade. Jesse watched what looked like a picture of his life inside that window. He watched his family and the woman and child who had become a part of that family.

They all talked and smiled. They exchanged hugs. A moment later Laura and Abigail walked back through the doors, and he was still standing there. He brushed a hand through his hair and managed a smile for Abigail.

"Is Granny Myrna going to be okay?" Abigail's eyes filled with tears.

Jesse squatted next to her. He put his stethoscope around her neck and let her listen to her own heart.

"Cool, huh?"

She nodded, big gray eyes luminous with unshed tears. He looked up at her mom and saw a twin look of grief in her eyes. He smiled at them both.

"She's going to be fine. I promise."

Laura shook her head. "Jesse."

He knew her hang-up with promises. He took the stethoscope off Abigail's neck and stood.

"Laura, I promise."

She started to object and he shook his head. "I'm telling you, she's fine. If there weren't a dozen people crowded in that room, I'd take Abigail in and show her. I can't do that so I'm telling you—Granny Myrna is good."

"We'll be able to see her tomorrow?" Abigail's little hand found its way into his.

"Yes, you will." He smiled down at her. "So you take your mom home, cuddle up and get some sleep."

Abigail slipped her hand from his and reached for her mom. He watched them walk across the parking lot, get in their car and leave. He watched as a little hatchback pulled through the parking lot, slowed down and then took off.

When he turned around, Jackson was waiting for him.

"You never know what God's going to do, brother." Jackson pounded him on the back. "And for a planner like you, that's pretty rough."

Jesse shook his head and walked inside, away from his all-too-happily married brother.

Chapter Fifteen

People were streaming into Dawson Community Church when Laura pulled into the parking lot on Sunday. She saw a few cars she recognized. Jackson's family was there, as was Reese's. She searched for the black truck that belonged to Jesse and saw it on the far side of the parking lot.

He had called her this morning to let her know his grandmother was doing well. He'd stayed at the hospital with her.

Laura parked her car and looked back at Abigail, who smiled because she didn't know that last night Ryan had followed them to the gas station where he'd approached Laura while she pumped gas. He wanted money. He had to have money. She had thought about calling the police but then she worried that he'd find a way to frame her, to make sure she lost Abigail for good.

"Mommy, it's time to get out of the car."

Laura nodded and unbuckled her seat belt. "You're right. We need to hurry."

She and Abigail were together. They were going to church together. They had a home. Ryan couldn't take that away from them. She wouldn't let him.

Abigail reached for her purple Bible and her doll. "Do they have a class for me?"

"I'm sure they do."

Laura led her daughter up the steps of the church. The man standing in the vestibule smiled and handed them a program.

"We have children's church for the little ones." He looked inside the sanctuary. "Let me see if I can find someone to show you where the class is."

"I'm sure we can find it." Laura smiled down at her daughter. "Can't we?"

Abigail nodded and held tightly to her hand.

"It's through the door, right over there." He pointed. "To the end of the hall and then left. They meet in the fellowship hall for Children's Church."

"Thank you."

Laura knew that everyone turned to watch

them. She kept her eyes focused on the door, and Abigail hurried along behind her.

"Mommy, I can stay with you."

"Do you want to stay with me?" Laura slowed her pace and whispered the question. "It's up to you."

Abigail chewed on her bottom lip and then shook her head.

"No, I want to meet other kids."

"Okay, Children's Church it is." Laura hurried Abigail through the door and down the hall to the big fellowship hall with tables and chairs pushed up against the walls to make room for the kids who were already lined up and starting to sing.

"Abigail!" Jade Cooper hurried to greet them. Laura smiled at the young teen with the sandy-blond hair and big hazel eyes.

"Hi, Jade. I'm sure Abigail's glad she picked Children's Church now."

Jade reached for Abigail's hand. "I told her I'd be here helping the teachers today."

Laura hugged her daughter one last time. "Be good for Jade."

Another step that should have been easy but wasn't. Letting go. Laura told herself to walk away. Abigail would be fine. They'd be together for lunch, and then Laura would take her back to the Coopers for another week. Soon she would have her every day.

"Laura, wait."

Laura turned and smiled at the woman running toward her. Long brown hair, a sweet smile, long flowing skirt.

"Madeline, hello." Jackson Cooper's wife.

"Sit with me?" Madeline drew in a breath as she got close. "I know how hard it is walking into church, not knowing anyone or where to sit."

Laura nearly sighed with relief. "It isn't easy."

Madeline linked an arm through Laura's. "It gets easier. People are curious, but they want you here. And of course they want to know what's going on between you and one of the most eligible bachelors in Oklahoma."

Laura stopped walking. "But there's nothing going on. Jesse's leaving and I have Abigail to think about."

"Laura, I get it, I really do. I shouldn't have said anything."

"It isn't your fault." She managed a smile. "Let's face the music."

They walked through the door together. People were seated, and the music had started. Laura searched for an empty pew. There were a few at the back. Madeline seemed oblivious, and she had a strong grip on Laura's arm.

"This way," Madeline whispered. "The Coopers always sit in the front two pews."

"I'm not a…" Cooper. But Madeline didn't give her a chance to object.

"You're an honorary member." Madeline led her down the aisle. "And that's a blessing, I promise."

The Coopers stood as they approached, giving them a chance to squeeze in and take the empty spaces in the middle of the second pew. They were sitting, getting settled, when everyone stood again.

Laura grabbed her Bible and thought she'd move down or to the back of the church. Instead Madeline gripped her arm.

"Stay, there's room. It's just Jesse."

Jesse slid into the space next to Laura, smiled and sat down. He looked tired. Whiskers shadowed his lean cheeks and his hair looked to have been brushed with his hands after sleeping in a chair all night.

"Glad you made it," he leaned to whisper.

"Me, too."

The choir went forward and the service started. Laura focused on the music, on the cross at the front of the sanctuary and then on the message about hope. She found herself in that message. Because hope was all she'd had for so long. Hope that she'd find a way back to her life. Hope that she'd get her daughter back.

Hope.

And in that hope, she'd found faith. The two were intertwined, keeping her steadfast in the darkest hours of her life.

Jesse reached for her hand, lacing his fingers through hers for a brief moment that seemed like forever. Intertwined. She drew in a deep, shaky breath and closed her eyes. Because this wasn't real. Love wasn't real. She'd grasped at it over the years, trying to hold it, to keep it. It had always evaporated like mist in the summer sunshine.

When church ended, she stood and looked for an escape route to go get Abigail. Jesse's phone rang and he looked at it and headed for the door.

Surrounded, Laura couldn't follow. She greeted people whose names she wouldn't remember but whose smiles welcomed her into their community. Eventually she broke away, walking through the door that led back to the fellowship hall.

She closed the door behind her and leaned on the wall for a minute to get her bearings after the overwhelming surge of people. She closed her eyes and took a deep breath, letting it out slowly.

"Too much?"

She opened her eyes and smiled at Jesse. He still held his phone and she nodded. "A little."

"I'm sure Mom is going to invite you for lunch." He walked with her when she turned toward the room where it sounded as if kids were still in the middle of a lesson.

"I thought I'd go check on your grandmother."

"She's at the ranch with my mom."

"She's okay?" Laura's heart squeezed at the thought of losing Myrna.

"I think so. We're going to do more tests but thanks to you we've hopefully saved her from having a major stroke."

"I didn't do anything."

"What you did last night made all of the difference. If you hadn't told me, Laura, the outcome could have been completely different."

"I hope she's forgiven me."

"She's forgiven you and then some. And this morning she had a visitor. Seems my grandmother has a beau. Winston James from down the road. I never suspected he was the one."

Laura smiled but didn't say anything. She'd known exactly what Myrna was up to and who she was seeing. She glanced toward the room where her daughter had just peeked out to look for her. Laura raised one finger and Abigail slipped back into the room with the other children.

"I need to get her."

"Okay, and then head out to the ranch for lunch with the family. You'll both enjoy it."

"Jesse, they aren't my family. It would feel strange without..." Heat flooded her cheeks. *Without him.* Why should he be her anchor with the Coopers?

From the end of the hall came a "pssst."

Laura glanced that way and saw Abigail peek around the corner. "Mom, we're not going to miss lunch at Cooper Creek."

Next to her, Jesse chuckled. "I think you're not getting out of lunch."

When they had reached the fellowship hall, Abigail exploded with information and stories about the fun she'd had and what they'd done. Laura listened and looked at the pages her daughter had colored. When she turned to say something to Jesse, he was already gone.

Jesse hadn't managed to get out of church as quickly as he planned. On his way out a side door he had gotten caught by Jason Bradshaw. The two of them were planning a canoe trip for the church youth and Jason had a question. When he finally walked out the front doors of the church, the parking lot was nearly empty. He saw their pastor, Wyatt Johnson, talking to a small crowd a short distance away. Jesse's family had all left.

One car caught his attention. An old hatchback was parked next to Laura's little blue sedan. The same hatchback he'd seen last night. A man got out and stood next to the car. Jesse walked down the sidewalk, keeping an eye on the man who leaned casually against the car.

The guy, in his early twenties, grinned and waved as Jesse got closer.

"Can I help you?" Jesse stopped in front of Laura's car and aimed for a casual smile. He turned back toward the church and saw no sign of Laura. She must still be talking to one of the children's ministry workers.

"I'm waiting for my sister."

So this was Ryan. Jesse inhaled deeply to clear the anger that boiled up inside of him at the thought of what this man had done to Laura. There he stood, smiling as though it was any spring day and he just wanted a family reunion, but he was the guy who had put Laura behind bars and caused her to lose her daughter.

There was one thing to do with a man like Ryan, and Jesse knew what it was. Fortunately for Ryan, Jesse had never been the Cooper brother itching to fight. He'd always been the peacemaker.

But today the peacemaker in him seemed to be missing.

"I tell you what, Ryan, why don't you get in that car and head on down the road?"

"Or what?"

"Well, I think I'd start by calling the police."

Ryan eased back a step, his smile fading. "I'm just here to see my sister."

"I don't think you're interested in a visit. What do you want from her?"

Ryan shrugged one thin shoulder. Jesse didn't like the guy. He didn't like his sallow face, his greasy hair or his baggy clothes. He looked like a guy who hadn't quite come down from his last high.

"I need some money to leave the state," Ryan admitted, his eyes darting to the road and then back to Jesse.

"Are you in trouble?"

"Listen, I just want to talk to Laura."

"Laura isn't going to talk to you. You aren't going to call her again. You aren't going to come near her."

Ryan smirked and his eyes lit up. "What's she to you?"

"A friend. And she works for me."

"Yeah, right." Ryan smirked a little more. "I'm sure that's what she…"

Jesse took a fast step forward. "Don't—not if you know what's good for you."

"I know what's good for me. And I know

what it takes to get Laura thrown back in jail and that cute kid of hers put back in foster care."

Jesse stepped back from Ryan because it was the only sane thing to do.

Ryan stood for a long minute like a man weighing his odds and then he got back into the hatchback. After a few rattling attempts, the car started and then pulled away.

Jesse heard a child's voice, light with laughter. He turned and smiled at Laura and Abigail. Laura's smile faded and he knew that she'd seen the car leaving and she knew who was in it. She leaned to listen to her daughter's story, pasting on a smile to let her little girl think that everything was okay.

He waited for them while Laura helped her daughter into the back seat of the car, making sure she was strapped in her booster seat. When she joined him on the sidewalk, her face had regained some of the color it lost when she saw her brother.

"I guess you know that was your brother."

She nodded, her back to the car and Abigail. "He followed me to a convenience store last night."

"He wants money."

"I don't have money. I'm not sure what more he can take from me."

Jesse stepped close. "He isn't taking anything else. We'll make sure of that."

"But what if he does something? I'm so close to having Abigail back."

"He won't take that from you." He opened the car door for her. "Don't worry."

She nodded but he knew she would worry. Until he could figure this out, he would worry, too.

Once she was behind the wheel of her car, he closed the door. He waited for her to back out and get on the road before he climbed in his truck and followed.

When he pulled up in front of the house at Cooper Creek, Laura stood on the porch waiting for him. He got out of his truck and she walked down to meet him.

"You can go on in."

"I can't, Jesse." She glanced over her shoulder at the big house. "You have the sweetest family in the world but they aren't my family. For now they are Abigail's."

"My grandmother would be real hard-pressed not to argue with you on that. She considers you her honorary granddaughter. She'll want you to visit with her at some point today. Might as well get it over with."

"Get it over with? That sounds like a visit I could do without."

"She does get some funny ideas." Like a sapphire ring.

She looked down at the ground and then back up. "What do I do about my brother?"

"Several things. On my way here I called the police, so they can be looking for his car. I have a new phone ordered for you. It should be here tomorrow. Meanwhile, if he calls, you don't answer. If you see him, you stay clear and call the police."

"I'd love a simple life without drama, without worrying what will happen next."

"Give it time." He glanced at his watch. "I have to be at a meeting in an hour but let's go inside and get lunch. I'll be your buffer."

"Thank you." She looked from him to the house. "It's going to be hard leaving her after being with her all weekend."

"It won't be long and you won't have to leave her at all."

Jesse led her into the house and through the living room to the dining room, where the tables had been set for Sunday lunch. His sister Sophie smiled at them as they walked through the room. She'd recently gotten married and they were already expecting a baby to add to the little girl that her husband, Keeton, had from a previous marriage.

The Cooper family was growing.

Laura paused at the door to the kitchen. He saw what she saw—Abigail surrounded by his family, smiling and telling stories. It didn't take a child long to become part of the Coopers.

"Mommy, did you know that Jackson has a new baby? They adopted him."

"I did know that." Laura leaned to hug her daughter.

Abigail shot him a look and Jesse waved. The little girl grinned quickly but then gave her mom a serious look.

"You're going to have lunch with us, aren't you?" Abigail studied her mom's face and then she gave him another look. "And Jesse, too?"

"Of course we're staying," Jesse answered for them both.

He turned to hug his mom and bumped into Jade. She grinned that grin of hers that, if he hadn't known better, he would say she got from Jackson. Maybe she got it from being around him so much.

"What are you grinning at?" he asked as he reached for a glass.

"Abigail had a great prayer request today." Jade smirked a little.

"A prayer request?" He wanted to be clueless, but he had a feeling he knew what a six-year-old girl prayed for.

"Yeah, so if God answers, congratulations. I think Laura and Abigail are great."

"I think you're great." Jesse hugged her. "And I think you are your father's daughter."

She looked at Jackson, who stood across the room talking to their father. "Yeah, I am just like him."

Jesse looked around the room for Laura. She and his mother had disappeared. Probably to go check on his grandmother. That gave him a few minutes to step outside and make a couple of phone calls and say a few prayers of his own.

Chapter Sixteen

Laura made good use of the next two weeks when Abigail would remain at Cooper Creek, visiting her only on weekends. She spent time with her aunt Sally and she helped keep an eye on Myrna. Both kept her from thinking about Abigail not living with her and dwelling on Jesse's imminent departure. The first trip he had to take would only be for ten days. It was the second trip, to Honduras, that made her heart ache.

It was her own fault, she lectured herself every chance she got. She should have kept her distance from him. She had known better.

Now he would be leaving, possibly for a year, and she and Abigail would both miss him. They would both suffer slightly broken hearts. But a year would give them time to heal. A year would give her time to get her life back on track.

The day before he left, Jesse knocked on her door. She opened it and motioned him inside.

"I thought I'd stop by. I'm not sure how much time I'll have before I leave tomorrow."

"I have the list you left, of everything that needs to be done. Don't worry, you'll have a home to come back to." She kept her tone light and it wasn't easy.

"That isn't why I'm here, Laura. I wanted to say goodbye—not give you last-minute instructions. I think we need to talk."

"About?" She walked away because it made it easier. In the kitchen she poured two glasses of tea. She took hers and walked out to the back deck. Jesse followed.

"Are you trying to make this difficult?"

"No, I'm trying to make it easier, but you won't let me. You have to let me, Jesse."

"Easy? This is going to be anything but easy. I'm planning a trip out of the States for a year. At the same time, a little girl is praying for a daddy and looking at me like I'm the answer to those prayers. Every time I touch you, I feel like you're the answer to mine."

"Jesse…"

He stopped her. "I don't want to hurt you. I don't want to hurt Abigail. I don't want to walk away feeling guilty because everyone thought this was a relationship."

"The only two people who think we're a couple would be my daughter and your grandmother." She managed to smile but it hurt deep inside, where promises are made and broken. But he hadn't made promises. From the beginning she had known his plans.

She leaned against the rail, wishing he would let this go. It would be easier if she didn't have to think about him being gone. He stopped in front of her and she looked up, her gaze connecting with his.

"Laura, I don't know what this is." While she stood there waiting for him to break her heart, he brushed a rough and yet tender hand down her arm. "I'm a planner. I've always planned. This is the year I planned a mission trip. I'll be thirty-four in a few months. I planned on meeting someone when I turned thirty-five. That's when I thought I'd be ready for marriage and kids."

Laura smiled at his honesty. She even laughed a little. "What you're saying is that you didn't plan on a woman and a child landing on your doorstep or in your life. You probably even had the type of woman you'd fall for planned."

Beneath his dark skin she saw a hint of red climb into his cheeks. "Possibly."

Before he could say more, his cell phone

buzzed. It was the front gate. He listened and then buzzed in the visitor.

"Laura, it's your probation officer."

She shook her head. "Why would he be here?"

"I'm not sure." With a hand on her back he guided her to the front of the house.

"Two days, Jesse. Abigail is moving in with me full-time in two days." It hurt to breathe and her face felt hot and her hands felt cold. She shivered and Jesse kept her close. He opened the door and the probation officer stood on the front porch and a female officer stood behind him.

"Laura, I'm sorry to do this but we've had a report that you're using."

"Frank, you know that isn't true." Laura's voice and hands shook. "It's Ryan. He's trying to get back at me for not giving him money."

"Laura, we have to do the test." He motioned the female officer forward. "If you could do this for me."

"Of course I can. But, Frank, what about Abigail? I'm so close to getting her back."

"Are you clean?"

"I've always been clean. I've never used drugs. You know that."

"Do the test, Laura. We'll clear this up."

She stared at the bag the probation officer had handed her, made eye contact with the female officer, then turned to Jesse because he had plans and she was pretty sure this wasn't in them.

"Go." She shook her head when he tried to interrupt. "Please, Jesse. I don't want you here. This is my life and you didn't ask for it to be yours. I can't do this with you looking at me like that."

Frank stood aside and motioned Jesse out the door. Laura watched him go and then she walked down the hall with the female officer behind her.

Jesse didn't want to leave her alone, but he recognized that look on her face. She was holding on to her pride. She needed him gone. He got that. He got in his truck and headed down the drive, not even sure where he was headed.

His cell phone rang. He looked at the display on the dash of his truck and shook his head. If he ignored it, Jeremy would just call back. There was no getting away from him.

"What now?" he answered as he pulled out on the road.

"Could you sound any more excited?"

"Not really. It's been a rough day. I'm on my way to the ranch to check on Abigail."

"Could you stop by here? I wanted to show you what I've managed to do in three short weeks." Jeremy cleared his throat. "I just want your thoughts on what I need to do next. I've talked to Doc Brannon and he's interested in volunteering."

"I see." Jesse flipped his blinker and headed down a back road that led from Grove to Dawson and came out on Back Street. "I'll be there in a few minutes."

"Thanks."

The line went dead. Jesse hit the stereo volume on the steering wheel and Brad Paisley filled the cab of the truck. He sang along, glad to be alone for just a few minutes. It gave him time to think and time to pray.

He needed the prayer time. He needed to get his head on straight and decide his next move.

When he pulled up in front of the metal building that now had a sign, Back Street Medical, he sighed. Jeremy knew how to make things happen. He stepped out of his truck and walked up to the building. Jeremy opened the door, smiling as he waved him inside.

There were three rooms in the clinic—a waiting room, office and exam room. A small bathroom was tucked between the office and exam room. He walked through each room and nodded at what his brother had accomplished.

"What do you need me to tell you, Jeremy?"

"First, tell me what's going on with you. You look like a hundred dollars of old money."

"Thanks. Laura's probation officer showed up

at the house to have her do a drug test. Seems someone called her in for using."

"She's clean, Jesse."

"I know that." He brushed a hand across his face. Did Laura know that he believed her? He should have ignored her pride and stayed.

"What are you doing here?"

"She showed me to the door. Actually, she had her PO show me the door."

"She's got to be humiliated. I don't blame her for not wanting anyone to see. But what about Abigail? I hope this doesn't change things for the two of them."

"Me, too. I'm going to have Mom make some calls."

"Jess, it'll work out."

"I know." He put his hat back on his head and looked around the office. "What do you need?"

"Could you help me fill in the gaps? What do I still need? What medical equipment? What supplies?"

"This wasn't cheap to put together."

"No, but we had several donors."

"I admire what you're doing."

Jeremy shrugged it off. "I'm just the guy pushing it through. There are several people making it happen."

"Gotcha." Jesse was impressed. And then he had a crazy urge to be here, to be a part of something that would be so huge for their community. He thought about the kids who needed care. He thought about parents who sometimes felt trapped. They had bills to pay, families to feed and not enough money to make the daily necessities happen, let alone foot the bill for a doctor's visit.

"Jess, don't get that look on your face. This isn't about trapping you into something. I know you have plans and this will be here when you get back. Until then Brannon and a few others can keep it going."

"I know." He walked out of the clinic, back into the warm June sunshine. "I'll make you a list. I'm really glad you're doing this."

"So am I." Jeremy walked him back to his truck. When they got there, Jeremy stared off at the field for a minute and then he grinned. "You know, you should head back to the house. When a woman says go, she usually means stay."

"Not this woman."

"Right, she's different from all other women. I'm just saying, you should probably check on her. Did you take Gran up on the offer of the sapphire ring?"

"Does everyone in town know about that ring?"

"She did mention it in front of the entire town."

"Yeah, she did do that." He shook his head.

"You're lucky she didn't know about you and Beth until it was too late."

"We got our ring after the fact." Jeremy leaned against the door of the truck. "You have to do what's right for you, Jesse. And I don't envy you. I know it's going to be tough."

"Yeah, it'll be tough."

He backed out of the parking space and pointed his truck toward Cooper Creek.

After her probation officer left, Laura splashed water on her face and then leaned over the sink, trying to get it together. Everything would be fine. God would get her through this. She looked up.

"Please, please don't let them take Abigail." She closed her eyes and stood there for a moment, praying for peace.

Her cell phone rang. She answered without thinking, without looking at the caller ID.

"Like my little surprise?" Ryan's voice chilled her to the core.

"Stay away from me. I'm going to get a restraining order."

"Don't be silly. Look, I need money to get out of the state. That's all I want from you. And if you don't, the next time your PO shows up, he'll have the police with him and a search warrant to find the drugs you're hiding."

"I don't have drugs, Ryan."

"You will. I'll figure out a way. Or you can give me the money to leave Oklahoma."

"Why are you doing this?" But she knew the answer. He was desperate. He was high. And he was more like his father than she'd ever realized.

"Because I don't have any other options, sis."

She shook her head and slammed the phone down on the counter. She wouldn't let him take her daughter.

She closed her eyes, blocking his voice and the threats. He was just like his father. They were both abusive, mean people. She'd just never seen it in Ryan. Or in Alex, her ex-husband, another abuser, another person who used her and walked out on her. He also walked out on Abigail. Without a backward glance he packed up and left the state.

A knock on the front door jolted her. She jumped a little and froze. Fear held her in one spot as the door rattled with another loud knock, a fist pounding on the wood.

"Laura, are you in there?"

Jesse. Tears sprung to her eyes. She wiped them away as she walked to the door and peeked out. When she saw him, she turned the dead bolt and opened the door.

She wouldn't throw herself into his arms. She

wouldn't cry. She would be strong because she had to be. He glanced back at his truck and then stepped inside and closed the door behind him.

"You okay?"

She nodded because if she opened her mouth she'd cry. She'd want him to hold her.

"Laura?

"I'm good." She took a deep breath and got past the emotion.

"You're pale. You're shaking. I don't call this good."

"I am." She shrugged. "I will be."

"I brought you a surprise that might help." He opened the door and waved.

Laura peeked out and her heart did amazing flips at the sight of Abigail jumping out of the truck. She was wearing boots, shorts and a T-shirt. She had a fishing pole and a brown paper bag.

"Mom, Jesse is taking us fishing." Abigail ran straight into her arms.

"If you want to go, that is," he offered with a smile that made everything a little better.

"Yeah, I'd love to go." Laura hugged her daughter again, avoiding the fishing pole that she waved around. "I'll pack us a picnic."

"Sounds good. I'm going to feed the animals and give the two of you time to get things ready to go."

He reached for the door. Laura touched his arm, stopping him.

"Thank you."

"No problem."

She could have argued that it was a problem. Her heart made it a problem. Instead she closed the door and waited until he was in his truck before she locked it.

"Mommy, have you been crying?"

Laura turned from the locked door and smiled at her daughter. "Only because I'm happy you're here."

"Are you sad because Jesse's leaving?"

"He'll only be gone ten days."

Abigail frowned. "Maybe a whole year."

"Yes, a whole year. But that's his life and what he wants to do. This is our life. Together. We have a new house. We have a car. We're going to church together. I'm even going to take college classes and be a nurse."

"But we'll still miss him."

She smiled at her daughter. Only to herself did she admit that she would miss him.

"Let's get ready to go fishing."

"I'm ready." Abigail smiled and pulled a plastic container out of the paper bag.

"What's that?" Laura pointed to the container.

"Worms!"

"Eww, gross. Where did you get those?"

"Jesse bought them for me." Abigail lifted the lid and showed her the dirt and a few earthworms crawling to the surface.

"Put the lid back on." Laura shuddered. "I'm going to make lunch, but now I feel all creepy crawly."

And so much better than she had an hour ago.

Abigail followed her into the kitchen. Laura made sandwiches and packed drinks and chips, homemade cookies and apples. Abigail watched with wide eyes.

"Do you think we'll catch fish?"

Laura shrugged. "I have no idea."

"I hope so. I want to eat a fish I caught."

Laura picked up the soft-sided cooler and leaned to hug her daughter. "If you catch fish, I'll figure out how to fry them."

"Deal!" Abigail held out a hand. Laura took it in hers. Abigail watched her closely and Laura put on a smile for her sake.

"Are you ready to go?"

"Yep. Are we walking?"

"I think so." Laura opened the door and they walked out together. She reached back in, locked the door and pulled it closed behind them. It was the first time she'd locked the door.

"What about the puppy?" Abigail stuck out her hand and a black-and-white puppy, one of the border collie puppies from the Cooper ranch, ran to Abigail's side.

"When did we get a puppy?"

"Jackson said it doesn't need its mommy anymore and I could bring it here."

"Nice of Jackson. I'll have to thank him."

Abigail reached for her hand. "I like Jackson."

"Yes, and it was nice of him to give us a puppy. But when did the puppy get here?"

Abigail grinned. "Jesse brought it when he brought me."

The puppy bounded along behind them, nipping at their heels and being a real nuisance. Laura would definitely thank Jackson and Jesse for this little surprise. But she smiled because Jesse had brought Abigail to her because he had known she needed her daughter.

"Should puppies go fishing?" she asked Abigail as they walked down the paved driveway toward Jesse's house. "It seems like he might be a lot of trouble at the lake."

"We can't leave him alone." Abigail walked fast to keep up with Laura.

"What's his name?"

Abigail bit down on her bottom lip and shrugged. "I just call him puppy. So I guess Rufus is good."

"Rufus? Are you sure?"

Abigail looked at the puppy and nodded her head. "I like Rufus."

They walked down the long driveway, Rufus running ahead, then around them. Laura carried worms, trying not to shudder, and Abigail carried the fishing pole.

They walked up the back steps of the big log home. Laura could hear country music on the radio and water running in the sink. She knocked on the back door and waited for Jesse to yell for them to come in.

Instead he opened the door. She stared up at him, unable to process this man in her life, even as a friend. He smiled, white teeth flashing in his suntanned face. Instead of his customary jeans and boots he wore khaki shorts, a T-shirt and no shoes.

"Let me get shoes." He motioned them inside. Abigail stayed on the porch with her puppy.

"Do you think we should do something with the puppy?" Laura sat on the edge of a bar stool as he slipped his feet into leather running shoes near the door.

"Sure, we can put him in the kennel with my dog. It would be better if they stayed here and weren't down there jumping in the water every few minutes."

"Thanks. And thank you for bringing her." Laura looked out the window and watched as her daughter raced around the yard with a fishing pole and the puppy chasing after her. "She's happier than she's ever been."

"Laura, we won't let Ryan take that away from her."

She smiled and nodded. "I know."

He stood and so did she. And they were together in the house, alone. The refrigerator hummed and country music played softly from the radio on the counter. Outside, Abigail laughed. Laura felt her breath hanging heavily in her lungs and she backed away from Jesse and the moment.

"We should go."

He smiled and touched her cheek. "I know."

Within minutes they were heading down a trail to the lake and the private dock where Jesse assured them they could catch fish without having to take the boat out.

Abigail hurried ahead of them, examining different flowers and plants. The puppy had been left behind, in a kennel Jesse used for his dog when he didn't want the animal to follow. The two dogs had barked at first but were quiet now.

Laura stopped at the edge of the covered dock with the short fishing pier extending from the end. Abigail had kneeled next to the water to examine rocks and the quickly escaping water turtles.

"Here we go." Jesse handed Abigail her pole. "Let's get you a life jacket."

She wrinkled her nose. "I'm six and I can doggy-paddle."

"I know, but this water gets deep and I think life jackets are better than trying to dog-paddle in deep water."

Another heavy sigh. "Okay."

Laura forced her gaze to the lake, the setting sun and the waterfowl that skimmed the water, occasionally swooping and coming back up.

Somehow God had known what she and Abigail needed. They had needed this town, these people. And Jesse Cooper. She watched the man who had entered their lives reluctantly but who now seemed to play an important role.

Laura wanted to break the cycle of broken relationships and lack of trust for her daughter's sake. Even as a friend, Jesse was doing that for them. Abigail could see in him that there were good men in the world.

Jesse interrupted her thoughts, taking her by the hand and leading her onto the dock. She stood for a moment, getting her bearings.

"It's safe," he assured her, still holding her hand.

"Of course it is." And somehow she managed to make the statement about the dock and not the dangerous waters her heart seemed to be treading.

Chapter Seventeen

Jesse led Abigail and Laura to the end of the private dock. Laura quickly took a seat on the bench. Abigail was ready to cast out and catch a fish. He smiled as she tried to get the bait and the line to sail across the water.

"Let me show you." He leaned behind her, eased her arms back and helped her cast.

The worm sank with a plop into the mirror surface of the lake water.

"Like that." He stepped back. "Reel it in slowly. Don't get in a rush or you'll miss the fish."

She nodded and cranked with a definite purpose. "Like this?"

"Perfect." He picked up his pole and baited the hook. "Laura, are you sure you don't want to fish?"

"I'll just watch." She stood and eased close

to the rail that surrounded the deck they were standing on.

Jesse stepped close, and his shoulder brushed hers. She didn't look up but he felt her tense. He put distance between them and cast his line, letting it drop easily into the water. For a long time they fished and Laura leaned on the rail, watching.

After a while she walked up behind Abigail and whispered, "Want to eat?"

Abigail shook her head. "We're fishing."

"But it's dinnertime." Laura opened the cooler they had carried down. "Sandwiches?"

Jesse took one, unwrapped it and handed it to Abigail. "We can eat and fish at the same time."

Abigail grinned. "Cool."

Laura smiled at him and he winked.

Abigail finished her sandwich and reeled her line in again. "I need another worm."

He figured they were almost out. He'd baited her hook several times.

"Do you want to do this one?" he asked as he grabbed the plastic container off the bench. The sun had gone down and the sky was now dark blue twilight with a band of deep orange over the hills on the western horizon. He held the container near one of the lights mounted on the wood rails.

Abigail hurried to his side and he looked up to

see Laura cringe a little. But her daughter, a true angler, had a worm out of the container and was waiting for him to show her how it was done.

"Okay, it's easy but takes some grit. I think you have grit." He smiled at her mother. "I'm not sure your mom could handle it. What do you think?"

Abigail shook her head quickly and held the worm up to the hook, her mouth set in a determined line. She did it and he felt a huge dose of pride in her work.

"Perfect. Now cast it on out there and catch a fish."

She eased the rod back, swung and released.

"You're a pro." Jesse placed a hand on her arm. "Remember, reel it in slowly."

"Okay. Do you think we'll catch fish tonight?"

"I hope so. If we do, I'll clean them so your mom can cook them for you."

Abigail nodded, her lip caught between her teeth. "You're leaving tomorrow?"

Jesse sighed. "Yes, but only for ten days."

"To the school?"

"Yep, I'll learn a lot about the mission field while I'm there."

"And then you'll go to South America?"

Jesse kneeled to put himself on her level. "I think so. I'll decide this week."

"Oh." She grabbed the fishing pole as the string tightened and the end dipped. "What's that?"

He liked to call it a break. "It's a fish. Reel it in. I'm behind you if you need help."

She reeled and reeled. The pole bent a little more. Jesse stayed behind her, aware of Laura at their side. The fish fought the line but Abigail kept at it. Jesse reached to help her crank it in and then he grabbed the net and scooped up the bass that hung precariously over the water.

"I caught dinner!" She nearly dropped the rod, doing a victory dance around the dock.

"You definitely caught dinner." Jesse grabbed the pole and the fish. As he removed the fish from the hook, his phone buzzed.

He let it go to voice mail as he slipped Abigail's fish into the live well at the end of the dock. He rinsed off his hands and then he replayed the message left by the hospital.

"I'm afraid my fishing is over. They've been slammed with patients at the emergency room and they need reinforcements."

Abigail's little face drooped, but then she smiled. "We can try again tomorrow night."

"I'll leave you a key for the storage room." He pointed to the little room at the end of the boat stalls. "You can fish anytime you want. Abigail, do you want to let this fish go so he can get a little bigger?"

She nodded and as the fish splashed into the water, Abigail hugged him tight.

"Thanks, Jesse. I love fishing."

"I love taking you fishing." He handed the pole to Laura. "How about a lift up the hill?"

Abigail nodded so he scooped her up and placed her on his back. She giggled and held tight to his shoulders as they trudged back up the path. The flashlight he'd brought cast a yellow glow on the trail. Laura walked behind them and every now and then he glanced back to check on her.

"You okay back there?" He turned and walked backward a few steps.

"I'm good. The fresh air has made me tired."

"Yeah, I'm going to have to fill my thermos with coffee before I head out."

"I can get that started for you while you get ready to leave."

"Thanks."

They reached the house and Jesse set Abigail back on her own two feet. She smiled up at him, her eyes sleepy.

"Abigail, I don't have homemade cookies, but I do have cookies and milk in here."

Laura had slipped off her shoes at the back door. Jesse left his next to hers. Abigail sighed and pushed hers off. He smiled at her and she managed a sleepy smile back. Without asking, he picked her up again and carried her inside the house.

"Are you too sleepy for cookies and milk?" He felt her head nod against his shoulder. Laura had already filled the coffeepot and the machine spurted and hissed as the coffee brewed.

"She'll be fine. The excitement is wearing off and it's way past bedtime." Laura glanced at the clock. "I'll fill the thermos up for you before I head back to the house with her."

Jesse sat Abigail on one of the bar stools and she hugged her knees to her chest, her eyes growing heavier. He smiled at the little girl's mother.

"Take her to the house and use the golf cart. It's charged. There's no need to carry her. I can get the coffee."

"Thanks, Jesse." She put the thermos on the counter next to the coffeepot. "I'll see you tomorrow."

"Do you want me to carry her out to the golf cart?"

"No, I can do it." She picked up her daughter. "She isn't supposed to stay with me."

"My mom will pick her up in the morning. She got this approved."

They were at the door. He pushed it open but

he couldn't move away. Laura looked up at him, Abigail clinging to her neck.

"If I don't get to see you before I leave…"

She shook her head. "Have a good trip. I'll be praying for you."

He nodded and let her go with that easy good-bye that didn't feel easy at all.

Sleep was not Laura's friend that night. Too many thoughts raced through her mind. Ryan and what he might do to her, to Abigail, Jesse leaving and the thought of him being gone for a year. Loneliness.

As the sun came up, she rolled over in bed and then sat up. Forget it. She would get up, work in the garden before the sun got hot and then make a big breakfast for herself and Abigail. She didn't know what time Angie would pick up her daughter, but she thought probably soon after breakfast.

And then Laura would really be alone.

She put on a pot of coffee and walked outside. The sun was barely peeking over the dark green of the trees at the edge of the field. She stood quietly and watched as two deer grazed near the edge of the field.

A door slammed, and the deer raised their beautiful heads and raced off into the woods. Laura turned toward the barn. She watched

Jesse toss hay for the horses in the field. He'd said the grass was getting pretty slim now. They needed rain.

He turned, saw her and waved. She swallowed the lump that lodged in her throat and returned the wave, smiling because maybe it wouldn't hurt so much if she waved and smiled, pretending it didn't matter.

She'd taken this job knowing that he might leave. She'd known not to get attached. But how did a woman not get attached to someone like Jesse?

The garden. She turned to her garden, smiling because she had done something so worthwhile for herself and her daughter. The tomato plants had tiny green tomatoes and the zucchini were sprouting by the dozens. She didn't know how to make zucchini bread, but she would learn.

By the end of summer she and Abigail would be baking together.

She turned and watched as Jesse pushed the wheelbarrow back into the barn. She kneeled in the garden and pulled the few weeds that had sprouted, even though she'd put down feed sacks and covered them with straw. One row at a time she pulled the weeds and she checked the tomatoes for aphids the way Myrna had taught her.

"Hey, do you have any coffee?"

She smiled up at the man standing behind her. Her heart beat a little too fast just looking at him. He pulled off his hat and swiped a hand through his hair. She nodded and stood.

"I put on a pot before I came out here."

"Mind if I have a cup?"

Mind? Yes, a little. Because she had wanted him to leave without saying goodbye. She'd wanted to practice life without him. She'd gotten too used to his presence, to the cowboy in faded jeans and a worn button-up shirt, to the doctor in khaki pants and a starched shirt with a tie.

She'd gotten used to his presence in her life— and to his kept promises.

She walked ahead of him, slipping off her flip-flops as she walked into the house. He stood with one hand on the door, pushing off his left boot and then the right.

Laura poured his coffee and handed it to him. She added sugar to hers. "Do you want a cookie?"

She pushed the container across the counter and he took one.

"Laura, the mission trip…"

She shook her head. "Let's not talk about it. And keep your voice down. I don't want Abigail up this early. She'll be a grouch for your mom if she doesn't get more sleep."

"She's never a grouch."

Laura managed a smile at that. "Yes, she is."

They walked outside, closing the door quietly behind them so that it didn't bang. But the puppy had woken up and it raced across the lawn, chasing grasshoppers.

"I didn't expect this," Jesse said as they sat down on the glider swing.

"What?"

He sipped his coffee and leaned back, taking off his hat and dropping it on the table next to the swing. "This is harder than I thought it would be."

He started to say something else and then he shook his head. Laura didn't look at him—she couldn't. They finished their coffee in silence.

"You'll be okay while I'm gone. The police are aware that Ryan is in the area. The security system gives you an extra layer of protection."

"I'm not afraid." But she was. Of so many things. Him leaving. Ryan. Losing Abigail.

A car pulled up the driveway.

"That's either Mom or Isaac. Both of them have the code to access the gate."

She nodded and stood to follow him inside.

There were two cars driving past her house. His mother's car and an old sedan she didn't recognize.

Jesse's hand was on her shoulder. "That would be Isaac."

"So, I'll see you in ten days." She smiled past her fear and her heartache.

"Yes, ten days."

The front door flew open and Abigail hurried out, still in her pajamas. "Don't leave."

Jesse held out his arms. "I have to, kiddo. But I'll be back soon."

"And then you'll leave again."

He hugged her tightly and Laura's heart fractured a little.

"You should go." She held her arms out and took her daughter.

"I should." He kissed the top of Laura's head and touched his forehead to Abigail's. "I've always known I'd go to the mission field."

She nodded, knowing he was trying to explain, but it didn't help.

"Bye, Jesse." Abigail swiped at her tears. "We love you."

Laura closed her eyes at words spoken so easily but with so much meaning. He wasn't chocolate cake or a sunny day. He was Jesse and they loved him because he had shown them how to trust. She opened her eyes as Jesse walked down the steps.

An hour later Jesse stood on his back porch staring out at the land he'd bought, the house he'd built, Isaac standing next to his aging sedan. Isaac with his curling blond hair, goatee and safari attire. Jesse smiled at his friend who sometimes appeared to be on the edge of poverty but could probably buy half the county.

"Ready?"

"As I'll ever be." He tossed his suitcase in the trunk of Isaac's car and climbed in the passenger seat, avoiding springs that stuck up through the upholstery.

Isaac cranked the car to life and backed out of the driveway.

"What's up?" Isaac squinted and then pulled on sunglasses.

"Second thoughts, I guess. I'm not worried about this school. I know the culture in Honduras."

"Yeah, but a lot changes in twenty or thirty years."

"True."

But he'd seen all sides of the culture. He'd lived the first six years of his life in a house that could have been a palace. He'd ridden in a car with armed guards. He'd watched his dad gunned down by a rival cartel. He'd lived in poverty with his mother and sister when they raced away from that palatial home, escaping with their lives and the clothes on their backs. He'd lived in the orphanage after his mother abandoned him.

He'd been adopted by the Coopers.

"Jesse, we've both known from the beginning that you weren't going to jump right into this. You said you needed to know for sure that you were supposed to go. I've taken that to mean you weren't sure if you were called to this. And going for the wrong reasons...man, that's the wrong thing to do. I have people who are called. They know without a doubt."

"They never doubt?"

Isaac shrugged and looked both ways before pulling out on the highway. "Everyone doubts. That's not what I mean. You can doubt a little, but when it comes right down to it, you have to know that you *know*. This is a big leap."

"Yeah, it is."

"So what's causing the doubts?"

He didn't want to get into that.

Laura, who had made it pretty clear that she needed space because there was more than one heart on the line. Abigail, a little girl who prayed for a daddy.

"There are a lot of ways to serve God, Jesse. It doesn't have to be a foreign mission field." Isaac shot him a look. "I stopped by and saw Jeremy. He showed me the clinic. He said he already has a few doctors rounded up."

"He's doing a great thing with that clinic."

"Yeah, he is. And that clinic is a mission,

too." Isaac watched him for a long minute. "Man, I've known you for years and I have to ask—what are you hoping to find in Honduras?"

"I'm not hoping to find anything." Jesse pulled his own sunglasses out of his pocket. "But maybe I am. There's a part of me that hopes I'll find my family."

"Yeah, I get that. I want you to go with me to this school, but while we're there, I want you to really think about what you're doing. Is this something God has called you to do, Jesse, or is this a burden?"

A call or a burden. He did feel a burden for the people in South America. For the people in Honduras. A burden led to answering the call.

Or maybe sometimes, the burden led to prayer or giving so that someone else could answer the call.

"Does this have something to do with the housekeeper?"

"Don't call her that."

"Sorry."

"Isaac, I've been planning this trip for years. What do I say, 'Sorry, God, but I've met this woman, and she has a kid and I think I just can't do what You've called me to do'?"

"I guess that's a conversation you need to have with God. Maybe take a closer look at the part *you've* been planning." Isaac cleared his throat. "You could tell her how you feel and ask her to wait for you. Long-distance relationships can work. Not that they've worked for me."

"Thanks for the advice, Isaac. You're a real encourager."

"Hey, it's a thought, right?"

Yeah, a thought.

But not a good one. He tried to imagine a conversation with Laura. One where he asked her to wait a year.

He tried to imagine a year without her in it. A woman he'd known for weeks, and yet she'd possibly changed everything.

Chapter Eighteen

Laura had Abigail again on Friday. Jesse had been gone for a few days. They had been sitting at the house staring at each other when Laura got the bright idea that they needed to go visit Myrna.

When they walked up her steps, Myrna opened the door and smiled. Her smile quickly faded as she looked them over.

"Well, look at you. The two of you look sadder than an old hound dog I used to have." Myrna leaned on the cane the family had convinced her to use. "Shall we sit on the porch? My dogs need to come outside and we can watch them while they play with Abigail."

Abigail and the dogs were already racing across the yard. Laura followed Myrna to the wicker furniture and they sat down next to each other on the love seat.

"It's hot out here." Myrna shook her head. "I'd give anything to be a kid and run through a sprinkler on a day like this."

"We could hook up the hose. I'd play in the sprinkler with you," Laura offered.

Myrna patted her leg. "I know you would. It might get that sadness out of your eyes if you let yourself have fun from time to time."

Laura watched Abigail roll in the grass and the dogs scramble over her, licking her face. "Abigail, you'll get chiggers."

"What's a chigger?" Abigail stopped rolling and sat up.

"A tiny bug that lives in the grass. They bite and make you itch."

"Eww. I don't like chiggers." Abigail did like puppies, though. "But it's okay."

"Don't complain tonight."

Myrna laughed. "She'll be itching and complaining by the time the sun goes down."

"I'm sure she will."

"Hair spray will kill them."

"Thank you." Laura smiled at her friend. "You look great. How do you feel?"

"Right as rain. I'm on my new medicine and haven't had another spell since the last one."

"And how is your beau?"

"My beau is the most handsome man in Dawson." Myrna patted Laura's hand. "Well, maybe second to that handsome grandson of mine. But my beau knows what he wants and isn't afraid to say it."

"Myrna…"

"Don't try to deny it, Laura White. I know that moony look in a girl's eyes. And I've seen the same look on my grandson's face. I think it happened to him that very first day, standing in my kitchen."

"I think that first day he was afraid I would rob you blind. And for good reason—you took in a complete stranger."

Myrna watched Abigail for a minute and a slow smile spread across her face. Her eyes twinkled. "I couldn't have planned that accident any better if I'd tried. Look at how things have worked out for you. God has indeed been at work in my family. He brought Jade and Madeline into Jackson's life. Travis and Elizabeth met when she had been nearly left at the altar. Sophie is married to the last man she thought she'd fall in love with. And Reese bumped into Cheyenne at a diner in Vegas."

"They're all very blessed."

Myrna laughed a bell-like laugh. "And so shall you be. Abigail and I are praying and I do believe God is listening."

"Myrna, Jesse is going to the mission field."

"I know he's called to do the Lord's work. I think he's just a little confused about where."

"I think he knows exactly what he plans on doing."

"Perhaps he does." Myrna watched Abigail for a few minutes. "When are you going to start taking those nursing classes?"

"In the fall."

"I'm so proud of you."

"Myrna, I'm not sure where I'd be if it hadn't been for you."

"Don't give me credit for God's handiwork."

"You could have left me on the side of the road. Or called the police to deal with me."

"I reckon I could have, but I wouldn't have. The minute I looked in those gray eyes of yours, I knew you were a special person in my life."

Laura brushed away the few tears that hovered. "You're special to me, too."

Myrna stood, leaning a little on the cane. "Let's stop talking like one of us has a foot in the grave. It makes me a little nervous. I think we should go shopping. We need to get our minds off our troubles."

"Shopping it is." Laura stood and hooked her

arm through Myrna's. "Abigail, let's go shopping. Can you help us get the dogs in?"

Abigail nodded and soon had the two dogs scooped up in her arms. And they were an armful.

"Let them walk, Abigail."

Laura's daughter put the dogs down. "Come on, fluffy white dogs."

Myrna chuckled. "I'm sure she learned that from Jesse and I'm sure he also calls my precious babies 'yappy.'"

"Only sometimes," Laura admitted. She opened the door and Myrna walked through, followed by those same yappy dogs. Abigail eased in with the dogs.

That night, when Laura put Abigail to bed in her new nightgown they bought on the shopping trip meant to lift their spirits, Abigail's eyes filled with tears.

"I don't want Jesse to go away." Abigail reached under the blanket and scratched at her legs. "I want you to tell him we love him, Mommy, and beg him to stay here with us. We don't have to marry him. Tell him that. Tell him we just want him here so we can go fishing and ride the pony."

"We can't keep Jesse here for our own selfish reasons."

Abigail frowned and continued to scratch, now her arms.

"It isn't selfish. Love isn't selfish. I learned that in Sunday school. Love believes all things and hopes all things."

"Wow, that's very good," Laura said in real amazement.

"I like the verses about love. Love suffers, too."

Laura leaned to hug her daughter and she agreed—love sometimes did feel like suffering. "I don't think that's what it means, Abigail. Love can put up with a lot. I think that's more what the verse means."

"We can put up with Jesse being gone, I guess."

"Yeah, we don't really have a choice." She sighed because how much did you explain to a six-year-old? She couldn't tell Abigail that Jesse didn't owe them anything. They weren't his responsibility.

"Can we pray that Jesse won't go?" Abigail rolled over on her side and started to scratch again. Laura put a hand on her daughter's hand.

"Stop scratching. And no, we can't do that. We can pray for Jesse, that he'll be safe and that he'll know God's will. We can't pray that he won't go."

Abigail grinned big. "Unless it's God's will that he doesn't go."

She had Laura with that. "Stay still—we're going to try Myrna's hair-spray trick and see if it stops the itching."

"It'll burn."

"No, it suffocates the chiggers, and tomorrow when you get up, we'll put itchy medicine on the bites."

Abigail got out of bed and followed Laura to the bathroom.

"Mommy, do you love Jesse?"

Laura found the hair spray and when she turned, Abigail had tears in her eyes. Laura breathed in deeply and exhaled. "That's a very big question for a little girl. I love you. I love chocolate cake."

Abigail smiled and snorted a little.

"I love him, too, Mom. And even if he's gone a year, I will still love him. Even more than chocolate cake."

Laura blinked away tears. She had meant to protect Abigail from this heartache. She had failed.

"Let me spray your legs with this." Laura sprayed her daughter's itchy legs and then led her back to bed where she tucked her in tightly with the quilt.

"Close your eyes and I'll say bedtime prayers with you."

Abigail nodded, her eyes closed. Laura said a prayer and kissed her cheek again. "Night, angel."

"Night, Mommy."

Laura stood at the door for a moment, watching Abigail drift off to sleep. She turned and walked back to the living room where she turned on a lamp and sat down to find a mindless TV program that she could drift off to sleep with.

She dozed toward the end of the show but woke to the sound of a car coming up the drive. No one had buzzed to be let in. She glanced at the clock on the fireplace mantel. It was later than she thought, almost one in the morning. The car pulled into her drive.

She eased to the door and peeked out, her heart pounding and her legs trembling. She reached into her pocket for her phone and it wasn't there. She'd left it on the counter.

As she headed that way to grab it, someone pounded on the door. Laura held her breath, her skin tingling as her heart beat harder.

"It's Ryan. Let me in."

Laura shook her head and stood there. If she didn't answer, maybe he'd go away. Instead he pounded harder.

"Laura, I saw you in there. Let me in. Don't be stupid—I won't hurt you."

He already had. He'd stolen her trust. His father, her stepfather, had stolen her trust. Ryan had left her to pay the consequences of his actions and she'd lost her daughter, three months of her life and her future.

"Ryan, go away."

"I just need money. You can get me money. Or you can sit in there and wonder what I'll do next. Let me in or I'll put what I have in your car and call the police."

"I don't have money."

"You're living off one of the richest families in northeast Oklahoma. You have money."

"No, I have a home and a chance to get my life back on track. I don't have money."

"I need to leave the state, Laura. You're my sister, so you have to help me."

She had been down this path before. She had given in to the pleading. She'd been living her life giving in to people who used her. Tonight she wanted to stand her ground, but what if standing her ground got Abigail hurt, or worse?

"I'm not letting you in, Ryan. Because of you, I lost my daughter for six months of her life. I won't trust you again."

"Why do I bother with you?"

"I don't know. Since it seems pointless, why don't you leave?"

"Mommy?"

Laura turned. Abigail, sleepy and hair wispy around her face, stood in the doorway. Laura briefly closed her eyes and prayed a quick prayer. She had to stay calm. And only God could keep them safe now.

"Abigail, go to the bathroom and lock the door." She said it as calmly as she could.

"Is that Uncle Ryan?"

"Abigail, please do what I ask. And get my phone off the counter and take it with you."

Abigail nodded and raced from the room, her bare feet pitter-pattering on the tile. Laura heard her daughter race down the hall and heard the bathroom door close and lock.

The front doorknob jiggled. Ryan pounded again. She reached to lock the dead bolt as he kicked and the door shook with the pressure of his body pounding against it.

"Ryan, I'm calling 911."

"Go ahead. I'll be gone before they get here." He rammed the door again.

In the distance she heard sirens. She whispered a quiet thank-you and looked up, her smile as shaky as her legs. Ryan swore and then his footsteps pounded as he ran.

Laura turned the dead bolt in case he came

back for one last attempt. She peeked out the window as two police cars pulled up. Two officers jumped from one car and ran after Ryan as he fled on foot.

The other officer walked up to the door. Laura's hands shook as she twisted the locks and opened the door.

"Ma'am, I'm Officer Rogers. Are you alone in the house?"

She shook her head. "My daughter is in the bathroom."

He smiled. "Yes, she's on the phone with our dispatcher."

"She called?"

He nodded and stepped inside. "There's no one else in here?"

His hand remained on his weapon as he glanced around the house.

"No, just my daughter and me. My stepbrother, Ryan Baldwin, is the one outside. He tried to kick the door down."

"Do you know what he was after?"

"Money to leave the state."

The officer nodded. "Can you take a seat for me while I make a call?"

"My daughter. She'll be afraid."

"I'll bring her out." He stepped away and talked into the mic on his collar as he walked through the house.

A minute later Abigail raced into the living room and threw herself at Laura. "Mommy, I called 911."

"I know you did." She looked up at the officer. "But she only called a few minutes before you got here."

"The gate is attached to a security system monitored by a private company. When the gate opened without a security code activation, the alarm went off and the company notified our county dispatch."

Laura hugged her daughter tightly. She could hear yelling outside. One of the voices belonged to her stepbrother. The officer who had remained with them walked back to the door.

"Guys, we have an active warrant on Mr. Baldwin."

"A warrant?" Laura continued to hold Abigail tight.

"Yeah, a felony drug warrant."

She closed her eyes but relief didn't last long. "Could you please check my car and make sure he didn't put anything in there?"

"Do you suspect that he would?" The officer stood at the door writing on a notebook."

"He threatened. And he did it once before."

"I'll check the car." He stepped back to the door. "I've had a call that there's someone on the way to stay with you tonight."

"Someone, who?"

He shifted to look out the door. "Mia Cooper is here."

Mia? Laura shook her head. She'd only met Mia once.

"I'm here." Mia was tall with long dark hair and an easy smile. She had a gun strapped to her side. She smiled at the officer and he smiled back, an easy smile as if they'd known each other awhile.

"Hi, Laura and Abigail." Mia took over in a way that didn't seem like taking over. "I'm just here until Jesse can get home."

"Jesse won't be home for a week," Laura explained, covering up her daughter, who had curled against her side and whose eyes were getting heavy with sleep. "Mia, you don't have to stay. We're used to…"

"Taking care of yourself?" Mia finished the sentence. "Yeah, that's what Jesse said. But everyone needs help. Let's call this a slumber party."

The police left a short time later. Laura sipped the water Mia had brought her. "You said Jesse asked you to stay here until he gets back?"

Mia smiled. "Yeah. He got the call from the security company. He immediately called me. I'm in town this week."

"I'm sure babysitting us isn't what you planned to do while you were home."

"Laura, Ryan is gone. They're probably processing him at the county jail right now. You're safe. I'm just here because no one wants to be alone when they've gone through something like this."

She had to admit that it did help. "You're right—being alone wouldn't have been at the top of my list tonight."

Mia grinned and reached for the remote. "How about a chick flick?"

"Romance?" Laura scrunched her nose and shook her head.

Mia laughed and flipped through the channels. "So true—who needs romance? It's messy and makes you feel horrible."

"I take it you've experienced it."

Mia stopped flipping through the channels and landed on an action movie. "Yeah, I've experienced it. The guy couldn't handle a woman with a gun. A strong woman."

"I want to be strong. If we're strong, we don't have to worry about needing a man."

The movie paused mid-action. Mia looked her over, settled her gaze on Abigail and smiled. "Sometimes a girl finds a guy who will love her no matter what."

Laura smiled at the sudden optimism. "I'll take your word on that."

"You should." Mia hit Play and the movie continued with a car going over a cliff. Laura somehow managed to sleep but it was restless with dreams of Ryan peering in the window and Jesse boarding a plane for South America.

Chapter Nineteen

Jackson had picked Jesse up at the school. As they pulled up his driveway, past the gate that now leaned to the side, Jackson shot him a look. Jesse shook his head.

"I shouldn't have left her here alone." He ran a shaky hand through his hair. "Maybe I should have given him the money to leave."

"You had no way of knowing her stepbrother would do something like this. Seriously, Jesse, you've been planning this trip for a long time. If you hadn't gone, you wouldn't have found the answers you needed."

"Yeah, sure."

"You found answers, right?" Jackson was only a year older than Jesse but was always playing the big brother.

"I found answers." He unbuckled his seat belt

as they pulled up to the cottage. He glanced at the clock. Barely six in the morning.

"If you aren't careful, Mia will shoot you."

"I'll be careful. Thanks for the ride."

"Are you heading back today?" Jackson parked the truck but he didn't kill the engine.

"I don't know." He opened his door. "I'll let you know."

"I've got a few horses to haul down south. If you can't get me, call Jeremy."

"Thanks, Jackson." Jesse closed the door and reached into the back of the truck for his suitcase. He walked up the sidewalk and hesitated before knocking.

Jackson waved and backed out of the driveway. Jesse stared at that closed door. Once he knocked he'd have to think quickly what to say. He didn't have a plan.

It was a crazy feeling standing there, not knowing what his next move would be.

The door opened. Abigail smiled up at him, her dark hair in ragged pigtails, her bare feet sticking out from under her princess nightgown.

"You're back," she whispered loudly.

"I am back." He held his finger to his lips. "Is your mom still sleeping?"

Abigail nodded. "On the couch. I'm not supposed to open the door when she's sleeping, but it's you and that's okay, isn't it?"

"I think it is. I'm going to take off my boots and we'll tiptoe inside and make her breakfast. How does that sound?"

Abigail nodded again and opened the door wider. He left his boots on the front porch and followed her inside. Mia was curled up in the big chair with the ottoman. Laura was stretched out on the couch with an afghan over her.

Jesse followed Abigail into the kitchen. She pointed to a chair at the dining room table. He picked it up and carried it to the counter. He lifted her up so that she could stand on the seat.

"I'm glad you're back." She held on to the counter and watched as he opened cabinet doors and the fridge.

"Me, too." He stood with the refrigerator door open. "What do you think I should make?"

"Pancakes?"

He shook his head. "Only if you have the kind that heat up in the microwave."

"We have cereal," she offered.

He pulled out a carton of eggs. "I make a pretty good omelet."

She shrugged and then nodded. "Okay, but not too much cheese."

"You got it." He pulled milk and cheese out of the fridge. He found a package of ham that he could cut up.

"Do I get to help?"

He nodded and searched drawers until he found a whisk. "I'll crack eggs and you can whip them up while I find a pan."

He cracked eggs into a bowl, added milk and slid it to Abigail to mix. "Before I find a pan, we should start the coffee."

"Yeah, 'cause Mommy is cranky without coffee."

He poured water in the reservoir of the coffeemaker. "Yeah, we don't want her to be cranky."

When he turned from the coffeepot, Abigail was watching him, her eyes huge and full of tears. He hadn't really known what to say to her about the previous evening, or if he should even bring it up. The tears meant that even though they were having fun, she had a lot of little-girl worry building up.

"Last night was tough, huh?" He stepped close and she held out her arms to him. Little-girl trust. She should always know how to trust.

She leaned her head on his shoulder. "I was afraid. Uncle Ryan was mean."

"Yes, he was. But not all men are mean, Abigail. Real men, the kind that you'll marry someday, protect and love women—they don't hurt them."

"I want to marry a cowboy." She smiled as she made the announcement.

"Or a doctor?"

She nodded. "A cowboy and a doctor. Like you."

"Yeah, like me."

"I don't want you to go." Tears filled her blue-gray eyes again. He wanted to promise her that he wouldn't go, but he couldn't make that promise.

Behind them he heard footsteps. He turned and smiled at Laura. She stood in the doorway, her long hair a mass of loose curls, her eyes hazy with sleep.

"Jesse? What are you doing here?"

Obviously Mia hadn't told her. "Surprise? Good or bad?"

Laura stepped farther into the room. "Good. Mia said she would stay with us until you got back. I thought…"

She bit down on her bottom lip, and he recognized someone trying to hold it together. Her gaze focused on his face and then switched to look at her daughter. Abigail held up the whisk, letting egg drip back into the bowl.

"I'm making you breakfast."

Laura smiled at Abigail. "I see that."

"I wanted to let you sleep a little longer." Jesse put the milk on the counter. "Hey, Abigail, do you think you could give us a minute?"

Abigail stepped down off the chair. "I'll wake Mia up."

"Good idea." Jesse smiled as the little girl skipped away. He listened as she tried to wake Mia. He heard Mia's groggy reply, soft voices and then a minute later the click of the front door.

Mia, always smart.

Laura stood in the doorway, still watching the cowboy in stocking feet. He filled up her kitchen, her house, her life. She had heard him tell her daughter that someday she would have a husband, a man who was strong, someone she could trust.

Laura couldn't help but compare that someone to him. Her heart ached looking at him.

He opened his arms to her, strong arms, a solid chest, a good heart. "I'm here for you."

The words broke her down. She walked into the kitchen and into his arms. Her cheek rested against the soft, worn cotton of the pale blue shirt, the collar frayed at the seams. It smelled like Jesse, like the outdoors, like cedar and warm sunshine on the grass.

His hands held her close. His arms were strong. She never wanted to leave those arms.

"What are you doing here?" She looked up and

he smiled down at her. He brushed his cheek, rough because he hadn't shaved, against hers.

"I'm here because you needed me."

"Are you always there for a woman when she needs you?"

"Always. I'm always going to be here for you. As long as you want me here."

"Jesse, don't make promises."

"I'm not making promises. I'm telling you that I want to be here. I want to be in your life. I want to hold you and make you feel strong and help you to trust that there are people who won't hurt you, won't walk out on you."

"That sounds like a promise."

"I guess it is. And I don't break my promises."

He pulled her close, inhaling deeply and then sighing. She wanted to stay in his arms, but she couldn't. He was here and none of it really added up.

"What about the school? What about South America?"

"The school was great. South America is a continent in our southern hemisphere and I hope to someday travel there. But not alone. And I do hope to find my mother and sister. Also, not alone."

"You aren't going?"

"My mission is here. I realized that a couple

of days ago. I was sitting in one of their chapel services and it hit me that Jeremy is doing exactly what I've always wanted to do."

"You're staying?" she asked, trying to process what this meant for her life.

"I'm staying. My plans have changed." He stepped close and she held her breath as he leaned, his hands on her back holding her close. She rested her hands on his shoulders, waiting.

"Are you going to kiss me or not?" She laughed a shaky laugh because it sounded so desperate. But she needed for him to make this real.

He smiled and moved one hand to her cheek. Slowly he lowered his head and kissed her. Laura closed her eyes as the moment lasted. He brushed his lips across her cheek and rested his cheek against hers, his mouth close to her ear.

"I love you." His voice, husky with emotion, made her shiver as the words sank in. He loved her.

Eventually he pulled back. Maybe because there was a pan on the stove that was starting to smoke. He reached back and turned it off, moving it off the burner.

"I want to be the man you can trust to always be in your life."

Laura's world spun in a crazy way that made

it hard to process what he was telling her. She closed her eyes and shook her head.

He placed a finger under her chin and tilted her head. She opened her eyes and looked at him, saw in his face the reflection of what he'd said.

"Laura, I'm getting a little worried. I said I love you. There's a proper response when a guy says that and the proper response triggers the next question. Honey, if you could just help me out here."

She stood on tiptoe and touched her lips to his, tasting him, loving him. "I love you, too."

He grabbed her up and held her tight. "That's good to know."

"Is it?"

He nodded as he backed away from her and reached into his pocket. "It's very good to know. I've been planning this all night but in my plans, you gave the proper response. I was a little worried."

He reached for her hand and she shivered at his touch. He smiled at her. "I know we need a little time to get to know each other, but I also know that there are times in life when you know your heart. There are times you see God at work and you just know that He's done something amazing."

"Jesse?" she whispered, swallowing the well of emotion that found itself lodged in her chest.

"Shh." He looked up as he dropped to one knee. He held her hand and slid a diamond and sapphire ring onto her finger.

"Myrna's ring." She blinked back the tears that blurred her vision.

"Shh." He held her hand in his. "She hunted this ring down after she got out of the hospital and she told me to take it and pray about what to do with it."

"And did you do that?" Her eyes watered and she could feel her pulse in her neck.

"I did. I realized that the most important thing God has given me to do is to serve Him. But I also realized He brought you and Abigail into my life and showed me that He had something for me that went beyond what I ever thought I would have. God has given me two people to love and protect."

Laura closed her eyes as he slipped the ring on her finger. He pulled her down to his level. They were both on the floor facing each other.

"I don't want a plan that's about next year or five years from now. I want a plan that includes the three of us *now*."

"Jesse." Her voice trailed off and he leaned to kiss her again.

"Don't say no." He whispered close to her ear. "I know this is sudden, but please, don't say no."

She shook her head. "I'm not saying no."

"Are you saying yes?" He held her close and she felt him tremble in her arms.

"I'm saying yes."

From behind them, someone shouted, "She's saying YES!"

Laura turned to smile at her daughter. "Abigail."

Abigail ran into the room and straight into Jesse's waiting arms. "Mia, she said yes!"

Mia peeked around the door and waved. "Hey. Just wanted to say congratulations before I leave. I just got a call."

Mia hurried into the room and hugged Laura and then her brother.

Jesse stood and held his sister for a long moment. "Be careful."

"Will do, Jesse Pooh."

He watched her walk out of the room, concern settling over him. Laura had stood and she touched his arm. He pulled her close to his side.

"She'll be safe," she offered, and he turned and held her. He picked up Abigail in his other arm. Laura smiled at the daughter who had her arms around Jesse's neck.

"Love hopes all things, believes all things," Abigail whispered to Jesse.

"Yes, Abigail, it certainly does. Love never fails."

Laura looked up and Jesse smiled and leaned to kiss her again. And again.

They were going to be a family.

* * * * *

*If you enjoyed this story by Brenda Minton,
be sure to look for the next book in her
COOPER CREEK series,
coming soon from Love Inspired books!*

Dear Reader,

Welcome back to Cooper Creek! *The Doctor's Healing Ways* is the fourth book in the series, and I hope you've enjoyed reading the story of Jesse Cooper and Laura White as much as I enjoyed writing it! Dr. Jesse Cooper is one of my favorite heroes. He is reluctant, and yet he is the kind of man who always comes to the rescue. What could be better than a reluctant hero and a heroine who is surprised by love? I hope you enjoy this story of second chances and happy endings.

Brenda Minton

Questions For Discussion

1. Laura White takes Myrna Cooper up on her offer and then regrets that decision. She has to face her own insecurity and Dr. Jesse Cooper. What are the reasons for her insecurities?

2. Jesse Cooper is obviously worried about his grandmother, a woman who makes decisions based on her heart and not always with the best judgment. How is this good? How is this bad?

3. Laura comes looking for help from an aunt she hasn't been in touch with in years. The outcome isn't what she expects, and things fall apart. How does she deal with this changing situation? Did she make a mistake?

4. Jesse finds that he has to put himself out there, rather than closing himself off. Why does this happen and how?

5. Laura is in a place where she has to take help from strangers. How does she reconcile this with the situation she finds herself in?

6. Jesse is considering major changes in his life. How does meeting Laura change things for him?

7. What causes Jesse's guilt in the situation with Gayla? Is it founded or unfounded?

8. How do the Coopers change Laura's life—not materially, but emotionally?

9. Laura has more to consider than her own heart. Why does she worry about her daughter's heart in this relationship with Jesse?

10. When does Laura really begin to see Jesse as someone she could fall in love with? What changes things in their relationship?

11. When does Jesse begin to see that maybe God is doing something unexpected in his life and that Laura is more than just a person who needs his help?

12. Jesse is understandably curious about his birth mother and the sister he lost track of. How does this affect his decisions in life?

13. Jesse can see that there is a difference between a burden and a call to ministry. What

are the differences, and how does he make the decision to go or not to go?

14. When Laura's stepbrother comes after her, she has to trust more than the police, more than herself. She has relied on herself for a long time. How is it good that she has learned to rely on others?

REQUEST YOUR FREE BOOKS!

2 FREE INSPIRATIONAL NOVELS
PLUS 2
FREE
MYSTERY GIFTS

Love Inspired

YES! Please send me 2 FREE Love Inspired® novels and my 2 FREE mystery gifts (gifts are worth about $10). After receiving them, if I don't wish to receive any more books, I can return the shipping statement marked "cancel." If I don't cancel, I will receive 6 brand-new novels every month and be billed just $4.49 per book in the U.S. or $4.99 per book in Canada. That's a savings of at least 22% off the cover price. It's quite a bargain! Shipping and handling is just 50¢ per book in the U.S. and 75¢ per book in Canada.* I understand that accepting the 2 free books and gifts places me under no obligation to buy anything. I can always return a shipment and cancel at any time. Even if I never buy another book, the two free books and gifts are mine to keep forever.

105/305 IDN FVYV

Name _____ (PLEASE PRINT)

Address _____ Apt. #

City _____ State/Prov. _____ Zip/Postal Code

Signature (if under 18, a parent or guardian must sign)

Mail to the Harlequin® Reader Service:
IN U.S.A.: P.O. Box 1867, Buffalo, NY 14240-1867
IN CANADA: P.O. Box 609, Fort Erie, Ontario L2A 5X3

**Are you a subscriber to Love Inspired books
and want to receive the larger-print edition?
Call 1-800-873-8635 or visit www.ReaderService.com.**

* Terms and prices subject to change without notice. Prices do not include applicable taxes. Sales tax applicable in N.Y. Canadian residents will be charged applicable taxes. Offer not valid in Quebec. This offer is limited to one order per household. Not valid for current subscribers to Love Inspired books. All orders subject to credit approval. Credit or debit balances in a customer's account(s) may be offset by any other outstanding balance owed by or to the customer. Please allow 4 to 6 weeks for delivery. Offer available while quantities last.

Your Privacy—The Harlequin® Reader Service is committed to protecting your privacy. Our Privacy Policy is available online at www.ReaderService.com or upon request from the Harlequin Reader Service.
We make a portion of our mailing list available to reputable third parties that offer products we believe may interest you. If you prefer that we not exchange your name with third parties, or if you wish to clarify or modify your communication preferences, please visit us at www.ReaderService.com/consumerchoice or write to us at Harlequin Reader Service Preference Service, P.O. Box 9062, Buffalo, NY 14269. Include your complete name and address.

LIDIR13

KIMBERLY WILLIS HOLT

PIPER REED
CAMPFIRE
GIRL

Illustrated by
CHRISTINE DAVENIER

SCHOLASTIC INC.
New York Toronto London Auckland
Sydney Mexico City New Delhi Hong Kong

ISBN 978-0-545-41930-7

12 11 10 9 8 7 6 5 4 3 2   11 12 13 14 15 16/0

Printed in the U.S.A.   40

First Scholastic printing, September 2011

For the Retreat Girls—
Kathi Appelt, Rebecca Kai Dotlich,
Jeanette Ingold, and Lola Schaefer:
Love and Pie

—K. W. H.

CONTENTS

1

ALL ABOUT STANLEY

Halloween was just two weeks away. Trick-or-treating and jack-o'-lanterns—that was all I could think about. But I still hadn't decided on my costume. I thought about dressing as a Blue Angel pilot for the U.S. Navy since that's what I planned to be when I grew up. But I didn't own a Blue Angel's uniform.

On the way to school, I asked, "Do you think the base is going to do anything special for Halloween?"

We lived at NAS Pensacola because our dad was a Navy chief.

"I'm going to be someone that I've never been before," my little sister, Sam, said.

"Who?"

"Princess Elizabeth."

"What's new about that?" I asked. "You're a princess every year." Sam would use any excuse to wear her crown.

Sam frowned. "I've never been Princess Elizabeth before."

"I thought she was Queen Elizabeth." I knew some things about the royal family.

"Queens have to be princesses first," said Sam.

"What are you going to be?" I asked Tori.

My big sister was sitting in the front seat with Mom. We had to drop her off at the middle school before Mom drove us to the elementary school where we went and where she worked as the art teacher.

Tori didn't answer me so I spoke louder. "Well, what are you going to be?"

She turned around and rolled her eyes. "Piper, Halloween is for little kids. I'm almost thirteen. I don't do dress up."

"You mean you have to stop having fun when you're a teenager?" I was sure glad I was in fifth

grade. That meant I still had a few good years left.

"I'll stay home and give out the candy," Tori said.

"Gosh," I said, "the trick-or-treaters won't stand a chance." My sister loved to eat. She'd probably empty the candy bowl before the first goblin rang our doorbell.

Tori glared at me. "Piper Reed, you're mean." Then her head snapped in Mom's direction. "Mom!"

Mom wasn't a morning person. She needed coffee. Lots of coffee. She probably didn't hear one word I said, but she went into her warning tone. "Girls, behave. It's too early for this."

Before the bell rang I met the other Gypsy Club members. We gathered in our usual spot near the front of the school sign. The twins, Michael and Nicole, were already there. But this time there was someone else standing in our circle—a boy with hair that stuck straight up like he forgot to comb it.

Hailey hopped off the bus and raced across the school yard. When she caught up with me, she asked, "Who's that boy?"

"I don't know, but he's in our meeting place."

"Hi, Piper." Nicole flashed her braces. She must have gone to the orthodontist because yesterday her rubber bands were fuchsia. Today she wore orange and black ones.

"Hi," I said, but I was staring at the new kid. He had the thickest glasses I'd ever seen on anyone.

"This is Stanley Hampshire," Michael said. "He just moved here." He punched Stanley's shoulder. He acted like Stanley was his new best friend.

"Oh," I said. "Hi, Stanley. I'm sorry, but this is a Gypsy Club meeting spot."

Hailey snapped, "Piper, you're mean!"

That was the second time I'd heard that today and the morning bell hadn't even rang yet. Hailey was right. I was being mean. My dad was a Navy chief. I knew what it was like being the new kid. I'd moved a zillion times.

"I . . . I was thinking," Michael stammered. "I was thinking Stanley could be in our Gypsy Club."

I gave Stanley a good look over. I'd only lived in Pensacola a year. That first day was hard until I started the Gypsy Club.

"He meets all the qualifications," Michael said. "His dad is in the Navy. He moves a lot, too. And he already knows the Gypsy Club creed."

"What?" I yelled.

Everyone stared at me.

"You taught him the Gypsy Club creed without asking permission of your fellow Gypsy Club members?"

Michael folded his arms across his chest. "I don't remember that being a rule."

"Well, some rules shouldn't have to be spoken."

"Am I supposed to read your mind?"

Stanley stared down at the ground. He was probably real smart and read a lot. Smart people had to wear glasses because they wore out their eyes from reading all those books. That meant my eyes had a lifetime guarantee.

Nicole spoke up. "I don't see anything wrong with Stanley being in the Gypsy Club. It's hard to be new and make friends."

Without saying a word, Stanley glanced around the playground. I guess he was the silent type. The smart, silent type, who had replaced me as Michael's best friend.

Everyone scowled at me. My face burned. I knew when I was outnumbered. Sometimes even a captain has to listen to her soldiers. I saluted him. "Welcome to the Gypsy Club, Stanley!"

All of a sudden, Stanley opened his mouth real wide and shouted, "Get off the bus!"

Then he started to talk very fast. "I mean thanks. You're really not going to regret this. I've never been a member of a club before, but I think I'll be good at it. I once was in the Boy Scouts of America. That's not really a club. The Boy Scouts of America is an organization, but, anyway, I was only a member for a short while. I never earned a badge though. I wanted to earn the knot-tying badge. I really wanted that one bad because my dad is a sailor. I mean, he's an officer, but he sails for a hobby. I go with him sometimes, but I'm not very good at it. Now my brother, Simon——"

The school bell rang. Kids raced by us and went inside the building. I usually dreaded that sound, but now I knew what it meant to be saved by the bell!

Nicole took off for her class while Hailey and

I followed the boys. I wasn't sure about this new kid, Stanley. He'd already weaseled his way into the Gypsy Club. Now he was going to be in my class, too. That added up to a lot of Stanley Hampshire. At least he lived in the officer housing instead of the enlisted housing. That way I wouldn't be bumping into him on my street.

As usual Ms. Gordon made a big to-do about Stanley being the new kid. She always made it sound like a new kid was a gift to our class.

"Students," she said, "may I present Stanley Hampshire. He moved here from Norfolk, Virginia. Stanley, would you like to tell us a little about yourself?"

Uh-oh. For a teacher, Ms. Gordon sure had a lot to learn.

Stanley stood like he was running for mayor of Pensacola, Florida. He pushed up his glasses.

He cleared his throat. "Well, my name is Stanley Hampshire, but you already know that. I was born in Germany, but I don't remember a thing about it because we moved by the time I was six months old, although my mom said I lived there long enough to develop a taste for Wiener schnitzel. But my dad says that's a fairy tale. Next we moved to Bremerton, Washington, and apparently we could see Mount Rainier from our backyard, but I don't remember that either because we moved before I was three. Then after that——"

Ms. Gordon said, "Okay, Stanley, thank you."

"But I didn't get to tell you about the other

places I lived or what my favorite color is or my favorite television show."

Ms. Gordon's right eyelid started twitching. "That's quite all right, Stanley. We need to start our day."

Stanley looked disappointed. "Well, all right, if you say so." He sat down.

Right off, I could see that I was going to have to make a new rule for the Gypsy Club—Gypsy Club members must not be blabbermouths.

At lunch, Michael, Hailey, Nicole, and I learned everything the rest of the class missed.

Stanley had also lived in Groton, Connecticut, and in Hawaii. His favorite color was blue, not the blue of the sky but the blue on his fourth-grade geography textbook. He had two brothers and, according to Stanley, his oldest brother was the smartest human being in the world. "Simon will probably be president of the United States someday."

Stanley told us his favorite song was "Yankee Doodle." How could my favorite song be the same as his?

" 'Yankee Doodle' makes me want to spin," said Stanley.

Hailey was about to take a bite when he said that. She put her sandwich down and asked, "Why?"

Stanley shrugged. "Beats me. I guess the rhythm makes me want to spin."

" 'Yankee Doodle' makes me want to march," said Nicole.

"That's because 'Yankee Doodle' is a marching song," I said.

"If you say so," said Stanley. He chomped on his carrot and swallowed quickly. I knew what was coming next. More about Stanley Hampshire.

Right after lunch, Ms. Mitchell came into our classroom. I glanced at the clock. It was one thirty. I had already been to her room. She must miss me. Every morning I go to Ms. Mitchell's room. While the other kids have to read together in our classroom, I get to read alone with Ms. Mitchell. That's because I have dyslexia.

I love Ms. Mitchell's room. It has an orange beanbag chair I sit in while I read. And she stashes stickers in her drawer—zillions of stickers. She lets me pick out a sticker for my notebook every time I read good . . . I mean, read well. That means I get a sticker every day because I've improved a lot since I started working with her last year. I grabbed my notebook and went to meet her at the front of the class.

"Hi, Piper," Ms. Mitchell said, smiling.

"Sit down, Piper," Ms. Gordon said.

"But I need to go to Ms. Mitchell's class," I told Ms. Gordon.

"Piper, I'm afraid it's not your turn," Ms. Mitchell said.

"But—"

Ms. Gordon's eye twitched. "Piper, please return to your seat." Then she said, "Stanley Hampshire, please come here and meet Ms. Mitchell."

Stanley stood and we passed each other on my return to my seat.

Ms. Gordon said, "Stanley Hampshire, this is your reading teacher, Ms. Mitchell."

Then Ms. Mitchell—my Ms. Mitchell— held out her hand. "Stanley, I can't wait to get to know you."

Uh-oh.

"Well," Stanley started, "I was born in Germany, which I don't remember a thing about because we moved when I was six months—"

"That's enough, Stanley," Ms. Gordon said. "You'll have plenty of time this year to tell Ms.

Mitchell about yourself. For now it's time to read."

"But—"

"Go along now." Even from where I sat, I could see both of Ms. Gordon's eyes twitch.

2

~~~

The New Hampshires

After school, Sam and I waited for Mom at the van. We always waited until the buses left and Mom was finished in her room. One by one, the yellow buses pulled away from the curb and left the parking lot. The roar of engines faded away, and the school grounds became as quiet as a church on Monday.

A few minutes later what looked like a box with legs moved toward us. It was Mom. I ran up to help her.

"Thanks, Piper," Mom said as I grabbed hold
of one side of the box.

I peeked inside. Dried flower petals, seeds,

and plastic cups—stuff we'd used for our spring art projects.

"I need to make room in my cabinets for this year's projects," Mom said.

We put the box in the back of the van and headed to Tori's middle school.

On the way, Mom asked Sam, "What did you do today?"

"We read a book about falling leaves and talked about patterns, but we didn't talk about Halloween."

"You can talk about it now," Mom said. "How was your day, Piper?"

"Okay, I guess." Then I added, "We have a new boy."

"What's his name?" Mom asked.

"Stanley."

"Tell me about him." Mom liked to know about the new students before she met them in art class. She said she wanted to make them feel as special as she hoped teachers made us feel every time we moved to a new school.

"Oh, nothing interesting."

"Just remember," Mom said. "You know what it's like to be new."

"I let him be in the Gypsy Club."

"That's the Gypsy spirit!" Mom said. "I'm proud of you."

At least someone thought I'd done the right thing. Making Stanley a Gypsy Club member was probably the biggest mistake of my life. But I'd have to live with it.

Sam perked up. "We have a new boy, too. I almost forgot."

"What's his name?" Mom asked.

"Kirby. Kirby Hampshire."

"Hampshire?" I asked. "His last name is Hampshire?" Then I remembered Stanley said he had two brothers. And how could I forget Simon, the perfect older brother?

"Yes," Sam said. "Like *New* Hampshire. Only it's Kirby Hampshire."

"Well, I hope he talks less than his brother Stanley."

"He doesn't talk at all. Unless the teacher talks to him, then his face turns red."

"Lucky you," I muttered. Figures. I had to get the Hampshire kid who couldn't shut up.

At the middle school, Tori floated into the car with a silly grin. That could mean one of two things. Either she got a poem published in the school paper or she had a new crush.

"Hi, Tori," Mom said. "Anything special happen today?"

"Nothing much." She stared out the window. "Well, we did get a new student."

"Oh," Mom said. "Seems this is the day for new students."

"What's his name?" I asked. "Simon Hampshire?"

Tori turned around, her eyes popping wide. "How did you know that?"

"I'll bet he has two brothers—Kirby and Stanley." Seems Hampshires were taking over Pensacola, Florida.

"I have no idea," Tori said smugly. "I just know Simon is the smartest guy I've ever met. He's in all of my honors classes."

Tori never missed a chance to remind me that she was a brain. Actually my sister was smart. She read books all the time, but she hadn't worn out her eyes yet. I guess Tori pretty much shot down my theory that everyone who was smart wore glasses.

Tori said, "Simon was the student body president at his last school in Norfolk, and he's already joined three clubs at our school. This is his first day. There's no telling what he'll accomplish by the end of the week. He's even joined the Poetry Club."

"Hmm," I said. "Aren't *you* a member of the Poetry Club?"

Tori ignored me.

"He loves Ted Kooser's poems."

"Ted who?" I asked.

Tori snapped her tongue against the roof of her mouth. "Good grief, he won a Pulitzer and was the Poet Laureate of the United States."

"Of course, how could I forget that," I said under my breath.

"What is a poet laureate?" Sam asked.

Tori's voice softened. She usually reserved her mean voice for lucky me. "It's an honor given to a gifted poet."

"Oh," Sam said. "Sort of like someone who wins the spelling bee?"

Sam was a spelling bee prodigy and she never let us forget it.

We reached the base and the gate guard signaled us through. I turned and saluted him as we rode by.

When we got out of the car, our three-year-old neighbor, Brady, waved from his front yard. "Hi, Piper!"

"Hi, Brady."

"Hi, Sam!"

"Hi, Brady."

Tori stood with her books in her hands, waiting. Finally she said, "Hi, Brady."

Brady walked all the way over to the edge of our yards where his mom, Yolanda, told him he must not step over without her permission.

"Hey, Sam, guess what I'm going to be for twick-or-tweat?"

Tori shook her head and walked toward the house. "I swear that kid doesn't like me. What have I ever done to him?"

Brady might be only three, but he knows a grump when he sees one.

"Twee guesses, Sam!" Brady said.

"A ghost?" Sam asked.

"Nope."

"A vampire?" I asked.

Brady giggled. "No, silly. One more guess."

"How about the president of the United States of America?" Sam asked.

Brady raised his chin and stared straight at Sam. "A pwince."

"A prince?" Sam shrieked. She acted like he'd yanked the crown right off her head.

"Yep." Brady nodded "A pwince."

"Oh." Sam seemed lost for words. Then she told him, "It's really hard to be a member of the royal family. There's a lot of responsibilities."

"Like what?" I asked.

Sam frowned at me. "You have no idea."

"Sam, we're talking about Halloween," I said.

"It's not like he wants to take over a country."

Brady stepped over the imaginary line. Then, as if he remembered, he jumped back. "Hey, Sam?"

"What?" she asked.

"Can I be *your* pwince?"

Sam put her finger to her chin. "I'll have to think about it."

"Just tell him *yes*," I said. "Yes, he can be your prince."

"I told him I'd think about it, didn't I?" Sam marched into the house.

I started to follow her, then I turned and told Brady, "You're going to make a great prince."

Inside the house, Sam picked up the container of fish flakes. She stood on her tiptoes as she sprinkled flakes into her goldfish Peaches the Second's bowl.

I couldn't believe how snotty she was about Brady wanting to be her prince for Halloween.

Sam put the container down with a thump. "I'm thinking about it."

Bruna came over and stared up at me with a look that told me she wanted to go outside.

I grabbed her leash and took her for a walk.

We left our street and headed for the base park. Two weeks until Halloween and I still hadn't figured out my costume. All I knew was that I wanted to be something different. Something no one would think of in a million years. Whenever I thought really hard about something, I entered a dreamlike world. Mom did that, too. Once she forgot and left the car running in the garage for two hours. Chief said we were lucky the house didn't blow up.

What could I be for Halloween? A witch? Nah, too ordinary. A Blue Angel pilot? I'd need a real uniform. I kept thinking of the possibilities.

And that's how it happened.

That's how I walked smack into Stanley Hampshire like he was nothing but air. He fell flat on his back.

I looked down. "Stanley?"

He looked up. "That sure is a cute dog you have. I always wanted a dog, but my dad says I can't have one because I'd forget to feed it, but I'm certain I wouldn't. Although I did forget to eat breakfast once. But I was starving by the time lunch came around and I've never forgotten to eat a—"

"Stanley, why don't you shut up—I mean *get* up?" I held out my hand to him.

Bruna licked his knobby knees. "Stanley, I have to get home. My mom doesn't know where I am." That wasn't a lie. I'd forgotten to tell her. I dashed away, but Stanley hollered, "Hey, when's the next Gypsy Club meeting?"

I could have pretended not to have heard. Instead I hollered, "Saturday at my house."

"What's your address?" he asked.

And then I told him. Great! Now Stanley Hampshire knew where I lived.

3

THE BIG SURPRISE

Mom was on a health-food kick. That night she fixed tofu stir-fry. Last week we had steamed fish and vegetables and eggplant lasagna with fake cheese.

It was my turn to set the table. While I tried to remember which side of the plate to place the napkins, I heard Mom on the phone with Chief. Before she hung up, she said, "That's a wonderful idea, Karl. The girls will love it."

What were we going to love? A trip to

Disney? Paris? Maybe we were going to get a house with four bedrooms. Then I wouldn't have to share a room with Sam anymore. Or maybe we were going to a haunted house for Halloween. Before or after trick-or-treating, of course.

After Chief came home, we sat for dinner. I could hardly eat because I was so excited. I looked down at my plate and stirred the slices of rubbery tofu into the cabbage, celery, and bean sprouts.

Finally Chief said, "Girls—"

I dropped my chopsticks. "He's got something exciting to tell us," I blurted.

Chief glanced toward Mom, "Did you already tell them, Edie?"

"No," she said, looking confused.

"We're going camping," he announced.

"Uncle Leo is letting us borrow his Airstream," Mom added.

"Get off the bus!" I hollered. I stared down at my plate. "I'm so excited, I can't eat another bite."

Mom's left eyebrow shot up.

"But it's delicious," I quickly added.

Tori wrinkled her nose. "Camping? Do you mean, like, in the great outdoors?"

"Is there any other kind of camping?" I asked. Tori's idea for camping was sitting by the pool with a bag of chocolate-dipped Oreos.

"I can't wait!" Sam said. "I've never been camping before."

"You can't wear your crown," I told her. Sam used to wear her crown everywhere until she got teased at school when we moved to Pensacola.

Sam lowered her eyebrows, frowning. "I wouldn't wear my crown camping."

I'd never camped either. Sleeping on Grandma and Grandpa Reed's screened porch was the closest I'd been to camping. I didn't know I wanted to go so badly until Chief mentioned it.

"When are we going?" I asked him.

"In two weeks. Y'all have a three-day break. It will be perfect. There's a park a few hours away in Alabama. Hopefully it will be a little cooler by then."

Two weeks from now? Why did that sound familiar?

Sam's eyes grew wide. "But two weeks from now is Halloween."

Bingo!

Tears welled up in Sam's eyes. "We can't miss Halloween."

"Girls," Chief said, "there will be other Halloweens. This is  a chance to go fishing and sit around a campfire. Breathe some fresh air."

 "But there's only one Halloween a year," I told him. "Can't we go another time?"

Tori sighed.

Chief's shoulders lowered and he sighed. He reminded me of a balloon losing air. "Girls, if I'd known you'd feel this way I wouldn't have gone through so much trouble. Now it's too late to back out."

"Why is it too late?" I asked.

"I've already paid a deposit on the campsite. Plus I've arranged to meet your uncle halfway for the trailer."

"But we can't miss trick-or-treating," Sam said. "We'll miss the candy."

"We'll buy some candy and take it camping," Mom said.

"It's not the same," I told her. "Plus, we'd have to hide it from Tori."

Tori narrowed her eyes at me, and Mom started to speak, but I beat her to it. "Sorry."

Mom put down her fork and leaned over her plate. "There are going to be other kids there."

"Who?" Tori asked.

"Nicole and Michael's family, and Isabel and Abe."

"Is Brady getting to stay and go trick-or-treating?" Sam asked.

"Brady is going camping," Mom said. "Isabel and Abe wouldn't leave him behind."

Sam sighed. "Brady will cry. He was going to be my prince."

I looked at her.

Sam glared back. "I said I would think about it."

"Great," Tori said. "A bunch of little kids and no one for me."

"I'd let you invite a friend, Tori," Mom said, "but we'll barely have enough room as it is. Uncle Leo's Airstream sleeps four comfortably. And there's five of us."

"How about Bruna?" I asked.

"Well," Chief said, "we thought about boarding her at the kennel. That way we wouldn't have to worry about her."

"I'll watch her," I said. I didn't want Bruna to go to the kennel.

"I'll help," Tori said. "Since I can't take any friends."

"Do you girls know what a responsibility that will be?" Chief asked. "There's a leash policy so you can't let her roam loose."

"No problem," I said. I glanced at Tori.

"We'll take shifts," Tori said.

Chief nodded. "Okay. If you're both fine with that, I'll make a schedule list."

"How about Peaches the Second?" Sam asked.

"Peaches will be fine," said Mom. "She's a goldfish. We'll feed her a little extra before we leave."

Sam folded her arms across her chest. "That's not fair. Bruna can go camping, but not Peaches the Second. Just because she's a fish?"

Mom sighed and gazed at Chief across the table. "Who would have thought camping would be so complicated?" Then she turned her focus to Sam. "How about if I ask Mr. Sanchez at the pet store? He probably wouldn't mind one more fish."

Sam nodded. "Okay, if I have to go camping and miss trick-or-treating."

I should've been excited, but I wasn't. Even

though part of the Gypsy Club would be there, I didn't want to miss trick-or-treating. And besides, the way Tori talked, I had only a few Halloweens left. The Gypsy Club had a new mission for the next meeting. We had to figure out a way to change our parents' mind about ruining Halloween.

Saturday, Stanley showed up two hours early for the Gypsy Club meeting. Mom and Chief liked to sleep late on Saturdays, so Mom wasn't so happy when Stanley rang the doorbell at eight o'clock in the morning.

The doorbell woke me, too. I slipped on my robe and walked into the living room. Leaning against the doorway, Mom listened to Stanley tell his story. "And then we moved to Norfolk, Virginia, where I learned to ride a bike and . . ."

When Mom noticed me, she muffled a yawn and motioned me over. "Piper, Stanley is here for the meeting."

"Stanley," I said, "it doesn't start until ten o'clock."

"Simon says it's better to be early than late."

I was really beginning to dislike this Simon and I hadn't even met him.

Mom rubbed her eyes. "Stanley, why don't you wait in the living room while Piper changes her clothes. Have you eaten breakfast?"

"I had a Pop-Tart, but I could always eat."

"Why don't you stay? Piper's dad makes the best pancakes."

"Well, if you insist . . ."

Great! I was stuck with Stanley for two whole hours before the rest of the club arrived. At breakfast I listened to his life story again as he repeated the saga for my family. Tori kept

her nose stuck in a poetry book the entire time
that he talked. But Sam was fascinated.

"Did you ever live in England?" she wanted
to know.

"No, but I've been to the Heathrow Airport," Stanley told her. Then he told her how

he'd eaten sushi there, the kind that floated on little boats around the sushi bar.

Sam blinked. "Did you see any of the royal family at the airport?"

"No," Stanley said.

"Oh," Sam sounded disappointed. "Are you going trick-or-treating?"

Then Stanley said the worst thing he could have said. "Michael asked me to go on a camping trip."

Finally 10:00 arrived. We met in the new club tent in our backyard. We recited the Gypsy Club creed.

We are the Gypsies of land and sea.
We move from port to port.
We make friends everywhere we go.
And everywhere we go, we let people know
That we're the Gypsies of land and sea.

"Everyone in favor of starting the meeting?" I asked.

"Aye!"

"Any nays?"

Silence.

Then Stanley spoke. "I just wanted to say I'm very honored to be a part of the Gypsy Club. I prom—"

"Stanley," I said, "I'm sorry to cut you off, but we have to start our meeting now."

He looked down at the grass and pushed at his glasses.

"We're glad to have you, Stanley," I said. "Now about this camping trip. All in favor of trying to convince our parents that another weekend would be better?" I said, "Aye!"

Hailey said, "Aye!"

Nicole said, "Aye!"

Michael said, "Aye!"

Stanley didn't say anything.

I couldn't believe what was happening. I slowly asked, "Any nays?"

Stanley pointed his arm toward the ceiling. "Nay."

"What?" we all asked.

"I want to go camping. I've only been once. With the Boy Scouts. And I wasn't very good at it then. I wanted to earn that campfire badge, but I didn't."

"Stanley," I told him, "we don't earn badges in the Gypsy Club."

"Maybe you should," he said. "We could have special shirts and as we earn badges we could have them sewn on the collars. Then when people asked about them we could tell them how we earned them. We could make it challenging to earn them, but not too hard. We could . . ."

I stared out the window as he went on and on. My head pounded. My stomach felt queasy. Stanley Hampshire was ruining my life.

4

Rendezvous in Yazoo

We were going camping. Halloween wouldn't happen this year. Sam pouted, but it didn't change Chief's mind. Yolanda told Mom that Brady cried when he found out he would miss out on his very first trick-or-treating.

A few nights after Chief's announcement, Sam and I lay in our beds, wide awake. Sam said, "I wonder what will happen when kids come to our door and no one answers."

That wasn't hard to figure out. I told her,

"They'll turn around, leave, and go to the next house."

"But Brady's family isn't going to be home either."

I sighed. "Then they'll turn around, leave, and go to the next house."

"But—"

"Sam, I'm trying to sleep."

But I couldn't sleep. My mind was on Halloween, too. One of my friends in San Diego said they'd moved during Halloween. Since

they were staying at a hotel, their mom let them dress up in their costumes and go to the mall. The awesome surprise was that all the stores gave out candy. So they trick-or-treated store-to-store. Turned out, Halloween happened after all. That's when it came to me—my big idea.

The next day I called for an emergency Gypsy Club meeting at recess. After we gathered, Stanley opened his mouth as if a ton of words were going to tumble out. I held up my hand to stop his words.

Stanley shut his mouth.

I felt like Superman stopping bullets.

"I have an idea," I told them. "If we can't stay home and trick-or-treat, who says that we can't celebrate Halloween while we camp?"

Silence.

The entire Gypsy Club stared at me as if I'd

said something stupid. Then all together they yelled, "Get off the bus!"

At home, everyone made lists. Well, everyone but Mom. She hated lists, especially since Chief tried to make lists for her.

Chief's List
1. Lanterns
2. Bug repellent
3. Tackle box
4. Rods and reels
5. Bait
6. Pop-up chairs
7. Charcoal
8. Lighter fluid and matches

Tori's List
1. Journal
2. Notebooks
3. Book of poems by Ted Kooser
4. Sunglasses

<u>Sam's List</u>

1. Crown
2. Costume
3. Magic wand

<u>My List</u>

1. Candy
2. Sheets for ghosts
3. Pumpkins
4. Apples
5. Masks

I still wasn't sure what I was going to be for Halloween, but I decided I'd make it when I got to the campgrounds. So I added to my list:

6. Scissors
7. Paints
8. Muslin
9. Needle
10. Thread

Then I thought about Bruna. She needed

treats. Not just any treats—her favorite treats.

11. Liver Lumps

The plan was to drive in our van and meet Uncle Leo at the halfway point in Yazoo, Alabama, while everyone else headed to the campgrounds. Uncle Leo would meet us with the trailer at 0900 hours in the post office parking lot. After we hitched the trailer to our van, we'd take off and meet up with everyone else at the campgrounds in time for lunch.

All the families met at dawn at the base entrance so that we could caravan to Yazoo.

Hailey and Stanley were with Michael and Nicole because they had a huge camping trailer that slept six. Brady's family took a pop-up tent that they'd rented for the weekend.

Tori and Sam dozed, but I was wide awake. I sat in the back seat by myself. Michael's family's RV was behind us, and since Michael was sitting in the front seat with his dad, I turned around and stuck out my tongue.

Then Michael crossed his eyes and touched his nose with his tongue. I still hadn't learned to do that. Michael was the Freaky Face Champion.

The first hour on the road flew by, but even making freaky faces gets boring. Not to mention my tongue became sore.

When we arrived at Yazoo, we waved good-bye to everyone else. Then we pulled into the post office parking lot. No Uncle Leo.

"Oh, dear," Mom said. "I was afraid of this."

"There are five minutes until 0900, Edie," Chief said. "Give him a chance."

Mom sighed. "We're talking about Leo. Remember, he has a terrible sense of direction."

"Why doesn't he use a GPS?" I asked.

Mom shook her head. "Piper, Uncle Leo wouldn't know how to program a GPS."

"What do you expect?" Tori said. "He's the absent-minded professor."

"I've never been absent," Sam said.

"Yes, you have," I told her. "Remember when we moved from San Diego last year? You missed a week of school."

"Well, I haven't been absent this year."

"It's only October. You might get some terrible disease like the creepy crawly disease."

"What's the creepy crawly disease?" she asked.

"You can only catch it around Halloween time," I told her.

To my surprise, Tori joined in. "Yes, that's right. You break out in pink spots all over your body."

"Well, I don't plan to get it," Sam said. "I'm going to be very careful and wash my hands a hundred times a day with soap."

"Good luck!" I told her.

Tori winked at me. "Yep. Good luck."

While we waited, I counted all the blue cars passing by.

"What time is it?" I asked.

"Ten o'clock," Mom said through gritted teeth. "He's lost. I just know it."

"Can't we call him?" I asked.

"Uncle Leo doesn't have a cell phone," Mom said. "He owned one once, but lost it. He said he never used it anyway."

When 11:00 arrived, I was thinking about hollering "Uncle Leo!" at the top of my lungs. It couldn't hurt. I was missing out on the fun. The other Gypsy Club members would be there by now and they'd be able to start putting our plan into action.

Thirty minutes later, I spotted an old beat-up truck with a silver trailer coming down the road. "There he is!" I hollered. "There's Uncle Leo!"

Then he drove right past the post office without even stopping.

"Was that him?" Sam asked.

"Yes." Mom and Chief groaned at the same time.

"Should we catch him?" I asked.

"Yazoo isn't that big. He'll turn around and figure it out," said Chief.

Mom frowned at Chief. "Don't bet on it."

Then I said, "Remember when Uncle Leo forgot how to get to Grandma's home?"

"And he grew up in that house," Tori said.

"Let's get out of the car, girls, so that he'll see us when he turns around."

We climbed out of the van and waited. Sure enough, ten minutes later Uncle Leo came back our way. We waved our arms high above our heads. We looked like we were signaling airplanes.

"Uncle Leo!" We yelled.

But Uncle Leo drove right on by.

Mom shook her head. "How could he miss us?"

Finally Chief said, "Let's catch him."

We climbed back into the van and Chief pressed the accelerator. Our van turned into a

NASCAR racecar. The wind blew through the open windows. Our hair and Bruna's ears flew like kite tails.

"Watch out, Karl," Mom said. "I wonder what the speed limit is in this little town?"

That's when our family met the sheriff of Yazoo, Alabama.

5

CAMP Chic-a-Dee

Chief pulled over to the side of the road.

"Are we going to jail?" asked Sam.

"Behave yourselves, girls," Chief said as the sheriff approached our van.

Chief pulled out his wallet and gave the sheriff his driver's license.

"Mr. Reed," the sheriff said, "we may be a small town, but we have laws."

"Yes, sir," Chief said. "I'm sorry. I was trying to catch up with——"

The sheriff held up his palm.

Chief stopped explaining. That hand trick must work on everyone.

Just as the sheriff handed a ticket to Chief, Uncle Leo drove up.

"Finally," I said.

Uncle Leo rolled down his window. "Excuse

me, sir. Could you tell me where I could find the Yazoo branch of the United States Post Office?"

Mom leaned over Chief and waved her hand out the window. "Leo! We're right here."

Uncle Leo squinted in our direction. "Oh, hi, Edie."

"Hi." Mom sounded mad.

"Hi, Karl."

"Hi, Leo."

"Hi, girls."

"Hi, Uncle Leo."

After the sheriff drove away, we headed to the post office. Uncle Leo helped Chief attach the Airstream to our van. Then we stopped at a diner for a soft drink before heading to the camp. My stomach growled as I watched the waitress serve hamburgers to another group. But Mom wouldn't let us order anything, except a drink, because she had told Yolanda we'd be there by lunchtime. I gulped down my cola while Mom and Chief asked Uncle Leo about Grandma and Grandpa Morris. But Uncle Leo always seemed to answer by telling them something else about hummingbirds. Most people are interested in all kinds of things. Not Uncle Leo. He's interested in only one thing—hummingbirds. Uncle Leo is a hummingbird expert. He's even traveled around the world studying different species, like the Stripe-tailed Hummingbird. Finally we took off for the campgrounds.

A couple of miles out of town, Chief glanced in the rearview mirror. Then he quickly looked again. "I hate to tell you this, Edie, but Leo is following us."

Chief pulled over on the shoulder of the road. Uncle Leo just waved and kept driving in the wrong direction.

"Maybe he wants to take the scenic route," I said.

Mom sighed. I thought it was bad having sisters like Tori and Sam. I guess even really smart people are dumb about some things. Uncle Leo knew everything about hummingbirds, but he couldn't read a map or find his way back home.

At two o'clock we pulled into the campgrounds.

"Where were you?" Hailey asked.

"We were worried," Nicole said.

"Did you stop at McDonald's?" Michael asked. "We had to eat turkey sandwiches. There's only one time a year that I want to eat turkey— Thanksgiving. And I don't even want it then."

"We didn't stop anywhere to eat," I said. "I'm starved." Even a turkey sandwich sounded delicious.

Mom shook her head and said, "Leo."

Chief explained what happened. Everyone laughed.

"I hope Uncle Leo finds his way home," I said.

"We tried waiting to eat as long as we could," Yolanda said, "but we got hungry. I don't know why we forgot to get each other's cell phone numbers."

While I ate my turkey sandwich, the other Gypsy Club members walked to the dock. I hurried and finished. Then I started to take off to join them at the lake.

"Piper, don't forget Bruna," Mom said.

I turned around and walked back.

Mom held out the leash. Bruna was at her feet, wagging her tail.

"You have the first shift," said Mom. "We didn't bring her so that she would be tied to a tree all day."

Bruna stretched up, resting her paws against my legs.

"Sit," I said.

Bruna sat.

Then I snapped the leash onto her collar. We ran toward the dock. The lake was sparkly with a few rowboats filled with people fishing. The trees were tall and thick around us. Before we got to the campgrounds, I could think only about Halloween. Now it was hard to think of anything but camping. I couldn't wait to go fishing and roast marshmallows.

Tori wandered up, holding her notebook. She was probably going to write some boring poems about water.

"Do you think we'll go fishing today?" Hailey asked.

"I don't know," I said. "It's kind of late. When Chief goes fishing he usually leaves early in the morning."

"My dad doesn't like to fish," Stanley said, "but he likes to sail."

"Does your brother like to sail?" Tori asked. Her voice sounded sweet and gooey. I almost didn't recognize it.

"Kirby doesn't like the water," said Stanley.

Tori shook her head. Her face turned red. "Not Kirby. S-Simon."

Stanley looked down at the water, fiddling with his glasses. "Oh, Simon is a good sailor. Simon is good at everything."

"Really?" Tori asked as if she hadn't gone

on and on about him all week. *Simon this.* *Simon that.* I'd had about enough of Simon Hampshire. Before long, he'd probably be the youngest inventor of a new candy bar.

Stanley got real quiet and stared at the clouds. I thought it was hard having two sisters who did great in school, but I knew I could do a lot of things they couldn't. I could draw better. I could teach Bruna tricks. I could run and swim faster than both of them together. But poor Stanley didn't seem to be good at anything.

Stanley looked at Bruna. "Does your dog bite?"

"Nope," I told him. "Want to make friends with her?"

Stanley nodded.

"Let her sniff you first," I said.

"Huh?"

"Like this, Stanley." Michael put his hand under Bruna's nose and Bruna smelled it.

Stanley slowly put his hand under Bruna's nose.

Bruna sniffed and sniffed at his fingers. Then she licked them.

Stanley laughed. "Hey, that tickles."

Nicole started to sneeze. "I'm allergic to dogs."

Michael sighed. "Yep, she's allergic to the whole world."

Nicole sneezed again. And again. She always

triple sneezed. Nicole was a champion sneezer.

Hailey tugged at Nicole's T-shirt. "Come on, Nicole. We'd better get you away from Bruna."

Nicole followed Hailey off the dock and toward the campgrounds. Someone had made a fire.

Keeping the entire Gypsy Club together and taking care of Bruna was going to be harder than I'd realized. Especially when one of the Gypsy Club members was allergic to dogs. I couldn't wait until it was Tori's turn.

I played with Bruna for a while, running back and forth along the lake. When she started panting and slowing down, I walked over to the campsite. I tied her leash to the leg of one of the picnic tables and joined my friends.

Tori stood smack in the middle of them. Tori, who thought she was too old for my friends. Tori, who thought the Gypsy Club was silly. Tori, who had no business sitting where I should have been sitting, announced, "We should write haikus."

"Hi who?" Stanley asked.

I knew what a haiku was because I had Tori Reed for a sister. I guess all her poetry talk dripped on me or something. "Haiku is a type of Japanese poem," I told him.

"It's usually about nature," Tori said, sounding just like the know-it-all she thinks she is.

"Doesn't each line have a certain number of syllables?" Hailey asked.

"Well," Tori said, "real haiku poets don't use this form, but to make it simple we could go with 5-7-5."

"Huh?" Stanley scratched his head.

"Five syllables for the first line," Hailey explained. "Then seven for the second, and five for the third."

"Oh, okay," Stanley said. "I think I remember Simon talking about haikus."

"Really?" The mere mention of Simon's name caused Tori's eyelashes to flutter. "What did Simon say about haikus?"

There was that name again. *Simon.*

Stanley shrugged. "Aw, I don't remember. But Simon won a poetry contest when we lived in Norfolk. They printed his poem in the newspaper and everything."

Sam rose on her tiptoes, trying to meet Stanley's eyes. "My picture has been in the newspaper."

"Well," Stanley said, "Simon's picture has been in the paper a lot for poetry and track and sailing and for earning the most Boy Scout badges and—"

"Okay, Stanley, we get the idea," I said. "Simon can do anything."

"Yeah," Stanley said, "he can. He'll probably be a famous author one day."

"No doubt," said Tori.

"I'm already an author," Sam said.

"You are?" Stanley asked, truly impressed. "What's your book? Maybe I've read it."

"*Princess Samantha, Ruler of the Fair Land of NAS Pensacola.*"

"Oh," Stanley said. "I haven't read that."

"Most people haven't," I told him.

"Well, how about it?" Tori asked. "We don't have to work hard at it. We'll just let the haikus come to us like all good poetry. Pretty soon you'll find haikus everywhere."

We just stared at her.

Tori sighed and walked away.

That night we all sat around the campfire and roasted hot dogs on stakes that Chief and Michael's dad made from wire clothes hangers.

"Enjoy these hot dogs, folks," Chief said. "Tomorrow we're having fish."

"Are we going to get to catch them?" I asked.

"You bet," Chief said.

Sam wiggled. "I don't think I should fish. Peaches the Second wouldn't like it if I caught one of her relatives."

"Sam," I said, "there are no goldfish in that lake."

Sam folded her arms in front of her chest. "They could be distant relatives."

After dinner we slid marshmallows on the wire stakes and roasted them over the fire.

"Piper," Chief said, "be careful. I think your marshmallow is about to catch fire."

I took it out of the flames. It was burnt black to the crisp. "Ah, just like I like them. Crispy on the outside. Gooey on the inside."

Tori laughed. "Let's write a haiku about that. It could start: Gooey marshmallows."

Everyone was quiet for a moment. Then Nicole said, "Burnt black in the campfire flames."

"The way Piper likes," Stanley said.

Everyone clapped. Except me.

"That's great, Stanley," Tori said. "See? Writing haikus is exciting."

I should have known Tori would ruin this camping trip. She was going to squeeze out every bit of fun and use my friends to do it.

6

GONE FISHING

The next morning, it was still dark outside when Mom said, "Rise and shine, Gypsy girls."

I popped up. Even inside the trailer, I could smell last night's campfire. I slipped into my jeans and long-sleeved T-shirt.

Chief had to order Tori and Sam to get up. "Come on, team. The early bird catches the worm!"

Tori groaned. "Remind me, again, why I'm doing this."

Sam kept her eyes squeezed tight. "I don't want to catch a goldfish."

"No problem there," I told her. "If you find a goldfish in that lake, we've got another problem."

"Tori and Sam," Mom said, "fishing is fun. My fondest memories are fishing with my dad on Blue Lake. Leo never wanted to go, though. Maybe you both take after your uncle."

Tori's and Sam's eyes popped wide open and their feet hit the floor. It was amazing how being compared to Uncle Leo woke them up. They yanked off their pajamas and quickly dressed like they were hurrying down to open presents under the Christmas tree.

Everyone at our campsite was going fishing except Yolanda and Brady. They said they would watch Bruna.

I snapped the leash to Bruna's collar and walked her over to Yolanda and Abe's pop-up tent. Abe was outside gathering his fishing equipment. I could hear Brady whining inside the tent. "But I want to go fishing!"

Brady wanted to go fishing as much as Sam didn't. They should trade places.

"Hi, Piper," Abe said, giving me a salute. I'd saluted Abe when I first met him and he'd never forgotten.

"Good morning, sir," I said, saluting back.

"Brady isn't too happy about not going fishing," he said.

"Maybe Mom would let him go with us," I told him.

Abe smiled. "Thanks, Piper, but maybe next year Brady can go after a few more swimming lessons."

Brady cried louder, "But I could wear my floaties!"

"I'm a great swimmer," I said. "I'd save Brady if he fell into the water."

"Thanks, Piper, but Yolanda will take him on the dock later."

Yolanda unzipped the tent's opening and slipped out. "Good morning, Piper."

"Top of the morning to you," I told her.

Brady stuck his head through the opening. "Piper, I want to go swimming."

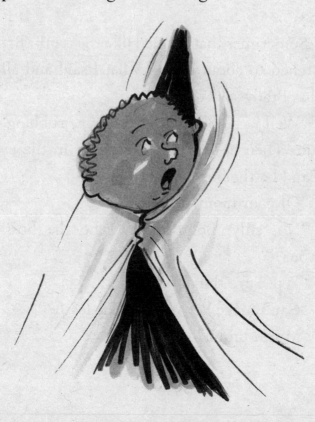

I had to think fast. "But, Brady, who would watch Bruna?"

"Mommy," Brady said.

I cupped my hand around my mouth as if I was telling Brady a secret even though I knew Abe and Yolanda could hear me. "Brady, Bruna might not listen to your mom. She likes you best."

Sometimes that seemed like the truth. Bruna listened to about half of what I said and all of what Brady said.

"Well . . ." Brady stared down, rubbing his chin. Then he looked me straight in the eyes. "Can I be the boss of her?"

"Of your mom?" I asked.

"No, silly. Boona. Can I be the boss of Boona?"

"Yep. Sure thing."

"Can I make her walk on the leash?"

"Mmm-hmm."

"Can I tell her to woll over?"

"Certainly."

"Okay!" Brady said.

Bribing a little kid was exhausting work.

By the time we met at the dock, the sun was just starting to peek above the horizon. It was too early for breakfast, but we waited for Mom and Chief to drink coffee. I didn't mind. Mom without coffee in the morning was not a pretty sight. They quickly drank a cup and then poured the rest of the coffee into two thermoses. Mom took the blue one and Chief took the green.

Everyone gathered on the dock and then divided into small groups. Hailey and Nicole went with Mr. and Mrs. Austin. Michael and Stanley went with Abe and Chief. That meant I was stuck in Mom's boat with my sisters who didn't want to fish. There's nothing worse than being stuck with people who don't want to do

something you want to do. Those people were
bubble busters.

"Here, Piper," Mom said, "take an oar and
make yourself useful."

I took hold of the oar. Mom gave the other
one to Tori. We began to row.

"You're going too fast!" Tori yelled.

"Hurry up then, slowpoke," I said, continuing my pace.

"Girls, you need to find a rhythm and stick to it. Piper, slow it down a bit."

"See," Tori said, her eyes turning into slits.

"Tori," Mom said, "pick up the pace a bit."

I didn't say a word. I just smiled.

A few yards away Chief handed Michael an oar while Abe offered one to Stanley.

Stanley shook his head. "No, I better not. I wouldn't be any good. I'm terrible at sailing. Rowing would be the same. If my brother Simon was here, he could do it. He——"

Abe interrupted him, still holding out the oar. "How are you going to know if you don't try?"

Stanley shrugged. "Well, if you say so." He grabbed the oar with such gusto he knocked Abe off balance. Abe tipped to the side, but held on to the edge to keep from falling into the water.

"Sorry about that." Stanley dipped the oar into the water and stirred as if he was cooking a pot of soup.

"Not like that, Stanley," Michael said. "Like this." Michael had been fishing with his dad a lot. He was an expert rower.

"Oh, okay. I get it." Stanley stroked the water with such force that the oar escaped out of his hands and started to float away. Chief grabbed hold of it, just as it was about to be out of reach.

"Oops," Stanley said. "I told you I wouldn't be any good at it. There's not much that I do well. If you would have asked my brother Simon he could have rowed you anywhere you wanted. My brother is an excellent sailor. He's also won trophies for all kinds of things and earned a whole mess of them. . . ."

Simon, Simon, Simon. I was glad we'd rowed our boat away from the guys' boat and I couldn't hear Stanley's gibber about his perfect big brother anymore.

"Let's stop right here," Mom said. She pointed to a log covered with moss that had fallen in the water. "That would be a great place to find fish."

"There aren't any goldfish in that spot, are there?" Sam asked.

"No," Mom said. "Just some perch."

Sam might be a spelling bee prodigy, but she doesn't know much about science. What did she think a lake was? A giant koi pond?

Mom dug in the bait box and pulled out real, live, wiggly worms. She baited Tori's and Sam's hooks, but I wanted to do my own.

My right hand held the hook. My left hand searched in the bait box. When I found a worm, I gently pulled it out. It wiggled and wiggled. I moved the hook toward the worm. But when the hook reached an inch from the worm, I froze. The worm wiggled and wiggled. I could have sworn I heard it squeaking: "Help me, help me!"

I guess I never thought about what happened to a worm once it was on a hook. Now that's all I could think about. It was as if *I* was that worm. The stab. *Ouch, ouch!* The water. *Gurgle, gurgle!* The fish. *Chomp, chomp.*

While I held the worm and the hook, Sam hollered, "I got one! I got a fish!"

Her float bobbed under the water a few times.

"You sure do, Sam," Mom said. "Hold the rod tight." Still seated, Mom scooted to Sam's side and fixed her hands over Sam's. Together, they yanked. Then Mom let go and Sam reeled by herself. Soon a silver fish appeared above the water.

"Now reel him in quickly," Mom told her.

Sam turned the handle. But before she finished, she pointed her rod straight in the air and the fish swung back and forth above our heads. Sam squealed, still reeling.

The fish swung toward me and hit me in the face. I dropped my worm a few inches from Tori's sneakers.

"Ahh!" she screamed.

"It's just a worm," I told her.

Mom grabbed the fish. "It's a beauty, Sam."

Sam rubbed her hands together. "I'm going to eat him!"

I tried to dig for another worm, but my fingertips barely touched the surface of the dirt. Now that I saw what happened to Sam's worm, I felt like a murderer.

Mom watched me. Finally she said, "Piper, why don't you be my guinea pig and try this new bait." She handed me a box. I wondered what was in this one. Crickets? Grasshoppers? Maybe I wasn't cut out for fishing.

"Aren't you going to open the box?" Tori asked.

"Sure, I am." I held my breath. Slowly, I lifted the lid and stared down at the worms—fake worms, red, yellow, and green worms. This was more like it.

The sunrise turned the sky pink and blue. I

heard Bruna barking and I looked toward the dock. Brady and Yolanda were there with her. Yolanda waved to us. Brady held a fishing pole that must have been three times taller than he was.

"Look, Piper," he yelled. "I'm fishing!"

"Get off the bus, Brady!"

"Look, Sam!" he shouted. "I'm fishing!"

"That's great, Brady. Me too. I even caught a big fish."

"Look, Mrs. Reed," Brady hollered. "I'm fishing."

"My, my!" Mom said. "Leave some fish for us, please."

"Okay," Brady said. Then he was quiet.

Tori's tongue made a snapping noise. "What did I ever do to him?"

I cast my fishing line into the lake. "The kid has good instincts."

Suddenly we heard Yolanda yell, "Oh no!"

We looked toward the dock, but she was pointing to the lake. One of the boats had flipped over. Chief, Abe, Michael, and Stanley were in the water, and Stanley was saying, "I'm sorry. I knew I'd be lousy at fishing."

7

PROJECT STANLEY

Chief and Abe gathered the oars and flipped the boat back over. Michael swam to the edge and climbed in. I wish Stanley would have been with us. Then I could have gone swimming.

Stanley was still a few yards away from the boat, treading water, the orange life vest framing his head.

Chief held out an oar and told him, "Grab hold, Stanley."

Stanley gripped the oar, and Chief pulled

him toward the boat. Then Abe and Michael helped drag Stanley into the boat.

"I guess Stanley isn't that good at swimming either," Sam said.

Mom's right eyebrow shot up. "Sam, we can't all be good at everything."

"That's true," said Sam, "but I'm good at a bunch of things."

"Like what?" I should have known better than to ask.

Sam gently placed her fishing rod on the floor of the boat and began to count on her fingers. "One, spelling. Two, writing stories. Three, dancing. Four, reading. Five, taking care of Peaches the Second—"

"Peaches the Second is a goldfish!" I told her. "What's the big deal about taking care of a gold-fish?"

"It's a very important job," she said.

"And don't forget about Peaches the First," I told her. "God rest her soul."

Tori squinted her eyes at me. "Piper Reed, you are mean."

"Fact is fact," I said.

"Okay, girls, that's enough," Mom said. Then she let out a great big sigh.

Tori shook her head. "It's strange that Stanley isn't good at swimming. His brother Simon is a champion—"

"Stop!" I said, "Don't tell me another thing about Simon. Stanley Hampshire is going to do something wonderful and fabulous before we leave this camp. I'm going to see to it, if it's the last thing I do."

I could hardly believe the words that were coming out of my mouth. One minute ago I was wishing Stanley wasn't a Gypsy Club member, that he wasn't in my class, that he wasn't on our camping trip. Now all I could think about was how I was going to make him shine.

All of a sudden, Sam's fishing pole started moving.

"Get your pole, Sam!"

Sam grabbed hold of her pole and yanked. The red-and-white float bobbed up and down. "Oooo! I think I have a big fish." She pulled and pulled.

Mom helped her reel. The

handle seemed to become harder and harder to turn.

"Oh, my goodness!" Sam said. "It must be really big!"

Figures! I hadn't caught one miserable fish and Sam was on her second. At least Tori hadn't caught any either.

Suddenly Sam's big catch appeared above the water's surface—a great big stick!

"Sam, you forgot something on the things you're good at list," I said. "Six, catching sticks."

Even after the boat turned over, Chief and the guys caught a dozen fish altogether. Although Stanley was quick to point out that he didn't catch any.

By mid-morning, Mom caught two and Tori and I caught one each. Sam caught one fish and two sticks.

"You've got a real knack for that stick catching," I told her.

I was starting to feel sorry for Stanley. "Don't worry," I told him later. "Not everyone can be good at everything. You're good at something."

"If you say so," Stanley said. "I just wish I knew what that was."

I was starting to wonder, too. What could it be? It wasn't sailing, swimming, fishing, or making a campfire. But that left a lot of things. Now I just had to think of them.

After we got back from fishing, Chief, Abe, and Michael's dad cleaned the fish. "Do you want to learn to clean fish, Stanley?"

"Not really. I have a queasy stomach."

He wasn't the only one with a queasy stomach. Nicole was feeling sick. "I wonder if I'm allergic to fishing," she said.

Mrs. Austin told her to go lie down in their trailer. After she checked on Nicole, she came back out. "She has a bit of a fever. Could Hailey stay with you?" she asked Mom.

"Of course," Mom said. "Do you think it could be serious?"

"I'm going to keep an eye on her. But right now I don't want to get alarmed. She might've just gotten overexcited."

Mrs. Austin was a lieutenant, but she always said, "I'm a mom first."

Once Chief overheard her say that, and he said, "Yep, and I'm a dad first."

"Piper," Chief called out. "Do me a favor? Could you put these cleaned fish in the ice chest near the Airstream?"

"Sure," I said, then I had a great idea. I'd let Stanley do it. It was a small job, but maybe it would build his confidence. Accomplishing a small task could lead to a bigger one.

I took the plastic bags of fish from Chief. Then I hollered to Stanley. "Stanley, could you do an important favor for me?"

"Me?"

"Yes, you. Could you put these bags of fish in the ice chest by our camper? It's really important. We're going to have them for dinner."

"Are you sure you trust me to do that?"

"Absolutely."

Stanley pushed at the bridge of his glasses, then reluctantly took the bags. I pointed to our trailer and left him.

I felt better already. Building up Stanley was going to be a lot easier than I thought. Every time I had something important to do, I'd pass the job to him. Soon he would be walking proud. Soon no one would care about Simon Hampshire. Everyone would be talking about Stanley.

"Piper," Mom said, "don't forget about Bruna."

I started to walk over to Yolanda, but then I noticed Stanley had returned from his first task. "Stanley, could you go get Bruna from Yolanda?"

"Your dog?" Stanley asked.

"Yep."

"I like your dog."

"That's why I thought you might want to help keep an eye on her for me."

"Sure." Stanley walked away, heading toward Yolanda's tent where Bruna's leash was attached to the picnic table.

He brought Bruna back to me. "Gee, thanks, Stanley. I really appreciate it."

"No big deal," he said.

He was right. It really wasn't a big deal to fetch Bruna from Yolanda and walk her a few yards. But it was another little step in building up Stanley.

8

No Easy Job

"Is everyone ready for the nature hike?" Mom asked.

Brady rose on his tiptoes "Yes!" Then he whispered, "Will we see any bears?"

"Let's hope not," Tori said. "I didn't sign on for any bear hunt."

"Well, I did," I said. Then I chanted, "I'm going on a bear hunt."

Sam joined in, then Brady. Soon we were all walking and singing about going on a bear hunt. Even Tori joined in. And when she did, Brady said to her, "You're silly."

Tori stopped singing and looked down at him.

Then Brady smiled up at her. "I like silly."

Brady stretched out his hand to her and Tori took hold of it. Together they began again, "I'm going on a bear hunt."

Walking through the woods may not sound very interesting, but Mom and Abe both knew a lot about plants and birds and they made it like a treasure hunt. Mom must have pointed out eight different woodpeckers. Maybe she had more in common with Uncle Leo than she wanted to admit.

Before we knew it, Chief announced, "We'd better return to the campsite and get started on dinner. I can almost taste those perch."

"How are you going to cook them?" Yolanda asked.

"The best way," Chief said. "The only way—fried."

"You can take the boy out of Louisiana," said Mom, "but you can't take Louisiana out of the boy." Mom and Chief grew up in Piney Woods, Louisiana, population 492. And both our grandmothers believed in the same cooking motto: *If it ain't fried, it ain't cooked.*

It would have been a perfect day, if Nicole hadn't gotten sick. Just as I was heading to her trailer window, Chief yelled, "Piper! Piper Reed!"

I knew that tone. It was not the *Piper Reed, you are an outstanding camper* tone. It was not the *Piper Reed, don't tell your sisters, but you are our favorite kid* tone. It was the *Piper Reed, you're in trouble* tone. But I had no idea why. I swung around and saluted. "Yes, sir?"

"Get over here."

I rushed to where Chief was standing next

to the ice chest. It was open and it was empty.

"I thought I told you to put the fish in the ice chest."

"I did. I mean, Stanley did."

"What do you mean *Stanley did*? I asked you to do it."

Stanley stood by, studying the ground, his eyes darting about as if he was following an ant.

Chief folded his arms across his chest. "The fish are gone, Piper."

My face burned. "Stanley, didn't you put the fish in the ice chest?"

Stanley slowly raised his chin. "In? You said *in*? I thought you said *on* the ice chest."

Chief started scouting around the campsite. I decided to help him. Maybe Mrs. Austin noticed the bags of fish on top of the ice chest and put them in theirs. But as I was about to go ask her, I found a plastic bag caught on a lower tree branch. An empty plastic bag. Then Chief found the other one. There had been only two bags, but he kept searching, brushing the ground with his hand.

"Just as I suspected," he said. "Raccoons."

"What?"

"See." He pointed to their tracks on the ground.

"Get off the bus!" I'd never seen raccoon tracks. "Can I take a picture of them?"

Chief frowned. I guess finding something as cool as raccoon tracks didn't matter when the raccoons ate your dinner.

Sam trotted over to us. "Did the raccoon eat *my* fish?"

"Of course, Sam," I told her. "They didn't know you were special."

Stanley didn't say a word. He just dug his heel in the dirt.

Brady walked over and squatted for a closer view of the tracks. "I want to eat fwied fish."

Stanley moved away from all of us like he was trying to disappear. He walked toward the dock.

I took off after him. I was looking forward

to Chief's fried fish and hush puppies, too. But I felt sorry for Stanley. Now I was going to have to work extra hard to build him up.

When I met him on the dock, he was throwing stones into the water.

"I'm really sorry. I guess I messed up big this time."

"It's okay, Stanley. You didn't mess up big. You only messed up by one word. On and in. In and on. They sound so much alike. And really you only messed up by one letter."

Stanley looked up at me. "Gee, Piper. You're a good friend."

I'd had a lot of friends in my life, but I never had any of them tell me that. I was trying to make Stanley feel good about himself and he surprised me and made me feel good.

Mom joined us on the dock. "Stanley, please don't worry. This means we'll have Just in Case Stew tonight."

"Just in case?" I asked.

"Just in Case We Don't Catch Enough Fish Stew. I bought ingredients to make a batch."

Although I guess in this situation it should be called Just in Case the Raccoons Eat Our Fish Stew.

Mom and Yolanda cooked some ground beef in a big pot. Then they added vegetables—corn, beans, peas, carrots. I hated to admit it, but dinner smelled delicious. Fishing and hiking were like swimming. They made me hungry. And even though we didn't have fish, Chief still fried his famous hush puppies.

After dinner, we fixed s'mores with chocolate bars and toasted marshmallows and graham crackers. At least raccoons didn't eat marshmallows.

This was the best camping trip ever. I'd

almost forgotten about Halloween. "Hey, what about tomorrow?"

"What about tomorrow?" Mom asked as if she had no idea, but I could tell she was just teasing. "Is there anything special going on tomorrow?"

"Halloween!" Brady and Sam said together.

I hoped Stanley didn't ruin Halloween. If

Stanley couldn't do a simple task like putting fish in the ice chest, I don't know how he could get through Halloween without messing up something. I had other things to worry about though. I still hadn't figured out what my Halloween costume was going to be.

9

CAMPSITE HALLOWEEN

After breakfast on Halloween morning, Mom surprised us. She gave each of us a pumpkin and a black marker.

"Real jack-o'-lanterns are supposed to be carved," I told her.

It was amazing how Mom could send a warning with her eyebrows. She didn't have to say a word.

I quickly added, "But there's a lot to be said about being original."

Sam studied her pumpkin and then she announced, "I'm going to make a pr—"

"Don't tell me," I said. "A princess."

Sam frowned. "Wrong! I'm going to make a pr—"

"A prince," I said.

"No!" Sam let out a heavy sigh. "I'm going to make a *pretty* goldfish just like Peaches the Second."

"Sam, how are you going to make a goldfish from a pumpkin?"

"Just wait," she said as she drew long eyelashes on the pumpkin.

Mom asked Hailey and me to carry a pumpkin over to the Austins' trailer for Nicole. She was still sick.

"How is Nicole?" I asked Mrs. Austin.

"She said her throat feels a little itchy." Mrs. Austin turned to Hailey. "Are you feeling ill, Hailey? You were in the boat with her yesterday."

"No. My mom says I have a strong immune system. I've never even had a cold."

"Everyone has had a cold," I said.

"Well, I haven't," said Hailey. She always had to be the best at everything.

We returned to the group and worked on on our pumpkins. When we were finished, we had three smiling jack-o'-lanterns, a laughing jack-o'-lantern, two scary jack-o'-lanterns, and a goldfish. We also had a jack-o'-lantern covered with lots of scribbles.

"My jacky-latwen is silly!" Brady said, pointing to it and bursting into a fit of giggles.

I grinned at him.

"You crack yourself up, don't you, Brady?"

"Yep."

I paid special attention to Stanley's. If there was ever a smug jack-o'-lantern, Stanley had drawn one. The right corner of the pumpkin's mouth turned up into a smirk.

"My jack-o'-lantern is named Simon," said Stanley.

At the mere mention of Simon's name, Tori's head swung in the direction of Stanley's pumpkin. When she noticed the snotty grin, she frowned.

"It looks just like him," Stanley said.

"You mean your brother has a pumpkin head?" I asked.

Stanley nodded. "Yeah, I would say so."

By lunchtime I knew what my costume was going to be. I had brown pants and a brown T-shirt in my suitcase, just right for an apple tree. We'd brought more than enough apples for the apple-bobbing game. Now I just needed a bunch of leaves.

I started to take off for my leaf gathering when Tori yelled, "Piper Reed, don't forget Bruna! It's your turn."

Tori walked over with Bruna. She slapped the leash in my hand and dug in her pocket. "Here are the L-I-V-E-R L-U-M-P-S," she spelled.

"Liver Lumps!" Sam yelled. She could never resist showing off her reading skills.

Bruna barked and wagged her tail. I gave her a Liver Lump. Then we started on the trail.

"Don't go alone," Mom called out from the Airstream window.

"I'm not. Bruna is with me."

"Take a friend, and don't go too far."

At her trailer window, Nicole called out, "I'd go with you, Piper, if I weren't sick."

"How are you feeling today?" I asked.

"Better, but not a hundred percent."

Nearby, Hailey was writing on a piece of paper.

I went over to her. "Do you want to walk with me?"

Hailey didn't even look up. "I've got to finish my homework. My mom said if I went camping, I had to make sure I finished it."

Mom overheard and asked, "Do you have homework, Piper?"

"Nah, I don't have any." It was true. I didn't have any homework with me. I left out the part about forgetting to bring it. I rushed off so she didn't have a chance to ask more questions.

Michael couldn't go either. He had to help his dad collect wood for that night's fire.

Stanley was sitting under a tree, listening to Sam read her book to him. Nicole was at the window listening, too. I could tell Nicole was interested even though she had her own copy of *Princess Samantha, Ruler of the Fair Land of NAS Pensacola*. But Stanley was digging his heel in the dirt. He'd made a pretty big hole, probably looking for a way to escape underground.

"Hey, Stanley," I yelled, "do you want to walk with me?"

Stanley jumped to his feet. A grin spread across his face.

Sam stared up, frowning. "He's listening to my story."

Stanley's shoulders slumped as he sat down.

"Mom said I can't walk by myself," I told her. "He can hear your story later."

"I promise I will," Stanley said, standing once again.

"When?" Sam asked.

"Before we go back home," said Stanley.

"I want to hear the rest," Nicole said.

Stanley and I walked quickly away.

"Don't you love Halloween, Stanley?"

"Yep, I do."

We walked along the trail and I started picking leaves from trees on the lower branches and Stanley helped. Most of the leaves hung from higher branches that we couldn't reach.

"Trick-or-treating is my favorite thing to do on Halloween," said Stanley. "Are we going to trick-or-treat?"

"Well, there are only two trailers and a pop-up tent at our campsite. And I don't think the parents are going to let us go to the other campsites."

"I like to trick-or-treat until my sack fills up. Then I go home and dump it and go back for some more."

"You're not supposed to go back to the same houses, Stanley."

"I didn't know there were any official Halloween rules."

"I guess there aren't any official rules. It's just one of those things everyone knows."

Stanley shrugged. "If you say so."

Most of the leaves were on branches that towered above our heads, but soon we discovered a patch of vines wrapped around the trunk and growing on the ground at the foot of the tree.

"Look!" Stanley pointed at the vine.

"Great find, Stanley! See, your Boy Scout skills have come in handy."

"Those leaves look familiar," said Stanley, "but I can't remember why."

Each leaf had three points and there were plenty of them. We picked and picked until we filled up the sack. Then we headed back.

"That was easy," Stanley said.

"Thanks to you," I told him.

Stanley held his head high as we made our way back to camp.

My hands began to itch. "I wish I'd used insect

repellant before we left." I scratched, and when I did, the itchy feeling traveled up my wrists.

"Me, too." Stanley dug his fingernails into his arms.

"Those were sneaky bugs. They attacked and left before I got a glimpse of them. Did you see them?"

"Nope," Stanley said. "I wonder if it was a brown recluse spider. Simon said a brown recluse is very tiny but if they bite, you could lose a body part."

I counted my fingers. They were all there. But they sure did itch.

After lunch, I took a needle and thread from Mom's sewing kit and sewed each leaf onto my T-shirt. Then I tripled the thread and tied it around the stem of the apples, attaching them to the T-shirt and my baseball cap. Now not only did my hands and wrists itch, but so did

my forearms. By the time I was finished sewing on the leaves, my entire arms felt like I'd been bitten by a bunch of brown recluse spiders. I sure hoped I didn't lose both of my arms. If I did, how would I ever be a Blue Angel pilot?

When it was time to put on my costume, my arms and hands were covered in red dots. I tried hard not to scratch, but it was useless. I decided not to say anything. If my parents suspected I'd been bitten by a brown recluse I'd probably have to go to the hospital. At the very least, I'd be stuck in the trailer like Nicole. That was no way to spend Halloween. I went outside to join my friends.

Stanley wore a Superman costume. "Hey, Super Stanley!" I said. "I'm Superman," he told me.

"I like Super Stanley better," I told him.

Stanley pushed at his glasses. "It's Halloween. I can pretend to be who I want."

Michael was dressed as a dill pickle, his favorite food. "How are you doing, Dill?"

"Not so sweet," Michael said.

"Hardy-har-har," I said. "I thought you'd sour for Halloween."

"Are you an apple tree?" asked Stanley.

"Yes," I stood tall and stretched my arms to the side. A few apples hung from my sleeves.

"Oh." He didn't sound impressed. Suddenly my idea didn't seem as fabulous as I thought it was. And I was itching like crazy. It seemed to get worse after I put on my costume.

Even though Hailey wasn't feeling well, she wore her mom's lieutenant uniform shirt and hat and waved to us from the open window. Dressed in his crown and cape, Prince Brady settled next to Princess Elizabeth.

Our parents pulled out the lawn chairs and sat. It was time for the costume parade. Sam and Brady were first. I wish I'd been first. That way I could get out of my itchy costume.

"Princess Elizabeth and Prince Brady!" Tori announced in her anchorwoman's voice. I liked how Tori thought she was too old for trick-or-treat, but didn't want to miss out on all the fun.

"Pwince Billy Bob," Brady said.

"Billy Bob?" Sam was not pleased. "There is no Prince Billy Bob."

"Yep," Brady said. "That's me."

They walked together in front of the parents. Brady held his crown as he inched carefully by, but Sam had lots of practice with a crown on her head. She pranced a few steps in front of him. I guess Princess Elizabeth didn't want to be caught walking side by side with a prince named Billy Bob.

"Mr. Dill Pickle," Tori called out with a wave of her arm.

Michael wiggled as he walked, a kind of pickle dance, I guessed.

When Michael finished, Tori said, "Is it a bird?"

Everyone yelled, "No!"

"Is it a plane?"

"No!"

"There's no need to fear. Superman is here!"

Stanley climbed atop the picnic table, jumped, and flexed his skinny biceps. Then he stretched out his arms and ran by the adults, stopping just short of a tree. Blue sleeves hid his arms, but I could see his pink polka-dotted hands. I looked down at my hands. They were covered with the same pink dots. So were my arms. I hummed "Yankee Doodle" to try and keep my mind off the itching.

"An apple tree," said Tori. She said it as if she was having to fight off a yawn.

My body itched all over. I continued to hum. I felt like twirling to keep from wanting to scratch. Then I had an idea. I wasn't just an apple tree.

"Apple tree in a tornado," I whispered to Tori.

"Huh?" She wrinkled her nose. "Okay. Apple tree in a TORNADO."

I closed my eyes and hummed "Yankee Doodle." I twirled and twirled. The apples fell off to the ground with a thump. Get off the bus! I was like a real tornado.

Even though I was dizzy, I peeked, trying to see Chief's reaction. His mouth dropped open. "Piper, what on earth did you get into?"

I stopped and tried to focus. Everything and everyone was still spinning. The lake looked like it flew into the sky. I fell to the ground.

"Are those real leaves?" Abe asked, standing above me.

"Yep. Stanley and I found them on the trail."

Mom bent over and took a close look. She gasped. "Piper! That's poison ivy all over your costume! Get out of those clothes quick!"

At first I froze. Then I rushed into the trailer

and shed my clothes. From inside, I heard Stanley say, "I knew there was something familiar about those leaves. We learned about poison ivy in Boy Scouts."

Then Abe hollered, "Stanley, you must have gotten into it, too. Run to our tent and change."

Mom put on Chief's work gloves and threw my apple tree clothes and hat in a garbage sack. She spread pink lotion over my arms and hands. She made me swallow some medicine for the infection. And then she took the lotion and medicine over to Abe so that he could help Stanley. His parents' note said he wasn't allergic to anything. It was a good thing his name wasn't Nicole Austin.

A few minutes later, dressed in plain clothes, Stanley and I joined the others. That was the quickest amount of time I had ever worn a Halloween costume.

Suddenly Sam said, "I know what Piper and Stanley are."

"What?" I asked.

"Pink polka-dot monsters with the creepy crawly disease."

Everyone laughed. I was just glad the pink lotion made most of the itching go away.

Later we bobbed for apples. When it got dark, we sat in a circle around the fire and listened to Tori tell scary stories. Only they weren't scary.

"She opened the door and BOO!" Tori said. But Brady and Sam grabbed hands and squealed. Even Nicole squealed. From her window.

Just when I thought I couldn't take another of Tori's boring stories, something hit my head. Worms! It was raining big glowing worms. We all screamed then. Until we discovered Chief and Abe up in the tree above us.

Then we went trick-or-treating. When we knocked on the Airstream door, Mom and

Chief answered. Mom wore a witch's hat and a cat mask covered Chief's face.

At the tent, Yolanda and Abe were dressed like a caveman and cavewoman.

Mr. and Mrs. Austin wore cowboy hats. "Howdy, partners," they said, tipping their hats.

After they dropped candy in our bags, I glanced down in my sack. This was the puniest amount of candy I'd ever got on Halloween. Then I announced, "Hey, maybe we should trick-or-treat Stanley style."

Everyone followed Stanley and me as we rushed back to the Airstream. We held our sacks out, ready to shout, "Trick or treat!"

The door slowly opened, and to our surprise, a ghost stood there.

"Ahh!" we yelled, jumping back.

"Aw, it's only Tori under a sheet," I said. But secretly I wanted to yell "Get off the bus!"

My sister had actually surprised me, only for a second, though.

Yolanda and Abe became firemen on their second round. The Austins put on redbird masks. We returned, again and again, to the trailers and tent, never knowing who we'd find behind the doors. It really felt like we were trick-or-treating at different homes. Only it was better.

Suddenly Mom said, "Piper, where is Bruna?"

I jumped up and gasped. "Bruna!"

The last time I'd seen her was hours ago when I was still an apple tree and Stanley was still Super Stanley.

10

CALLING BRUNA

Little beams from our flashlights bounced against the woods.

"Bruna! Bruna!" We called out.

"Boona," cried Brady.

We were all there except for Nicole and Mrs. Austin who stayed behind at the campsite.

My heart felt like it had dropped into my stomach. It was my fault. I was in charge of Bruna. I'd been the one to convince Mom and

Chief to let her come camping with us. Now she was lost.

I thought about the day we went to pick her up at the poodle lady's house. I'd wanted a German shepherd instead of a poodle until I saw those little floppy ears and her bobbed tail with a pom-pom. I thought about how she slept with me and kept my cold feet warm at the foot of the bed. I thought about the tricks I'd taught her and how we almost won the Gypsy Club Pet Show. A big lump lodged in my throat. It was so big, I couldn't even call out her name.

The wind blew through the tree branches and made a crackle sound. Above our heads I heard a *hoot-hoot*.

"What's that?" asked Sam.

"An owl," Mom said. Then she and Sam went back to calling, "Bruna! Bruna!"

A thin cloud drifted in front of a full moon. It felt like a Halloween night with all the eerie sounds and sights. Now I really was scared. I was scared for Bruna.

That big knot in my throat kept me from joining in with the others. Then I noticed Stanley wasn't calling her name either. He was fiddling with the flashlight, turning it on and off.

I walked closer to him.

"I'm thinking," Stanley said.

"About what?" I asked.

"Bruna. You know if I was a dog, it might scare me if a whole bunch of people were yelling my name. I'd think I was in trouble."

Stanley had a point. He continued explaining. "And if I was a dog out exploring in the woods, having a fun time, I'd have to have a real good reason to stop."

"Yes?"

Stanley shined his flashlight under his chin so that his entire face glowed. "What does Bruna like better than anything in the whole world?"

I thought hard, trying to think of what it was that Bruna liked the most. I slipped my hands in my pockets. That's when I knew.

Then above everyone's voices calling out "Bruna!" I yelled, "Get off the bus!"

Every flashlight turned toward me. It was so bright I covered my eyes until they pointed them to the ground.

"What's wrong, Piper?" Chief asked.

"I have a great idea. I mean Stanley has a great idea."

"You're kidding," Hailey said.

"No." I frowned at her and continued. "It's a really, really great idea. Stanley said we should think about what Bruna wants more than anything in the world."

"And just what would that be?" Tori asked.

"Liver Lumps!" I said.

Mom nodded, smiling. "Great idea, Stanley. Piper, why don't you give it a try? And the rest of us will keep quiet."

I took a deep breath and yelled at the top of my voice. So loud that everyone covered their ears. "Bruna, Liver Lump! Liver Lump, Bruna! Liver Lump, Liver Lump!"

We began to walk again, the light from our flashlights dotting the trail. My voice was the only one, calling, "Liver Lump, Bruna." I made sure to make my voice sound happy like Bruna had done something good even though running away was bad. Still we couldn't blame her for wanting to explore. She was a dog, after all.

My arms felt itchy again. I scratched and scratched as we walked and walked. I was starting to think Stanley's brilliant idea wasn't so brilliant. That big knot came back and my eyes went all blurry. I didn't want to know what it was like to not have Bruna in my life. But it looked like I was going to have to find out.

Then I heard a bark. A familiar bark. Sam covered her mouth with both hands, but she jumped up and down. Brady joined her, covering his mouth, too.

Soon we heard some bushes rustling. We pointed our flashlights in the direction of the shaking bush. And then we saw the little floppy ears, the bobbed tail with the pom-pom.

Get off the bus!

Bruna walked over to me and sat. Dried leaves stuck to her coat. She looked up.

I patted her head. "Good girl."

She stood and wagged her tail.

"Good girl," I said again.

She barked.

"What's wrong, Bruna?" I asked.

Then our entire group of campers yelled, "She wants a Liver Lump!"

"Genius," muttered Tori.

"Oh, I knew that." I dug in my pocket and pulled out five Liver Lumps. And although I usually gave her only one or two a day, this time, I gave her every one of them. It was Halloween, after all.

And it was the best Halloween ever—poison ivy and pink polka dots and finding Bruna. And it wouldn't have happened without Stanley's great idea. Finally Stanley could do something special that none of us could do. Not even his pumpkin head brother Simon. Stanley Hampshire could think like a dog!

11

Happy Trails

While Chief cooked pancakes for breakfast the next morning, I took paper, scissors, and markers, and made something for Stanley. The idea came to me after we found Bruna. Michael and Hailey agreed we should do it.

I gobbled down three pancakes. Then I put Bruna on her leash and together we walked to the lake. After what happened last night, I didn't want her out of my sight.

The Gypsy Club met me on the dock. Nicole

must have gotten better because she was there, too.

"Today we have a special presentation for our newest member—Stanley Hampshire."

Stanley's eyes popped wide. "Me? Gosh, what did I do that was so special? I mean I'm not saying that I don't want to have a special presentation, but I just can't possibly think of what I could have done to deserve this. I—"

My hand went up, the palm facing him. "Stanley!"

"What?"

"Be quiet." Then I added. "Please."

"If you say so," Stanley said.

I cleared my throat. "Stanley, as founder of the Gypsy Club, I'm proud to present our very first badge to you."

"A badge," Stanley started. "I can—"

I held up my palm and he pressed his lips together tight.

Then I held up the badge. "Stanley, you have earned the Think Like a Dog badge. If it weren't for your suggestion, we might never have found Bruna. It was a simple idea, but most great ideas are. Why, look at the invention of Velcro. That came about because of some grass burrs sticking to a man's clothing. Just think if that simple idea had never happened and look at——"

Hailey sighed and showed me her palm.

"Okay," I said. "Anyway, Stanley, you deserve this badge. If you hadn't thought of that idea, I would have never said *Liver Lump*."

Bruna barked and wiggled her tail.

"And," I continued, but Hailey interrupted.

"That's right," she said. "We're proud of you, Stanley."

"I'm proud of you, too," said Nicole.

"Just remember," Michael said, "I was the one who invited him to the Gypsy Club."

"You don't get a badge for that," I told him.

I pinned the badge on Stanley's shirt and we all saluted him. Then I counted, "One, two, three!" And we all said, "Get off the bus, Stanley Hampshire!"

An hour later we formed our caravan. The Austins first, then Brady's family, then us. When we arrived in Yazoo, Alabama, everyone else drove on while we waited for Uncle Leo in the post office parking lot.

"I wonder if Uncle Leo will get lost again," said Sam.

"Probably," Mom said.

Chief smiled at her and she laughed.

"I have an idea," I said. "It worked once before."

"What?" Tori asked.

"We could holler Liver Lump."

"Hardy-har-har," said Tori.

Just then we spotted Uncle Leo's car coming down the road.

"He's bound to see us now," Chief said. "We've got the Airstream."

But Uncle Leo drove right on by, not even glancing our way.

Chief groaned. "Oh, no!"

All of us jumped out of the car, getting ready for him to pass again. This time we knew better than to call his name.

I had a hunch about what would work. Thank goodness Uncle Leo's car window was down. When he made a U-turn and headed back, I cupped my hands around my mouth and hollered, "Hummingbird!"

Then, all of us, even Chief hollered, "Hummingbird! Hummingbird!"

Uncle Leo screeched on the brakes, stopping

in time to make the turn into the parking lot. He pulled up next to us.

"Did anyone say hummingbird?" he asked, staring as if he was expecting us to hand over a stripe-tailed one.

Stanley Hampshire's genius idea had worked again! But I don't even think Stanley would want a Think-Like-an-Uncle-Leo badge.

Later, back in our car, I said, "It's too bad Uncle Leo doesn't have a cell phone anymore."

Sam leaned forward. "Daddy, can I use your cell phone? I have an important call to make."

Chief chuckled. "Sounds very important." He handed his phone to Sam.

"What's Mrs. Austin's cell phone number?" Sam asked.

Mom told the number and Sam began to dial. "Hi, Mrs. Austin. May I please speak to Stanley?"

Sam opened her copy of *Princess Samantha, Ruler of the Fair Land of NAS Pensacola* and began to read. "Then the princess thought about all the people on the base . . ."

I sighed. Maybe there shouldn't be a Think-Like-an-Uncle-Leo badge, but after this, Stanley definitely deserved a Surviving-Sam's-Story badge!

Kimberly Willis Holt

Are Tori, Piper, and Sam Reed based on your own family growing up?
Yes. Although most of the book comes from my imagination, the setup is very autobiographical. My dad was a Navy chief and I am one of three girls. However, I'm the oldest. Growing up, I was the serious one, the bossy one, the one who worried about her weight. I didn't think that point of view would be as interesting as my middle sister's. She was the funny one, the confident one, the clever one.

Being the middle sister has its advantages and disadvantages, but ultimately Piper seems stronger as a result of her position in the family. Do you agree?
I do. All the sisters are planners, but Piper has the most guts. She's not afraid to speak her mind and she does what

she sets out to do. She doesn't always get the results she hoped for, but she goes for it.

As a child, you lived on many different Navy bases because your father was stationed all over the world. What did you like most and least about being a "Navy Brat"?

I don't think I truly appreciated what a military life offered me while I was growing up. I hated moving. I was shy and didn't make friends easily. About the time I would start to feel at home, we moved, again. Now I look back on that experience and realize how rich a childhood I had. I was exposed to many cultures. And I learned to be adaptable and tolerant. I'm interested in people. Even though I was shy growing up, now I feel like I can talk to anyone. I believe that is because of my childhood.

What are some of the ways in which the life of a Navy family is different today than it was back when you were growing up?

One major difference is that when the parents are away on an assignment, military kids today can stay in touch with them more easily. I interviewed several groups of Navy kids whose parents were serving on a ship. They told me how they e-mailed their mom or dad every day. A couple of kids even played Internet games with their military parent. Now that's a huge improvement. I can remember when my dad was away we looked forward to the mail—snail mail.

Another difference is that there are a lot of kids with moms serving in the military today. That wasn't common when I was a kid. That's why I wrote about two of Piper's friends having their moms serve on the same ship as Piper's dad.

Is there really such a thing as Sister Magic?
Sure. I think it really has to do more with shared life experiences than genes, though. My sisters and I might laugh at something that no one else would think was funny.

When did you realize you wanted to be a writer?
In seventh grade, three teachers encouraged my writing. That was when I first thought the dream could come true. Before that, I didn't think I could be a writer because I wasn't a great student and I read slowly.

What's your first childhood memory?
Buying an orange Dreamcicle from the ice-cream man. I was two years old.

What's your most embarrassing childhood memory?
In fourth grade, I tried to impress the popular girls that I wanted to be friends with by doing somersaults in front of them. (I never learned to do cartwheels.) They called me a showoff so I guess it didn't work. If only I'd known how to do a cartwheel.

What was your first job?
I was in the movies. I popped popcorn at the Westside Cinemas.

How did you celebrate publishing your first book?
I'm sure my family went out to dinner. We always celebrate by eating.

Where do you write your books?
I write several places—a big soft chair in my bedroom, at a table on my screen porch, or at coffee shops.

Where do you find inspiration for your writing?
Most of the inspirations for my writing come from moments in my childhood.

Which of your characters is most like you?
I'm a bit like most of them. However, I fashioned Tori in the Piper Reed books after me. But Tori is bossier than I was and she certainly makes better grades than I did.

What's your idea of the best meal ever?
That's a toss-up. My grandmother's chicken and dumplings, and sushi.

Which do you like better: cats or dogs?
I'm a dog person. I have a poodle named Bronte who is the model for Bruna.

Who is your favorite fictional character?
Leroy in Mister and Me because he is forgiving. And that's a trait many of us don't have.

What's the best advice you have ever received about writing?
A writer once told me, "Readers either see what they read or hear what they read. Writers have to learn to write for both." When I started following that advice, my writing improved.

What do you want readers to remember about your books?
The characters. I want them to seem like real people. I want them to miss them and wonder what happened to them.

What would you do if you ever stopped writing?
I plan on dying with a pen in my hand.

What do you wish you could do better?
I wish I could do a cartwheel.

What would your readers be most surprised to learn about you?
I send gift cards with positive messages to myself when I order something for me.